ALSO BY LAURENT BINET

HHhH

THE
SEVENTH FUNCTION
OF LANGUAGE

THE
SEVENTH FUNCTION
OF LANGUAGE

■

LAURENT BINET

TRANSLATED FROM THE FRENCH BY SAM TAYLOR

FARRAR, STRAUS AND GIROUX   NEW YORK

Farrar, Straus and Giroux
18 West 18th Street, New York 10011

Copyright © 2015 by Éditions Grasset et Fasquelle
Translation copyright © 2017 by Sam Taylor
All rights reserved
Printed in the United States of America
Originally published in 2015 by Éditions Grasset et Fasquelle, France,
as *La septième fonction du langage*
English translation published in the United States by Farrar, Straus and Giroux
First American edition, 2017

Library of Congress Cataloging-in-Publication Data
Names: Binet, Laurent, author. | Taylor, Sam, 1970– translator.
Title: The seventh function of language / Laurent Binet ; translated from the
    French by Sam Taylor.
Other titles: Septième fonction du langage. English
Description: First American edition. | New York : Farrar, Straus and Giroux,
    [2017]
Identifiers: LCCN 2016050811 | ISBN 9780374261566 (hardcover) |
    ISBN 9780374715083 (e-book)
Subjects: LCSH: Barthes, Roland—Death and burial—Fiction.
Classification: LCC PQ2702.I57 S4713 2017 | DDC 843/.92—dc23
LC record available at https://lccn.loc.gov/2016050811

Designed by Jonathan D. Lippincott

Our books may be purchased in bulk for promotional, educational, or business use.
Please contact your local bookseller or the Macmillan Corporate and Premium
Sales Department at 1-800-221-7945, extension 5442, or by e-mail
at MacmillanSpecialMarkets@macmillan.com.

www.fsgbooks.com
www.twitter.com/fsgbooks • www.facebook.com/fsgbooks

1 3 5 7 9 10 8 6 4 2

There are interpreters everywhere. Each speaking his own language, even if he has some knowledge of the language of the other. The interpreter's ruses have an open field and he does not forget his own interests.   —Jacques Derrida

PART I

PARIS

■

1

Life is not a novel. Or at least you would like to believe so. Roland Barthes walks up Rue de Bièvre. The greatest literary critic of the twentieth century has every reason to feel anxious and upset. His mother, with whom he had a highly Proustian relationship, is dead. And his course on "The Preparation of the Novel" at the Collège de France is such a conspicuous failure it can no longer be ignored: all year, he has talked to his students about Japanese haikus, photography, the signifier and the signified, Pascalian diversions, café waiters, dressing gowns, and lecture-hall seating—about everything but the novel. And this has been going on for three years. He knows, without a doubt, that the course is simply a delaying tactic designed to push back the moment when he must start a truly literary work, one worthy of the hypersensitive writer lying dormant within him and who, in everyone's opinion, began to bud in his *A Lover's Discourse: Fragments*, which has become a bible for the under-25s. From Sainte-Beuve to Proust, it is time to step up and take the place that awaits him in the literary pantheon. Maman is dead: he has come full circle since *Writing Degree Zero*. The time has come.

Politics? Yeah, yeah, we'll see about that. He can't really claim to be very Maoist since his trip to China. Then again, no one expects him to be.

Chateaubriand, La Rochefoucauld, Brecht, Racine, Robbe-Grillet, Michelet, Maman. A boy's love.

I wonder if the area was already full of Vieux Campeur shops back then.

In a quarter of an hour, he will be dead.

I'm sure he ate well, on Rue des Blancs-Manteaux. I imagine people like that serve pretty good food. In *Mythologies*, Roland Barthes decodes the contemporary myths erected by the middle classes to their own glory. And it was this book that made him truly famous. So, in a way, he owes his fortune to the bourgeoisie. But that was the petite bourgeoisie. The ruling classes who serve the people are a very particular case that merits analysis; he should write an article. Tonight? Why not right away? But no, first he has to organize his slides.

Roland Barthes ups his pace without paying attention to the world around him, despite being a born observer, a man whose job consists of observing and analyzing, who has spent his entire life scrutinizing signs of every kind. He really doesn't see the trees or the sidewalks or the store windows or the cars on Boulevard Saint-Germain, which he knows like the back of his hand. He is not in Japan anymore. He doesn't feel the bite of the cold. He barely even hears the sounds of the street. It's a bit like Plato's allegory of the cave in reverse: the world of ideas in which he shuts himself away obscures his awareness of the world of the senses. Around him, he sees only shadows.

These reasons I mention to explain Roland Barthes's anxiety are all well known. But I want to tell you what actually happened. If his mind is elsewhere that day, it's not only because of his dead mother or his inability to write a novel or even his increasing and, he thinks, irreversible loss of appetite for boys. I'm not saying that he's not thinking about these things; I have no doubts about the quality of his obsessive neuroses. But, today, there is something else. In the absent gaze of a man lost in his thoughts, the attentive passerby would have recognized that state which Barthes thought he was destined never to feel again: excitement.

There is more to him than his mother and boys and his phantom novel. There is the *libido sciendi*, the lust for learning, and, awoken by it, the flattering prospect of revolutionizing human knowledge and, perhaps, changing the world. Does Barthes feel like Einstein, thinking about his theory as he crosses Rue des Écoles? What is certain is that he's not really looking where he's going. He is less than a hundred feet from his office when he is hit by a van. His body makes the familiar, sickening, dull thudding sound of flesh meeting metal, and it rolls over the pavement like a rag doll. Passersby flinch. This afternoon—February 25, 1980—they cannot know what has just happened in front of their eyes. For the very good reason that, until today, no one understands anything about it.

2

Semiology is a very strange thing. It was Ferdinand de Saussure, the founding father of linguistics, who first dreamed it up. In his *Course in General Linguistics*, he proposes imagining "a science that studies the life of signs within society." Yep, that's all. For those who wish to tackle this, he adds a few guidelines: "It would form a part of social psychology and, consequently, of general psychology; I shall call it *semiology* (from the Greek *semeion*, 'sign'). It would show what constitutes signs, what laws govern them. Since it does not exist yet, no one can say what it will be; but it has a right to existence, a place staked out in advance. Linguistics is only a part of this general science; the laws discovered by semiology will be applicable to linguistics, and the latter will circumscribe a well-defined area within the mass of anthropological facts." I wish Anthony Hopkins would reread this passage for us, enunciating each word as he does so well, so that the whole world could at least grasp all its beauty if not its meaning. A century later, this brilliant intuition, which was almost incomprehensible to his contemporaries when the course was taught in 1906, has lost none of its power or its obscurity. Since then, numerous semiologists have attempted to provide clearer and more detailed definitions, but they have contradicted each other (sometimes without realizing it themselves), got everything muddled up, and ultimately succeeded only in lengthening (and even then, not by much) the list of systems of signs beyond language: the highway code, the international maritime code, and bus and hotel numbers have been added to military ranks and the sign language alphabet . . . and that's about it.

Rather meager in comparison with the original ambition.

Seen this way, far from being an extension of the domain of linguistics, semiology seems to have been reduced to the study of crude proto-languages, which are much less complex and therefore much more limited than any real language.

But in fact, that's not the case.

It's no accident that Umberto Eco, the wise man of Bologna, one of the last great semiologists, referred so often to the key, decisive inventions in the history of humanity: the wheel, the spoon, the book . . . perfect tools, he said, unimprovable in their effectiveness. And indeed, everything suggests that in reality semiology is one of the most important inventions in the history of humanity and one of the most powerful tools ever forged by man. But as with fire or the atom, people don't know what the point of it is to begin with, or how to use it.

3

In fact, a quarter of an hour later, he still isn't dead. Roland Barthes lies in the gutter, inert, but a hoarse wheeze escapes his body. And while his mind sinks into unconsciousness, probably full of whirling haikus, Racinian alexandrines, and Pascalian aphorisms, he hears—maybe the last thing he will hear, he thinks (he does think, surely)—a distraught man yelling: "He thrrrew himself under my wheels! He thrrrew himself under my wheels!" Where's that accent from? Around him, the passersby are recovering from the shock, have gathered in a circle and are leaning over what will soon be his corpse, discussing, analyzing, evaluating:

"We should call an ambulance!"

"No point. He's done for."

"He thrrrew himself under my wheels—you werrre all witnesses!"

"Doesn't look too good, does he?"

"Poor guy . . ."

"We have to find a pay phone. Anyone got some coins?"

"I didn't even have to time to brrrake!"

"Don't touch him. We must wait for the ambulance."

"Let me through! I'm a doctor."

"Don't turn him over!"

"I'm a doctor. He's still alive."

"Someone should inform his family."

"Poor guy . . ."

"I know him!"

"Was it suicide?"

"We have to find out his blood group."

"He's a customer of mine. He comes to my bar for a drink every morning."

"He won't be coming anymore . . ."

"Is he drunk?"

"He smells of alcohol."

"A glass of white, sitting at the bar. Same thing every morning, for years."

"That doesn't help us with his blood group . . ."

"He crrrossed the rrroad without looking!"

"The driver must remain in control of his vehicle at all times. That's the law here."

"Don't worry, man, you'll be fine. As long as you've got good insurance . . ."

"Yeah, there goes his no-claims bonus, though."

"Don't touch him!"

"I'm a doctor!"

"So am I."

"Look after him, then. I'll go and call an ambulance."

"I have to deliverrr my merrrchandise . . ."

Most of the world's languages use an apico-alveolar *r*, known as the rolled *r*, in contrast to French, which adopted the dorso-velar *R* about three hundred years ago. There is no rolled *r* in German or English. Nor in Italian or Spanish. Portuguese, maybe? True, it does sound a little guttural, but the man's intonation is not nasal or singsong enough; it's quite monotonous, in fact, so much so that it's hard to make out the notes of panic.

So he's probably a Russian.

4

Born of linguistics and almost doomed to be the runt of the litter, used only for the study of the most rudimentary, limited languages, how at the last possible moment was semiology able to turn itself into a neutron bomb?

By means Barthes was familiar with.

To begin with, semiology was devoted to the study of non-linguistic systems of communication. Saussure himself told his students: "Language is a system of signs expressing ideas, and in this way is comparable to writing, the sign language alphabet, symbolic rites, forms of politeness, military signals, et cetera. It is simply the most important of these systems." This is more or less true, but only if we limit the definition of systems of signs to those designed to communicate explicitly and intentionally. The Belgian linguist Eric Buyssens defines semiology as "the study of communication processes; in other words, means used to influence others and recognized as such by the others in question."

Barthes's stroke of genius is to not content himself with communication systems but to extend his field of inquiry to systems of meaning. Once you have tasted that freedom, you quickly become bored with anything less: studying road signs or military codes is about as fascinating for a linguist as playing gin rummy would be for a poker player, or checkers for a chess player. As Umberto Eco might say: for communicating, language is perfect; there could be nothing better. And yet, language doesn't say everything. The body speaks, objects speak, history speaks, individual or collective destinies speak, life and death speak to us constantly in a thousand different ways. Man is an interpreting machine and, with a little imagination, he sees signs everywhere: in the color of his wife's coat, in the stripe on the door of his car, in the eating habits of the people in the apartment next door, in France's monthly unemployment figures, in the banana-like taste of Beaujolais nouveau (it always tastes either like banana or, less often, raspberry. Why? No one knows, but there must be an explanation, and it is semiological), in the proud, stately bearing of the black woman striding ahead of him through the corridors of the metro, in his colleague's habit of leaving the top two buttons of his shirt undone, in some footballer's goal celebration, in the way his partner screams when she has an orgasm, in the design of that piece of Scandinavian furniture, in the main sponsor's logo at this tennis tournament, in the soundtrack to the credits of that film, in architecture, in painting, in cooking, in fashion, in advertising, in interior decor, in the West's representation of women and men, love and death, heaven and earth, etc. With Barthes, signs no longer need to be signals: they have become clues. A seismic shift. They're everywhere. From now on, semiology is ready to conquer the world.

5

Superintendent Bayard reports to the emergency room of Pitié-Salpêtrière, where he is given Roland Barthes's room number. The case he is investigating can be summarized as follows: a man, sixty-four years old, knocked over by a laundry van, Rue des Écoles, Monday afternoon, while on a pedestrian crossing. The driver of the van, one Yvan Delahov, of Bulgarian nationality, tested positive for alcohol but was below the limit: 0.6 g, while the legal maximum is 0.8. He admitted that he was running late, delivering his shirts. Nevertheless, he claimed that he was not driving at more than 60 kilometers per hour. The victim was unconscious when the ambulance arrived, and had no papers on his person, but he was identified by one of his colleagues, a certain Michel Foucault, a lecturer at the Collège de France and a writer. The man, it turns out, was Roland Barthes, also a lecturer at the Collège de France and a writer.

So far, nothing justified sending an investigator, never mind a superintendent from the Renseignements Généraux, the French police's intelligence service. Jacques Bayard's presence is, in truth, down to one detail: when Roland Barthes was run over, on February 25, 1980, he had just eaten lunch with François Mitterrand, on Rue des Blancs-Manteaux.

In theory, there is no link between the lunch and the accident, nor between the Socialist candidate for the following year's presidential election and some laundry firm's Bulgarian driver, but it is the habit of Renseignements Généraux to gather information about everything, and especially, during this lead-up to the election campaign, about François Mitterrand. Michel Rocard is more popular in the opinion polls (Sofres survey, January 1980: "Who is the best Socialist candidate?" Mitterrand 20 percent, Rocard 55 percent), but presumably those in high places do not believe that he will dare to cross the Rubicon: the French Socialists believe in following the rules, and Mitterrand has been re-elected as leader of the party. Six years ago, he gained 49.19 percent of the vote against Giscard's 50.81 percent: the smallest margin of defeat recorded in a presidential election since the establishment of universal suffrage. So it's impossible to dismiss the risk that a left-wing president could be elected for the first time in the history of the Fifth Republic; that is why the RG have sent an investigator. Jacques Bayard's mission consists essentially in verifying whether Barthes drank too much at Mitterrand's apartment or, better still, whether he took part in a sadomasochistic orgy involving dogs. The Socialist leader has been involved in so few scandals in recent years that one might almost imagine he was deliberately watching his step. The fake kidnapping in the Observatory Gardens has been forgotten. The Francisque medal awarded by the Vichy regime is now taboo. They need something new. Officially, Jacques Bayard's task is to establish the circumstances of the accident, but he doesn't need to have spelled out what is expected of him: to find out if there is any way of damaging the Socialist candidate's credibility by investigating and, if necessary, smearing him.

When Jacques Bayard reaches the hospital room, he discovers a line several yards long outside in the corridor. Everyone is waiting to visit the victim. There are well-dressed old people, badly dressed young people, badly dressed old people, well-dressed young people, people of all kinds, long-haired and short-haired, some North African types, more men than women. While waiting their turn, they talk among themselves, speaking in loud voices, sometimes yelling, or they read books, smoke cigarettes. Bayard is yet to fully appreciate just how famous Barthes is and must be wondering what the hell is going on. As is his prerogative, he walks to the front of the line, says "Police," and enters the room.

Jacques Bayard notes immediately: the surprisingly high bed, the tube stuck in the throat, the bruises on the face, the sad look. There are four other people in the room: the younger brother, the editor, the disciple, and some kind of young Arab prince, very chic. The Arab prince is Youssef, a mutual friend of the master and his disciple, Jean-Louis, whom the master considers the most brilliant of his students, or at least the one he feels the greatest affection for. Jean-Louis and Youssef share an apartment in the Thirteenth Arrondissement, where they organize parties that brighten up Barthes's life. He meets so many people there: students, actresses, lots of celebrities, often the director André Téchiné, sometimes Isabelle Adjani, and always a crowd of young intellectuals. For now, these details do not interest Superintendent Bayard, who is here simply to reconstruct the circumstances of the accident. Barthes regained consciousness after his arrival at the hospital. He declared to his close friends, who rushed to his bedside: "How stupid of me! How stupid!" Despite the multiple contusions and a few broken ribs, his condition did not appear too worrying. But Barthes has an "Achilles' heel," as his younger brother puts it: his lungs. He had tuberculosis in his youth, and he is a prodigious cigarette smoker. Result: a chronic respiratory weakness that catches up with him that night: he starts suffocating, has to be intubated. When Bayard arrives, Barthes is awake but no longer able to speak.

Bayard talks quietly to Barthes. He is going to ask him a few questions; all he need do is nod or shake his head to indicate yes or no. Barthes stares at the superintendent with his sad spaniel eyes. He gives a weak nod.

"You were on your way to your place of work when the vehicle hit you, is that correct?" Barthes nods. "Was the vehicle moving quickly?" Barthes tilts his head slowly from side to side, and Bayard understands: he doesn't know. "Were you distracted?" Yes. "Was your inattention connected to your lunch?" No. "To the course you had to prepare?" A pause. Yes. "Did you meet François Mitterrand at that lunch?" Yes. "Did anything special or unusual happen during that lunch?" A pause. No. "Did you consume alcohol?" Yes. "A lot?" No. "One glass?" Yes. "Two glasses?" Yes. "Three glasses?" A pause. Yes. "Four glasses?" No. "Did you have your papers with you when the accident happened?" Yes. A pause. "Are you sure?" Yes. "You did not have any papers on you when you were found. Is it possible you forgot them, left them at home or somewhere else?" A longer pause. Barthes's gaze is suddenly charged with a new intensity. He shakes his head. "Do you remember if someone touched you while you were on the ground, before the ambulance arrived?" Barthes seems not to understand or perhaps not to hear the question. He shakes his head again: no. "No, you don't remember?" Another pause, but this time, Bayard thinks he can identify the expression on the man's face: it is incredulity. Barthes replies no. "Was there any money in your wallet?" Barthes stares at his interrogator. "Monsieur Barthes, can you hear me? Did you have any money on you?" No. "Did you have anything valuable with you?" No response. Barthes's gaze is so unwavering that were it not for a strange fire in the back of his eyes one would think him dead. "Monsieur Barthes? Did you have something valuable in your possession? Do you think something might have been stolen from you?" The silence that fills the room is broken only by Barthes's hoarse breathing in the ventilator tube. There's another long pause. Slowly, Barthes shakes his head, then looks away.

6

On his way out of the hospital, Superintendent Bayard thinks: there's a problem here. It strikes him that what should have been a routine investigation will perhaps not be completely super-fluous, after all; that the disappearance of the papers is a curi-ous gray area in what otherwise looks like an ordinary accident; that he will have to interview more people than he'd imagined in order to clear this up; that his investigation should begin on Rue des Écoles, outside the Collège de France (an institution whose existence was entirely unknown to him before today, and whose nature he therefore hasn't quite grasped); that he will have to start by meeting this Monsieur Foucault, "professor of the history of systems of thoughts" [sic]; that, after this, he will have to interrogate a whole gang of hairy students, plus the accident witnesses, plus the victim's friends. He is simultaneously baffled and annoyed by this extra work. But he knows what he saw in that hospital room. What he saw in Barthes's eyes: fear.

Superintendent Bayard, absorbed by his thoughts, pays no

attention to the black DS parked on the other side of the boulevard. He gets in his official vehicle, a Peugeot 504, and heads toward the Collège de France.

7

In the entrance hall, he spots a list of course titles: Nuclear Magnetism, Neuropsychology of Development, Sociography of Southeast Asia, Christianity and Gnosis in the Pre-Islamic East . . . Perplexed, he goes to the faculty room and asks to see Michel Foucault, only to be told that he is busy giving a class.

The lecture hall is packed. Bayard cannot even get in. He is held back by a solid wall of students, who react furiously when he tries to force his way through. Taking pity on him, one explains in a whisper how it works: if you want a seat, you need to arrive two hours before the lecture starts. When the hall is full, you can always fall back on the hall across the corridor, where the lecture is broadcast over speakers. You won't get to see Foucault, but at least you'll hear him speak. So Bayard walks over to Lecture Hall B, which is also pretty full, though there are a few empty seats remaining. The audience is a colorful mix: there are young people, old people, hippies, yuppies, punks, goths, Englishmen in tweed waistcoats, Italian girls with plunging necklines, Iranian women in chadors, grandmothers with their little dogs . . . He sits next to two young male twins dressed as astronauts (though without the helmets). The atmosphere is studious: people scribble in notebooks or listen reverently. From time to time they cough, as if at the theater, but there is no one on the stage. Through the speakers, the superintendent hears a nasal, slightly 1940s-sounding voice; not Chaban-Delmas exactly, more like a mix of Jean Marais and Jean Poiret, only higher-pitched.

"The problem I would like to pose you," says the voice, "is this: What is the meaning, within an idea of salvation—in other words, within an idea of illumination, an idea of redemption, granted to men on their first baptism—what could be the meaning of the repetition of penitence, or even the repetition of sin?"

Very professorial: Bayard can sense that. He tries to grasp what the voice is talking about, but unfortunately he makes this effort just as Foucault says: "In such a way that the subject moving toward the truth, and attaching itself to it with love, in his own words manifests a truth that is nothing other than the manifestation in it of the true presence of a God who, Himself, can tell only truth, because He never lies, He is completely honest."

If Foucault had been speaking that day about prison, or power, or archaeology, or green energy, or genealogy, who knows? . . . But the implacable voice drones on: "Even if, for various philosophers or views of the universe, the world might well turn in one direction or another, in the life of individuals time has only one direction." Bayard listens without understanding, rocked gently by the tone, which is simultaneously didactic and projected, melodious in its way, underpinned by a sense of rhythm, an extremely precise use of silences and punctuation.

Does this guy earn more than he does?

"Between this system of law that governs actions and relates to a subject of will, and consequently the indefinite repeatability of the error, and the outline of the salvation and perfection that concerns the subjects, which implies a temporal scansion and an irreversibility, there is, I think, no possible integration . . ."

Yes, without a doubt. Bayard is unable to suppress the bitterness that instinctively makes him detest this voice. The police have to battle people like this for taxpayers' funds. They're functionaries, like him, except that he deserves to be remunerated by society for his work. But this Collège de France, what is it exactly? Founded by François I, okay: he read that in the entrance hall. Then what? Courses open to all, but of interest only to work-shy lefties, retired people, lunatics, or pipe-smoking teachers;

improbable subjects that he's never even heard of before . . . No degrees, no exams. People like Barthes and Foucault paid to spout a load of woolly nonsense. Bayard is already sure of one thing: no one comes here to learn how to do a job. *Episteme*, my ass.

When the voice wraps up by giving the date and time of next week's lecture, Bayard returns to Lecture Hall A, elbows his way through the flood of students pouring out through the swing doors, finally enters the lecture hall, and spots a bald, bespectacled man at the very back of the room wearing a turtle-neck sweater under his jacket. He looks at once sturdy and slen-der. He has a determined jaw with a slight underbite and the stately demeanor of those who know that they are valued by the world. His head is perfectly shaved. Bayard joins him on the stage. "Monsieur Foucault?" The big baldy is gathering his notes in the relaxed manner of a teacher whose work is done. He turns welcomingly toward Bayard, aware of what levels of shyness his admirers must sometimes overcome in order to speak to him. Bayard takes out his card. He, too, is well aware of its effect. Foucault stops dead for a second, looks at the card, stares at the policeman, then goes back to his notes. In a theatrical voice, as if for the attention of what's left of the audience, he declares: "I refuse to be identified by the authorities." Bayard pretends he hasn't heard him: "It's about the accident."

The big baldy shoves his notes in his satchel and exits the stage without a word. Bayard runs after him: "Monsieur Fou-cault, where are you going? I have to ask you a few questions!" Foucault strides up the steps of the lecture hall. He replies without turning around, loud enough for all the remaining students to be able to hear him: "I refuse to be confined by the authorities!" The audience laughs. Bayard grabs his arm: "I just want you to give me your version of the facts." Foucault stands still and says nothing. His entire body is tensed. He looks down at the hand gripping his arm as if it were the most serious human rights vio-lation since the Cambodian genocide. Bayard does not loosen his hold. There are murmurs around them. After a minute or so

16

of this, Foucault finally speaks: "My version is that they killed him." Bayard is not sure he's understood this correctly.

"Killed him? Killed who?"

"My friend Roland."

"But he's not dead!"

"He is already dead."

From behind his glasses, Foucault stares at his interrogator with the intensity of the shortsighted. And slowly, emphasizing each syllable, as if concluding a long argument whose secret logic he alone knows, he announces:

"Roland Barthes is dead."

"But who killed him?"

"The system, of course!"

The use of the word *system* confirms to the policeman exactly what he feared: he's surrounded by lefties. He knows from experience that this is all they talk about: society's corruption, the class struggle, the "system" . . . He waits unenthusiastically for the rest of the speech. Foucault, magnanimously, deigns to enlighten him:

"Roland has been mercilessly mocked in recent years. Because he had the power of understanding things as they are and, paradoxically, inventing them with unprecedented freshness, he was criticized for his jargon, he was pastiched, parodied, caricatured, satirized . . ."

"Do you know if he had enemies?"

"Of course! Ever since he joined the Collège de France—I brought him here—the jealousy has intensified. All he had were enemies: the reactionaries, the middle classes, the fascists, the Stalinists, and, above all, above all, the rancid old critics who never forgave him!"

"Forgave him for what?"

"For daring to think! For daring to question their outdated bourgeois ideas, for highlighting their vile normative functions, for showing them up for what they really were: prostitutes sullied by idiocy and compromised principles!"

"But who, in particular?"

"You want names? Who do you think I am? The Picards, the Pommiers, the Rambauds, the Burniers! They'd have executed him themselves given the chance. Twelve bullets in the Sorbonne courtyard, beneath the statue of Victor Hugo!"

Suddenly, Foucault strides off again and Bayard is caught off-guard. The professor gets a head start of several yards, leaves the lecture hall and races up the stairs. Bayard runs after him, close behind. Their footsteps ring loudly on the stone floors. The policeman calls out: "Monsieur Foucault, who are those people you mentioned?" Foucault, without turning around: "Dogs, jackals, mules, morons, nobodies, but above all, above all, above all! the servants of the established order, the scribes of the old world, the pimps of a dead system of thought who seek to make us breathe the stench of its corpse forever with their obscene sniggers." Bayard, clinging to the banister: "What corpse?" Foucault, storming up the stairs: "The corpse of the dead system of thought!" Then he laughs sardonically. Trying to find a pen in the pockets of his raincoat while keeping up with the professor, Bayard asks him: "Could you spell Rambaud for me?"

8

The superintendent enters a bookstore to buy some books but he is unused to such places and struggles to find his way among the aisles. He cannot find any works by Raymond Picard. The bookseller, who seems relatively knowledgeable, mentions in passing that Raymond Picard is dead—something Foucault had omitted to tell him—but that he can order *New Criticism or New Fraud*? On the other hand, he does have a copy of *Enough Decoding!* by René Pommier, a disciple of Raymond Picard who lays into structuralist criticism (that, in any case, is how the bookseller sells him the book, which doesn't get him much further), and most notably, *Roland Barthes Made Easy*, by Rambaud and Burnier. This is quite a slim book with a green cover, a photograph of Barthes staring out severely from an orange oval. Coming out of the frame, a Crumb-style cartoon character says "hee-hee," grinning and laughing, mockingly, one hand over his mouth. In fact, I've checked, and it is Crumb. But Bayard has never heard of Fritz the Cat, the countercultural cartoon strip and film, in which black people are saxophone-playing crows and the hero is a cat in a turtleneck who, Kerouac-style, smokes joints and fucks anything that moves in Cadillacs, against a back-drop of urban riots and burning Dumpsters. Crumb is famous, though, for the way he drew women, with their big, powerful thighs, their lumberjack shoulders, their breasts like mortar shells, and their mares' asses. Bayard is no cartoon-strip connoisseur, and does not make the connection. But he buys the book, and the Pommier, too. He doesn't order the Picard, because at this stage of the investigation dead authors don't interest him.

The superintendent sits in a café, orders a beer, lights a Gitane, and opens *Roland Barthes Made Easy.* (Which café? The little details are important for reconstructing the atmosphere, don't you think? I see him at the Sorbon, the bar opposite the Champo, the little arthouse cinema at the bottom of Rue des Écoles. But, in all honesty, I don't have a clue: you can put him wherever you want.) He reads:

> *R.B. (in his writing, Roland Barthes calls himself R.B.) ap-peared in its archaic form twenty-five years ago, in the book entitled* Writing Degree Zero. *Since then it has, little by little, detached itself from French, from which it is partially descended, forming an autonomous language with its own grammar and vocabulary.*

Bayard takes a drag on his Gitane, swallows a mouthful of beer, turns the pages. At the bar, he hears the waiter explain to a customer why France will descend into civil war if Mitterrand is elected.

Lesson one: The basics of conversation.
1—How do you formulate yourself?
French: What is your name?
2—I formulate myself L.
French: My name is William.

Bayard more or less understands the satirical intent and also that in theory he ought to be on the same wavelength as the authors of this pastiche, but he is wary. Why, in "R.B.," does "William" call himself "L"? It's a puzzle. Fucking intellectuals.

The waiter to the customer: "When the Communists are in power, everyone with money will leave France and put it somewhere else, somewhere they won't have to pay taxes and where they're sure they won't get caught!"

Rambaud and Burnier:

3—What "stipulation" locks in, encloses, organizes, arranges
the economy of your pragma like the occultation and/or
exploitation of your egg-zistence?
French: What is your job?
4—(I) expel units of code.
French: I am a typist.

This makes him laugh a little, but he hates what he instinctively perceives as a principle of verbal intimidation. Of course, he knows that this kind of book is not aimed at him, that it's a book for intellectuals, for those smart-assed parasites to have a good snigger among themselves. Mocking themselves: the last laugh. Bayard is no idiot; he's already doing a bit of a Bourdieu without even realizing it.

At the bar, the speech continues: "Once all the money's in Switzerland, we won't have any capital left to pay wages, and it'll be civil war. And the Socialists and Commies will have won, just like that!" The waiter stops pontificating for a minute to go and serve someone. Bayard returns to his reading:

5—My discourse finds/completes its own textuality through
R.B. in a game of smoke and mirrors.
French: I speak fluent Roland Barthes.

Bayard gets the gist: Roland Barthes's language is gibberish.
But in that case why waste your time reading him? And, more
to the point, writing a book about him?

6—The "sublimation" (the integration) of this as (my) code
constitutes the "third break" of a doubling of cupido, my
desire.
French: I would like to learn this language.
7—Does the R.B. as macrology serve as "fenceage" to the
enclosed field of Gallicist interpellation?
French: Is Roland Barthes too difficult for a French person
to learn?
8—The scarf of Barthesian style tightens "around" the code
as it is confirmed in its repetition/duplication.
French: No, it's pretty easy. But you have to work at it.

The superintendent's perplexity increases. He doesn't know
who he hates more: Barthes or the two comics who felt the need
to parody him. He puts the book down, stubs out his cigarette.
The waiter is back behind the bar. Holding his glass of red, the
customer objects: "Yeah, but Mitterrand'll stop them at the border. And the money will be confiscated." The waiter scolds the
customer, frowning: "You think the rich are idiots? They'll pay
professional smugglers. They'll organize networks to ship their
money out. They'll cross the Alps and the Pyrenees, like Hannibal! Like during the war! If it's possible to get Jews over the border, they won't have any trouble getting bundles of cash over, will
they?" The customer does not seem too convinced, but as he obviously doesn't have a comeback he settles for a nod, then finishes
his glass and orders another one. The waiter takes out an open
bottle of red and puffs himself up: "Oh yes! Oh yes! Personally,

I don't give a toss. If the pinkos win, I'm out of here. I'll go and work in Geneva. They won't get my money, no way. Over my dead body! I don't work for pinkos! What do you take me for? I don't work for anyone! I'm free! Like de Gaulle!"

Bayard tries to remember who Hannibal is and notes mechanically that the little finger on the waiter's left hand is missing a phalanx. He interrupts the waiter's speech to order another beer, opens the René Pommier book, counts the word *nonsense* seventeen times in four pages, and closes it again. In the meantime, the waiter has begun opining on another subject: "No civilized society can get by without the death penalty!" Bayard pays and exits the café, leaving his change on the table.

He passes the statue of Montaigne without seeing it, crosses Rue des Écoles and enters the Sorbonne. Superintendent Bayard understands that he understands nothing, or at least not much, about all this rubbish. What he needs is someone to explain it to him: a specialist, a translator, a transmitter, a tutor. A professor, basically. At the Sorbonne, he asks where he can find the semiology department. The person at reception sharply replies that there isn't one. In the courtyard outside, he approaches some students in navy-blue sailor coats and boat shoes to ask where he should go to attend a semiology course. Most of them have no idea what it is or have only vaguely heard of it. But, at last, a long-haired young man smoking a joint beneath the statue of Louis Pasteur tells him that for "semio" he has to go to Vincennes. Bayard is no expert when it comes to academia, but he knows that Vincennes is a university swarming with work-shy lefties and professional agitators. Out of curiosity, he asks this young man why he isn't there. The man is wearing a large turtleneck sweater, a pair of black trousers with the legs rolled up as though he's about to go mussel fishing, and purple Dr. Martens. He takes a drag on his joint and replies: "I was there until my second second year. But I was part of a Trotskyite group." This explanation seems to strike him as sufficient, but when he sees from Bayard's inquiring look that it isn't, he adds: "Well, there were, uh, a few problems."

Bayard does not press the matter. He gets back in his 504 and drives to Vincennes. At a red light, he sees a black DS and thinks: "Now, *that* was a car!"

9

The 504 joins the ring road at Porte de Bercy, gets off at Porte de Vincennes, goes back up the very long Avenue de Paris, passes the military hospital, refuses to yield to a brand-new blue Fuego driven by some Japanese men, skirts around the chateau, passes the Parc Floral, enters the woods, and parks outside some shack-like buildings that resemble a giant 1970s suburban high school: just about humanity's worst effort in architectural terms. Bayard, who remembers his distant years spent studying law in the grandeur of Assas, finds this place utterly disorienting: to reach the classrooms, he has to cross a sort of souk run by Africans, step over comatose junkies sprawled on the ground, pass a waterless pond filled with junk, pass crumbling walls covered with posters and graffiti, where he can read: "Professors, students, education officers, ATOS staff: die, bitches!"; "No to closing the food souk"; "No to moving from Vincennes to Nogent"; "No to moving from Vincennes to Marne-la-Vallée"; "No to moving from Vincennes to Savigny-sur-Orge"; "No to moving from Vincennes to Saint-Denis"; "Long live the proletarian revolution"; "Long live the Iranian revolution"; "Maoists=fascists"; "Trotskyites=Stalinists"; "Lacan=cop"; "Badiou=Nazi"; "Althusser=murderer"; "Deleuze=fuck your mother"; "Cixous=fuck me"; "Foucault=Khomeini's whore"; "Barthes=pro-Chinese social traitor"; "Callicles=SS"; "It is forbidden to forbid forbidding"; "Union de la Gauche=up your ass"; "Come to my place, we'll read *Capital*! signed: Balibar" . . . Students stinking of marijuana accost him aggressively, thrusting thick pamphlets at him: "Comrade, do you know what's going on in Chile? In El Salvador? Are you concerned about Argentina? And Mozambique? What, you don't care about Mozambique? Do you know where it is? You want me to tell you about Timor? If not, we're having a collection for a literacy drive in Nicaragua. Can you buy me a coffee?" Here, he feels less at sea. Back when he was a member of Jeune Nation, he used to beat the crap out of filthy little lefties like these. He throws the tracts in the dried-out pond that serves as a trash can.

Without really knowing how he got there, Bayard ends up at the Culture and Communications department. He scans the list of "course units" displayed on a board in the corridor and finally finds roughly what he came for: Semiology of the Image, a classroom number, a weekly timetable, and the name of a professor—Simon Herzog.

10

"Today, we are going to study figures and letters in James Bond. If you think of James Bond, which letter comes to mind?" Silence, as the students consider the question. At least Jacques Bayard, sitting at the back of the classroom, is familiar with James Bond. "What is the name of James Bond's boss?" Bayard knows this! He is surprised to find himself wanting to say the answer out loud, but several students get there before him, giving the response simultaneously: M. "Who is M, and why M? What does M signify?" A pause. No answer. "M is an old man, but is a feminine figure. It's the M of *Mother*, the nurturing mother, who provides and protects, the one who gets angry when Bond does something silly but who always indulges him, who Bond wants to please by succeeding in his missions. James Bond is a man of action but he is not a lone gunman, he is not on his own, he is not an orphan (he is biographically, but not symbolically: his mother is England; he is not married to his homeland, he is its beloved son). He is supported by a hierarchy, an organization, an entire nation that assigns him impossible missions—which the country takes great pride in him carrying out (M, the metonymical representation of England, the representative of the queen, often repeats that Bond is his best agent: he is the favorite son)—but that provides him with all the material means necessary to accomplish them. James Bond, in fact, has his cake and eats it, too, and that is why he is such a popular fantasy, an extremely powerful contemporary myth: James Bond is the adventurer-functionary. Action *and* security. He commits offenses, misdemeanors, even crimes, but he is permitted, he has the authority; he won't be punished because he has the famous 'license to kill' signified by his identification number. Which brings us to those three magic figures: 007.

"Double 0 is the code for the right to commit murder, and here we see a brilliant application of the symbolism of figures. How could the license to kill be represented by a figure? Ten? Twenty? A hundred? A million? Death is not quantifiable. Death is nothingness, and nothingness is zero. But murder is more than mere death, it is death inflicted on another. It is death times two: his own inevitable death, whose probability is increased by the dangers of his job (we are often reminded that the life expectancy of double 0 agents is very low), and that of the other. Double 0 is the right to kill and to be killed. As for 7, it was obviously chosen because it is traditionally one of the most elegant numbers, a magical number charged with history and symbolism; but in this case, it complies with two criteria: it is an odd number, of course, like the number of roses we give to a woman, and prime (a prime number is divisible only by one and by itself) in order to express a singularity, a uniqueness, an individuality that confounds the whole impression of interchangeability suggested by an identification number. Let's cast our minds back to the series *The Prisoner*, with its protagonist, Number 6, who desperately, rebelliously repeats: 'I am not a number!' James Bond, on the other hand, is perfectly comfortable with his number, all the more so as it confers upon him extraordinary privileges, making him an aristocrat (in Her Majesty's service, naturally). 007 is the antithesis of Number 6: he is satisfied with the extremely privileged place society gives him, he works devotedly for the preservation of the established order, without ever questioning the enemy's nature or motivation. Where Number 6 is a revolutionary, 007 is a conservative. The reactionary 7 here opposes the revolutionary 6, and as the meaning of the word *reactionary* supposes the idea of posteriority (the conservatives 'react' to the revolution by working for a return to the *ancien régime*, i.e., the established order), it is logical that the reactionary figure succeeds the revolutionary figure (to put it as plainly as possible: that James Bond is not 005). The function of 007 is, therefore, to guarantee the return of the established order, threatened by a menace that destabilizes the world order. The end of each episode coincides always with a return to 'normality,' i.e., 'the old order.' Umberto Eco calls James Bond a fascist. In actual fact, we can see that he is, above all, a reactionary . . ."

A student raises his hand: "But there's also Q, the guy in charge of gadgets. Do you see a meaning in that letter too?"

With an immediacy that surprises Bayard, the professor goes on:

"Q is a paternal figure, because he is the one who provides James Bond with weapons and teaches him how to use them. He passes on his savoir faire. In this sense, he ought to be called F, for *Father* . . . But if you watch the scenes involving Q carefully, what do you see? A distracted, impertinent, playful James Bond, who doesn't listen (or pretends not to). And, at the end, you have Q, who always asks: 'Questions?' (or variations on the theme of 'Do you understand?'). But James Bond never has any questions; although he plays the dunce, he has assimilated what has been explained to him perfectly because he is an extraordinarily quick study. So Q is the *q* of 'questions'—questions that Q calls for and that Bond never asks, except in the form of jokes, and his questions are never those that Q is expecting."

Another student speaks up now: "And in English, Q is pronounced exactly the same way as the word *queue*, which implies shopping. People queue outside the gadget store, they wait to be served; it is a dead time, a playful time, between two action scenes."

The young professor waves his arms enthusiastically: "Exactly! Well observed! That's a very good idea! Don't forget that one interpretation never exhausts the sign, and that polysemy is a bottomless well where we can hear an infinite number of echoes: a word's meaning never runs dry. And the same's true even for a letter, you see."

The professor looks at his watch: "Thank you for your attention. Next Tuesday we'll talk about clothes in James Bond. Gentlemen, I'll expect you in tuxedos, naturally [laughter in the classroom]. And ladies, in Ursula Andress–style bikinis [men whistling, women protesting]. See you next week!"

While the students leave the hall, Bayard goes up to the young lecturer with a discreetly malicious smile that the lecturer does not understand, but which means: "I'm going to make you pay for that baldy's bad attitude."

11

"Just to be clear, Superintendent, I am not a specialist in Barthes, nor strictly speaking am I a semiologist. I have an MAS in modern criticism of the historical novel, I'm preparing a linguistics thesis on acts of language, and I also run a tutorial. This semester, I'm giving a specialized course in semiology of the image, and last year I ran an introductory course on semiology for first-year students. I taught them the basics of linguistics because that's the foundation of semiology; I told them about Saussure and Jakobson, a bit of Austin, a bit of Searle; we worked mainly on Barthes because he's the most accessible and because he often chose his subjects from popular culture, which are more likely to pique my students' interest than, say, his critiques of Racine or Chateaubriand, because these kids are doing media studies, not literature. With Barthes, we could spend a lot of time discussing steak-frites, the latest Citroën, James Bond . . . it's a more playful approach to analysis, and that is in a sense the definition of semiology: it applies literary criticism methods to non-literary subjects."

"He's not dead."

"I beg your pardon?"

"You said 'we could.' You were talking in the past tense, as if it were no longer possible."

"Um, no, that's not what I meant . . ."

Simon Herzog and Jacques Bayard walk side by side down the university's corridors. The young lecturer holds his satchel in one hand and a sheaf of photocopies in the other. He shakes his head when a student tries to hand him a leaflet. The student calls him a fascist, and he responds with a guilty smile, then corrects Bayard:

"Even if he did die, we could still apply his critical methods, you know . . ."

"What makes you think he might die? I didn't mention the seriousness of his injuries."

"Well, er, I doubt whether superintendents are sent to investigate all road accidents, so I deduce from that that it's serious, and that there's something fishy about the circumstances."

"The circumstances are pretty straightforward, and the victim's condition is really nothing to be worried about."

"Really? Ah, well, I'm glad to hear it, superintendent . . ."

"I didn't tell you I was a superintendent."

"No? I just thought Barthes was so famous that the police would send a superintendent . . ."

"I'd never even heard of this guy until yesterday."

The young postgrad falls silent. He looks disconcerted; Bayard is satisfied. A student in socks and sandals hands him another tract: *Waiting for Godard: A One-Act Play*. He puts it in his pocket and asks Herzog:

"What do you know about semiology?"

"Um, well, it's the study of the life of signs within society."

Bayard thinks about his *Roland Barthes Made Easy*. He grits his teeth.

"And in plain French?"

"But . . . that's Saussure's definition . . ."

"This Chaussure, does he know Barthes?"

"Er, no, he's dead. He was the inventor of semiology."

"Hmm, I see."

But Bayard does not see anything. The two men walk through the cafeteria. It looks like the ruins of a warehouse and smells strongly of merguez sausage, pancakes, and marijuana. A tall, awkward-looking guy in mauve lizard-skin boots is standing on a table. Cigarette in mouth, beer in hand, he harangues some students who listen, eyes shining. As Simon Herzog has no office, he invites Bayard to sit down and, automatically, offers him a cigarette. Bayard refuses, takes out a Gitane, and says:

"So, in concrete terms, what's the point of this . . . science?"

"Um, well . . . understanding reality?"

Bayard grimaces imperceptibly.

"Meaning?"

The young lecturer takes a few seconds to think about this. He gauges his interrogator's capacities for abstraction—clearly quite limited—and adapts his response accordingly. If not, they'll be going around in circles for hours.

"In fact, it's simple. There are loads of things in our environment that have, uh, a function of use. You see?"

Hostile silence from the policeman. At the other end of the room, the guy in mauve lizard-skin boots is telling his young disciples about the events of May '68, which, in his account, sound like a mixture of *Mad Max* and Woodstock. Simon Herzog tries to keep his explanation as simple as possible: "A chair is for sitting on, a table is for eating on, a desk for working at, clothes for keeping warm, et cetera. Okay?"

Icy silence.

"Except that, in addition to their function of . . . um, their usefulness . . . these objects also possess a symbolic value . . . as if they could speak, if you like: they tell us things. That chair, for example, that you're sitting on, with its zero design, its low-quality varnished wood, and its rusted frame, tells us that we are in a community that doesn't care about comfort or aesthetics and that has no money. Added to this, those mingled smells of bad food and cannabis confirm that we're in a higher-education establishment. In the same way, your manner of dressing signals your profession: you wear a suit, which indicates an executive job, but your clothes are cheap, which implies a modest salary and/or an absence of interest in your appearance; so you belong to a profession in which presentation doesn't matter, or not very much. Your shoes are badly scuffed, and you came here in a car, which signifies that you are not deskbound—you are out and about in your job. An executive who leaves his office is very likely to be assigned some kind of inspection work."

"I see," says Bayard. (A long silence, during which Herzog can hear the man in lizard-skin boots telling his fascinated audience how, back when he was head of the Armed Spinozist Faction, he defeated the Young Hegelians.) "Then again, I know where I am, because there's a sign saying 'University of Vincennes—Paris 8' over the entrance. And the word 'Police' is also written in bold on the red, white, and blue card I showed you when I came to talk to you after your lecture, so I don't really see where you're going with this."

Simon Herzog starts to sweat. This conversation brings back painful memories of oral exams. Don't panic, just concentrate. Don't focus on the seconds passing in silence; ignore the falsely sanctimonious attitude of the sadistic examiner who is secretly enjoying his institutional superiority and the suffering he's inflicting on you because in the past he suffered the same himself.

The young postgrad thinks fast, attentively observing the man facing him, and proceeds methodically, stage by stage, as he's been taught. Then, when he feels ready, he lets a few further seconds pass, and says:

"You fought in Algeria; you have been married twice; you are separated from your second wife; you have a daughter under twenty, with whom you have a difficult relationship; you voted for Giscard in both rounds of the last presidential election, and you'll do the same again next year; you lost a colleague in the line of duty, perhaps it was your own fault, in any case you blame yourself or feel bad about it, though your superiors decided it was not your responsibility. And you went to see the latest James Bond film at the cinema, but you prefer a good Maigret on TV or films starring Lino Ventura."

A very, very long silence. At the other end of the room, the reincarnation of Spinoza is recounting, to the cheers of the crowd, how he and his gang overcame the Fourier Rose group. Bayard mutters tonelessly:

"What makes you say that?"

"Well, it's very simple!" (Another pause, but this one is the young professor's. Bayard does not react at all, except for a slight quivering in the fingers of his right hand. The man in mauve lizard-skin boots starts singing a Rolling Stones song a cappella.) "When you came to see me at the end of the lecture earlier, you instinctively placed yourself in a position where you wouldn't have your back to the door or the window. You don't learn that at police school, but in the army. The fact that this reflex has stayed with you signifies that your military experience was not limited to the usual National Service but marked you sufficiently that you have kept some unconscious habits. So you probably went to war and you're not old enough to have fought in Indochina, so I think you were sent to Algeria. You're in the police, so you're bound to be right-wing, as confirmed by your hostility to students and intellectuals (which was plain from the minute we started talking), but as an Algerian veteran you considered de Gaulle's granting of independence as a betrayal. So you refused to vote for the Gaullist candidate, Chaban, and you are too rational (a condition of your job) to give your vote to a candidate like Le Pen, who has no chance of making it through to the second round, so your vote naturally went to Giscard. You came here alone, against all the rules of the French police, where officers always go about in twos, so you must have been given special dispensation, a favor that could only have been granted for a serious reason such as the death of a colleague. The trauma is such that you cannot bear the idea of having a new partner, so your superiors allow you to operate solo. That way, you can pretend to be Maigret, who, judging from your raincoat, is a role model, consciously or not. (Superintendent Moulin, with his leather jacket, is probably too young for you to identify with, and, well, you don't have enough money to dress like James Bond.) You wear a wedding ring on your right hand, but you still have a ring mark on your left ring finger. You presumably wished to avoid the feeling that you were repeating yourself by changing your ring hand for the second marriage, as a way of warding off fate, or something like that. But apparently it didn't work, because your rumpled shirt, this early in the day, proves that no one is doing the ironing at your house; and, in conformity with the petit-bourgeois model, which fits your sociocultural background, if your wife were still living with you, she would not have let you leave the house wearing an unironed shirt."

The silence that follows this speech feels as if it might last twenty-four hours.

"And my daughter?"

With an air of false modesty, Herzog waves this invitation away. "It would take too long to explain."

In fact, he was carried away by his momentum. He just thought a daughter seemed to fit the picture he had painted.

"All right. Follow me."

"I beg your pardon? Follow you where? Am I under arrest?"

"I'm requisitioning you. You strike me as being less stupid

than the rest of these long-haired louts, and I need a translator for all this bullshit."

"But . . . I'm sorry, but that's completely impossible! I have a class to prepare for tomorrow, and I have to work on my thesis, and there's a book I have to take back to the library . . ."

"Listen, you little jerk: you're coming with me. Got it?"

"Where?"

"We're going to interrogate the suspects."

"The suspects? But I thought it was an accident!"

"I meant the witnesses. Let's go."

The horde of young fans gathered around the man in boots chants "Spinoza fucks Hegel up the arse! Spinoza fucks Hegel up the arse! Down with dialectics!" On his way out, Bayard and his new assistant stand aside to let a group of Maoists pass; apparently they have decided to beat up the Spinozists.

12

Roland Barthes lived on Rue Servandoni, next to the Saint-Sulpice church, a stone's throw from the Jardin du Luxembourg. I am going to park where I suppose Bayard parked his 504, outside the front door of number 11. I'll spare you the now obligatory copy-and-paste of the Wikipedia page: the private mansion designed by such-and-such Italian architect for such-and-such Breton bishop, and so on.

It's a handsome building, nice white stone, impressive wrought-iron gate. Outside the gate, a Vinci employee is installing an entry keypad. (Vinci is not yet called Vinci and belongs to CGE, the Compagnie Générale d'Electricité, later known as Alcatel, but Simon Herzog can't know anything about all this.) They have to cross the courtyard and take Staircase B, on the right, just after the concierge's office. Herzog asks Bayard what they are looking for here. Bayard has no idea. They climb the stairs because there is no elevator.

The decoration in the third-floor apartment is old-fashioned. There are wooden clocks, it's very neatly kept, very clean, even the room that serves as an office—next to the bed is a transistor radio and a copy of Chateaubriand's *Memoirs from Beyond the Tomb*— but Barthes worked mostly in his attic room, on the seventh floor.

In the sixth-floor apartment, the two men are welcomed by Barthes's younger brother and his wife—an Arab, notes Bayard; pretty, notes Simon—who invites them in for tea. The younger brother explains that the apartments on the third and sixth floor are identical. For a while, Barthes, his mother, and his younger brother lived on the sixth floor, but when his mother fell ill she became too weak to climb all those stairs, so—as the third-floor apartment was available—Barthes bought it and moved in there with her. Roland Barthes had a wide social circle, he went out frequently, especially after their mother's death, but the younger brother says he doesn't know any of the people he hung around with. All he knows is that he often went to the Café de Flore, where he had work meetings and where he also met up with friends.

The seventh floor is actually two adjoining attic rooms knocked into one to create a small studio apartment. There is a trestle table that acts as a desk, an iron-framed bed, a kitchenette with a box of Japanese tea on top of the refrigerator. There are books everywhere, empty coffee cups next to half-full ashtrays. It is older, dirtier, and messier, but it does have a piano, a turntable, some classical music records (Schumann, Schubert), and shoeboxes containing files, keys, gloves, maps, press cuttings.

A trapdoor allows entry directly into the sixth-floor apartment without going out onto the landing.

On the wall, Simon Herzog recognizes the strange photographs from *Camera Lucida*, Barthes's latest book, which has just come out—among them, the yellowed snapshot of a little girl in a sunroom: his beloved mother.

Bayard asks Herzog to take a look through the files and the

library. Like any book lover entering someone's home for the first time, even if they've not gone there for that reason, Herzog is already curiously examining the books in the library: Proust, Pascal, de Sade, more Chateaubriand, not many contemporary writers, apart from a few works by Sollers, Kristeva, and Robbe-Grillet, and various dictionaries, critical works, Todorov, Genette, and books about linguistics, Saussure, Austin, Searle . . . There is a sheet of paper in the typewriter on the desk. Simon Herzog reads the title: "We always fail to talk about what we love." He quickly scans the text—it's about Stendhal. Simon is moved by the thought of Barthes sitting at this desk, thinking about Stendhal, about love, about Italy, completely unaware that every hour spent typing this article was bringing him closer to the moment when he would be knocked over by a laundry van.

Next to the typewriter is a copy of Jakobson's *Linguistics and Poetics*; inside it, a bookmark that makes Simon Herzog think of a stopped watch found on a victim's wrist: when Barthes was knocked over by the van, this is what was going through his mind. As it happens, he was rereading the chapter on the functions of language. Barthes's bookmark was actually a sheet of paper folded in four. Simon Herzog unfolds the sheet: notes scrawled in small, dense handwriting, which he doesn't even try to decipher. He folds the sheet up without reading it and carefully puts it back in the right place, so that when Barthes comes home he will be able to find his page.

Close to the edge of the desk are a few opened letters, lots of unopened letters, other pages covered with scribbles in the same dense handwriting, a few copies of the *Nouvel Observateur*, newspaper articles, and photographs cut from magazines. Cigarette butts are piled up like firewood. Simon Herzog feels overwhelmed by sadness. While Bayard rummages around under the little iron bed, he bends to look through the window. Down on the street, he spots a black DS double-parked and he smiles at the symbolism. The DS was the emblem of Barthes's *Mythologies*, and the most famous, the one he chose for the cover of his celebrated collection of articles. He hears a hammering sound from below: the Vinci employee is chiseling a notch in the stone that will house the metal keyboard. The sky has turned white. Above the rooftops, below the horizon, he can make out the trees of the Jardin du Luxembourg.

Bayard tears him from his reverie by dropping a stack of magazines on the desk. He found them under the bed. They are not back issues of the *Nouvel Obs*. With a snarl of satisfaction, he says to Simon: "He liked cock, this intellectual!" Spread out before him, Simon Herzog sees magazine covers featuring young, muscular naked men, posing and staring out insolently at him. I'm not sure how widely known Barthes's homosexuality was at the time. When he wrote his bestseller, *A Lover's Discourse*, he took care never to characterize his love object in terms of gender, striving to use neutral formulations such as "the partner" or "the other" (both of which, for what it's worth, are masculine words in French, meaning that the pronoun is always "he"). Unlike Foucault, whose homosexuality was very open, almost as a form of protest, I know that Barthes was very discreet, perhaps ashamed, in any case very preoccupied with keeping up appearances, until his mother's death at least. Foucault wanted him to be more open, and despised him a little for his reserve, I think. But I don't know if there were rumors in university circles or among the wider public, or whether everyone knew. Anyway, if Simon Herzog was aware of Barthes's homosexuality, he hadn't thought it necessary to inform Superintendent Bayard at this stage of the inquiry.

Just as the sniggering policeman is opening the centerfold of a magazine named *Gai Pied*, the telephone rings. Bayard stops. He puts the magazine on the desk without bothering to close it, and freezes. He looks at Simon Herzog, who looks back at him, while the handsome youth in the photograph grips his cock and looks out at both of them and the telephone continues to ring. Bayard lets it ring a few more times and picks up the receiver without a word. Simon watches as he remains silent for several seconds. He also hears the silence on the other end of the line and instinctively stops breathing. When Bayard finally says "Hello" there is an audible click, followed by the "beep-beep" that indicates the call has been ended. Bayard hangs up, puzzled. Simon Herzog asks stupidly: "Wrong number?" In the street, through the open window, they hear a car engine start. Bayard takes the porn magazines and the two men leave the room. Simon Herzog thinks: "I should have closed the window. It's going to rain." Jacques Bayard thinks: "Fucking queer intellectual bastards . . ."

They ring the bell at the concierge's office to return the keys, but no one answers. The workman installing the keypad offers to give them back to the concierge when she returns, but Bayard prefers to go back upstairs and hand them to the younger brother.

When he comes back down, Simon Herzog is smoking a cigarette with the workman, who's taking a break. Out in the street, Bayard does not get back in the 504. "Where are we going?" Simon Herzog asks him. "To the Café de Flore," replies Bayard. "Did you notice, the guy installing the keypad?" Simon says. "He had a Slav accent, didn't he?" Bayard grumbles: "As long as he's not driving a tank, I couldn't care less." As they cross Place Saint-Sulpice, the two men pass a blue Fuego and Bayard says, with the air of an expert: "That's the new Renault. It's only just gone on sale." Simon Herzog thinks automatically that the workers who built this car wouldn't be able to afford it even if ten of them got together. And, lost in his Marxist thoughts, doesn't pay attention to the two Japanese men inside the car.

13

At the Flore, they see a man squinting through thick glasses, seated next to a little blonde. He looks sickly, and his froglike face is vaguely familiar to Bayard, but he is not the reason they are there. Bayard spots some men in their twenties and goes over to talk to them. Most are gigolos who pick up clients in the area. Do they know Barthes? Yes, all of them. Bayard interrogates them a bit while Simon Herzog observes Sartre out of the corner of his eye: he is definitely not in good shape; he keeps coughing as he smokes his cigarette. Françoise Sagan pats his back solicitously. The last one to have seen Barthes is a young Moroccan: the great critic was negotiating with a new guy, he doesn't know his name, they left together the other day, he doesn't know what they did or where they went or where he lives but he knows where they can find him tonight: at the Bains Diderot, a sauna at the Gare de Lyon. "A sauna?" Simon Herzog asks, surprised, when suddenly a scarf-wearing maniac appears and begins yelling at anyone who will listen: "Look at them! Look at their faces! They won't look like that much longer! Seriously, I'm telling you: a bourgeois must reign or die! Drink! Drink your Fernet to the health of your company! Enjoy it while you can! Drink to your downfall! Long live Bokassa!" A few conversations come to an abrupt halt. The regulars observe this newcomer gloomily, and the tourists try to enjoy the show without really understanding what it's about, but the waiters ignore it and continue serving. His arm sweeps the room in theatrical outrage and, addressing an imaginary opponent, the scarf-wearing prophet proclaims victoriously: "No need to run, comrade. The old world is ahead of you!"

Bayard asks who this man is; the gigolo tells him it is Jean-Edern Hallier, some aristocratic writer who is always making a fuss and who reckons he will be a minister if Mitterrand wins next year. Bayard notes the inverted-V mouth, the shining blue eyes, the typical upper-class accent that verges on mispronunciation. He returns to his questioning: What is this new guy like? The young Moroccan describes him as an Arab with a southern accent, a small earring, and hair that falls over his face. Still shouting at the top of his voice, Jean-Edern haphazardly extols the virtues of ecology, euthanasia, independent radio stations, and Ovid's *Metamorphoses*. Simon Herzog watches Sartre watching

Jean-Edern. When the aristocrat notices that Sartre is there, he starts to tremble. Sartre stares at him contemplatively. Françoise Sagan whispers into his ear, like a simultaneous translator. Jean-Edern narrows his eyes, which makes him look even more weasel-like under his thick, frizzy hair, is silent for a few seconds, apparently thinking, and then starts shouting again: "Existentialism is a contagion! Long live the third sex! Long live the fourth! Don't despair, La Coupole!" Bayard explains to Simon Herzog that he must come with him to the Bains Diderot to help him find this unknown gigolo. Jean-Edern Hallier goes over to stand in front of Sartre, holds his arm up in the air, hand flat, clicks his loafers together, and yells: "Heil Althusser!" Simon Herzog protests that his presence is not absolutely essential. Sartre coughs and lights another Gitane. Bayard says, on the contrary, a queer little intellectual will be very useful in locating the suspect. Jean-Edern starts singing obscene lyrics to the tune of "The Internationale." Simon Herzog says it's too late to buy a pair of swimming trunks. Bayard laughs and tells him there's no need. Sartre unfolds *Le Monde* and starts doing the crossword. (As he is almost blind, it is Françoise Sagan who reads the clues to him.) Jean-Edern spots something in the street and rushes outside, yelling: "Modernity, I shit on you!" It is already seven o'clock, and night has fallen. Superintendent Bayard and Simon Herzog go back to the 504, parked outside Barthes's apartment block. Bayard yanks three or four parking tickets from under the windshield wiper and they head off toward Place de la République, followed by a black DS and a blue Fuego.

14

Jacques Bayard and Simon Herzog walk through sauna steam, little white towels tied around their waists, amid sweaty figures who furtively brush against one another. The superintendent left his card in the changing room, so they are incognito. The aim of the game is not to scare off the gigolo with the earring, if they find him.

In truth, they make a fairly credible couple: the old, beefy, hairy-chested guy, looking around inquisitively, and the skinny, young, clean-shaven one, who glances at his surroundings surreptitiously. Simon Herzog, looking like a frightened anthropologist, excites some lustful looks—the men who pass him stare for a long time, and circle back toward him—but Bayard gets a fair amount of attention too. Two or three young men shoot him flirtatious glances, and a fat man stares from a distance, fist balled around his penis: apparently the Lino Ventura look has its fans here. If Bayard is angry that this gaggle of queers can take him for one of them, he is professional enough to conceal it, merely adopting a faintly hostile expression intended to discourage approaches.

The complex is divided into different spaces: the sauna itself, a Turkish bath, a swimming pool, back rooms in various configurations. The fauna is quite varied too: all ages, all sizes, all degrees of corpulence are here. But in terms of what the superintendent and his assistant are searching for, there is a problem: half of the men here are wearing an earring, and for the under-30s the figure reaches almost 100 percent, nearly all of whom are North Africans. Unfortunately, the description of the man's hair is not much more useful: young men with bangs over their eyes are undetectable in here because it's a natural reflex to slick back wet hair.

And so to the final clue: the southern accent. But that requires, at some point, verbal contact.

In the corner of the sauna, on a tiled bench, two youths are kissing and wanking each other off. Bayard leans over them discreetly to check whether either is wearing an earring. They both are. But if they were gigolos, would they really be wasting their time on each other? It's possible. Bayard has never worked for the vice squad and is no specialist when it comes to this kind of behavior. He takes Simon on a tour of the premises. It's difficult to see much: the steam forms a thick fog, and some men are hidden away in back rooms where they can be observed only through barred windows. They pass an apparently half-witted Arab who tries to touch everyone's dicks, two Japanese men, two guys with mustaches and greasy hair, fat tattooed men, lascivious old men, velvet-eyed young men. The sauna's clients wear their towels around their waists or over their shoulders; everyone in the pool is naked; some have hard-ons, others don't. Here, too, all sizes and shapes are on display. Bayard tries to spot earring wearers and, when he's found four or five, he points one out to Simon and orders him to go and talk to the man.

Simon Herzog knows perfectly well that it would make more sense for Bayard to approach the gigolo rather than him but, seeing the cop's blank face, he realizes it would be pointless to argue. Awkwardly, he walks over to the gigolo and says good evening. His voice quavers. The gigolo smiles but does not reply. Outside his classroom, Simon Herzog is naturally shy, and he has never been much of a ladies' man (or a man's man, for that matter). He manages to make a few banal comments that immediately sound inappropriate or merely ridiculous. Without a word, the gigolo takes his hand and leads him toward the back rooms. All strength gone, Simon follows him. He knows he has to react quickly. In a toneless voice, he asks: "What's your name?" The man replies: "Patrick." No *o* or *eu* to help him detect a southern accent, and no use of the telltale word *con*. Simon follows him into a little cell where the young man grabs his hips and kneels down in front of him. In the hope of making him pronounce a full sentence, Simon stammers: "Wouldn't you prefer it if I went first?" The gigolo says no and his hand moves under Simon's towel. Simon shivers. The towel falls. With surprise, Simon notices that his cock, touched by the young man's fingers, is not completely flaccid. So he decides to go for broke: "Hang on! You know what I'd like to do?" "What?" the other asks. Still not enough syllables to detect his accent. "I'd like to shit on you!"

The gigolo looks surprised. "Can I?" And finally Patrick replies, without even a hint of a southern accent: "All right, but it'll be more expensive!" Simon Herzog picks up his towel and rushes out, calling: "Never mind! Another time?" If he has to do the same with the dozen potential gigolos patrolling the club, this could be a very long night. He passes the half-witted Arab again, who tries to touch his dick, and the two men with mustaches, the two Japanese men, the fat tattooed men, the velvet-eyed youths, and rejoins Bayard just as a loud, nasal, professorial voice intones: "A functionary of the powers that be showing off his repressive muscles in the service of biopower? What could be more normal?"

Behind Bayard, a wiry, square-jawed, bald man is sitting, naked, arms outstretched and resting on the back of a wooden bench, legs spread wide, being sucked off by a skinny young man who does have an earring but also has short hair. "Have you found anything interesting, Superintendent?" asks Michel Foucault, staring at Simon Herzog.

Bayard conceals his surprise, but doesn't know how to respond. Simon Herzog's eyes open wide. The silence is filled with the echoes of cries and moans from back rooms. The mustachioed men hold hands in the shadows, stealthily observing Bayard, Herzog, and Foucault. The Arab dick-toucher wanders around. The Japanese pretend to go for a swim in the pool with their towels on their heads. The tattooed men accost the velvet-eyed youths, or vice versa. Michel Foucault questions Bayard: "What do you think of this place, Superintendent?" Bayard does not reply. No sound but the echoes from the back rooms. "Ahh! Ahh!" Foucault: "You came here to find someone, but it looks to me like you've already found him." He points to Simon Herzog and laughs: "Your Alcibiades!" The back rooms: "Ahh! Ahh!" Bayard: "I'm looking for someone who saw Roland Barthes not long before his accident." Foucault, caressing the head of the young man hard at work between his legs: "Roland had a secret, you know . . ." Bayard asks what it was. The back-room panting grows louder. Foucault explains to Bayard that Barthes had a Western understanding of sex, i.e., something simultaneously secret and whose secret must be uncovered. "Roland Barthes," he says, "is the ewe that wanted to be a shepherd. And was! That's as brilliant as it gets! But for everyone else . . . as far as sex is concerned, he always remained a ewe." The back rooms moo. "Oh! Oh! Ooh! Ooh!" The Arab groper tries to slip his hand under Simon's towel, but is gently pushed away, so he goes over to the mustachioed men. "Essentially," says Foucault, "Roland had a Christian temperament. He came here like the first Christians went to Mass: uncomprehendingly but fervently. He believed in it without knowing why." (In the back rooms: "Yes! Yes!) "Homosexuality disgusts you, doesn't it, Superintendent?" ("Harder! Harder!") "And yet it was you who created us. The notion of male homosexuality didn't exist in Ancient Greece: Socrates could bugger Alcibiades without being seen as a pederast. The Greeks had a more elevated notion of the corruption of youth . . ."

Foucault throws back his head, eyes closed. Neither Bayard nor Herzog can tell if he's abandoning himself to pleasure or thinking. And still the back-room chorus rises in volume: "Oh! Oh!"

Foucault opens his eyes, as if he's just remembered something: "And yet the Greeks had their limits too. They used to deny the young boy his share of pleasure. They couldn't forbid it, of course, but they couldn't conceive of it, and in the end, they did what we do: they excluded it through decorum." (The back rooms: "No! No! No!") "At the end of the day decorum is always the most effective means of coercion . . ." He points at his crotch: "This is not a pipe, as Magritte would say, ha ha!" He pulls up on the head of the young man, who is still pumping away conscientiously: "But you like sucking me, don't you, Hamed?" The young man nods carefully. Foucault looks at him tenderly and says, stroking his cheek, "Short hair suits you." The young man smiles and replies, in a strong southern accent: "Thanks a lot!"

Bayard and Herzog prick up their ears. They are not sure

they heard him correctly, but the boy adds: "You're a nice guy, Michel, and you have a really lovely dick, *con!*"

15

Yes, he saw Roland Barthes, a few days ago. No, they didn't really have sexual relations. Barthes called it "boating." But he wasn't very active. More the sentimental type. Barthes bought him an omelet at La Coupole and afterward insisted on taking him back to his attic room. They drank tea. They didn't talk about anything special; Barthes was not very chatty. He seemed pensive. Before he left, Barthes asked him: "What would you do if you ruled the world?" The gigolo replied that he would abolish all laws. Barthes said: "Even grammar?"

16

It is relatively calm in the lobby of Pitié-Salpêtrière. Friends, admirers, acquaintances, and the merely curious line up to sit at the great man's bedside; they fill the hospital foyer, conversing in undertones, a cigarette or a sandwich or a newspaper in hand, or a book by Guy Debord or a Milan Kundera novel. Suddenly, three figures appear: a small-waisted woman, short-haired, full of energy, flanked by two men; one in a white shirt open to the navel and a long black coat, black hair billowing, and the other, beige-haired, birdlike, a cigarette holder between his lips.

The formation moves resolutely through the crowd. You can tell that something is about to happen. It's all a bit Operation Overlord. They plow into the coma wing. The people there to see Barthes look at one another, and the other visitors do the same. Barely five minutes have passed before the first yells are heard: "They're letting him die! They're letting him die!"

The three avenging angels return from the kingdom of the

dead raging: "This is a place for the dying! It's a scandal! Who are they trying to fool? Why didn't anyone warn us? If only we'd been there!" It's a shame there is no photographer in the room to immortalize this great moment in the history of French intellectuals: Julia Kristeva, Philippe Sollers, Bernard-Henri Lévy upbraiding the hospital staff for the disgraceful way they are treating a patient as prestigious as their great friend Roland Barthes.

Maybe you'll be surprised by the presence of BHL but, even back then, he is always where the action is. Barthes supported him as a "new philosopher" in slightly vague but nevertheless relatively official terms, and Deleuze took him to task for it. According to his friends Barthes was always weak, he never knew how to say no. When *Barbarism with a Human Face* comes out in 1977, BHL sends him a copy and he gives a polite response praising the book's style, while not lingering on its substance. No matter: BHL has the letter published in *Les Nouvelles littéraires*, teams up with Sollers, and here he is three years later, raising his voice in the Salpêtrière in a show of noisy concern for his friend the great critic.

Now, while he and his two acolytes continue making a scene by barking at the poor medical staff ("He must be transferred immediately! To the American Hospital! Call Neuilly!"), two figures in ill-fitting suits sneak down the corridor unnoticed. Jacques Bayard watches, baffled and slightly stunned, as the tall, dark-haired man whirls about and the two others squawk. Beside him, Simon Herzog, fulfilling the task he was requisitioned for, explains to Bayard who these people are, while the three avengers bang on, moving through the lobby in a grid pattern that appears erratic but which I wouldn't be surprised to discover actually obeys some obscure tactical choreography.

They are still barking ("Do you know who he is? Are you going to pretend that Roland Barthes can be treated like any other patient?" It's always the same with people like that, expecting privileges because of who they are . . .) when the two badly dressed figures reappear in the lobby before discreetly slipping away. And they are still there when a terrified nurse runs in, a blonde with slender legs who whispers something in the doctor's ear. Cue a mass movement: people push past one another, charge down the corridor, rush into Barthes's room. The great critic is lying on the floor, the tube and all his wires torn out, his flabby buttocks visible under the paper-thin hospital tunic. He groans as he is turned over and his eyes roll frantically, but when he sees Superintendent Jacques Bayard, who is standing among the doctors, he sits up, in a superhuman effort, grabs the policeman's jacket, forcing him to squat down, and pronounces weakly but distinctly, in his famous bass voice, only broken now and as if he is hiccupping:

"Sophia! *Elle sait . . .*"

But what does Sophia know?

In the doorway he sees Kristeva, next to the blond nurse. His eyes are fixed on her for several long seconds, and everyone in the room—doctors, nurses, friends, policeman—is frozen, paralyzed, by the intensity of his distraught gaze. Then he loses consciousness.

Outside, a black DS races off with a screech of tires. Simon Herzog, who has remained in the lobby, pays no attention.

Bayard asks Kristeva: "Sophia, that's you?" Kristeva says no. But as he just stands there waiting, she eventually adds—pronouncing it the French way, with the *j* and the *u* palatalized—"My name is Julia." Bayard can vaguely detect her foreign accent; he thinks she must be Italian, or German, or maybe Greek, or Brazilian, or Russian. He finds her face harsh; he doesn't like the piercing look she gives him; he is well aware that those little black eyes want him to understand that she is an intelligent woman, more intelligent than he is, and that she despises him for being a stupid cop. Mechanically, he asks: "Profession?" And when she replies disdainfully, "Psychoanalyst," he instinctively wants to slap her, but he suppresses the urge. He still has the two others to question.

The blond nurse puts Barthes back in his bed. He is still unconscious. Bayard puts two policemen on guard outside the room and forbids all visits until further notice. Then he turns to the two clowns.

Last name, first name, age, profession.

Joyaux, Philippe, aka Sollers, forty-three, writer, married to Julia Joyaux née Kristeva.

Lévy, Bernard-Henri, thirty-one, philosopher, former École Normale Supérieure student.

The two men were not in Paris when it happened. Barthes and Sollers were very close . . . Barthes contributed to Sollers's magazine *Tel Quel*, and they went to China together with Julia a few years ago . . . To do what? A study trip . . . Bloody Communists, thinks Bayard. Barthes wrote several articles praising Sollers's work . . . Barthes is like a father for Sollers, even if Barthes behaves like a little boy at times . . . And Kristeva? Barthes said one day that if he liked women, he would be in love with Julia . . . He adored her . . . And you weren't jealous, Monsieur Joyaux? Ha ha ha . . . Julia and I, we don't have that kind of relationship . . . And anyway, poor Roland, he already had enough problems with men . . . Why? He didn't know how to handle things . . . He always got taken for a ride! . . . I see. And you, Monsieur Lévy? I admire him greatly, he's a great man. Did you travel with him too? I was going to suggest several projects to him. What sort of projects? A project for a film about the life of Charles Baudelaire; I was planning to offer him the title role. A project for a joint interview with Solzhenitsyn. A project to petition NATO to liberate Cuba. Could you provide any evidence to substantiate these claims? Yes, of course, I spoke to Andre Glucksmann about them—he's a witness. Did Barthes have any enemies? Yes, lots, replies Sollers. Everyone knows he's our friend and we have lots of enemies! Who? The Stalinists! The fascists! Alain Badiou! Gilles Deleuze! Pierre Bourdieu! Cornelius Castoriadis! Pierre Vidal-Naquet! Uh, Hélène Cixous! (BHL: Oh, really? Did she and Julia fall out? Sollers: Yes . . . well, no . . . she's jealous of Julia, because of Marguerite . . .)

Marguerite who? Duras. Bayard notes down all the names. Does Monsieur Joyaux know a certain Michel Foucault? Sollers starts whirling around like a dervish, faster and faster, his cigarette holder still held between his lips, the incandescent end tracing graceful orange curves in the hospital corridor: "The truth, Superintendent? The whole truth . . . nothing but the truth . . . Foucault was jealous of Barthes's fame . . . and especially jealous because I, Sollers, loved Barthes . . . because Foucault is the worst kind of tyrant, Superintendent: a lackey . . . Can you believe, Mr. Representative of Public Order—*cough cough*—that Foucault gave me an ultimatum? 'You must choose between Barthes and me!' . . . One might as easily choose between Montaigne and La Boétie . . . Between Racine and Shakespeare . . . Between Hugo and Balzac . . . Between Goethe and Schiller . . . Between Marx and Engels . . . Between Merckx and Poulidor . . . Between Mao and Lenin . . . Between Breton and Aragon . . . Between Laurel and Hardy . . . Between Sartre and Camus (well, no, not them) . . . Between de Gaulle and Tixier-Vignancour . . . Between the Plan and the Market . . . Between Rocard and Mitterrand . . . Between Giscard and Chirac . . ." Sollers slows down. He coughs into his cigarette holder. "Between Pascal and Descartes . . . *cough cough* . . . Between Trésor and Platini . . . Between Renault and Peugeot . . . Between Mazarin and Richelieu . . . Hhhhh . . ." But just when it looks as if he is about to collapse, he finds a second wind. "Between the Left Bank and the Right Bank . . . Between Paris and Beijing . . . Between Venice and Rome . . . Between Mussolini and Hitler . . . Between andouille and mashed potato . . ."

Suddenly, there is a noise in the room. Bayard opens the door and sees Barthes twitching and jerking, talking in his sleep, while the nurse tries to tuck him in. He is saying something about "starred text," a "minor earthquake," "blocks of signification," the reading of which grasps only the smooth surface, imperceptibly bonded by the flow of phrases, the running speech of the narration, the naturalness of vernacular.

Bayard immediately brings in Simon Herzog to translate for him. Lying in bed, Barthes is becoming increasingly agitated. Bayard leans over him and asks: "Monsieur Barthes, did you see your attacker?" Barthes opens his madman's eyes, grabs Bayard by the back of the neck, and declares, in an anguished, breathless voice: "The tutor signifier will be cut up into a series of short, contiguous fragments, which we shall call lexias, since they are units of reading. This cutting up, it must be said, will be arbitrary in the extreme; it will imply no methodological responsibility, because it will be carried out only on the signifier, while the proposed analysis will be carried out only on the signified . . ." Bayard shoots a quizzical look at Herzog, who shrugs. Barthes whistles threateningly between his teeth. Bayard asks him: "Monsieur Barthes, who is Sophia? What does she know?" Barthes looks at him without understanding, or perhaps understanding all too well, and starts singing in a hoarse voice: "The text is comparable in its mass to a sky, at once flat and smooth, deep, without edges and without landmarks; like the soothsayer drawing on it with the tip of his staff an imaginary rectangle wherein to consult, according to certain principles, the flight of birds, the commentator traces through the text certain zones of reading, in order to observe therein the migration of meanings, the outcropping of codes, the passage of citations." Bayard curses Herzog, whose puzzled face reveals all too clearly that he is incapable of explaining this gobbledygook, but Barthes is on the verge of hysteria when he starts shouting, as if his life depended on it: "It's all in the text! You understand? Find the text! The function! Oh, this is so stupid!" Then he falls back on his pillow and quietly intones: "The lexia is only the wrapping of a semantic volume, the crest line of the plural text, arranged like a berm of possible meanings (but controlled, attested to by a systematic reading) under the flux of discourse: the lexia and its units will thereby form a kind of polyhedron faceted by the word, the group of words, the sentence of the paragraph, i.e., with the language which is its 'natural' excipient." And he faints. Bayard tries to shake him back to consciousness. The blond nurse has to force him to put the patient down, then she clears the room again.

When Bayard asks Simon Herzog to give him the lowdown, the young professor wants to tell him that he shouldn't take too much notice of Sollers and BHL, but at the same time he sees an opportunity, so he says with relish: "We should begin by interrogating Deleuze."

On his way out of the hospital, Simon Herzog bumps into the blond nurse who is looking after Barthes. "Oh, excuse me, mademoiselle!" She gives him a charming smile: "No prrroblem, monsieur."

17

Hamed wakes early. His body, still soaked with last night's steam and drugs, jolts him from a bad sleep. Dazed and groggy, disoriented, all at sea in this unfamiliar room, it takes him a few seconds to recall how he got here and what he did. He slides out of bed, trying not to wake the man next to him, puts on his sleeveless T-shirt and his Lee Cooper jeans, goes into the kitchen to make himself coffee, finishes a joint from the night before which he finds in a Jacuzzi-shaped ashtray, grabs his jacket, a black-and-white Teddy Smith with a large red *F* near the heart, and leaves, slamming the door behind him.

It's a beautiful day outside and a black DS is parked by the curb in the empty street. Hamed enjoys the fresh air while listening to Blondie on his Walkman and doesn't notice as the black DS starts up and slowly follows him. He crosses the Seine, passes the Jardin des Plantes, thinks that with a bit of luck there'll be someone at the Flore to buy him a real coffee. But at the Flore there are only his gigolo colleagues and two or three old guys who aren't in the market; Sartre is already there too, coughing and smoking his pipe, surrounded by a little circle of sweater-wearing students, so Hamed asks for a cigarette from a passerby who's walking a sad-eyed beagle, and smokes outside the Pub Saint-Germain, which is not yet open, with some other young gigolos who, like him, look as if they didn't get enough sleep, drank too much and smoked too much, and most of whom forgot to eat the night before. There's Saïd, who asks him if he went to the Baleine Bleue yesterday; Harold, who tells him he almost had it off with Amanda Lear at the Palace; and Slimane, who got beaten up, but can't remember why. They all agree that they're bored shitless. Harold would like to see *Le Guignolo* in Montparnasse or Odéon, but there's no showing before 2:00 p.m. On the opposite pavement, the two guys with mustaches have parked the DS and are drinking a coffee at the Brasserie Lipp. Their suits are crumpled as if they'd slept in their car and they still have their umbrellas with them. Hamed thinks he'd be better off going home and sleeping, but he can't be bothered to climb the six flights of stairs, so he bums another cigarette from a black guy coming out of the metro and wonders whether he should go to the hospital or not. Saïd tells him that "Babar" is in a coma, but that he might be happy to hear his voice; apparently people in comas can hear, like plants, when you play classical music to them. Harold shows them his black-and-orange reversible bomber jacket. Slimane says he saw a Russian poet they know yesterday with a scar, and that he was even more handsome like that, and this makes them giggle. Hamed decides to go to La Coupole to see if I'm there, and walks up Rue de Rennes. The two mustaches follow him, leaving their umbrellas behind, but the waiter catches up with them, yelling, "Gentlemen! Gentlemen!" He brandishes the umbrellas like swords, but no one pays any attention, even though it looks like it's going to be a sunny day. The two men get their umbrellas back and start tailing their target again. They stop outside the Cosmos, which is showing Tarkovsky's *Stalker* and a Soviet war film, and a little gap opens up between them and Hamed, but he keeps pausing to look in the windows of clothing stores, so there's no danger of them losing him.

Nevertheless, one of them goes back to fetch the DS.

18

At Rue de Bizerte, between La Fourche and Place Clichy, Gilles Deleuze receives the two investigators. Simon Herzog is thrilled to meet the great philosopher, in his own home, among his books, in an apartment that smells of philosophy and stale tobacco. The TV is on, showing tennis, and Simon notices lots of books about Leibniz scattered all over the place. They hear the *poc-poc* of balls. It's Connors versus Nastase.

Officially, the two men are here because Deleuze was implicated by BHL. The interrogation begins, then, with A for Accusation.

"Monsieur Deleuze, we've been informed of a dispute between yourself and Roland Barthes. What was it about?" *Poc-poc.* Deleuze lifts a half-smoked but extinct cigarette to his mouth. Bayard notices his abnormally long fingernails. "Oh, really? No, no, I didn't have any quarrel with Roland, beyond the fact that he supported that nonentity, the moron with the white shirt."

Simon notices the hat hanging on the hat rack. Added to the one on the coat rack in the entrance hall and the other on the dresser, that's a lot of hats, in various colors, similar to the one Alain Delon wore in *Le Samouraï*.

Poc-poc.

Deleuze settles himself more comfortably in his chair: "You see that American? He's the anti-Borg. Well, no, the anti-Borg is McEnroe: Egyptian service, Russian soul, eh? Hmm, hmm. [He coughs.] But Connors, hitting the ball full on, that constant risk-taking, those low, skimming shots . . . it's very aristocratic, too. Borg: stays on the baseline, returns the ball, well above the net, thanks to his topspin. Any prole can understand that. Borg is inventing a tennis for the proletariat. McEnroe and Connors, obviously, play like princes."

Bayard sits down on the sofa. He has a feeling he's going to have to listen to a lot of crap.

Simon objects: "But Connors is the archetype of the people, isn't he? He's the bad boy, the brat, the hooligan; he cheats, he argues, he whines; he's a bad sport, a scrapper, a fighter, he never gives up . . ."

Deleuze interrupts impatiently: "Oh yes? Hmm, that's an interesting point of view."

Bayard asks: "It's possible that someone wanted to steal something from Monsieur Barthes. A document. Would you know anything about that, Monsieur Deleuze?"

Deleuze turns toward Simon: "It is likely that the question *what?* isn't the right kind of question. It's possible that questions like *who? how much? how? where? when?* would be better."

Bayard lights a cigarette and asks in a patient, almost resigned voice: "What do you mean?"

"Well, it's obvious that if you have come to find me, more than a week after the event, to question me about a moronic philosopher's half-baked insinuations, it's because Roland's accident was probably not an accident at all. So you are searching for a culprit. Or, in other words, a motive. But you are a long way from *why*, aren't you? I suppose that the line of inquiry relating to the driver didn't get you anywhere? I heard that Roland had woken up. And he didn't want to say anything? So you change the *why*."

They hear Connors grunting each time he hits the ball. Simon glances out of the window. He notices a blue Fuego parked down below.

Bayard asks why, in Deleuze's opinion, Barthes does not want to reveal what he knows. Deleuze replies that he has no idea, but he does know one thing: "Whatever happens, whatever the situation, there are always pretenders. In other words, there are people who claim: as far as this goes, I am the best."

Bayard grabs the owl-shaped ashtray on the coffee table and

drags it toward him. "And what do you claim to be the best at, Monsieur Deleuze?"

Deleuze emits a small noise somewhere between a snigger and a cough: "One always claims to be what one cannot be or what one was once and will never be again, Superintendent. But I don't think that is the question, is it?"

Bayard asks what the question is.

Deleuze relights his cigarette: "How to choose from among the pretenders."

Somewhere in the building, they hear the echo of a woman screaming. They can't tell if it's from pleasure or anger. Deleuze points at the door: "It is a common misconception, Superintendent, that women are women by nature. Women have a *devenir-femme*." He stands up, panting slightly (yes, him, too), and walks off to pour himself a glass of red wine. "We're the same."

Bayard, suspicious, asks: "You think we're all the same? You think that you and me, we're the same?"

Deleuze smiles: "Yes . . . well, in a way."

Bayard, trying to show willingness but revealing a sort of reticence: "So you're searching for the truth too?"

"Oh my! The truth . . . Where it begins is where it ends . . . We're always in the middle of something, you know."

Connors wins the first set 6–2.

"How can we determine which of the pretenders is the right one? If you have the *how*, you'll find the *why*. Take the Sophists, for example: according to Plato, the problem is that they claim something they don't have the right to claim . . . Oh yes, they cheat, those little shits!" He rubs his hands together. "The trial is always a trial of pretenders . . ."

He downs the contents of his glass in a single gulp and, looking at Simon, adds: "This is as amusing as a novel."

Simon meets his gaze.

19

"No, it's absolutely impossible! I categorically refuse! I won't go!
That's enough now! There's no way I'm setting foot in that palace! You don't need me to decode that bastard's words! And
I don't need to hear him; let me summarize for you: I am the
groveling servant of capital. I am the enemy of the working
classes. I have the media in my pocket. When I'm not hunting
elephants in Africa, I hunt down independent radio stations. I
muzzle freedom of expression. I build nuclear power stations all
over the place. I am a populist pimp who invites himself into
poor people's homes. I receive diamonds from dictators. I like
pretending to be a prole by going on the metro. I like blacks, but
only when they're emperors or garbagemen. When I hear the
word *humanitarian*, I send in the paratroopers. I use the back
rooms of extreme right-wing organizations for my private purposes. I am . . . I am . . . a STUPID FASCIST PIG!"

Simon lights a cigarette, hands trembling. Bayard waits for
his tantrum to end. At this stage of the investigation, given the
available evidence, he handed in a preliminary report and had a
feeling that this case would turn into something big . . . but,
even so, he didn't expect that he would be summoned here. With
his young assistant in tow.

"Anyway, I won't go I won't go I won't go," says his young
sidekick.

20

"The President will receive you now."

Jacques Bayard and Simon Herzog enter a brightly lit corner
office with walls covered in green silk. Simon looks like he's in
shock, but he instinctively notes the two chairs facing the desk
behind which Giscard stands and, at the other end of the

room, more chairs with a sofa beside a coffee table. The student immediately grasps the possibilities: depending on whether the president wishes to maintain some distance between himself and his visitors or, alternatively, give the meeting a more convivial feel, he can welcome them from behind his desk, which acts as a sort of shield, or sit around the coffee table and eat cakes and biscuits with them. Simon Herzog also spots a book on Kennedy, placed ostentatiously on an escritoire to suggest the young, modern head of state that Giscard also aspires to embody; two boxes, one red and one blue, set on a roll-top desk; bronze statues here and there; stacks of files at a carefully calculated height: too low, they would give the impression that the president was lazy, too high, that he couldn't cope with his workload. Several old master paintings hang on the walls. Standing behind his massive desk, Giscard points to one representing a beautiful, severe-looking woman, arms outspread, dressed in a fine white dress open to the waist that barely covers her heavy, milk-white breasts: "I was lucky enough to obtain one of the most beautiful works in the history of French painting from the Museum of Bordeaux: *Greece on the Ruins of Missolonghi*, by Eugène Delacroix. Magnificent, isn't it? I'm sure you know Missolonghi: it's the city where Lord Byron died, during the war of independence against the Turks. In 1824, I believe." (Simon notes the false modesty of that "I believe.") "A terrible war. The Ottomans were so ferocious."

Without leaving his desk, without any attempt to shake their hands, he invites them to sit. No sofa or cakes for them. Still standing, the president goes on: "Did you know what Malraux said about me? That I had no sense of the tragic in history." From the corner of his eye, Simon observes Bayard in his raincoat, waiting silently.

Giscard goes back over to the painting, so the two visitors feel obliged to turn around to show they are following what he says: "Perhaps I don't have any sense of the tragic in history, but at least I feel the emotion of tragic beauty when I see that young woman, wounded in the side, bringing the hope of liberation to her people!" Unsure how to punctuate this presidential speech, the two men say nothing, which does not seem to perturb Giscard, used as he is to silent gestures of polite assent. When the man with the whistling voice turns on his heel to look out the window, Simon realizes that this pause is a form of transition, and that they are about to get to the point.

Offering his visitors only a view of the back of his bald head, the president continues: "I met Roland Barthes once. I had invited him to the Élysée. Such a charming man. He spent a quarter of an hour analyzing the menu and brilliantly deconstructed the symbolic value of each dish. It was absolutely fascinating. Poor man . . . I heard he found it hard to get over the death of his mother, isn't that right?"

Finally sitting down, Giscard speaks to Bayard: "Superintendent, on the day of his accident, Monsieur Barthes was in possession of a document that was stolen from him. I wish you to recover this document. It concerns a matter of national security."

Bayard asks: "What is the exact nature of this document, Monsieur President?"

Giscard leans forward and, with both fists resting on his desk, announces gravely: "It is a vital document that may pose a threat to national security. Used unwisely, it could cause incalculable damage and endanger the very foundations of our democracy. Unfortunately, I am not at liberty to tell you more than that. You must act in complete secrecy. But you will have carte blanche."

He looks at Simon at last: "Young man, I've heard that you are acting as a . . . guide to the superintendent? So you are well acquainted with the linguistic milieu in which Monsieur Barthes worked?"

Simon does not need to be asked twice: "No, not really."

Giscard shoots a quizzical look at Bayard, who explains:

"Monsieur Herzog has knowledge that could be useful to the inquiry. He understands how these people think and, well, what it's all about. And he can see things that the police wouldn't see."

Giscard smiles: "So you're a visionary, like Arthur Rimbaud, young man?"

Simon mutters shyly: "No. Not at all."

Giscard points at the red and blue boxes on the roll-top desk behind them, under the Delacroix. "What do you think is inside them?"

Simon does not realize he is being tested and, before considering whether it is in his interests to pass the test, answers instinctively: "Your Legion of Honor medals, I assume?"

Giscard's smile widens. He stands up and walks over to the boxes, opens one, and takes out a medal: "May I ask how you guessed?"

"Well, uh . . . The whole room is saturated with symbols: the paintings, the wall hangings, the moldings on the ceiling . . . Each object, each detail is intended to express the splendor and majesty of republican power. The choice of Delacroix, the photograph of Kennedy on the cover of the book on the escritoire: everything is heavily symbolic. But a symbol has value only if it's on display. A symbol hidden inside a box is pointless. In fact, I'd go further: it doesn't exist.

"At the same time, I don't suppose this room is where you keep your screwdrivers and spare bulbs. It seemed unlikely that the two boxes were for holding tools. And if they were for storing paper clips or a stapler, they'd be on your desk, where you could reach them. So the contents are neither symbolic nor functional. And yet they must be one or the other. You could put your keys in there, but I imagine that at the Élysée, the president isn't responsible for locking up, and you don't need your car keys either, because you have a chauffeur. So that left only one possibility: a dormant symbol, one that does not signify anything in itself here, but which would be activated outside of this room: the miniature, mobile symbol of what this place symbolizes. Namely, the grandeur of the republic. A medal, in other words. And, given where we are, it has to be the Legion of Honor."

Giscard exchanges a knowing look with Bayard. "I think I see what you mean, Superintendent."

21

Hamed sips his Malibu and orange as he talks a little about his life in Marseille, and his companion drinks in his words without really listening. Hamed knows what those spaniel eyes mean: he is this man's master, because the man is overcome by the desperate desire to possess him. He'll give himself to him later, or not, and maybe he'll find some pleasure in it, but that pleasure will undoubtedly be less than the feeling of power he is experiencing now by knowing he is the object of desire—and this is the upside of being young, handsome, and poor: without even thinking about it he can calmly despise all those prepared to pay, in one way or another, to have him.

The evening is in full flow and, as always, in this large bourgeois apartment, in the heart of the capital, as winter comes to an end, the feeling that he does not belong here intoxicates him with a cruel joy. What we steal is worth twice as much as what we earn through hard work. He returns to the buffet to pick up more slices of bread and tapenade, which reminds him vaguely of the South, fighting his way through the mob wiggling their hips to Bashung's "Gaby Oh Gaby." He finds Slimane there, swallowing handfuls of escargots while forcing himself to laugh at the jokes of a paunchy publisher who is discreetly fondling his arse. Next to them, a young woman guffaws, arching her neck exaggeratedly: "So he stops . . . and walks backwards!" At the window, Saïd is smoking a joint with a black man who looks like a diplomat. The opening words of "One Step Beyond" come through the speakers and a frisson of fake hysteria runs through the room; people cry out as if transported by the music, as if a wave of pleasure were moving through their bodies, as if the madness were a faithful dog, supposed lost but now running toward them wagging its tail, as if they could stop thinking or not thinking for the duration of an instrumental punctuated by blasts of throaty saxophone. After this, there will be a few disco tracks to keep the good mood going. Hamed helps himself to a plate of truffle tabbouleh, seeking out the guests most likely to offer him a line of cocaine or, failing that, a bit of speed. Both make him want to fuck, but the speed softens his hard-on, although that's not very important, he thinks. Just keep going as long as possible so he doesn't have to go home. Hamed goes over to the window to join Saïd. A streetlamp illuminates the advertising billboard, on the corner of Boulevard Henri-IV, showing Serge Gainsbourg in a suit and tie, above the words "A Bayard changes a man. Doesn't it, Monsieur Gainsbourg?" Hamed can't remember why that name is familiar. And, as he's a bit of a hypochondriac, he goes to look for a drink, reciting his previous year's schedule to himself out loud. Slimane contemplates a series of lithographs hanging on the wall representing dogs, in every color of the rainbow, eating from bowls filled with one-dollar bills, while he pretends to ignore the paunchy publisher, who is now rubbing against his backside and breathing into the back of his neck. From the speakers, Chrissie Hynde's voice orders any guests who may be sobbing to stop. Two long-haired guys discuss the death of Bon Scott and his possible replacement as AC/DC's singer by a fat truck driver in a flat cap. A young man with a side parting, wearing a suit, his tie untied, repeats excitedly to anyone who will listen that he has it on good authority that you can see Marlène Jobert's breasts in *La Guerre des Polices*. He's also heard that Lennon is making a new single with McCartney. A gigolo whose name Hamed has forgotten asks him if he has any grass, mocks the party briefly as too "designer Left Bank," and points out the window at the statue of the Spirit of Freedom atop the July Column: "You see the problem, buddy? I want us to be Jacobin as much as the next guy, but, you know, there are limits." Someone knocks a glass of blue curaçao onto the carpet. Hamed thinks about going back to Saint-Germain, but Saïd gestures toward the bathroom, where two girls and an old man are heading in together. As the girls know they are going in there not to fuck but to sniff (something the old guy pretends not to realize because, if he can't get what he wants, at least he'll enjoy the prospect for five minutes), Saïd and Hamed figure that, if they play their cards right, they'll be able to negotiate a line or maybe two. Someone asks a balding guy with a mustache if he's Patrick Dewaere. To get rid of the paunchy publisher, Slimane grabs a blonde in stretch jeans and dances with her to "Sultans of Swing" by Dire Straits. The surprised publisher watches the couple whirling around while trying to look simultaneously ironic and easygoing, an expression that fools nobody. He is alone, like all of us, but he can't hide it, and no one really notices him except to remark how lonely he looks. Slimane keeps his partner for the next dance, "Upside Down" by Diana Ross. Foucault enters the party with Hervé Guibert, just as the opening riff to the Cure's "Killing an Arab" comes on. He's wearing a big black leather jacket with chains and has a razor nick on his shaved head. Guibert is young and handsome, his beauty so exaggerated that only a Parisian could take him seriously as a writer. Saïd and Hamed hammer on the bathroom door and try to coax it open by lying to the people inside, coming up with ridiculous excuses, but the door remains hopelessly locked. All they hear behind it are furtive sounds of metal, enamel, and inhalation . . . "The sand was starting to stir under my feet . . ." Now as always, Foucault's arrival provokes a sort of fearful excitement, except for the few people too out of their heads on speed to notice, who jump around to what they imagine is a song about a beach holiday: "It was the same relentless sun, the same light on the same sand . . ." The bathroom door finally opens and the two girls emerge, looking scornfully at Saïd and Hamed, sniffing showily, with that pride typical of a high-society cokehead who has yet to feel the loss of the liters of serotonin evaporated from her brain, although, as the months and years pass, it will take longer and longer to replace it. "He was alone . . ." At the center of the circle that has already formed around them, Foucault is telling young Guibert a story, as if he hadn't noticed the turmoil his presence has aroused, continuing a conversation they'd begun on the way here: "When I was little I wanted to become a goldfish. My mother told me: 'But you know that's not possible, poppet. You hate cold water.'" Robert Smith's voice yelps: "Nothing mattered!" Foucault: "That plunged me into a quandary. I said to her: 'Please, just for one second, I'd really like to know what they think about.'" Robert Smith: "The Arab hadn't moved!" Saïd and Hamed decide to try elsewhere, maybe at La Noche. Slimane goes back to the publisher because, well, a boy has to eat. "I was staring down at the ground . . ." Foucault: "Someone has to confess. There's always one who confesses in the end . . ." Robert Smith: "Whether I stayed or went made no difference . . ." Guibert: "He was naked on the sofa, and couldn't find a single phone booth that worked . . ." "I turned back toward the beach and started walking . . ." "And when he did finally find one, he realized he didn't have a token . . ." Hamed looks outside again, through the curtains, sees a black DS parked below, and says: "I'm going to stay here a bit longer." Saïd lights a cigarette and in the frame of the window the two figures stand out perfectly, illuminated by the party.

22

"Georges Marchais? No one cares about Georges Marchais! Surely you know that!"

Daniel Balavoine is finally able to speak. He knows that in less than three minutes they will stop him speaking, one way or another, so he tears into his maniacal monologue, stating that politicians are old, corrupt, and completely missing the point.

"I'm not talking about you, Monsieur Mitterrand . . ."

But still . . .

"What I'd like to know, what would interest me, is who the immigrant workers pay their rent to that they pay . . . I'd like to . . . Who dares every month to ask seven hundred francs a month from immigrant workers to live in Dumpsters, in slums?" It's muddled, unstructured, full of grammatical errors, delivered way too fast, and it's magnificent.

The journalists, who as usual understand nothing, grumble when Balavoine reproaches them for never inviting young people (and there's the inevitable rhetorical snigger: well, obviously we do—you're here, you little twerp!).

But Mitterrand understands exactly what is happening. This young brat is showing them up for what they are—him, the journalists around the table, and all their kind—old farts who have been moldering in one another's company for so long that they've become dead to the world without even realizing it. He tries to agree wholeheartedly with the angry young man, but each attempt to get a word in edgewise ends up sounding like misjudged paternalism.

"Hang on, I'm trying to read my notes . . . In any case, what I want to give you is a warning . . ." Mitterrand fiddles with his glasses, bites his lip. This is being filmed, it's live on television, it's a disaster. "What I want to tell you is that despair is a motivating force and that when it's a motivating force, it's dangerous."

The journalist, with a hint of sadistic irony: "Monsieur Mitterrand, you wanted to speak with a young person. You've listened very carefully . . ." Now get out of that, you jerk.

And so Mitterrand starts to stammer: "What interests me very much is that this way of thinking . . . of reacting . . . and also of communicating!—because Daniel Balavoine also expresses himself through writing and through music—should have the rights of a citizen . . . should be heard and, in that way, understood." Keep digging, keep digging. "He says things his way! He is responsible for his words. He's a citizen. Like any other."

It is March 19, 1980, on the set of a Channel 2 news program. It is 1:30 p.m. and Mitterrand is a thousand years old.

23

What does Barthes think about as he dies? About his mother, they say. His mother killed him. Of course, of course, there's always the hidden personal business, the dirty little secret. As Deleuze says, we all have a grandmother who had amazing experiences . . . so what? "About his grief." Yes, sir, he is going to die of heartbreak and nothing else. Poor little French thinkers, trapped in your vision of a world reduced to the pettiest, most formulaic, most flatly egocentric domestic concerns. A world without enigma, without mystery. The mother—mother of all responses. In the twentieth century, we got rid of God, and put the mother in His place. What a great trade. But Barthes is not thinking about his mother.

If you could follow the thread of his hazy reverie, you would know that the dying man thinks about what he was, but above all about what he could have been. What else? He doesn't see his whole life in a flash, just the accident. Who ran the operation? He remembers that he was manhandled. And then the document disappeared. Whoever's responsible, we are probably on the brink of an unprecedented catastrophe. Whereas he, Roland, his mother's son, would have known how to make good use of it: a little for him, the rest for the world. His shyness defeated him in the end. What a waste. Even if he survives, it will be too late to celebrate.

Roland does not think about his mommy. This is not *Psycho*.

What does he think about? Maybe he sees this or that memory flash through his mind, things that are private or insignificant or known only to him. One evening—or was it still daylight?—he was sharing a taxi with his American translator, who was over in Paris for a brief stay, and Foucault. The three of them are sitting in the backseat, the translator in the middle, and Foucault, as usual, is monopolizing the conversation. He speaks in his animated, confident, nasal voice, like a voice from days of old, and he is the one in control, as ever. He improvises a little speech to explain how much he hates Picasso, how crappy Picasso really is, and he laughs, of course, and the young translator listens politely; in his own country he is a writer and a poet, but here, he listens deferentially to these two brilliant French intellectuals' speeches, and Barthes already knows that he's powerless to match Foucault's loquacity, but he has to say something all the same if he doesn't want to be left out, so he wins some time by laughing, too, but he knows that his laughter doesn't ring true, and he's embarrassed because he seems embarrassed, it's a vicious circle. It's been like this all his life. He wishes he could have Foucault's self-assurance. Even when he speaks to his students and they listen reverently, he shelters his shyness behind a professorial tone, but it is only when he writes that he feels sure of himself, that he is sure of himself, alone, in the refuge of his page, and all his books, his Proust, his Chateaubriand, and Foucault continues to babble on and on about Picasso, and so Barthes, in order not to be left out, says that he, too, hates Picasso, and when he says this he hates himself, because he can see exactly what's happening, it's his job to see what's happening: he's debasing himself in front of Foucault, and no doubt the young and handsome translator realizes it too. He spits on Picasso but only timidly, a small gob of spit, while Foucault roars with laughter, he agrees that Picasso is overrated, that he has never understood what people saw in him, and I can't be certain that he didn't think this; after all, Barthes was above all a classicist who, deep down, did not like modern life, but really—what does it matter? Even if he did hate Picasso, he knows that's not the point; the point is not to be outdone by Foucault; the point is that as soon as Foucault makes such a provocative statement, he would look like an old fart if he disagreed, so even if he genuinely didn't like Picasso, he now denigrates him and mocks him, in this taxi taking him God knows where, for the wrong reasons.

Perhaps that is how Barthes dies, thinking about that taxi ride, that is how he closes his eyes and falls asleep, sadly, with that sadness that has always filled him, never mind his mother, and perhaps he spares a brief thought for Hamed, too. What will become of him? And of the secret he now guards? He sinks slowly, gently into his final sleep and, well, it's not an unpleasant sensation, but while his bodily functions give out one by one, his mind continues to wander. Where else will this final reverie lead him?

Hey, he should have said that he didn't like Racine! "The French boast endlessly about having had their Racine (the man who used only two thousand words) and never complain about not having had their Shakespeare." There—that would have impressed the young translator. But Barthes wrote that much later. Ah, if only he'd had the function then . . .

The door opens slowly, but Barthes is in his coma and does not hear it.

It's not true that he's a "classicist": deep down, he doesn't like the seventeenth century's dryness, those heavily layered alexandrines, those finely chiseled aphorisms, those intellectualized passions . . .

He does not hear the footsteps approaching his bed.

Of course, they were peerless rhetoricians, but he doesn't like their coldness, their fleshlessness. The Racinian passions? Pfft, big deal. Phaedra, sure . . . well, the confession scene in the pluperfect subjunctive, tantamount to the conditional past . . . all right, sure, that was brilliant. Phaedra rewriting the story with her in Ariadne's place and Hippolytus in the place of Theseus . . .

He doesn't know that someone is leaning over his electrocardiogram.

But Berenice? Titus didn't love her anymore, that was blatantly obvious. It's so simple, you'd think it was Corneille . . .

He does not see the figure rummaging in his belongings.

And La Bruyère, so scholarly. At least Pascal conversed with Montaigne, Racine with Voltaire, La Fontaine with Valéry . . . But who would want to have a conversation with La Bruyère?

He does not feel the hand delicately turning the valve of the ventilator.

But La Rochefoucauld . . . him, yes. After all, Barthes owes a great deal to *Maximes*. He was a semiologist before his time, in that he knew how to decode the human soul through the signs of our behavior . . . The greatest master in French literature, no less . . . Barthes sees the Prince of Marcillac riding proudly beside the Grand Condé in the ditches of Faubourg Saint-Antoine, under fire from Turenne's troops, thinking, my word, what a beautiful day for dying . . .

What's happening? He can't breathe anymore. His throat has suddenly shrunk.

But the Grande Mademoiselle will open the city gates to let the Condé's troops in, and La Rochefoucauld, wounded in the eyes, temporarily blind, will not die, not this time, and will recover . . .

He opens his eyes. And he sees her, haloed by blinding light, like a representation of the Virgin Mary. He is suffocating. He tries to call for help, but no sound emerges from his mouth.

He'll recover, won't he? Won't he?

She smiles sweetly at him and presses his head against the pillow to prevent him from sitting up. Not that he has enough strength, anyway. This time it's for good, he knows it. He would like to surrender but his body goes into convulsions. His body wants to live. His frightened brain craves the oxygen that is no longer entering his bloodstream. Spurred by a final burst of adrenaline, his heart races, then slows down again.

"Always to love, to suffer, to expire." In the end, his final thought is a line of verse from Corneille.

24

The television news, March 26, 1980, 8:00 p.m., presented by Patrick Poivre d'Arvor:

"Ladies and gentlemen, good evening. A great deal of news that . . . [PPDA pauses for a second] affects our day-to-day lives.

67

So, some of it is good, some less so. I'll let you decide which is which." (From his apartment, next to Place Clichy, Deleuze, who never misses the evening news, replies from the comfort of his armchair: "Thank you!")

8:01 p.m.: "First of all, the rise in the cost of living for the month of February: 1.1 percent. 'It's not a very good sign,' said René Monory, the minister for the economy—although it is better [it would have been difficult to be worse, says PPDA, and, in front of his TV set, on Rue de Bièvre, Mitterrand thinks the same thing] than the figure for January: 1.9 percent. Also better than the corresponding figures for the United States and Great Britain and . . . the same as West Germany's." (At the mention of their German rivals, Giscard, who is signing documents at his desk in the Élysée, chuckles mechanically without looking up. In his attic room, Hamed is getting ready to go out, but can't find his second sock.)

8:09 p.m.: "There are strikes, too, in schools. Tomorrow, the teachers' union is calling on its members in Paris and the Essonne to protest against planned class closures for the next academic year." (Holding a Chinese beer in one hand, his cigarette holder in the other, Sollers curses from his sofa: "A nation of bureaucrats!" From the kitchen, Kristeva replies: "I'm making sauté de veau.")

8:10 p.m.: "Finally, some news that will come as a 'breath of fresh air,' so to speak [Simon rolls his eyes]: the significant reduction in atmospheric pollution in France over the last seven years. Sulfur emissions down thirty percent, according to Michel d'Ornano, the environment minister, and carbon dioxide down forty-six percent." (Mitterrand tries to put on a grimace of disgust, but in fact this doesn't alter his usual expression.)

8:11 p.m.: "So, foreign news . . . Today, in Chad . . . Afghanistan . . . Colombia . . ." (Various countries are mentioned but no one listens, except Foucault. Hamed finds his sock.)

8:12 p.m.: "A rather surprising victory for Edward Kennedy in the New York State primaries . . ." (Deleuze picks up his telephone to call Félix Guattari. At home, Bayard irons his shirt in front of the television.)

8:13 p.m.: "The number of road accidents rose last year, the Gendarmerie Nationale informs us: 12,480 deaths and 250,000 accidents in 1979 . . . that's equal to the entire population of a town like Salon-de-Provence dying in these accidents. [Hamed wonders why the newsreader chose Salon-de-Provence.] Figures that give us food for thought, with the Easter holidays approaching . . ." (Sollers lifts a finger and exclaims: "Food for thought! Food for thought, Julia, do you hear? . . . Isn't that marvelous? . . . Figures that give us food for thought, ha!" Kristeva replies: "Dinner's ready!")

8:15 p.m.: "A road accident that could have had very serious consequences: yesterday, a truck transporting radioactive materials collided with another truck before crashing into a ditch. But thanks to the safety systems, there has not been a radioactive leak." (Mitterrand, Foucault, Deleuze, Althusser, Simon, Lacan, all laugh loudly in front of their respective TV sets. Bayard lights a cigarette while continuing to iron shirts.)

8:23 p.m.: "And the interview with François Mitterrand in *La Croix*, with these little phrases that will go down in history [Mitterrand smiles with pleasure]: 'Giscard remains the man bound to a clan, a class, and a caste. Six years of stagnation, belly-dancing in front of the Golden Calf. And pshit, said Ubu.'" ("That is François Mitterrand saying that," PPDA makes clear. Giscard rolls his eyes.) "So that is what he said about the president. About Georges Marchais and his gang of three, well . . . 'When he wants to be,' says François Mitterrand again, 'Marchais is a world-class comic.' [In his apartment on Rue d'Ulm, Althusser shrugs. He shouts to his wife, in the kitchen: "Did you hear that, Hélène?" No response.] Finally, François Mitterrand, in response to a question about a possible Mitterrand-Rocard ticket for the Socialist Party, he pimply . . . [PPDA gets his words muddled, but continues impassively] simply replied that this American expression had no French equivalent in our institutions."

8:24 p.m.: "Roland Barthes . . . [PPDA pauses] died this afternoon in the Pitié-Salpêtrière hospital, in Paris. [Giscard stops signing documents, Mitterrand stops grimacing, Sollers stops rummaging around in his underpants with his cigarette holder, Kristeva stops stirring her sautéed veal and runs out of the kitchen, Hamed stops putting on his sock, Althusser stops trying to not yell at his wife, Bayard stops ironing his shirts, Deleuze says to Guattari: "I'll call you back!," Foucault stops thinking about biopower, Lacan continues smoking his cigar.] The writer and philosopher was the victim of a traffic accident last month. He was [PPDA pauses] sixty-four years old. He was famous for his work on modern writing and communication. Bernard Pivot interviewed him for *Apostrophes*: Roland Barthes was presenting his book *A Lover's Discourse*, a book that was extremely successful [Foucault rolls his eyes], and in the clip we are going to see now, he explained from a sociological point of view [Simon rolls his eyes] the relationships between sentimentality . . . [PPDA pauses] and sexuality. [Foucault rolls his eyes.] We'll listen to that now." (Lacan rolls his eyes.)

Roland Barthes (in his Philippe Noiret voice): "I maintain that a subject—and I say a subject in order not to specify the, er, sex of the subject, if you see what I mean—but a subject who is in love would have, uh, a lot more difficulty over . . . overcoming the sort of taboo about sentimentality, whereas the taboo about sexuality is, today, transgressed very easily."

Bernard Pivot: "Because to be in love is to be childish, silly?" (Deleuze rolls his eyes. Mitterrand thinks he should call his daughter, Mazarine.)

Roland Barthes: "Uh . . . yes, in a way, that's what the world does believe. The world attributes two qualities, or rather two faults, to the subject who is in love: the first is that they are often stupid—there is a silliness to being in love that the subject feels— and there is also the madness of people in love—and this is a very popular observation these days!—except that it is a polite madness, isn't it, a madness lacking the glory of a great, transgressive madness." (Foucault lowers his eyes and smiles.)

The clip ends. PPDA says: "So, we've seen, er, Jean-François Kahn, er, Roland Barthes was fascinated by everything, he talked about everything, er, we saw him, er, in films . . . playing roles . . . recently, er, but would you describe him as a Renaissance man?" (It's true: he played Thackeray in Téchiné's *Brontë Sisters*, a small role that he did not besmirch with his talent, Simon remembers.)

J.-F. Kahn (very excited): "Well, yes, apparently he is a Renaissance man! Yes, he dealt with, er, er, he wrote about fashion, about ties, or I don't know what, he wrote about wrestling! . . . He wrote about Racine, about Michelet, about photography, about cinema, he wrote about Japan, so, yes, he was a Renaissance man! [Sollers chuckles. Kristeva glares at him.] But in fact, it does all fit together. Take his last book! On lovers' discourses . . . on the language of love . . . well, in truth, Roland Barthes always wrote about language! But he found that . . . his tie . . . our tie . . . is a way of speaking. [Sollers, indignantly: "A way of speaking . . . Oh, come on!"] It's a way of expressing oneself, fashion. The motorbike: it's the way a society expressed itself. The cinema: obviously! Photography, too. So that's to say that Roland Barthes is, at heart, a man who spent his time tracking signs! . . . The signs a society, a community, uses to express itself. Expresses vague, confused feelings, even if it's not aware of it! In this sense, he was a very great journalist. He was the master of a science called semiology. That is, the science of signs.

"And then, of course, he was a very great literary critic! Because, the same thing applies: What is a literary work? A literary work is what a writer writes to express himself. And what Roland Barthes showed is that, essentially, in a literary work, there are three levels: there is the language—Racine wrote in French, Shakespeare wrote in English, that's the language. There is the style: this is the result of their technique, their talent. But between the style—which is a choice, you know, it's controlled by the author—and the language, there is a third level, which is the writing. And the writing, he said, is the place . . . of politics, in every sense of the word. In other words, even if the writer is not aware of it the writing is the thing through which he expresses what he is socially, his culture, his origins, his social class, the society around him . . . and even if he sometimes writes something because it seems self-evident—I don't know, in a Racine play, say: 'Let us retire to our rooms' or something that seems self-evident—ah, but it's not! It's not self-evident, says Barthes. Even if he says it's self-evident, don't believe it, because there's something being expressed beneath it."

PPDA (who has not been listening, or has not understood, or simply doesn't care), earnestly: "Because every word is dissected!"

J.-F. Kahn (who doesn't notice): "So, so, as well as that . . . what's great with Barthes is that this is a man who has written things that are very . . . mathematical, very cold in style, and who, at the same time, has produced veritable hymns to the beauty of style. But to conclude, let's say that he is a very important man. Who I think expresses the spirit of our age. And I'm going to tell you why. Because there are ages that are expressed through the theater, you know, really. [Here, Kahn makes an untranslatable gurgling sound.] Others through the novel: the 1950s, for example, Mauriac, er, Camus, er, et cetera. But I think the 1960s . . . in France . . . France's cultural spirit is expressed through the discourse on the discourse. On the *marginal* discourse. We're probably aware that we haven't produced any truly great novels . . . maybe not, or great plays; the best thing we have produced is a way of explaining what others have said or have done and, by better explaining what they've done or said or other things, revitalizing an ancient discourse."

PPDA: "In a few moments, soccer. At the Parc des Princes, France will play the Netherlands [Hamed leaves his apartment, slamming the door and hurtling down the stairs]: a friendly match that is much more important than you might think [Simon turns off his television], because the Dutch were the losing finalists, as we know, in the last two World Cups [Foucault turns off his television], and also, crucially, because France and the Netherlands are in the same qualifying group for the next World Cup, in 1982, in Spain. [Giscard starts signing documents again. Mitterrand picks up his phone to call Jack Lang.] You can watch a recording of that match after tonight's late news, which will be presented by Hervé Claude, at around ten fifty p.m." (Sollers and Kristeva sit down to eat. Kristeva pretends to wipe away a tear and says: "Rrreal life goes on." In two hours, Bayard and Deleuze will both watch the match.)

25

It is Thursday, March 27, 1980, and Simon Herzog is reading the newspaper in a bar full of young people sitting at tables with cups of coffee they finished hours ago. I would situate the café on Rue de la Montagne-Sainte-Geneviève, but, again, you can put him wherever you like, it doesn't really matter. It's probably more practical and logical to put him in the Latin Quarter, though, to explain all the young people. There's a pool table, and the sound of the balls colliding clicks like a pulse beneath the hubbub of late-afternoon conversations. Simon Herzog is also drinking coffee, because it still seems a bit early—given the expectations of his social class and individual personality—to order a beer.

The main headlines on the front page of *Le Monde* dated Friday, March 28, 1980 (it is always already tomorrow with *Le Monde*), concern Thatcher's "anti-inflationary" budget (setting out—surprise, surprise—a "reduction in public spending") and the civil war in Chad, but in the bottom of the right-hand column there is also a small mention of Barthes's death. The famous journalist Bertrand Poirot-Delpech's obituary begins with these words: "Just twenty years after Camus breathed his last in a glove box, literature has paid the chrome goddess a rather harsh price!" Simon rereads the phrase several times, and glances around the room.

Around the pool table, two boys of about twenty are facing off, watched by a girl who looks barely legal. Simon automatically identifies what's going on: the more smartly dressed boy desires the girl, who desires the more disheveled-looking boy, with his long hair and slightly grubby appearance, whose faintly arrogant detachment makes it difficult to tell whether he is interested in the girl—and is simulating a tactical indifference as a mark of his superiority, a statutory indifference linked to his condition as the dominant male who takes it for granted that the girl will be his by right—or if he is waiting for another girl, more beautiful, more rebellious, less shy, more suited to someone of his standing (the two hypotheses obviously not being incompatible).

Poirot-Delpech goes on: "If Barthes, along with Bachelard, is one of those who have done most to enrich criticism during the last thirty years, it is not as a theoretician of a still-hazy semiology but as the champion of a new pleasure in reading." The semiologist in Simon Herzog emits a grunt. Pleasure in reading, blah blah blah. Still-hazy semiology, my arse. Even if, well . . . "More than a new Saussure, he would have been a new Gide." Simon slams his cup into its saucer and the coffee spills over onto his newspaper. The noise is drowned out by the sound of the pool balls, so no one notices, except for the girl, who turns around. Simon meets her eye.

The two boys are both obviously bad pool players, but this does not prevent them from using the table as a sort of stage, frowning, nodding, bending to bring their chins close to the balls, phases of intense thinking leading to innumerable circuits of the table, technical and tactical calculations regarding the white ball's point of impact on the colored ball (itself chosen according to changeable criteria), repetition of practice shots with hard, jerky, too-fast movements evoking both the game's erotic stakes and the players' inexperience, followed by a shot whose speed cannot mask its clumsiness. Simon turns back to *Le Monde*.

Jean-Philippe Lecat, the minister of culture and communication, declared: "All his work on writing and thought was motivated by the deep study of mankind in order to help us know ourselves better and to live better in society." Another, better-controlled slamming of the cup into the saucer. Simon checks to see if the girl turns around (she does). Apparently no one at the Ministry of Culture could be bothered to come up with anything better than this platitude. Simon wonders if it is based on some sort of formula that, with minor variations, can be applied to any writer, philosopher, historian, sociologist, biologist . . . The in-depth study of mankind? Oh yes, bravo, my good sir, what a sterling effort! And you can trot it out again for Sartre, Foucault, Lacan, Lévi-Strauss, and Bourdieu.

Simon hears the smartly dressed boy contesting a rule: "No, you don't get two penalty shots if you pot a ball with your first shot." Sophomore law student (though he probably had to repeat his first year). Analyzing his clothes, jacket, shirt, Simon would plump for Panthéon-Assas University. Emphasizing each word, the other boy replies: "Okay, no problem, cool, whatever you want. I don't care. It's all the same to me, man." Sophomore psychology (or repeating his first year) at Censier or Jussieu (he's on home turf, clearly). The girl gives a faux-discreet smile that is intended to be knowing. She has two-tone Kickers, electric-blue turn-up jeans, a ponytail held in place by a scrunchie, and she smokes Dunhill Lights: modern literature, first year, Sorbonne or Sorbonne Nouvelle, probably having skipped a year of school.

"For an entire generation, he blazed a trail in the analysis of communication media, mythologies, and languages. Roland Barthes's work will remain in everyone's heart like a vibrant call to liberty and happiness." So Mitterrand is not very inspired either, but at least he gestures toward Barthes's fields of expertise.

After an interminable endgame, Assas wins haphazardly with an improbable shot (potting the black in off the cushion, following the imaginary rule invented by Breton drunkards to prolong the pleasure) and lifts his arms in imitation of Borg.

Censier tries to compose himself with a mocking expression, Sorbonne goes over to Censier and consoles him by rubbing his arm, and all three pretend to laugh, as if it were merely a game.

The Communist Party also made a statement: "It is to the intellectual who devoted the lion's share of his work to a new way of thinking about imagination and communication, the pleasure of the text, and the materiality of writing, that we pay tribute today." Simon isolates the most important element of this sentence immediately: "It is to" that intellectual that we pay tribute, not, the implication being, to the other one: the neutral, uncommitted man who ate lunch with Giscard and went to China with his Maoist friends.

Another girl enters the bar: long curly hair, leather jacket, Dr. Martens, earrings, ripped jeans. Simon thinks: history of art, first year. She kisses the disheveled young man on the mouth. Simon observes the ponytailed girl carefully. On her face he reads bitterness, suppressed anger, the irresistible feeling of inferiority that rises in her (unfounded, obviously) and manifests itself in the folds of her mouth, the unmistakable traces of the battle within between resentment and contempt. Once again, their eyes meet. The girl's eyes blaze for a second with an indefinable brilliance. She gets up, walks over to him, leans across the table, stares straight into his eyes, and says: "What's your problem, dickhead? You want my photo or what?" Embarrassed, Simon stammers something incomprehensible and starts reading an article on Michel Rocard.

26

The pretty village of Urt had never seen so many Parisians. They have taken the train to Bayonne. They have come for the funeral. An icy wind blows through the cemetery, the rain hammers down, and the mourners gather in small groups, none having thought to bring an umbrella. Bayard has made the trip too, and brought Simon Herzog with him, and the two of them observe the soaked fauna of Saint-Germain. We are 485 miles from the Café de Flore, and to see Sollers nervously chewing his cigarette holder or BHL buttoning his shirt, you feel that the ceremony had better not go on too long. Simon Herzog and Jacques Bayard are able to identify almost everyone: there's the Sollers/Kristeva/BHL group; the Youssef/Paul/Jean-Louis group; Foucault's group, containing Daniel Defert, Mathieu Lindon, Hervé Guibert, and Didier Eribon; the university group (Todorov, Genette); the Vincennes group (Deleuze, Cixous, Althusser, Châtelet); Barthes's brother, Michel, and his wife, Rachel; his editor, Eric Marty, and two students and former lovers, Antoine Compagnon and Renaud Camus, as well as a group of gigolos (Hamed, Saïd, Harold, Slimane); film people (Téchiné, Adjani, Marie-France Pisier, Isabelle Huppert, Pascal Greggory); two male twins dressed like astronauts in mourning (neighbors who work in television, apparently), and some villagers . . .

Everyone in Urt liked him. At the cemetery gate, two men get out of a black DS and open an umbrella. Someone in the crowd spots the car and exclaims: "Look, a DS!" A delighted murmur runs through the gathering, who see in it an homage to Barthes's *Mythologies*, published with the famous Citroën on the front cover. Simon whispers to Bayard: "Do you think the murderer is in the crowd?" Bayard does not reply. He looks at every mourner and thinks they all look guilty. To get anywhere in this investigation, he knows that he has to understand what he's searching for. What did Barthes possess of such value that someone not only stole it from him but they wanted to kill him for it too?

27

We are in Fabius's magnificent apartment in the Panthéon, which as I imagine it has moldings all over the place and herringbone parquet flooring. A group of Socialist Party advisers have met to discuss their candidate's strengths and weaknesses, in terms of image and—at the time, the term is still a little vulgar—"communication."

The first column is almost empty. The only thing written there is *Denied de Gaulle a first-round victory*. And Fabius remarks that this achievement dates back fifteen years.

The second column is much fuller. In ascending order of importance:

Madagascar
Observatoire
Algerian War
Too old (too Fourth Republic)
Canines too long (looks cynical)
Loses all the time

Bizarrely, back then, his Francisque medal, received directly from General Pétain, and his functions in the Vichy regime, however modest, are never mentioned, neither by the media (amnesiac, as usual) nor by his political enemies (who perhaps don't want to upset their own constituency with unpleasant memories). Only the very small group on the extreme right are spreading what the new generation considers a calumny.

The meeting begins. Fabius has served hot drinks, cookies, and fruit juice on a large varnished wooden table. To indicate the size of their task, Moati takes out an old editorial on Mitterrand by Jean Daniel, which he cut out of a *Nouvel Obs* from 1966: "Not only does this man give the impression that he believes in nothing: when you are with him, he makes you feel guilty for believing in something. Almost involuntarily, he insinuates that nothing is pure, all is sordid, and that no illusions are allowed."

All the men gathered around the table agree that they have a job on their hands.

Moati eats Palmitos.

Badinter pleads Mitterrand's cause: in politics, cynicism is only a relative handicap; it can also suggest shrewdness and pragmatism. After all, compromise doesn't have to be unprincipled. The very nature of democracy necessitates flexibility and calculation. Diogenes the Cynic was a particularly enlightened philosopher.

"Okay. So what about the Observatoire?" asks Fabius.

Lang protests: this murky affair about a faked attack was never cleared up, and it was all based on the dubious testimony of an ex-Gaullist turned right-wing extremist who changed his story several times. And Mitterrand's car had been found riddled with bullets! Lang seems genuinely indignant.

"Agreed," says Fabius. So that's his shady past dealt with. But there remains the fact that, up to now, he has not come across as especially likable or especially socialist.

Jack Lang reminds them that Jean Cau said Mitterrand was a priest and his socialism was "the flip side of his Christianity."

Debray sighs. "What a load of crap."

Badinter lights a cigarette.

Moati eats Chokinis.

Attali: "He decided to move to the left. He thinks it's necessary to contain the Communist Party. But it puts off moderate left-wing voters."

Debray: "No, what you call a moderate left-wing voter, I would call a centrist. Or a radical Valoisian, at a push. Those people will vote for the Right, no matter what. They're Giscardians."

Fabius: "Including left-wing radicals?"

Debray: "Naturally."

Lang: "All right, and the canines?"

Moati: "We've booked him an appointment with a dentist in the Marais. He's going to give him a smile like Paul Newman's."

Fabius: "Age?"

Attali: "Experience."

Debray: "Madagascar?"

Fabius: "Who cares? Everyone's forgotten it."

Attali: "He was minister of the colonies in '51, and the massacres took place in '47. Sure, he said some unfortunate things, but he doesn't have blood on his hands."

Badinter says nothing. Neither does Debray. Moati drinks his hot chocolate.

Lang: "But there's that film where you see him in a colonial helmet in front of Africans in loincloths . . ."

Moati: "The TV stations won't show those images again."

Fabius: "Colonialism is a bad subject for the Right. They won't want to get into this."

Attali: "That's true for the Algerian War too. First and foremost, Algeria is de Gaulle's betrayal. It's sensitive. Giscard won't take any risks with the *pied-noir* vote."

Debray: "And the Communists?"

Fabius: "If Marchais plays the Algerian card, we'll play Messerschmitt. In politics, as in every other aspect of life, it's not in anyone's interests to dig up the past."

Attali: "And if he insists, we'll hit him with the Nazi-Soviet Pact!"

Fabius: "Okay, fine. And the positives?"

Silence.

They pour themselves more coffee.

Fabius lights a cigarette.

Jack Lang: "Well, his image is of a man of letters."

Attali: "Who cares? The French vote for Badinguet, not for Victor Hugo."

Lang: "He's a great orator."

Debray: "Yeah."

Moati: "No."

Fabius: "Robert?"

Badinter: "Yes and no."

Debray: "He's a crowd-pleaser."

Badinter: "He's good when he has the time to develop his line of thought, and when he's feeling confident."

Moati: "But he's no good on TV."

Lang: "He's good when he goes head-to-head."

Attali: "But not face-to-face."

Badinter: "He's uncomfortable when anyone resists or contradicts him. He knows how to construct an argument, but he doesn't like being interrupted. As powerful as he can be at a rally, with the crowd behind him, he can be equally abstruse and boring with journalists."

Fabius: "That's because on TV he usually despises whoever's interviewing him."

Lang: "He likes to take his time, to warm up slowly. Onstage, he can do that, feel his way forward, test out his rhetoric, adapt to his audience. On TV, that's impossible."

Moati: "But TV's not going to change for him."

Attali: "Well, not in the next year anyway. Once we're in power . . ."

All: ". . . we fire Elkabbach!" (laughter)

Lang: "He has to think about TV like a giant rally. He has to tell himself that the crowd is right behind the camera."

Moati: "He needs to watch out for waxing lyrical, though. It's okay at a rally, but it doesn't work in a studio."

Attali: "He has to learn to be more concise and direct."

Moati: "He has to improve. He has to train for it. We'll make him rehearse."

Fabius: "Hmm, he's going to love that."

28

After four or five days, Hamed finally decides to go home, at least to check whether he might have a clean T-shirt lying around somewhere, so he drags himself up the six or seven flights of stairs that lead to his attic room, where he can't take a shower because there's no bathroom but he can at least collapse on his bed for a few hours to purge himself of physical and nervous fatigue and the vanity of the world and existence. But when he turns the key in the lock, he feels something odd and notices that the door has been forced, so he gently pushes it open—it creaks discreetly—and finds his room in a state of chaos: the bed turned over, the drawers pulled out, the baseboard torn off, his clothes spread all over the floor, his fridge open with a bottle of Banga left intact in the door, the mirror over the sink broken into several pieces, his cans of Gini and 7 Up scattered to the far corners of the room, his collection of *Yacht Magazine* torn out page by page as well as his comic-book history of France (the volume on the French Revolution and the one on Napoleon seem to have disappeared), his dictionary and his books thrown haphazardly around, the tape from his music cassettes unraveled and his stereo partially dismantled.

Hamed respools a Supertramp tape, puts it in the cassette player, and presses PLAY to see if it still works. Then he collapses onto his upside-down mattress and falls asleep, fully clothed, door wide open, to the opening chords of "The Logical Song," thinking that when he was young he, too, thought that life was a miracle, beautiful and magical, but that, while things have certainly changed, he doesn't yet feel very responsible nor very radical.

29

A line thirty feet long has formed outside the Gratte-Ciel, which is guarded by a bulky, severe-looking black bouncer. Hamed spots Saïd and Slimane with a tall, wiry lad known as "the Sergeant." Together, they skip the line, greeting the bouncer by name and telling him that Roland, no, Michel, is waiting for them inside. The doors of the Gratte-Ciel open for them. Inside, they are assailed by a strange smell, like a mix of curry, cinnamon, vanilla, and fishing port. They meet Jean-Paul Goude, who leaves his belt in the cloakroom, and they can tell instantly that he is wasted. Saïd leans toward Hamed to tell him, no, the

Giscard years must come to an end, the cost of living is too high, but he has to get some dope. Slimane sees the young Bono Vox at the bar. On the stage, a gothic reggae group is playing a vulgar, ethereal set. The Sergeant is nonchalantly wiggling his hips to the drum machine, behind the beat, watched by the curious, miserable-looking Bono. Yves Mourousi talks to Grace Jones's stomach. Brazilian dancers slalom between the customers, executing the fluid movements of capoeira. A former minister of some standing under the Fourth Republic tries to touch the breasts of a young, almost famous actress. And there is always that procession of boys and girls wearing live lobsters on their heads or walking them on leashes, the lobster being, for reasons unknown, *the* fashionable animal in Paris, 1980.

At the entrance, two badly dressed men with mustaches slip the bouncer a five-franc note and he lets them in. They leave their umbrellas in the cloakroom.

Saïd asks Hamed about drugs. Hamed gestures to relax and rolls a joint on a coffee table shaped like a naked woman on all fours, like the one in the Moloko Bar in *A Clockwork Orange*. Next to Hamed, on a corner sofa, Alice Sapritch takes a drag through her cigarette holder, an imperial smile on her lips, a boa around her neck (a real boa, thinks Hamed, but he also thinks it is a stupid affectation). She leans toward them and yells: "So, my darlings, is this a good night?" Hamed smiles as he lights his joint, but Saïd replies: "For what?"

At the bar, the Sergeant has managed to get Bono to buy him a drink, and Slimane wonders what language the two of them are speaking. In fact, though, they do not appear to be talking to each other. The two mustachioed guys have gone to a corner of the room and ordered a bottle of Polish vodka, the one with bison grass in it, which has the effect of attracting a group of young people of various sexes to their table, with one or two B-list stars in their wake. Near the bar, Victor Pecci (dark-haired, shirt open, diamond earring) is chatting with Vitas Gerulaitis (blond, shirt open, clip earring). Slimane waves to a young anorexic girl who is talking to the singer of Taxi Girl. Just next to him, leaning against a concrete pillar designed to look like a square Doric column, Téléphone's bassist doesn't bat an eyelid as a girl licks his cheek, trying to explain to him how people drink tequilas in Orlando. The Sergeant and Bono have disappeared. Slimane is buttonholed by Yves Mourousi. Foucault emerges from the toilets and begins a heated conversation with one of the singers from ABBA. Saïd shouts at Hamed: "I want some drugs, dope, blow, crack, smack, speed, poppers, whatever, but get me *something*, for fuck's sake!" Hamed hands him the joint, which he grabs angrily, as if to say "This is what I think of your joint" and puts it to his mouth, sucking greedily, disgustedly on it. In their corner, the two mustaches are hitting it off with their new friends, clinking glasses and exclaiming *"Na zdravie!"* Jane Birkin is trying to say something to a young man who looks like he could be her brother, but the man makes her repeat it five times before shrugging helplessly. Saïd yells at Hamed: "What's left? The PAC? Is that the plan?" Hamed realizes Saïd will be unbearable until he's had his fix, so he grabs him by the shoulders and says, "Listen," staring into his eyes as he would with someone in a state of shock or smashed out of their mind, and he takes a folded sheet of paper from his back pocket. It's an invitation for the Adamantium, a club that has just opened opposite the Rex, where a dealer he knows ought to be this evening, supplying the atmosphere for what the flyer calls, above a large drawing of a face that vaguely resembles Lou Reed, a special '70s night. He asks Alice Sapritch for a pen and carefully writes the name of the dealer on the back of the flyer in block capitals, which he hands solemnly to Saïd, who slides it tenderly into his inside jacket pocket and takes off immediately. In their corner, the two badly dressed men with mustaches look like they're having a great time; they have invented a new pastis-vodka-Suze cocktail, and Inès de La Fressange has joined them at their table, but when they see Saïd heading toward the exit, they suddenly stop laughing, politely brush aside the attentions of the drummer from

Trust, who wants to kiss them while yelling *"Brat! Brat!,"* and stand up together.

On the Grands Boulevards, Saïd walks determinedly, blind to the two men who are following him at a distance, armed with their umbrellas. He calculates the number of tricks he'll have to perform in the Adamantium's toilets in order to pay for his gram of cocaine. Maybe he'll have to take amphetamines: they're not as good, but not as expensive either. Though they last longer. But anyway. Five minutes to pull a client, five minutes to locate an empty cubicle, five minutes for the trick, so a quarter of an hour altogether, three tricks should be enough, maybe two if he finds a couple of really horny rich guys—and surely the Adamantium wants to attract VIPs? It doesn't look like a cheap lesbian junkie kind of place. All being well, he'll have the drugs in an hour. But the two men have drawn closer, and just as he is about to cross Boulevard Poissonnière, the first one points his umbrella down and stabs him in the leg through his stonewashed jeans while the second—as Saïd cries out, startled by the sudden pain—reaches inside his jacket and purloins the flyer from the pocket. By the time he has turned around, the two men have already run to the other side of the pedestrian crossing, and Saïd feels his leg throbbing. He also felt the furtive touch of the man's hand on his chest, so he thinks the two men must have been pickpockets, and he checks that he still has his papers (he has no money), but his head starts to spin when he realizes they've stolen his invitation, and he runs after them, shouting, "My invitation! My invitation!" But he grows dizzy, feels weak, his vision blurs, his legs give way beneath him, and he stops in the middle of the road, puts his hand over his eyes, and collapses amid the blare of car horns.

Tomorrow, in *Le Parisien Libéré*, there will be stories about the deaths of two people: a twenty-year-old Algerian, victim of an overdose in the middle of the street, and a drug dealer tortured to death in the toilets of the Adamantium, a recently opened nightclub, which has now been closed by the authorities.

30

"Those guys are looking for something. The only question, Hamed, is why they didn't find it."

Bayard chews his cigarette. Simon fiddles with paper clips.

Barthes run over, Saïd poisoned, his dealer murdered, his apartment trashed . . . Hamed decided it was time to go to the police, because he didn't tell them everything he knew about Roland Barthes: during their last meeting, Barthes gave him a paper. The clatter of typewriters echoes through the offices. The Quai des Orfèvres hums with police and administrative activity.

No, the people who searched his apartment didn't find it. No, it is not in his possession.

How can he be sure, then, that they haven't got hold of it? Because it wasn't hidden in his room. And for a very good reason: he burned it.

Okay.

Did he read it first? Yes. Can he tell them what it's about? Sort of. What's it about? Silence.

Barthes asked him to learn the document by heart and destroy it immediately. Apparently, the semiologist believed that the southern accent was a mnemonic technique that facilitated memorization. Hamed did it because even if Roland was old and ugly with his paunch and his double chin, deep down he liked him, this old man who talked about his mother like a heartbroken kid, and anyway he was flattered that this famous professor should entrust him with a mission that didn't, for a change, involve the insertion of a penis into his mouth, and also because Barthes had promised him three thousand francs.

Bayard asks: "Could you recite the text to us?" Silence. Simon has stopped his construction of a paper-clip necklace. Beyond the door, the clatter of typewriters continues.

Bayard offers the gigolo a cigarette, which he accepts with his gigolo's reflex, even though he doesn't like dark tobacco.

Hamed smokes the cigarette and remains silent.

Bayard repeats that he is clearly in possession of an important piece of information that has caused the deaths of at least three people and that until this information is made public his life is in danger. Hamed objects that, on the contrary, as long as his brain is the sole repository of this information, he cannot be killed. His secret is his life insurance policy. Bayard shows him the photographs of the dealer who was tortured in the toilets of the Adamantium. Hamed stares at them for a long time. Then he tips backwards on his seat and begins to recite: "Happy who like Ulysses has explored / Or he who sought afar the golden fleece . . ." Bayard shoots a questioning look at Simon, who explains that it is a poem by Du Bellay: "When shall I hail again my village spires / The blue smoke rising from that village see . . ." Hamed says he learned the poem at school and he still remembers it. He seems quite proud of his memory. Bayard makes it clear to Hamed that he can hold him in custody for twenty-four hours. Hamed tells him to go ahead and do it. Bayard lights another Gitane with the butt of the last one and mentally adjusts his tactics. Hamed cannot go back home. Does he have a safe place to stay? Yes, Hamed can sleep at his friend Slimane's place, in Barbès. He should go there and lie low for a while, not go out to his usual haunts, not open the door to any strangers, be careful when he does go out, turn around frequently in the street . . . he should hide, basically. Bayard asks Simon to accompany Hamed in the car. His intuition tells him that the gigolo will confide more easily in a young non-cop than in an old cop, and anyway, unlike all those cops in novels and films, he has other cases on the go; he can't devote 100 percent of his time to this one, even if Giscard has made it a priority, and even if Bayard voted for him.

He gives the necessary orders for them to be provided with a vehicle. Before he lets them leave, he asks Hamed if the name Sophia means anything to him, but Hamed says he doesn't know any Sophias. A uniformed bureaucrat with one finger missing takes them to the garage and issues the keys to an unmarked R16. Simon signs a form, Hamed gets in the passenger seat, and they leave the Quai des Orfèvres in the direction of Châtelet. Behind them, the black DS, which had been waiting patiently, double-parked by the side of the road, without any of the policemen on guard duty taking the slightest notice, sets off. At the crossroads, Hamed says to Simon (in his southern accent): "Oh! A Fuego, *con*!" It is blue.

Simon crosses the Île de la Cité, passes the law courts, and reaches Châtelet. He asks Hamed why he came to Paris. Hamed explains that Marseille is a tough place for queers; Paris is better, even if it's no panacea (Simon notes the gigolo's use of the word *panacea*): queers are treated better here, because in the provinces, being queer is worse than being Arab. And besides, in Paris, there are loads of queers with loads of money, and there's more fun to be had. Simon drives through a yellow light at the Rue de Rivoli crossing and the black DS behind him runs the red to remain in close pursuit. The blue Fuego, though, stops. Simon explains to Hamed that he teaches Barthes at university and says carefully: "What's it about, that document?" Hamed asks for a cigarette and says: "To be honest, I don't know."

Simon wonders if Hamed is stringing them along, but Hamed tells him that he learned the text by heart without seeking to understand it. His instructions were that if anything ever happened to Barthes, Hamed had to go somewhere to recite the text to one particular person, and no one else. Simon asks him why he hasn't done this. Hamed asks what makes him think he hasn't. Simon says he doesn't believe Hamed would have gone to the police if he had. Hamed admits that he hasn't done it, because the place is too far away: the person doesn't live in France, and he didn't have enough money. He chose to spend the three thousand francs Barthes gave him on other things.

In his rearview mirror Simon notices that the black DS is still behind them. At Strasbourg-Saint-Denis, he runs a red light and the DS does the same thing. He slows down, it slows down. He double-parks, just to be sure. The DS stops behind him. He feels his heart begin to pound a little. He asks Hamed what he wants to do later, when he has enough money, if that ever happens. Hamed doesn't understand why Simon has stopped the car, to begin with, but he doesn't ask questions and tells him that he'd like to buy a boat and organize trips for tourists, because he loves the sea, because he used to go fishing in little coves with his father when he was young (but that was before his father threw him out). Simon starts up suddenly, making his tires screech, and in his rearview mirror he sees the large black Citroën's hydraulic suspension lifting it up from the tarmac. Hamed turns around and catches sight of the DS and then he remembers the car parked below his apartment, and below the party in Bastille, and he realizes that it has been following him for weeks and that they could have killed him ten times by now, but that that doesn't mean they won't kill him the eleventh time, so he grabs hold of the handle above the passenger-side window and says simply: "Take a right."

Simon turns without thinking and finds himself in a little side street parallel to Boulevard Magenta, and what scares him most now is that the car behind him is not even attempting to conceal its presence. And so, as it moves closer again, guided by a vague inspiration, he slams on the brakes and the DS crashes into the back of the R16.

For a few seconds, the two cars are immobile, one behind the other, as if they had lost consciousness, and the passersby, too, seem petrified, stunned by the accident. Then he sees an arm emerge from the DS and a shiny metallic object and he thinks: that's a gun. So he shoves the car into gear, missing first, which produces a horrible crunching noise, and the R16 leaps forward. The arm disappears and the DS also takes off.

Simon runs every traffic light he sees, honking his horn constantly, so much so that it sounds like an air-raid siren warning the Tenth Arrondissement of an imminent bombardment. Behind, the DS stays close to him, like a fighter plane that's locked an enemy plane in its crosshairs. Simon hits a 505, bounces off a van, skids onto the pavement, almost runs over two or three passersby, and enters Place de la République. Behind him, the DS weaves between obstacles like a snake. Simon slaloms through traffic, avoiding pedestrians, and yells at Hamed: "The text! Recite the text!" But Hamed can't concentrate; his hand is clinging to the handle above the window and not a single word escapes his lips.

Simon tries to think as he drives around Place de la République. He doesn't know where the nearest police stations are, but he remembers attending a July 14 party in the fire station near the Bastille, in the Marais, so he piles down Boulevard des Filles-du-Calvaire and barks at Hamed: "What's it about? What's the title?" Hamed is pale, but manages to articulate: "The seventh function of language." But just as he starts to recite it, the DS comes up alongside the R16, the passenger-side window opens, and Simon sees a man with a mustache pointing a pistol at him. Just before the gunshot, Simon slams on the brakes with all his strength and the DS overtakes them as the bullet leaves the gun, but a 404 behind him crashes into the back of the R16, shunting it forward until it is, once again, level with the DS, so Simon yanks the steering wheel to the left and sends the DS into the line of oncoming traffic. By some miracle, however, the DS avoids a blue Fuego coming the other way and escapes into a side road at Cirque d'Hiver, then disappears in Rue Amelot, which runs parallel to Boulevard Beaumarchais, an extension of Filles-du-Calvaire.

Simon and Hamed believe they've shaken off their pursuers, but Simon is still heading toward the Bastille—it doesn't cross his mind to lose himself in the labyrinth of little streets in the Marais—so when Hamed starts to recite mechanically "There exists a function that eludes the various inalienable factors of verbal communication . . . and which, in a way, encompasses all of them. This function we shall call . . . ," at that very moment, the DS speeds out of a perpendicular street and smashes into the side of the R16, which collides with a tree in a howl of steel and glass.

Simon and Hamed are still in shock when a mustachioed

man armed with a pistol and an umbrella bursts out of the smoking DS, rushes over to the R16, and pulls open the loose passenger door. He aims his pistol, straight-armed, at Hamed's face and squeezes the trigger, but nothing happens. His pistol jams. He tries again—click click—but it doesn't work, so he wields his closed umbrella like a sword and attempts to stick it between Hamed's ribs, but Hamed protects himself with his arm, knocking aside the umbrella's point, which sinks into his shoulder. The sudden pain provokes a high-pitched cry. Then, his fear turning to rage, he wrenches the umbrella from the man's hands, releasing his safety belt in the same movement, launches himself at his aggressor, and stabs him in the chest with the umbrella.

While this is happening, the other man has gone around to the driver's door. Simon is conscious and tries to get out of the R16, but his door is blocked—he's trapped inside—and when the second mustachioed man aims his gun at him, he is paralyzed with terror and stares at the black hole the bullet will emerge from before perforating his head, and he has time to think "A lightning flash, then night!" when suddenly a buzzing noise fills the air and a blue Fuego crashes into the man, who is sent flying and lands in a crumpled heap on the pavement. Two Japanese men get out of the Fuego.

Simon escapes through the passenger door and crawls over to Hamed, who is slumped over the body of Mustache No. 1. He turns Hamed over and discovers, to his relief, that he is still alive. One of the Japanese men comes over and supports the wounded young gigolo's head. He feels his pulse and says "*Poison*," but Simon initially hears "*poisson*" and he thinks of Barthes's analyses of Japanese food before understanding dawns on him as he looks at Hamed's yellow complexion and yellow eyes and the spasms that shake his body, and he yells for someone to call an ambulance and Hamed tries to say something to him, he struggles to sit up a bit, and Simon leans over and asks about the function but Hamed is completely incapable of reciting a word because everything is whirling inside his head: he sees his poor childhood in Marseille again and his life in Paris, his friends, his tricks, the saunas, Saïd, Barthes, Slimane, the cinema, croissants at La Coupole, and the silken reflections of the oiled bodies that he rubbed himself against, but just before dying, while the sirens scream in the distance, he has time to whisper: "Echo."

31

When Jacques Bayard arrives, the police have secured the area but the Japanese have disappeared and so has Mustache No. 2, the man knocked over by the Fuego. Hamed's body is still laid out flat on the pavement alongside his attacker's, whose umbrella is sticking out of his chest. Simon Herzog is smoking a cigarette, a blanket wrapped around him. No, he has nothing. No, he doesn't know who those Japanese guys are. They didn't say anything, they just saved his life and then left. With the Fuego. Yes, the second mustachioed man is probably injured. He must be hard as nails to have gotten up after being hit like that in the first place. Jacques Bayard contemplates the two wrecked cars, perplexed. Why a DS? Production of that model ended in 1975. The Fuego, on the other hand, is so new that it's fresh from the factory and is not yet on sale. Someone draws an outline in chalk around Hamed's corpse. Bayard lights a Gitane. So the gigolo's calculation was wrong: the information he possessed did not protect him. Bayard concludes that the men who killed him did not want to make him talk but to shut him up. Why? Simon tells him Hamed's last words. Bayard asks what he knows about this seventh function of language. Still in shock, but professorial by instinct, Simon explains: "The functions of language are linguistic categories that were once the subject of a theory by a great Russian linguist named . . ."

Roman Jakobson.

Simon goes no further in the lecture he was about to give. He remembers the book on Barthes's desk, *Essays in General Linguistics* by Roman Jakobson, opened at the page on the functions of language, and the sheet of notes that served as a bookmark.

He explains to Bayard that the document for which four people have already been killed was perhaps right under their noses when they searched the apartment on Rue Servandoni, and pays no heed to the policeman standing behind them who then walks away to make a telephone call once he's heard enough. He cannot see that the policeman has a finger missing on his left hand.

Bayard, too, thinks he's heard enough, even if he still doesn't really understand this thing about Jakobson; he pushes Simon inside his 504 and zooms off toward the Latin Quarter, escorted by a van full of uniformed officers, including the one with the severed finger. They arrive in Place Saint-Sulpice, sirens howling, and that is probably a mistake.

There is an entry code beside the heavy double doors, and they have to hammer on the window of the concierge's office. She opens it for them, stupefied.

No, nobody has asked to see the attic room. Nothing special has happened since the installation of the entry code by a Vinci technician last month. Yes, the one with the Russian accent, or maybe it was Yugoslav, or maybe Greek. Actually, it's funny, he came back today. He said he wanted to do an estimate for installing an intercom. No, he didn't ask for the key to the seventh-floor room, why? It's hanging on the board, with the others, look. Yes, he went upstairs not five minutes ago.

Bayard takes the key and climbs the stairs two by two, followed by half a dozen policemen. Simon remains downstairs with the concierge. On the seventh floor, the door to the attic room is locked. Bayard inserts the key in the lock, but it's obstructed by something: another key, *on the inside*. The key that was not found on Barthes, thinks Bayard, as he bangs on the door and shouts, "Police!" They hear a noise inside. Bayard orders the door smashed down. The desk looks intact, but the book is no longer there, nor is the page of notes, and there is nobody in the room. The windows are shut.

But the trapdoor to the apartment below is open.

Bayard screams at his men to get downstairs but by the time they have turned around, their prey is already on the stairs and they bump into Barthes's brother, Michel, coming out of his apartment in a panic because an intruder just came through the hole in his ceiling. So the Vinci technician is now two floors below them, and on the ground floor, of course, Simon, who has no idea what is going on, is shoved out of the way by the man, who sprints out of the building at top speed, and when he slams the double doors shut behind him, the mechanism that he himself installed is triggered, locking them inside.

Bayard rushes into the concierge's office and grabs the telephone. He wants to call for backup, but it's a rotary phone and the time it takes him to compose the number feels enough for the man to have reached Porte d'Orléans, or maybe even the city of Orléans.

But the man is not going in that direction. He wants to escape by car, but two policemen left on guard outside prevent him from picking up his vehicle, parked at the end of the street, so he runs toward the Jardin du Luxembourg while behind him the two officers shout their first warnings. Through the double doors, Bayard shouts, "Don't shoot!" He wants the man alive, of course. When his men finally manage to free the mechanism, by pressing on the button embedded in the wall, the guy has disappeared but Bayard has sounded the alert. He knows that the area is being sealed off and the man won't get far.

The man runs through the Jardin du Luxembourg and he can hear the policemen blowing their whistles behind him, but the passersby, used to joggers and the park guards' whistles, pay no notice until he finds himself face-to-face with a cop. The cop tries to tackle him, but the man runs smack into him, like a rugby player, knocks him down, steps over him, and continues running. Where is he going? Does he know? He changes direction. One thing is sure: he has to get out of the park before all the exits are blocked.

Bayard is now in the van, giving orders by radio. Police officers have fanned out around the Latin Quarter. The fugitive is surrounded. He's screwed.

But this man is resourceful. He hurtles down Rue Monsieur-le-Prince, a narrow one-way street, which prevents any cars from following him. For some reason known only to him, he must cross over to the Right Bank. Coming out of Rue Bonaparte, he runs onto the Pont-Neuf, but that is where his race ends, because at the other end of the bridge, police vans block the way, and when he turns around he sees Bayard's van cutting off his retreat. He's trapped like a rat. Even if he jumps in the river, he won't get far, but maybe he has one last card to play, he thinks.

He climbs onto the parapet and holds out a piece of paper he has taken from his jacket. Bayard approaches him, alone. The man says one step farther and he'll throw the paper in the Seine. Bayard stops dead, as if he's just walked into an invisible wall. "Calm down."

"Don't come any nearrrer!"

"What do you want?"

"A car with a full tank of gas. If not, I thrrrow the document in the rrriver."

"Go ahead, throw it in."

The man's arm twitches. Bayard shivers, in spite of himself. "Wait!" He knows that this scrap of paper might solve the mystery of at least four deaths. "Let's talk, okay? What's your name?" Simon has joined him. At both ends of the bridge, the police have the man in their sights. Out of breath, chest wheezing from the effort, he moves his other hand to his pocket. At that precise instant, there is the sound of a gunshot. The man swivels. Bayard yells: "Don't shoot!" The man drops like a stone, but the paper flutters around above the river, and Bayard and Simon, who have rushed to the stone balustrade, lean over to watch the graceful curves of its erratic descent as if hypnotized. At last, it lands delicately on the water. And floats. Bayard, Simon, and the policemen who have instinctively understood that this document was their real objective, all stare, petrified, breath held, as the sheet of paper drifts along with the current.

Then Bayard tears himself from this contemplative torpor and, deciding that all hope is not yet lost, yanks off his jacket, his shirt, and his trousers, steps over the parapet, hesitates for a few seconds. And jumps. Disappears in a huge splash.

When he resurfaces, he is about sixty feet from the paper and, from up on the bridge, Simon and the policemen start shouting at him, all at the same time, indicating which direction to take, like supporters at a football match. Bayard starts swimming, as hard as he can. He tries to get closer, but the paper is carried away by the current. Still, the gap is gradually reduced. He's close now, he's going to catch it, only another ten feet, and then they disappear under the bridge and Simon and the policemen run to the other side and wait for them to reappear, and when they reappear the shouting starts up again. Three more feet and he'll have it, but at that moment a riverboat passes, creating little waves that submerge the paper just as Bayard is about to reach out and grab it. The paper sinks, so Bayard dives after it, and for a few seconds all they can see is the pair of underpants he's wearing, poking up out of the water. When he resurfaces, he is clutching the soaked paper in his hand and he swims doggedly over to the bank amid cheers and hurrahs.

But when he hauls himself onto the grass, he opens his hand and realizes that the sheet of paper is now merely a shapeless paste and that the writing has been dissolved because Barthes wrote with a fountain pen. This isn't *CSI* and there will not be any way of making the text reappear: no magic scanner, no ultraviolet light. The document is lost forever.

The officer who fired the shot comes over to explain: he saw the man reaching for a gun in his pocket and he didn't have time to think, so he fired. Bayard notes that the cop has a finger missing on his left hand. He asks him what happened. The policeman replies he had an accident while he was chopping wood at his parents' house in the countryside.

When the police divers fish the corpse out of the water, they will find in his jacket pocket not a firearm but Barthes's copy of *Essays in General Linguistics*, and Bayard, still drying himself, will ask Simon: "For fuck's sake, who is this Jakobson guy?" And so, at last, Simon will be able to finish his lecture.

32

Roman Jakobson was a Russian linguist, born at the end of the nineteenth century, who was at the inception of a movement named Structuralism. After Saussure (1857–1913) and Peirce (1839–1914), and along with Hjelmslev (1899–1965), he is probably the most important theoretician among the founders of linguistics.

Beginning with two stylistic devices taken from ancient rhetoric, namely the metaphor (replacing one word with another linked to it by some sort of resemblance, "raging bull" for the boxer Jake LaMotta, for example) and metonymy (replacing one word with another linked to it by contiguity: "having a glass" to say that one drinks the liquid in the glass—the container for the contents, for example), he succeeded in explaining the functioning of language according to two axes: the paradigmatic axis and the syntagmatic axis.

Broadly speaking, the paradigmatic axis is vertical and concerns the choice of vocabulary: each time you pronounce a word, you choose it from a list that you have in mind and which you mentally scroll through. For example, "goat," "economy," "death," "trousers," "I-you-he," or whatever.

Then you join it to other words: "belonging to Monsieur Seguin," "stagnant," "with his scythe," "creased," "undersigned," to form a phrase: this chain is the horizontal axis, the word order that will enable you to make a sentence, then several sentences, and finally a speech. This is the syntagmatic axis.

With a noun, you must decide if it needs an adjective, an adverb, a verb, a coordinating conjunction, a preposition . . . and you must choose which adjective or which adverb or which verb: you renew the paradigmatic operation at each syntagmatic stage.

The paradigmatic axis makes you choose from a list of words in the equivalent grammatical class: a noun or a pronoun, an adjective or a relative proposition, an adverb, a verb, etc.

The syntagmatic axis makes you choose the order of words: subject-verb-complement or verb-subject or complement-subject-verb, and so on.

Vocabulary and syntax.

Each time you formulate a phrase, you are subconsciously practicing these two operations. The paradigmatic axis uses your hard disk, if you like, and the syntagmatic your processor. (Although I doubt whether Bayard knows much about computers.)

But in this particular case that is not what interests us.

(Bayard grumbles.)

Jakobson also summarized the process of communication with an outline that consists of the following elements: the sender, the receiver, the message, the context, the channel, and the code. It was from this outline that he drew the functions of language.

Jacques Bayard has no desire to learn more, but for the sake of the investigation he has to understand at least the broad outlines. So here are the functions:

- The "referential" function is the first and most obvious function of language. We use language to speak about something. The words used refer to a certain context, a certain reality, which one must provide information about.
- The "emotive" or "expressive" function is aimed at communicating the presence and position of the sender in relation to his or her message: interjections, modal

adverbs, hints of judgment, use of irony, and so on. The way the sender expresses a piece of information referring to an exterior subject gives information about the sender. This is the "I" function.

- The "conative" function is the "you" function. It is directed toward the receiver. It is principally performed with the imperative or the vocative, i.e., the interpellation of whoever is being addressed: "Soldiers, I am satisfied with you!," for example. (And remember, by the way, that a phrase is hardly ever reducible to a single function, but generally combines several. When he addresses his troops after Austerlitz, Napoleon marries the emotive function—"I am satisfied"—with the conative—"Soldiers/with you!")

- The "phatic" function is the most amusing. This is the function that envisages communication as an end in itself. When you say "hello" on the telephone, you are saying nothing more than "I'm listening," i.e., "I am in a situation of communication." When you chat for hours in a bar with your friends, when you talk about the weather or last night's soccer game, you are not really interested in the information per se, but you talk for the sake of talking, without any objective other than making conversation. In other words, this function is the source of the majority of our verbal communications.

- The "metalinguistic" function is aimed at verifying that the sender and the receiver understand each other, i.e., that they are using the same code. "You understand?," "You see what I mean?," "You know?," "Let me explain . . ."; or, from the receiver's point of view, "What are you getting at?," "What does that mean?," etc. Everything related to the definition of a word or the explanation of a development, everything linked to the process of learning a language, all references to language, all metalanguage, is the domain of the metalinguistic function. A dictionary's sole function is metalinguistic.

- And finally, the last function is the "poetic" function. This considers language in its aesthetic dimension. Plays on the sounds of words, alliteration, assonance, repetition, echo or rhythm effects, all belong to this function. We find it in poems, of course, but also in songs, oratory, newspaper headlines, advertising, and political slogans.

Jacques Bayard lights a cigarette and says, "That's six."

"Sorry?"

"That's six functions."

"Ah . . . yes. Quite."

"Isn't there a seventh function?"

"Well, uh . . . apparently, there is, yes . . ."

Simon smiles stupidly.

Bayard wonders out loud what Simon is being paid for. Simon reminds him that he did not ask for anything and that he is there against his will, on the express orders of a fascist president who sits at the head of a police state.

Nevertheless, after thinking about it, or rather after rereading Jakobson, Simon Herzog does come up with a possible seventh function, designated as the "magic or incantatory function," whose mechanism is described as "the conversion of a third person, absent or inanimate, to whom a conative message is addressed." And Jakobson gives as an example a Lithuanian magical spell: "May this stye dry up, tfu tfu tfu tfu." Yeah yeah yeah, thinks Simon.

He also mentions this incantation from northern Russia: "Water, queen of rivers, aurora! Take the sadness beyond the blue sea, to the bottom of the sea, and never let it weigh down the happy heart of God's servant . . ." And, for good measure, a citation from the Bible: "Sun, stand thou still upon Gibeon; and thou, Moon, in the valley of Ajalon. And the sun stood still, and the moon stayed" (Joshua 10:12).

Fair enough, but that all sounds pretty anecdotal. You can't really consider it a separate function; at most, it is a slightly crazy use of the conative function for an essentially cathartic effect, poetic at best, but completely ineffective: the magical invocation works only in fairy tales, by definition. Simon is convinced that this is not the seventh function of language, and in any case Jakobson only mentions it in passing, in the interests of completeness, before returning to his serious analysis. The "magical or incantatory function"? A negligible curiosity. A nonsensical footnote. Nothing worth killing for, in any case.

33

"By the spirits of Cicero, tonight, let me tell you, my friends, it is going to rain enthymemes! I can see some have been revising their Aristotle, and I know some others who know their Quintilian, but will that be enough to overcome the lexical snares in the slalom race of syntax? Caw caw! The spirit of Corax is speaking to you. Glory to the founding fathers! Tonight, the victor will win a trip to Syracuse. As for the defeated . . . they will have their fingers trapped in the door. Well, it's always better than your tongue . . . And don't forget: today's orators are tomorrow's tribunes. Glory to the logos! Long live the Logos Club!"

34

Simon and Bayard are in a room that is half-laboratory, half-armory. In front of them, a man in a white coat is examining the mustachioed man's pistol, which should have obliterated Simon's brain. ("He's Q," thinks Simon.) The ballistics expert commentates as he inspects the weapon: "Nine millimeter; eight shots; double action; steel, finished in bronze, walnut butt; weight: 730 grams without the magazine." It looks like a Walther PPK, he says, but the safety is the other way around: it's a Makarov PM, a Soviet pistol. Except that . . .

Firearms, the expert explains, are like electric guitars. Fender, for instance, is an American firm that produces the Telecaster used by Keith Richards or Jimi Hendrix's Stratocaster, but there are also Mexican or Japanese models produced under franchise, which are replicas of the original U.S. version: cheaper and generally less well finished, although often well-made.

This Makarov is a Bulgarian, not a Russian, model, which is probably why it jammed: the Russian models are very reliable, the Bulgarian copies slightly less so.

"Now, you're going to laugh, Superintendent," says the expert, showing him the umbrella that was removed from the man's chest. "You see this hole? The point is hollow. It functions like a syringe, fed through the handle. All you have to do is press this trigger and it opens a valve that, with the aid of a compressed air cylinder, releases the liquid. The mechanism is impressively simple. It's identical to the one used to eliminate Georgi Markov, the Bulgarian dissident, two years ago in London. You remember?" Superintendent Bayard does indeed remember that the murder had been attributed to the Bulgarian secret services. At the time, they were using ricin. But now they have a stronger poison, botulinum toxin, which acts by blocking neuromuscular transmission, thus provoking muscle paralysis and causing death in a matter of minutes, either by asphyxia or by stopping the heart.

Bayard, looking pensive, fiddles with the umbrella's mechanism.

Would Simon Herzog happen to know any Bulgarians in the academic world?

Simon thinks.

Yes, he does know one.

35

The two Michels, Poniatowski and d'Ornano, have reported for duty in the president's office. Giscard stands anxiously by the ground-floor window, looking out on the Élysée Gardens. As d'Ornano is smoking, Giscard asks him for a cigarette. Poniatowski, sitting in one of the luxurious armchairs in the informal part of the office, has poured himself a whiskey, which he puts down on the coffee table in front of him. He speaks first: "I talked to my contacts, who are in touch with Andropov." Giscard says nothing because, like all men with this much power, he expects his employees to save him the bother of asking important questions. So Poniatowski replies to the silent question: "According to them, the KGB is not involved."

Giscard: "What makes you think that opinion is credible?"

Ponia: "Several things. The most convincing being that in the short term they would not have any use for such a document. At a political level."

Giscard: "Propaganda is critical in those countries. The document could be very useful to them."

Ponia: "I doubt it. You can't really say that Brezhnev has encouraged freedom of expression since he succeeded Khrushchev. There are no debates in the USSR, or only within the Party, and the public aren't aware of those. So what counts is not the power of persuasion but the relative strengths of political forces."

D'Ornano: "But it's perfectly imaginable that Brezhnev or another member of the Party might want to use it internally. The central committee is a vipers' nest. It would be a considerable asset."

Ponia: "I can't imagine Brezhnev wanting to assert his preeminence in that way. He doesn't need to. The opposition is nonexistent. The system is locked in place. And no Central Committee member could order such an operation for his own profit without the authorities being informed."

D'Ornano: "Except Andropov."

Ponia (irritated): "Andropov is a shadowy figure. But he has more power as head of the KGB than he would have in any other position. I can't see him embarking on a political adventure."

D'Ornano (ironic): "True. Shadowy figures rarely do things like that. Talleyrand and Fouché had no political ambitions at all, did they?"

Ponia: "Well, they didn't realize those ambitions."

D'Ornano: "That's debatable. At the Congress of Vienna—"

Giscard: "All right. What else?"

Ponia: "It seems highly improbable that the operation would have been carried out by the Bulgarian services without the approval of their big brother. On the other hand, it is possible to envisage Bulgarian agents selling their services to private interests. It is up to us to determine the nature of those private interests."

D'Ornano: "Do the Bulgarians have that little control over their men?"

Ponia: "Corruption is widespread. No part of society is free of it, least of all the intelligence services."

D'Ornano: "Secret agents working freelance in their spare time? Frankly . . ."

Ponia: "Secret agents working for several employers? It's not exactly unheard of." (He drains his glass.)

Giscard (stubbing out his cigarette in a little ivory hippopotamus that serves as an ashtray): "Agreed. Anything else?"

Ponia (leaning back in his chair, arms behind his head): "Well, it turns out Carter's brother is a Libyan agent."

Giscard (surprised): "Which one? Billy?"

Ponia: "Andropov seems to have got this from the CIA. Apparently, he thought it was hilarious."

D'Ornano (getting them back to the subject at hand): "So, what are we going to do? If in doubt, wipe them out?"

Ponia: "The president does not need the document. He just needs to know that the opposition doesn't have it."

As far as I know, no one has ever pointed out that Giscard's famous speech impediment became more pronounced during moments of embarrassment or pleasure. He says: "Of coursh, of coursh . . . But if we could find it . . . or at leasht locate it, and if poshible, get our handzh on it, I would resht more eazhily. For the shake of Fransh. Imagine if thish document fell into, uh, the wrong handzh . . . Not that . . . But, well . . ."

Ponia: "Then we have to make Bayard's mission clearer: get hold of the document, without letting anyone read it. Let's not forget that that young linguist he's hired is capable of deciphering it and therefore using it. Or of ensuring that every copy of it is destroyed. [He gets up and walks over to the drinks table, muttering.] A lefty. Bound to be a lefty . . ."

D'Ornano: "But how can we know if the document has already been used?"

Ponia: "According to my information, if someone used it we would know about it pretty damn quickly . . ."

D'Ornano: "What if they were discreet? Kept a low profile?"

Giscard (leaning against the sideboard under the Delacroix, and fingering the Legion of Honor medals in their boxes): "That doesn't seem very plausible. Power, of whatever kind, is intended to be used."

D'Ornano (curious): "Is that true for the atomic bomb?"

Giscard (professorial): "Especially the atomic bomb."

The mention of a possible end to the world plunges the president into a light daydream for a moment. He thinks of the A71 highway which must cross the Auvergne, of the mayor's office in Chamalières, of the France over which he rules. His two employees wait respectfully for him to start speaking again. "In the meantime, all our actions should be governed by a single objective: preventing the left from gaining power."

Ponia (sniffing a bottle of vodka): "As long as I'm alive, there will be no Communist ministers in France."

D'Ornano (lighting a cigarette): "Exactly. You should slow down if you want to get through the election."

Ponia (raising his glass): *"Na zdrowie!"*

36

"Comrade Kristoff . . . You know, of course, who is the greatest politician of the twentieth century?"

Emil Kristoff was not summoned to Lubyanka Square, but he would have preferred that.

"Naturally, Yuri Vladimirovich. It's Georgi Dimitrov."

The faux-intellectual tenor of his meeting with Yuri Andropov, the head of the KGB, in an old bar located in a basement, as nearly all the bars in Moscow are, is not designed to reassure him, and the fact that they are in a public place changes nothing. You can be arrested in a public place. You can even die in a public place. He is well placed to know this.

"A Bulgarian." Andropov laughs. "Who would have believed it?"

The waiter puts two small glasses of vodka and two large glasses of orange juice on the table, with two fat gherkins on a little plate, and Kristoff wonders if this is a clue. Around him, people smoke, drink, and talk loudly, and that is the first rule when you want to be sure that a conversation cannot be overheard: meet in a noisy place, full of random sounds, so that any microphones hidden nearby cannot isolate a particular voice. If you are in an apartment, you should run a bath. But the simplest solution is to go out for a drink. Kristoff observes the customers' faces and spots at least two agents in the room, but he presumes there must be more.

Andropov continues on the subject of Dimitrov: "If you think about it, it was there for all to see during the Reichstag trial. The conflict between Göring, who is summoned as a witness, and Dimitrov, in the dock, anticipated the fascist aggression to come, the heroic Communists' resistance, and our final victory. That trial is highly symbolic of the superiority of communism from every point of view, political and moral. Dimitrov is majestic and mocking, and masters the historical dialectic perfectly, even as he risks his life, faced with the angry, fist-waving Göring . . .

What a spectacle! Göring, who just happens to be president of the Reichstag, prime minister and minister of the interior for Prussia. But Dimitrov reverses their roles, and it is Göring who has to respond to his questions. Dimitrov completely demolishes him. Göring is furious: he stamps his feet, like a little boy who's been told he can't have any dessert. Facing him, imperious in the dock, Dimitrov reveals the madness of the Nazis to the world. Even the president of the tribunal realizes it. It's hilarious because you'd think he was asking Dimitrov to forgive fat Göring's behavior. He says to him—I remember this as if it were yesterday—'Given that you are spouting Communist propaganda, you should not be surprised if the witness is so agitated.' Agitated! And then Dimitrov says he is fully satisfied with the prime minister's response. Ha ha! What a man! What a talent!"

Kristoff sees allusions and deeper meanings everywhere, but he tries to keep things in perspective because he knows that his paranoia makes it difficult for him to assess the KGB chairman's words correctly. All the same, the fact that he was summoned to Moscow is, indisputably, a clue in itself. He does not wonder if Andropov knows something. He wonders what he knows. And that is a much harder question to answer.

"Back then, people all over the world said: 'There is only one man left in Germany, and that man is Bulgarian.' I knew him, Emil, were you aware of that? A born orator. A master."

While he listens to Andropov praising the great Dimitrov, Comrade Kristoff assesses his own situation. There is nothing more uncomfortable for someone preparing to lie than being uncertain how much the person he is about to lie to knows. At some point, he realizes, he will have to gamble.

And that moment arrives: ending his disquisition on Dimitrov, Andropov asks his Bulgarian counterpart for clarification on the latest reports that have reached his desk in Lubyanka Square. What exactly is this operation in Paris?

So, here we are. Kristoff feels his heart accelerate, but is careful not to breathe more quickly. Andropov bites into a gherkin.

He must decide now. Either admit the operation or claim to know nothing about it. But this second option has the disadvantage of making you look incompetent, which, in the world of intelligence, is never a good idea. Kristoff knows exactly how a good lie works: it must be drowned in an ocean of truth. Being 90 percent truthful enables you to render the 10 percent you are attempting to conceal more credible, while reducing the risks of contradicting yourself. You buy time and you avoid becoming muddled. When you lie, you must lie about one point—and one only—and be perfectly honest about the rest. Emil Kristoff leans toward Andropov and says: "Comrade Yuri, you know Roman Jakobson? He's a compatriot of yours. He wrote some very nice things about Baudelaire."

37

My Julenka,

I got back from Moscow yesterday. The visit went well, or at least I think it did. I got back, in any case. We had a few drinks, me and the old guy. He was friendly and seemed pretty drunk by the end of the night, but I don't believe he really was. I do the same thing sometimes, pretending to be drunk in order to win people's trust or get them to lower their guard. But as you can probably guess, I didn't lower mine. I told him everything he wanted to know except, obviously, I didn't mention you. I said I didn't believe in the manuscript's power, and that was why I didn't inform him about the Paris mission, because I wanted to be sure first. But as certain agents in my service did believe in it, I decided it was better to be safe than sorry, so I sent a few agents, and I told him that they'd been overzealous. Apparently, the French services are investigating at the moment, but Giscard is pretending not to know anything about it. Maybe you can use your husband's connections to find out? Either way, you should be very careful, and now that the old man is watching me, I won't be able to send you any extra men.

The van driver got here safely, and so did the fake doctor who gave you the document. The French will never be able to find them— they've gone on holiday to the Black Sea, and they are the only people who could possibly lead anyone to you, along with the two other agents who died and the one who's stayed there to oversee the investigation. I know he was wounded, but he's tough. You can count on him. If the police find anything, he'll know what to do.

Allow me to give you some advice. You must file away a copy of that document. We are used to keeping and hiding precious documents that must absolutely not be lost but whose contents cannot under any circumstances be divulged to anyone else. You must make a copy of it, one only, and give it for safekeeping to someone trustworthy who has no idea what it's about. Keep the original on you.

One other thing: look out for Japanese people.

All right, that is my advice for you, my Juleshka. Make good use of it. I hope you're well and that everything will go as planned, even if I know from experience that nothing ever goes as planned.

Your old father who watches over you,
Tatko

PS: Write back to me in French. It's safer, and anyway I need to practice.

38

There is some faculty housing at the École Normale Supérieure, behind the Panthéon. We are in a large apartment, and the weary-looking, white-haired man with bags under his eyes says:

"I'm alone."

"Where is Hélène?"

"I don't know. We had another row. She had a horrible tantrum about something absurd. Or maybe that was me."

"We need you. Can you keep this document? You mustn't open

it, you mustn't read it, and you mustn't talk to anyone about it, not even Hélène."

"Okay."

39

Hard to imagine what Julia Kristeva is thinking in 1980. The idea that Sollers's histrionic dandyism, his so-very-French libertinism, his pathological boasting, his adolescent-pamphleteer style, and his shock-the-bourgeoisie habits could have seduced the young Bulgarian girl, newly arrived from Eastern Europe . . . yes, I can buy that. Fifteen years later, one might suppose that she is somewhat less under his spell, but who knows? What seems obvious is that their partnership is solid, that it has functioned perfectly from the beginning, and that it is still functional now: a tightly knit team with clearly defined roles. For him, the pretentious bullshit, society parties, and clownish nonsense. For her, the icy, venomous, structuralist Slavic charm, the arcana of academia, the management of mandarins, the technical, institutional, and, inevitably, bureaucratic aspects of their rise. (He "doesn't know how to write a check," so the story goes.) Together, they are a formidable political war machine already, working toward the heights of an exemplary career in the next century: when Kristeva receives the Legion of Honor from the hands of Nicolas Sarkozy, Sollers, also present, will be sure to mock the president for pronouncing "Barthès" instead of "Barthes." Good cop, bad cop. They get their cake full of honors and they eat it with insolence. (Later, François Hollande will elevate Kristeva to the ranks of *commandeur*. Presidents come and go, people with meaningless medals remain.)

In summary: an infernal duo, and a political double-act. Let's keep that in mind.

When Kristeva opens the door and sees that Althusser has come with his wife, she cannot or prefers not to suppress a grimace of displeasure. Hélène, Althusser's wife, is well aware of what these people think of her and gives an evil grin in return, the two women's instinctive hatred instantly bordering on a sort of complicity. For his part, Althusser looks like a guilty child as he hands over a small bouquet of flowers. Kristeva rushes off to put them in a sink. Visibly under the influence of the aperitifs he's had, Sollers welcomes the two arrivals with phony exclamations of delight: "So, my dear friends, how are you? . . . We were just waiting for you to come . . . before we sat down to eat . . . Dear Louis, a martini . . . as usual? . . . red! . . . oh wow! . . . Hélène . . . what would you like to drink? . . . I know . . . a Bloody Mary! . . . hee hee! . . . Julia . . . will you bring the celery . . . my darling? . . . Louis! . . . how's the Party?"

Hélène observes the other guests like an old, nervous cat, recognizing no one but BHL, who she's seen on the television, and Lacan, who has come with a tall young woman in a black leather suit. Sollers makes the introductions while they sit down, but Hélène doesn't bother trying to remember anyone's name: there is a young New York couple in sports clothes, a Chinese woman who either works for the embassy or as a trapeze artist for the Peking Circus, a Parisian publisher, a Canadian feminist, and a Bulgarian linguist. "The avant-garde of the proletariat," Hélène says to herself, laughing.

The guests have barely sat down when Sollers unctuously begins a discussion about Poland: "Now that is a subject that will never go out of fashion! . . . Solidarnosc, Jaruzelski, yes, yes . . . from Mickiewicz and Slovacki to Walesa and Wojtyla . . . We could be talking about it in a hundred years, a thousand years, but it will still be bowed beneath the yoke of Russia . . . it's practical . . . it makes our conversations immortal . . . And when it's not Russia, it's Germany, of course, hmm? . . . Agh, come on, come on . . . comrades . . . To die for Gdansk . . . to die for Danzig . . . What delicious nonsense! . . . What's that phrase again? . . . Oh yes: six of one and half a dozen of the other . . ."

The provocation is aimed at Althusser, but the old philosopher is so dull-eyed as he sips his martini that he looks like he might drown in it. So Hélène, with the boldness of a small wild animal, replies on his behalf: "I understand your solicitude toward the Polish people: I don't think they sent any members of your family to Auschwitz." And as Sollers hesitates for a second (just one) before following up with some provocative insult to the Jews, she decides to drive home her advantage: "But what about this new pope, do you like him?" (She plunges her nose into her plate.) "I wouldn't have thought so." (She imitates a working-class intonation.)

Sollers opens his arms wide, as if beating his wings, and declares enthusiastically: "This pope is just my type!" (He bites into an asparagus spear.) "Isn't it sublime when he gets off his plane and kisses the ground? . . . Whichever country he's in, the pope gets down on his knees, like a beautiful prostitute preparing to give you a blow job, and he kisses the ground . . ." (He waves his half-eaten asparagus.) "What can you do? This pope is a kisser . . . How could I not like him?"

The New York couple giggle as one. Lacan lifts his hand and squeaks like a little bird, but decides not to speak. Hélène, who like any good Communist is single-minded, asks: "And you think he likes libertines? Last I heard, he wasn't very open on sexuality." (She glances over at Kristeva.) "Politically, I mean."

Sollers laughs noisily, the sign that he is about to embark on his usual strategy of abruptly changing the subject to pretty much anything that comes to mind: "That's because he's badly advised . . . Anyway, I'm sure he's surrounded by homosexuals . . . The homosexuals are the new Jesuits . . . but on things like that, they're not necessarily that well advised . . . Except . . . apparently there's a new disease that's decimating them . . . God said: be fruitful and multiply . . . The rubber johnny . . . What an abomination! . . . Sterilized sex . . . Horny bodies that don't touch each other anymore . . . Pfft . . . I've never used a rubber in my life . . . Wrap up my dick like some meat in a supermarket? . . . Never!"

At this moment, Althusser wakes up:

"If the USSR attacked Poland, it was for highly strategic reasons. They had to prevent Hitler from moving close to the Russian border at all costs. Stalin used Poland as a buffer: by taking up a position on Polish soil, he was insuring himself against the coming invasion . . ."

"And that strategy, as everyone knows, worked like a dream," says Kristeva.

"After Munich, the Nazi-Soviet Pact had become a necessity. More than that, an inevitability," Althusser continues.

Lacan makes a sound like an owl. Sollers pours himself another drink. Hélène and Kristeva stare at each other. It is still not clear if the Chinese woman speaks French, nor, for that matter, the Bulgarian linguist or the Canadian feminist or even the New York couple, until Kristeva asks them, in French, if they've played tennis recently (they are, we discover, doubles partners, and Kristeva talks for quite a while about their last match, when she proved herself astonishingly combative, to her own surprise, as she is essentially not a very good player, she's at pains to make clear). But Sollers, always happy to change the subject, does not let the couple reply:

"Ah, Borg! . . . The messiah who came in from the cold . . . When he falls to his knees on Wimbledon's grass . . . arms outstretched . . . that blond hair . . . his bandana . . . his beard . . . it's Jesus Christ on Centre Court . . . If Borg wins Wimbledon, it's for the redemption of all mankind . . . And, as there's a lot of redeeming to do, he wins every year . . . How many victories will it take to wash our sins away? . . . Five . . . Ten . . . Twenty . . . Fifty . . . A hundred . . . A thousand . . ."

"I thought you prefer McEnroe," says the young New Yorker in his New York–accented French.

"Ah, McEnroe . . . the man you love to hate . . . a dancer, that one . . . the grace of the devil . . . But he should have actually flown around the court . . . McEnroe is Lucifer . . . the most beautiful of all the angels . . . Lucifer always falls in the end . . ."

While he embarks on a biblical exegesis in which he compares St. John with McEnroe, Kristeva slips into the kitchen with the Chinese woman on the pretext of serving the main course. Lacan's young mistress takes off her shoes under the table. The Canadian feminist and the Bulgarian linguist look at each other questioningly. Althusser plays with the olive in his martini. BHL bangs his fist on the table and says: "We must intervene in Afghanistan!"

Hélène looks around at everyone.

She says: "And not in Iran?" The Bulgarian linguist adds mysteriously: "Hesitation is the mother of the fantastical." The Canadian feminist smiles. Kristeva returns with the leg of lamb and the Chinese woman. Althusser says: "The Party was wrong to support the invasion of Afghanistan. You shouldn't invade a country with a press release. The Soviets are smarter than that: they'll withdraw." Sollers asks mockingly: "The Party? How many divisions have they got?" The publisher looks at his watch and says: "France is slow." Sollers smiles as he looks at Hélène and says: "One is not serious at seventy." Lacan's mistress uses her bare foot to caress BHL's crotch. He is hard within seconds.

The conversation drifts toward Barthes. The publisher delivers an ambiguous eulogy. Sollers explains: "Lots of homosexuals have given me the same strange impression, now and then—as if they're being eaten up from inside . . ." Kristeva points out to the eleven guests: "As I'm sure you know, we were very close. Roland adored Philippe and [she sounds suddenly modest and mysterious] he liked me very much." BHL insists on adding: "He could *never* stand Marxism-Leninism." The publisher: "He adored Brecht, though." Hélène, venomously: "And China? What did he think of China?" Althusser frowns. The Chinese woman looks up. Sollers replies in a relaxed way: "Boring. But no more than the rest of the world." The Bulgarian linguist, who knew Barthes well: "Except for Japan." The Canadian feminist, who did her master's under Barthes, remembers: "He was very welcoming and very lonely." The publisher says knowingly: "Yes and no. He knew how to surround himself . . . when he wanted to. He wasn't without resources, in spite of everything." Lacan's mistress slides farther down her chair to massage BHL's balls with her toes.

BHL is imperturbable: "It's good to have a master. But you must know how to detach yourself from him. With me, for example, at the École Normale—" Kristeva interrupts him with a dry laugh: "Why are the French so obsessed with their education? They can't go two hours without mentioning it. It reminds me of old soldiers." The publisher agrees: "That's true. In France, we're all nostalgic for our school days." Sollers says teasingly: "Well, some stay in school all their lives." But Althusser doesn't react. Hélène grinds her teeth at this middle-class compulsion: imagining their own experience holds for everyone. She didn't like school, and she didn't stay there long either.

The doorbell rings. Kristeva gets up to open it. In the entrance hall, she can be seen talking to a badly dressed man with a mustache. The conversation lasts less than a minute. Then she comes back to the table as if nothing happened, saying simply (and her accent resurfaces for a second): "Sorrrry, just some borrring work stuff. For my office." The publisher goes on: "In France, academic success has too much influence on social success." The Bulgarian linguist stares at Kristeva: "But thankfully, it is not the only factor. Isn't that true, Julia?" Kristeva says something in Bulgarian. Then the two of them begin talking in their native language: brief, muttered replies. If there is any hostility between them, the ambience around the table makes it impossible for the other guests to detect it. Sollers intervenes: "Come on, now, children, no whispering, ha ha . . ." Then he addresses the Canadian feminist: "So, my dear friend, how is your novel going? I agree with Aragon, you know . . . The woman is the future of the man . . . and therefore of literature . . . because the woman is death . . . and literature is always on the side of death . . ." And while he vividly imagines the Canadian peeling back his foreskin, he asks Kristeva if she would like to go and fetch dessert.

Kristeva gets to her feet and starts clearing the table, helped by the Chinese woman, and while the two women disappear once again into the kitchen, the publisher takes out a cigar and cuts the end off it with the bread knife. Lacan's mistress continues to perform contortions on her chair. The New York couple hold hands and smile politely. Sollers imagines a foursome with the Canadian and tennis rackets. BHL, hard as a rock, says they should invite Solzhenitsyn next time. Hélène scolds Althusser: "You pig! You made a stain!" She wipes his shirt with a napkin dipped in a little sparkling water. Lacan quietly sings a sort of Jewish nursery rhyme. The others pretend not to notice. In the kitchen, Kristeva grabs the Chinese woman by the waist. BHL says to Sollers: "When you think about it, Philippe, you're better than Sartre: Stalinist, Maoist, papist . . . He always seems to be wrong, but you! . . . You change your mind so quickly that you don't have time to be wrong." Sollers sticks a cigarette in his cigarette holder. Lacan mumbles: "Sartre does not exist." BHL continues: "In my next book, I—" Sollers interrupts him: "Sartre said that all anti-Communists are dogs . . . I say that all anti-Catholics are dogs . . . Anyway, it's very simple: there is not a Jew of any worth who hasn't been tempted to convert to Catholicism . . . Isn't that true? . . . Darling, are you going to bring us dessert?" From the kitchen, Kristeva's muffled voice replies that it's coming.

The publisher says to Sollers that he might publish Hélène Cixous. Sollers replies: "Poor Derrida . . ." BHL again sees fit to tell everyone: "I have a great deal of affection for Derrida. He was my tutor at the École. Along with you, dear Louis. But he is not a philosopher. I can think of only three French philosophers who are still alive: Sartre, Levinas, and Althusser." Althusser does not react to this flattery. Hélène conceals her irritation. The American man asks: "What about Pierre Bowrdieu—isn't he a good philosopher?" BHL replies that he went to the École Normale but he is certainly not a philosopher. The publisher explains to the American that Bourdieu is a sociologist who did a lot of work on invisible inequalities, and cultural, social, symbolic capital . . . Sollers makes a show of yawning. "Above all, he is boring beyond belief . . . His *habitus* . . . Yes, we are not all equal—who would have guessed? And, allow me to let you all in on a little secret . . . shhh . . . gather around and listen . . . It has always been like that and it always will be . . . Incredible, huh?"

Sollers becomes more and more garbled: "Rise above! Rise above! Abstraction, quick! . . . We're not Elsa and Aragon, no more than Sartre and Beauvoir. Wrong! . . . Adultery is a criminal conversation . . . Oh yeah . . . oh yeah . . . And while we're at it . . . Here. Now. Really here . . . Really now . . . Fashion is often true . . ." His gaze wavers between the Canadian and Hélène. "The Maoist affair? It was our age's entertainment . . . China . . . Romanticism . . . I've had to write some incendiary things, it's true . . . I'm a great heckler . . . The best in the country . . ."

Lacan is miles away. His mistress's foot is still caressing BHL's crotch. The publisher waits for it all to stop. The Canadian and the Bulgarian feel united in silent solidarity. Hélène endures the great French writer's monologue in mute rage. Althusser feels something dangerous rising within him.

Kristeva and the Chinese woman finally return with an apricot tart and a clafouti; their hastily reapplied lipstick burns passionately. The Canadian asks how the French will vote in next year's elections. Sollers explodes: "Mitterrand has only one destiny: defeat . . . he will fulfil it completely . . ." Always prompt to issue reminders, Hélène asks him: "You've had lunch with Giscard, haven't you? What's he like?"

"Who, Giscard? . . . Pfft, a hypocrite and a degenerate . . . You know the aristocratic bit of his name is from his wife? . . . Our dear Roland had it right . . . a very successful bourgeois specimen, he said . . . Ah, we wouldn't be safe from a new May '68 . . . if we were still in '68 . . ."

"The structures . . . in the street . . ." murmurs Lacan, on his last legs.

"In America, his public image is as a brilliant, dynamic, and ambitious patrician," says the American woman. "But up to now he hasn't made much of an impression internationally."

"He hasn't bombed Vietnam, that's for sure," rasps Althusser, wiping his mouth.

"He did intervene in Zaire, though," says BHL. "And he loves Europe."

"Which brings us back to Poland," says Kristeva.

"Oh no, we're not going to talk about Poland anymore to-night!" says Sollers, taking a drag through his cigarette holder.

"Yes, we could talk about East Timor, for example," says Hélène. "That would make a change. I haven't heard the French government condemning the massacres committed by Indonesia."

"Think about it," says Althusser, apparently emerging from his fog once again. "One hundred and thirty million inhabitants, a huge market, and a precious ally of the United States in a region of the world where they don't have many."

"That was delicious," says the American woman, finishing her clafouti.

"Another cognac, gentlemen?" asks Sollers.

Suddenly, the young woman who is still playing footsie with BHL's balls asks who this Charlus is who everyone's talking about in Saint-Germain. Sollers smiles: "He's the most interesting Jew in the world, my dear . . . And another faggot, as it happens . . ."

The Canadian says that she would like a cognac, too. The Bulgarian offers her a cigarette, which she lights with a candle. The house cat rubs against the Chinese woman's legs. Someone mentions Simone Veil: Hélène hates her, so Sollers defends her. The American couple think that Carter will be reelected. Althusser starts trying to seduce the Chinese woman. Lacan lights one of his famous cigars. They talk for a bit about soccer, and young Platini, who everyone agrees is promising.

The evening draws to a close. Lacan's mistress will go home with BHL. The Bulgarian linguist will accompany the Canadian feminist. The Chinese woman will go back alone to her delegation. Sollers will fall asleep and dream about the orgy that didn't happen. Out of nowhere, Lacan makes this observation, in a tone of infinite weariness: "It's curious how a woman, when she ceases being a woman, can crush the man she has under her thumb . . . Yes, crush him. For his own good, of course." There is embarrassed silence among the other guests. Sollers declares: "The king is he who wears on his sleeve the most vivid experience of castration."

40

This thing about the severed fingers must be cleared up, so Bayard decides to put a tail on the policeman who shot the Bulgarian on the Pont-Neuf. But as he has the uneasy feeling that the police force has been infiltrated by an enemy whose identity—and, in truth, whose nature—he knows nothing about, he doesn't ask his superiors to organize this tail, but tells Simon to do it. As usual, Simon protests, but this time he thinks he has a valid objection: that policeman saw him on the Pont-Neuf; Simon was with the others when Bayard dived into the Seine, and then the two of them were seen together, deep in discussion, after he emerged from the water.

Never mind. He can disguise himself.

How?

They'll cut his hair and get him out of those rags that make him look like an overgrown student.

This is too much. He's been fairly easygoing up to now, but Simon is categorical: it's absolutely out of the question.

Bayard, who knows about public employment, brings up the thorny question of transfers. What will become of young Simon (or not so young, actually; how old is he?) once he has finished his thesis? He could easily be transferred to a secondary school in Bobigny. Or maybe they could help get him tenure at Vincennes?

Simon doesn't believe things work like that in National Education, and that string-pulling by Giscard in person (especially

Giscard!) will not help him get a job at Vincennes (the university of Deleuze, of Balibar!), but he is not entirely sure. On the other hand, he is sure that a transfer to somewhere unappealing as a form of punishment is perfectly possible. So he goes to the hairdresser and gets his hair cut—short enough that he feels genuinely uneasy as he contemplates the results, as if he were a stranger to himself, recognizing his face but not the identity that he has unwittingly constructed, year after year—and he lets the Ministry of the Interior pay for a suit and tie. Despite not being cheap, the suit is rather so-so, inevitably a bit big in the shoulders, a little short at the ankles, and Simon has to learn not only to tie his tie but to make the wide part cover the narrow part neatly. And yet, once his metamorphosis is complete, standing in front of the mirror, he surprises himself by feeling—beyond that sensation of strangeness mixed with repulsion—a sort of curiosity and interest in this image of himself, himself without being him, a him from another life, a him who decided to work in a bank or in insurance, or for a government organization, or as a diplomat. Instinctively, Simon adjusts the knot of his tie and, beneath the cuffs of his jacket, pulls at the sleeves of his shirt. He is ready for his mission. And the part of him that appreciates the playful aspects of existence decides to try enjoying this little adventure.

Outside the Quai des Orfèvres he waits for the policeman with the missing finger to finish his shift, and he smokes a Lucky Strike paid for by France, because the other upside of being under government orders is that he has the right to an expense account. So he has kept the receipt from the tobacconist (three francs).

Finally, the policeman appears. He's out of uniform, and the tailing operation begins, on foot. Simon follows the man as he crosses the Pont Saint-Michel and goes up the boulevard until he reaches the junction with Saint-Germain, where he takes a bus. Simon hails a taxi and, uttering the strange words "Follow that bus," he feels as if he has wandered into a movie, though what genre of movie he isn't yet sure. But the driver obeys without asking questions, and at each stop Simon has to make sure that the plainclothes policeman has not gotten off the bus. The man is middle-aged, of average height and build and not easy to spot in a crowd, so Simon has to be vigilant. The bus goes up Rue Monge, and the man gets off at Censier. Simon stops the taxi. The man enters a bar. Simon waits a minute before following him. Inside, the man is sitting at a table at the back. Simon sits near the door and immediately realizes this is a mistake because the man keeps looking over in his direction. It is not because he has identified him, just because he is expecting someone. In order not to attract attention, Simon looks out the window. He contemplates the ballet of students entering and emerging from the metro station, standing about smoking cigarettes or gathering in groups, still undecided about what will happen next, happy to be together, excited about the future.

But suddenly, it is not a student that he sees coming out of the metro but the Bulgarian who almost killed him during the car chase. He's wearing the same crumpled suit and apparently hasn't thought it worthwhile to shave off his mustache. He looks around the square, then comes toward Simon. He is limping. Simon hides his face behind the menu. The Bulgarian opens the door of the café. Instinctively, Simon shrinks back, but the Bulgarian passes without seeing him and heads to the back of the room, where he sits down with the policeman.

The two men begin a conversation in low voices. This is the moment that the waiter chooses to take Simon's order. The apprentice detective asks for a martini, without thinking. The Bulgarian lights a cigarette, a foreign brand that Simon doesn't recognize. Simon, too, lights up, a Lucky Strike, and takes a drag to calm his nerves, convincing himself that the Bulgarian hasn't seen him and that his disguise means no one has recognized him. Or maybe the whole café has spotted his too-short trouser hems, his too-baggy jacket, his shifty amateur air? It isn't difficult, he thinks, to perceive the dichotomy between the envelope he is wrapped in and the deeper reality of his being. Simon is overwhelmed by the awful feeling—yes, familiar but more intense this time—of being an impostor, on the verge of being unmasked. The two men have ordered beers. All things considered, they don't seem to have noticed Simon, just—to his great surprise—like the bar's other customers. So Simon pulls himself together. He tries to listen to the conversation by concentrating on the voices of the two men, isolating them amid the general hubbub, like a sound engineer isolating a single track on a mixing desk. He thinks he hears "paper" . . . "script" . . . "contact" . . . "student" . . . "service" . . . "carrr" . . . But perhaps he is the puppet of a sort of autosuggestion; perhaps he is only hearing what he wants to hear; perhaps he is constructing the elements of his own dialogue? He thinks he hears: "Sophia." He thinks he hears: "Logos Club."

Then he feels a presence, a shape that glides past him. He didn't notice the current of air released by the opening of the café door, but he hears the sound of a chair being pulled back. He turns and sees a young woman sitting down at his table.

Smiling, blond, high cheekbones, eyebrows in a V. She says to him: "You were with the policeman in Salpêtrière, weren't you?" Simon feels sick. He glances furtively over at the back of the room: the two men, absorbed by their conversation, can't possibly have heard her. "That poorrr Monsieur Barthes," she adds, and he shivers again. He recognizes her now: she is the nurse with the slender legs, the one who found Barthes with his tubes removed, the day when Sollers, BHL, and Kristeva turned up and made a scene. More important, he thinks, she recognized him, which undermines his confidence about the quality of his disguise. "He was so verrry sad." The accent is light, but Simon detects it. "Are you Bulgarian?" The young woman looks surprised. She has large brown eyes. She can't be more than twenty-one. "No, why? I'm Rrrussian." From the back of the room, Simon hears laughter. He risks another glance. The two men are clinking glasses. "My name is Anastasia."

Simon is a bit muddled, but all the same he does wonder

what a Russian nurse is doing in a French hospital, in 1980, a time when the Soviets have begun to relax certain restrictions, but not to the point of opening their borders. He also didn't know that French hospitals were recruiting from the East.

Anastasia tells him her life story. She arrived in Paris when she was eight. Her father was head of the Champs-Élysées Aeroflot office. He was authorized to bring his family with him, and when Moscow summoned him back to headquarters, he applied for political asylum and they stayed, along with her mother and her little brother. Anastasia became a nurse; her brother is still in high school.

She orders tea. Simon still doesn't know what she wants. He tries to calculate her age based on the date she arrived in France. She gives him a childlike smile: "I saw you through the window. I decided I had to talk to you." The sound of a chair scraping on the floor at the back of the room. The Bulgarian gets up, to piss or use the phone. Simon leans forward and puts his hand to his temple to mask his profile. Anastasia dips her tea bag in the hot water and Simon sees something graceful in the movement of the young woman's wrist. At the counter, a customer is talking about the situation in Poland, then Platini's performance against Holland, then the invincibility of Borg at Roland-Garros. Simon can sense that he is losing concentration. This young woman turning up has unhinged him, and his nervousness is increasing every minute. And now, God knows why, he has the Soviet national anthem in his head, with its cymbal crashes and its Red Army choirs. The Bulgarian comes out of the toilets and goes back to his seat.

"Soyuz nerushimy respublik svobodnykh . . ."

Some students enter the café and join their friends at a noisy table. Anastasia asks Simon if he's a cop. At first, Simon protests: of course he's not a cop! But then—he has no idea why—he makes clear that he is acting as, let's say, a consultant to Superintendent Bayard.

"Splotila naveki velikaya Rus' . . ."

At the table at the back, the policeman says "tonight." Simon thinks he hears the Bulgarian reply with a short phrase containing "Christ." He contemplates the girl's childlike smile and thinks that, through storm clouds, the sunlight of freedom is shining on him.

Anastasia asks him to tell her about Barthes. Simon says that he was very fond of his mother and of Proust. Anastasia knows Proust, of course. *And the great Lenin illuminated our path.* Anastasia says that Barthes's family was worried because he didn't have his keys on him, so they wanted to change the locks, which would cost money. *We were raised by Stalin to be true to the people.* Simon recites this couplet to Anastasia, who informs him that, after Khrushchev's report, the anthem's words were altered and the reference to Stalin removed. (This did not happen until 1977, however.) Whatever, thinks Simon, *we grew our army in battles . . .* The Bulgarian stands up and puts on his jacket; he's about to leave. Simon considers following him, but prudently decides to stick to his mission. *We shall in battle decide the fate of generations.* The Bulgarian looked him in the eyes when he tried to execute him. The policeman never did. It's less dangerous, more certain that way, and he knows, now, that the cop is mixed up in the business somehow. On his way out, the Bulgarian stares at Anastasia, who smiles at him sweetly. Simon feels death brush past him. His whole body stiffens, he lowers his head. Then the policeman leaves. Anastasia smiles at him, too. Well, she's a woman who is used to being looked at, Simon thinks. He watches the policeman head up toward Monge and knows he must react quickly if he doesn't want to lose him, so he takes out a twenty-franc note to pay for the tea and the martini and, without waiting for his change (but pocketing the receipt), he takes the nurse by the arm and leads her out of the café. She seems a little surprised but lets him do it. *"Partiya Lenina, sila narodnaya . . ."* Simon smiles at her. He felt like getting some fresh air and he's in a bit of a rush; would she like to accompany him? In his head, he finishes the chorus: " *. . . Nas k torzhestvu kommunizma vedyot!*" Simon's father is a Communist, but he doesn't see any need to mention this to the young woman, who thankfully seems amused by his slightly eccentric behavior.

They walk about thirty feet behind the policeman. Night has fallen. It's a bit cold. Simon is still holding the nurse's arm. If Anastasia finds his attitude strange or cavalier, she doesn't show it. She tells him that Barthes was very popular—too popular, in her opinion. There were always people trying to get into his room. The policeman turns off toward La Mutualité. She tells him that on the day of the incident, when he was found on the floor, the three people who came in and made a scene really insulted her. The policeman goes down a small street near the square outside Notre-Dame. Simon thinks about the friendship of peoples. He explains to Anastasia that Barthes was renowned for his ability to detect the symbolic codes that govern our behavior. Anastasia nods, frowning. The policeman comes to a halt outside a heavy wooden door, set just below the pavement. By the time Simon and Anastasia get there, he has disappeared inside. Simon stops. He still hasn't let go of Anastasia's arm. She says nothing, having noticed the rising tension in the air. The two young people look at the iron gate, the stone staircase, the wooden door. Anastasia frowns again.

A couple that Simon did not hear approaching walk around them, open the gate, descend the steps, and ring the doorbell. The door is half-opened, and a pasty-faced man of indeterminate age, a cigarette in his mouth, wool scarf wrapped around his neck, stares at the couple and then lets them through.

Simon wonders: "What would I do if I were in a novel?" He would ring the doorbell, obviously, and walk in with Anastasia on his arm.

Inside, there would be a secret gambling den. He'd sit at the policeman's table and challenge him to a game of poker while Anastasia sipped a Bloody Mary beside him. He would ask the man in a knowing voice what had happened to his finger. And the man, equally knowing, would reply threateningly: "Hunting accident." Then Simon would win the hand with a full house, aces over queens.

But life is not a novel, he thinks, and they carry on walking as if nothing had happened. When he turns around at the end of the street, however, he sees another three people ring the door-bell and enter. Equally, he does not see the dented Fuego parked on the opposite pavement. Anastasia starts telling him about Barthes again: when he was conscious, he asked for his jacket several times, as if he were looking for something. Does Simon have any idea what it might have been? Realizing that his mis-sion is over for tonight, Simon feels as if he is waking up and, finding himself standing next to the young nurse, he is discon-certed. He stammers that, maybe, if she's free, they could have a drink together. Anastasia smiles (and Simon is unable to interpret the sincerity of this smile): isn't that what they just did? Simon, piteously, suggests they have another drink, another time. Anas-tasia stares deeply into his eyes, smiles again, as if upping the ante on her natural smile, and tells him simply: "Maybe." Simon takes this as a rejection, and he is probably right because, repeat-ing "another time," she leaves without giving him her phone number.

In the street, behind him, the Fuego's headlights come on.

41

"Approach, great speakers, fine rhetoricians, deep-lunged orators! Take your place in the lair of madness and reason, the theater of thought, the academy of dreams, the school of logic! Come and hear the clamor of words, admire the interlacing of verbs and adverbs, taste the venomous circumlocutions of the duelers of discourse! Today, for this new session, the Logos Club is offering not one digital combat, not two, but three, yes, three digital combats, my friends! And now, to whet your appetite, the first joust pits two rhetoricians against

each other with the following thorny geopolitical question: Will Afghanistan be the Soviets' Vietnam?

"Glory to the logos, my friends! Long live dialectics! Let the party begin! May the verb be with you!"

42

Tzvetan Todorov is a skinny guy in glasses with a big tuft of curly hair on the top of his head. He is also a linguistics researcher who has lived in France for twenty years, a disciple of Barthes who worked on literary genres (fantasy, in particular), a specialist in rhetoric and semiology.

Bayard has come to interrogate him, at Simon's suggestion, because he was born in Bulgaria.

Having grown up in a totalitarian country evidently aided the development of a very strong humanist conscience, which comes out even in his linguistic theories. For example, he believes that rhetoric can truly blossom only in a democracy, because it requires a venue for debate that, by definition, neither a monarchy nor a dictatorship can offer. As proof, he cites the fact that in imperial Rome, and later, in feudal Europe, the science of discourse abandoned its objective of persuasion, focusing not on the receiver's interpretation but on the spoken word itself. Speeches were no longer expected to be effective, simply beautiful. Political issues were replaced by purely aesthetic issues. In other words, rhetoric became poetic. (This is what is known as the *seconde rhétorique*.)

He explains to Bayard, in immaculate French but with a still very noticeable accent, that the Bulgarian secret services (the KDC), as far as he knows, are active and dangerous. They are supported by the KGB and are therefore in a position to mount sophisticated operations. Assassinating the pope? Maybe not, but they are certainly capable of eliminating individuals whose existence is inconvenient. That said, he does not see why they would be involved in Barthes's accident. What possible interest could they have in a French literary critic? Barthes was not political and had never had any contact with Bulgaria. Sure, he went to China, but you couldn't say he returned a Maoist, any more than he did an anti-Maoist. He was neither a Gide nor an Aragon. When he came back from China, Barthes's anger, Todorov remembers, was focused mainly on the quality of Air France's in-flight meals: he even thought of writing an article on the subject.

Bayard knows that Todorov has pinpointed the central difficulty of his investigation: discovering a motive. But he also knows that in the absence of any other information he must make do with the objective evidence at his disposal—a pistol, an umbrella—and, even though in theory he sees no geopolitical implications in Barthes's murder, he continues to interrogate the Bulgarian critic about the secret services of his country of origin.

Who is in charge of them? A Colonel Emil Kristoff. His reputation? Not especially liberal, but not particularly well versed in semiology either. Bayard has the unhappy impression that he is going farther down a dead end. After all, if the two killers had been from Marseille or Yugoslavia or Morocco, what would he have deduced from that? Without knowing it, Bayard is thinking like a structuralist: he wonders if the Bulgarian connection is relevant. He mentally reviews the other clues that he has not yet investigated. Just to be sure, he asks:

"Does the name Sophia mean anything to you?"

"Well, yes, it's the city where I was born."

Sofia.

So the Bulgarian lead really is a lead, after all.

At this moment, a beautiful young Russian woman in a dressing gown makes her appearance and crosses the room, discreetly greeting the visitor. Bayard thinks he can detect an English accent. So maybe this bespectacled egghead doesn't lead such a boring life. He notes automatically the silent, erotic complicity between the Anglophone woman and the Bulgarian critic, the sign of a relationship that he assesses—not that he cares, it's just a professional reflex—as being either nascent or adulterous or both.

While he's at it, he asks Todorov if "echo," the last word pronounced by Hamed, means anything to him. And the Bulgarian replies: "Yes, have you heard from him recently?"

Bayard does not understand.

"Umberto. How is he?"

43

Louis Althusser holds the precious sheet of paper in his hand. The discipline of the Party, which formed him, his obedient temperament, his years as a docile prisoner of war, all command him not to read the mysterious document. At the same time, his rather un-Communist individualism, his fondness for enigmas, his historical propensity to cheat, all encourage him to unfold the page. If he did, not knowing but suspecting what it contains, his act would join the long list of dishonesties that started with a fraudulent 17/20 on a philosophy dissertation in his *classe préparatoire* for the École Normale Supérieure (a sufficiently important episode in his personal mythology that he thinks about it all the time). But he is afraid. He knows what they're capable of. He decides, wisely (spinelessly, he feels), not to read the document.

But, then, where should he hide it? He looks at the great mess piled up on his desk and thinks of Poe: he slips the page into an open envelope that had contained some flyer (for a local pizzeria, say, or maybe a bank; I don't remember what kinds of flyers we got in our mailboxes back then); what matters is that he places this envelope on his desk, clearly visible amid a clutter of manuscripts, works-in-progress, and rough drafts, almost all devoted to Marx, Marxism, and, in particular—in order to draw out the "practical" consequences of his recent "antitheoreticist autocriticism"—to the unpredictable material relationship between "popular movements" and the ideologies to which they have given themselves or in which they have invested. The letter will be safe here. There are also a few books—Machiavelli, Spinoza, Raymond Aron, André Glucksmann—that look as if they have been read, which is not the case (he thinks about this often, as part of his carefully constructed neurosis that he is an impostor) for most of the thousands of books that fill his shelves: Plato (well, he read that), Kant (never read), Hegel (leafed through), Heidegger (skimmed), Marx (read volume 1 of *Capital*, but not volume 2), etc.

He hears the key in the door. It's Hélène, coming home.

44

"What's it about?"

The bouncer looks like every other bouncer in the world except that he is wearing a thick wool scarf and he is white, age-less, gray-skinned, with a cigarette stub in his mouth, and his gaze is not expressionless, staring behind you as if you weren't there, but malignant and staring right into you, as if trying to read your soul. Bayard knows he cannot show his card, because he must remain incognito in order to see what happens behind this door, so he gets ready to invent some pathetic lie, but Simon, struck by sudden inspiration, beats him to it and says: *"Elle sait."*

The wood creaks, the door opens. The bouncer moves aside and, with an ambiguous gesture, invites them in. They enter a vaulted cellar that smells of stone, sweat, and cigarette smoke. The room is full, as if for a concert, but the people have not come to see Boris Vian and the walls have forgotten the jazz chords that once ricocheted from them. Instead, amid the vague hub-bub of preshow conversations, a voice like a circus ringmaster's declaims:

"Welcome to the Logos Club, my friends. Come demonstrate,

come deliberate, come praise and criticize the beauty of the Word! O Word that sweeps away hearts and commands the universe! Come attend the spectacle of litigants jousting for oratory supremacy and for your utmost pleasure!"

Bayard gives Simon a puzzled look. Simon whispers into his ear that Barthes's last words were not the beginning of a phrase, but two initials. Not "elle sait" (she knows), but "LC" for "Logos Club." Bayard looks impressed. Simon shrugs modestly. The voice continues to warm up the room:

"My zeugma is beautiful, and so is my asyndeton. But there is a price to pay. Tonight you will know the price of language once again. Because this is our motto, and this should be the law of the world: None may speak with impunity! At the Logos Club, fine words are not enough. Are they, my darlings?"

Bayard goes up to an old white-haired man who has two phalanges missing on his left hand. In a tone he hopes sounds neither professional nor like a tourist, Bayard asks: "What's going on here?" The old man stares at him without hostility: "First time? Then I would advise you just to watch. Don't rush to join in. You have plenty of time to learn. Listen, learn, progress."

"Join in?"

"Well, you could always play a friendly, of course—that won't cost you anything—but if you've never seen a session before, you'd be better off staying a spectator. The impression your first combat leaves will be the basis of your reputation, and reputation is important: it's your *ethos*."

He takes a drag from a cigarette held between his mutilated fingers while the invisible ringmaster, hidden in some dark corner of the stone vaults, continues at the top of his voice: "Glory to the Great Protagoras! Glory to Cicero! Glory to the Eagle of Meaux!" Bayard asks Simon who these people are. Simon tells him that the Eagle of Meaux is Bossuet. Bayard again feels an overriding desire to slap him.

"Eat stones like Demosthenes! Long live Pericles! Long live

131

Churchill! Long live de Gaulle! Long live Jesus! Long live Danton and Robespierre! Why did they kill Jaurès?" At least Bayard knows those people. Well, apart from the first two.

Simon asks the old man about the rules of the game. The old man explains to them: all the matches are duels; they draw a subject; it is always a closed question to which the answer is either yes or no, or a "for or against" type of question, so that the two adversaries can defend their opposing positions.

"Tertullian! Augustine! Maximilian! Let's go!" yells the voice.

The first part of the evening consists of friendly matches. The real matches come at the end. There is always one, sometimes two. Three is rare, but it does happen. Theoretically, there's no limit to the number of official matches but, for reasons that the old man thinks obviously don't need explaining, there is not exactly a long line of volunteers.

"Disputatio in utramque partem! *Let the debate begin! And here are two smooth talkers, who will do battle over the lively question: Is Giscard a fascist?"*

Shouting and whistling in the crowd. *"May the gods of antithesis be with you!"*

A man and a woman take their places on the stage, each behind a lectern, facing the audience, and start scribbling notes. The old man explains to Bayard and Herzog: "They have five minutes to prepare, then they make a presentation where they set out their point of view and the broad outlines of their argument. After that, the dispute begins. The duration of the contest varies and, like a boxing match, the judges can call a halt whenever they like. The person who speaks first has an advantage because he chooses the position he will defend. The other one is obliged to adapt and to defend the opposite position. For friendly matches featuring two opponents of the same rank, they draw lots to see who will begin. But in official matches between opponents of differing ranks, it is the lower-ranked player who goes first. You can tell from the kind of subject they get; this is a level-one meeting. Both of them are *speakers*. That is the lowest tier in the hierarchy of the Logos Club. Private soldiers, basically. Above that, there are the rhetoricians, and then the orators, the dialecticians, the peripateticians, the tribunes, and, at the very top, the sophists. But here, people rarely get past level three. I've heard there are very few sophists, only about ten, and they all have code names. Once you get to level five, it becomes very sealed off. I've even heard it said that the sophists don't exist, that level seven has been invented to give people in the club a sort of unreachable goal, so they'll fantasize about the idea of an unattainable perfection. Personally, I'm sure they exist. In fact, I reckon de Gaulle was one of them. He might even have been the Great Protagoras himself. That's what president of the Logos Club is called, so they say. I'm a rhetorician. I made it to orator one year, but I couldn't hold on to it." He lifts up his mutilated hand. "And it cost me dear."

The duel commences, everyone falls silent, and Simon is unable to ask the old man what he means by a "real match." He observes the audience: mostly male, but all ages and types are represented. If the club is elitist, its criteria are apparently not financial.

The first duelist's melodious voice rings out, explaining that in France, the prime minister is a puppet; that Article 49-3 castrated Parliament, which has no power; that de Gaulle was a benevolent monarch in comparison with Giscard, who is concentrating all the power in his own hands, including the press; that Brezhnev, Kim Il-Sung, Honecker, and Ceausescu were at least accountable to their parties; that the president of the United States possesses far less power than our own leader, and that while the president of Mexico cannot stand for reelection, the French president can.

He is up against a fairly young speaker. She responds that all one need do to verify that we are not in a dictatorship is read the newspapers (like *Le Monde*, earlier this week, which ran a headline about the government reading: "Failure across the board"; and there have been more severe criticisms than that . . .), and she offers as proof the attacks by Marchais, Chirac, Mitterrand, etc. For a dictatorship, there is a healthy amount of freedom of expression. And, talking of de Gaulle, let's not forget what was said about him: de Gaulle is fascist. The Fifth Republic is fascist. The Constitution is fascist. *The Permanent Coup d'Etat*, etc. Her peroration goes on: "To say that Giscard is a fascist is an insult to history; it is to spit on the victims of Mussolini and Hitler. Go and ask the Spanish what they think. Go and ask Jorge Semprun if Giscard is Franco! Shame on rhetoric when it betrays the past!" Prolonged applause. After a brief deliberation, the judges declare the young woman the victor. Looking thrilled, she shakes her opponent's hand, then gives the audience a little curtsy.

There is a series of debates. The candidates are happy or unhappy, the audience applauds or boos, there is whistling, there is yelling . . . and then we come to the climax of the night: the "digital duel."

Subject: *The written word versus the spoken word.*

The old man rubs his hands: "Ah! A metasubject! Using language to discuss language, there's nothing better. I adore that. Look, their levels are shown on the board: it's a young rhetorician challenging an orator so he can take his place. So it's the rhetorician who goes first. I wonder which point of view he'll choose. There is often one argument that's harder to make but if you want to impress the jury and the audience it can be a good idea to choose the difficult one. With the more obvious positions, it can be harder to shine, because what you say is likely to be more straightforward, less spectacular . . ."

The old man stops talking. The match is about to start. There is a fevered silence as everyone in the room listens intently. The aspirant orator begins his speech confidently:

"Religions of the Book forged our societies and we made their texts sacred: the Tablets of Stone, the Ten Commandments, the Torah scroll, the Bible, the Koran, and so on. To be valid, it must be engraved. I say: fetishism. I say: superstition. I say: dogmatism.

"It is not I who affirms the superiority of the spoken word, but he who made us what we are, o thinkers, o rhetoricians, the father of dialectics, our common ancestor, the man who without ever writing a single book laid the foundations of all Western thought.

"Remember! We are in Egypt, in Thebes, and the king asks: What is the point of writing? And the god responds: It is the ultimate cure for ignorance. And the king says: On the contrary! In fact, this art will breed forgetfulness in the souls of those who learn it because they will stop using their memories. The act of remembering is not memory, and the book is merely an aide-mémoire. It does not offer knowledge, it does not offer understanding, it does not offer mastery.

"Why would students need professors if they could learn everything they need from books? Why do they need what is in those books to be explained? Why are there schools and not just libraries? Because the written word alone is never enough. All thought is alive on the condition that it is exchanged; if it is frozen in place, it is dead. Socrates compares writing to painting: the beings created by painting stand in front of us as if they were alive; but when we question them, they remain petrified in a formal pose and don't speak a word. And the same goes for writing. One might believe that the written word can speak; but if we question it, because we wish to understand it, it always repeats the same thing, down to the last syllable.

"Language produces a message, which has meaning only to the extent that it has a recipient. I am speaking to you now; you are the raison d'être of my speech. Only madmen speak in the desert. And the madman also talks to himself. But in a text, to whom are the words addressed? To everyone! And thus to no one. When each discourse has been written down for good and all, it passes indifferently to those who understand it and those who have no interest in it. A text without a precise recipient is a guarantee of imprecision, of vague and impersonal words. How could any message be suited to everyone? Even a letter is inferior to any kind of conversation: it is written in a certain context, and received in another. Besides, both the author's and the recipient's situation will have changed later. It is already obsolete; it was addressed to someone who no longer exists, and its author no longer exists either, vanished in the depths of time as soon as the envelope was sealed.

"So that's how it is: writing is dead. The place for texts is in textbooks. Truth lives only in the metamorphoses of discourse, and only the spoken word is sensitive enough to capture thought's eternal developing flow in real time. The spoken word is life: I prove it, we prove it, gathered here today to speak and listen, to exchange, to discuss, to debate, to create living thought together, to be as one in the word and the idea, animated by the forces of dialectics, alive with that sonorous vibration we call speech, of which the written word is only the pale symbol, when all's said and done: what the score is to music, nothing more. And I will end with one final quotation from Socrates, as I am speaking under his high patronage: 'The appearance of knowledge, rather than true knowledge,' that is what writing produces. Thank you for your attention."

Prolonged applause. The old man seems excited: "Ah, ah! The kid knows his Classics. That was good stuff. Socrates, the guy who never wrote a book—a no-brainer, in this context! He's a bit like the Elvis of rhetoric, isn't he? And, tactically, he played safe because defending the spoken word legitimizes the club's activity, of course; the *mise en abyme*! The other one will have to respond now. He has to find something solid to base his argument on, too. If it were me, I'd do it like Derrida: strip the whole thing of context, explain that a conversation is no more personalized than a text or a letter because no one, when he speaks or when he listens, really knows who he is or who the other person is. There is never any context. It's a con! Context does not exist. That's the way to go! Well, that'd be how I'd refute it, anyway. First you have to demolish your opponent's beautiful edifice, and afterward, you just have to be precise. The superiority of writing is a bit academic, you see, it's pretty technical, but it's not exactly a bundle of laughs. Me? Yeah, I took night classes at the Sorbonne. I was a mailman. Ah! Shh, here it comes! Go on, my son, show us how you won your rank!"

And the whole room falls silent when the orator, an older, graying man, more composed and less ardent in his body language, stands ready to speak. He looks at the audience, his opponent, the jury, and he says, lifting his index finger, one word:

"Plato."

Then he says nothing, long enough to produce the feeling of unease that always accompanies a prolonged silence. And when he senses that the audience is wondering why he is wasting so many precious seconds of his speaking time, he explains:

"My honorable adversary attributed his quotation to Socrates, but you knew better, didn't you?"

Silence.

"He meant Plato. Without whose writings Socrates, his thought, and his magnificent defense of the spoken word in *Phaedo*, which my honorable adversary quoted for us almost in its entirety, would have remained unknown to us."

Silence.

"Thank you for your attention." He sits down.

The entire room turns toward his opponent. If he wishes, he can speak again and engage in a debate, but, looking very pale, he says nothing. He has no need to wait for the verdict of the three judges to know that he has lost.

Slowly, courageously, the young man walks forward and places his hand flat on the judges' table. The whole room holds its breath. The smokers suck nervously on their cigarettes. Everyone thinks he can hear the echo of his own breathing.

The man sitting in the middle of the jury lifts a cleaver and chops off the young man's little finger.

The victim does not cry out, but folds up in two. In a cathedral-like silence, his wound is immediately cleaned and bandaged. The severed phalanx is picked up, but Simon does not see if it is thrown away or kept somewhere, to be exhibited with others in labeled jars revealing the date and subject of the debate.

The voice rings out once again: *"Praise to the duelists!"* The audience chants back: "Praise to the duelists!"

In the graveyard silence, the old man explains in a whisper: "Generally, when you lose, you wait quite a while before you try your luck again. It's a good system: it weeds out the compulsive challengers."

45

This story has a blind spot that is also its genesis: Barthes's lunch with Mitterrand. This is the crucial scene that has not taken place. And yet it did take place . . . Jacques Bayard and Simon Herzog will never know, never knew what happened that day, what was said. They could barely even get hold of the guest list. But I can, maybe . . . After all, it's all a question of method, and I know how to proceed: interrogate the witnesses, corroborate, discard any tenuous testimonies, confront these partial memories with the reality of history. And then, if need be . . . You know what I mean. There is more to be done with that day. February 25, 1980, has not yet told us everything. That's the virtue of a novel: it's never too late.

46

"Yes, what Paris needs is an opera house."

Barthes wishes he were elsewhere. He has better things to do than make small talk. He regrets having agreed to this lunch: his leftist friends will give him hell again, although at least Deleuze will be happy. Foucault, of course, will utter a few contemptuous barbs, and make sure they are repeated by others.

"Arab fiction no longer hesitates to question its limits. It wants to struggle out of the straitjacket of classicism, break free from the conceptual novel . . ."

This is probably the price he has to pay for having eaten lunch with Giscard. "A very successful *grand bourgeois*"? Yes, certainly, but these bourgeois have done pretty well, too . . . Come on, once the wine's been poured, you have to drink it. And actually, it is pretty good, this white. What is it? Chardonnay, I reckon.

"Have you read the latest Moravia? I like Leonardo Sciascia. Do you read Italian?"

What distinguishes them? Nothing, in principle.

"Do you like Bergman?"

Look at the way they stand, speak, dress . . . Without a shadow of a doubt the *habitus* of the Right, as Bourdieu would say.

"With the possible exception of Picasso, no other artist can rival Michelangelo's critical standing. And yet nothing has been said about the democratic nature of his work!"

And me? Do I have right-wing *habitus*? Being badly dressed is not enough to get off the hook. Barthes touches the back of his chair to check that his old jacket is still there. Calm down. No one's going to steal it. Ha! You're thinking like a bourgeois.

"Modernity? Pfft! Giscard dreams of a feudal France. We'll see if the French people are looking for a master or a guide."

He doesn't so much speak as plead. Every inch a lawyer. Some good smells coming from the kitchen.

"It's coming, it's almost ready! And you, my good sir, what are you working on at the moment?"

On words. A smile. A knowing look. No need to go into details. A little Proust, that always goes down well.

"You won't believe me, but I have an aunt who knew the Guermantes." The young actress is quite spiky. Very French.

I feel tired. What I really wanted was to take an anti-rhetorical path. But it's too late now. Barthes sighs sadly. He hates being bored, and yet so many opportunities are offered to him, and he accepts them without really knowing why. But today is a little different. It's not as if he didn't have anything better to do.

"I'm friends with Michel Tournier. He's not at all as wild as you'd imagine, ha ha."

Oh, look, fish. Hence the white.

"Come and sit down, 'Jacques'! You're not going to spend the whole meal in the kitchen, are you?"

The curly-haired young man with goatlike features finishes serving his hot pot and comes to join us. He leans on the back of Barthes's chair before sitting down next to him.

"It's a *cautriade*: a mix of different fish. There's red mullet, whiting, sole, mackerel, along with shellfish and vegetables, spiced up by a dash of vinaigrette, and I put a bit of curry in it with a pinch of tarragon. Bon appétit!"

Oh yes, that's good. It's chic and at the same time working-class. Barthes has often written about food: steak-frites, the simple ham sandwich, milk and wine . . . But this is something else, obviously. It has an aura of simplicity, but it has been cooked and prepared with effort, care, love. And also, always, a show of strength. He has already theorized about this in his book on Japan: *Western food—accumulated, dignified, swollen into the majestic, linked to some prestigious operation—always tends toward excess, abundance, copiousness; Eastern food goes in the opposite direction, it blossoms into the infinitesimal: the future of the cucumber is not its piling up or its thickening, but its division.*

"It's a Breton fishermen's meal: it was cooked originally using seawater. The vinaigrette was meant to counterbalance the salt's thirst-inducing effect."

Memories of Tokyo . . . *To divide the baguette, pull it apart, pick at it, spread it open, instead of cutting and gripping it, as we do with our cutlery; never assault the food . . .*

Barthes does not object when his glass is filled again. Around the table, the guests eat in a somewhat intimidated silence, and he observes that little man with the hard mouth who vacuums up his mouthfuls of whiting with a light sucking sound that is proof of a good bourgeois education.

"I declared that power was property. That is not entirely false, of course."

Mitterrand puts down his spoon. The silent listeners stop eating to indicate to the little man that they are concentrating on what he says.

If Japanese cuisine is always prepared in front of the person who will eat it (a distinguishing mark of this cuisine), it is perhaps because it is important to consecrate the death of what we honor by this spectacle . . .

It's as if they're afraid to make a sound, like the audience at a theater.

"But it's not true either. As I think you know better than I do, isn't that so?"

No Japanese dish possesses a center (an alimentary center, implied for us by the rite that consists in ordering the meal, in surrounding or coating the dish); everything ornaments everything else: primarily because on the table, on the plate, the food is always a collection of fragments . . .

"The real power is language."

Mitterrand smiles. His voice has taken on a fawning tone Barthes didn't suspect it of possessing, and he realizes that the politician is talking directly to him. Farewell, Tokyo. The moment he feared (but which he knew was inevitable) has arrived: when he must give the reply and do what is expected of him; play the semiologist, or at least the intellectual vaguely specialized in language. Hoping his terseness will be taken for profundity, he says: "Especially under a democratic regime."

Still smiling, Mitterrand says, "Really?" It is hard to tell whether this is a request for elaboration, a polite agreement, or a discreet objection. The whipping boy, who is clearly responsible for this meeting, decides to intervene, out of fear, perhaps, that the conversation may die a premature death: "As Goebbels said, 'When I hear the word *culture*, I reach for my revolver' . . ." Barthes does not have time to explain the significance of this quotation in its context before Mitterrand dryly corrects his underling: "No, that was Baldur von Schirach." Embarrassed silence around the table. "You must excuse Monsieur Lang, who, although he was born before the war, is too young to remember it. Isn't that right, 'Jacques'?" Mitterrand narrows his eyes like a Japanese man. He pronounces "Jack" the French way. Why, at this instant, does Barthes have the impression that something is afoot between him and this little man with the piercing gaze? As if this lunch had been organized purely for him; as if the other guests were there only to allay suspicion, as if they were decoys or, worse, accomplices. And yet, this is not the first cultural lunch organized for Mitterrand: he has one every month. Surely, thinks Barthes, he didn't have all the others just to provide an alibi.

Outside, what sounds like a horse-drawn carriage is heard passing along Rue des Blancs-Manteaux.

Barthes analyzes himself quickly: given the circumstances and the document folded in the inside pocket of his jacket, it's only logical that he should be prone to surges of paranoia. He decides to speak again, partly to dilute the embarrassment of the young man with the curly brown hair, who's still smiling, if somewhat contritely: "The great eras of rhetoric always correspond with republics: Athens, Rome, France . . . Socrates, Cicero, Robespierre . . . Different kinds of eloquence, admittedly, linked to different eras, but all unfolded like a tapestry over the canvas of democracy." Mitterrand, who looks interested, objects: "Since our friend 'Jacques' decided to bring the war into our conversation, I ought to remind you that Hitler was a great orator." And, he adds, without giving his listeners any sign of irony they might cling to: "De Gaulle, too. In his way."

Resigned to playing along, Barthes asks: "And Giscard?"

As if he had been waiting for this all along, as if these preliminaries had no other purpose than to bring the conversation to exactly this point, Mitterrand leans back in his chair: "Giscard is a good technician. His strength is his precise knowledge of himself, of his strengths and weaknesses. He knows he is short of breath, but his phrasing is perfectly matched to the rhythm of his breathing. A subject, a verb, a direct complement. A period, no commas: because that would lead him into the unknown." He pauses to give the obliging smiles time to spread across his guests' faces, then goes on: "And there need not be any link between two sentences. Each is enough in itself, as smooth and full as an egg. One egg, two eggs, three eggs, a series of eggs, regular as a metronome." Encouraged by the prudent chuckles offered from around the table, Mitterrand begins to warm up: "The well-oiled machine. I knew a musician once who claimed his metronome had more genius than Beethoven . . . Naturally, it's a thrilling spectacle. And highly educational, into the bargain. Everyone understands that an egg is an egg, no?"

Eager to maintain his role as cultural mediator, Jack Lang intervenes: "That is exactly what Monsieur Barthes condemns in his work: the ravages of tautology."

Barthes confirms: "Yes, well . . . let's say the false demonstration *par excellence*, the useless equation: A equals A, 'Racine is Racine.' It's zero degree thought."

Though delighted by this convergence of theoretical viewpoints, Mitterrand is not sidetracked from the main flow of his speech: "Exactly! That's exactly it. 'Poland is Poland, France is France.'" He puts on a whiny voice: "Go on, then, explain the opposite! What I mean is that to a rare degree Giscard has the art of stating the obvious."

Barthes, obligingly, concurs: "The obvious is not demonstrated. It demonstrates."

Mitterrand repeats, triumphantly: "No, the obvious is not demonstrated." Just then, a voice is heard at the other end of the table: "And yet if we follow your demonstration it seems *obvious* that victory cannot escape you. The French people are not that stupid. They won't fall twice for that impostor's tricks."

The speaker is a young man with thinning hair and pouty lips, a bit like Giscard, who, unlike the other guests, does not seem impressed by the little man. Mitterrand turns spitefully toward him: "Oh, I know what you think, Laurent! Like most of our contemporaries, you think that he is the most dazzling performer of all."

Laurent Fabius protests, with an expression of disdain: "I did not say that . . ."

Mitterrand, aggressively: "Oh yes you did! Oh yes you did! What a good television viewer you make! It's because there are so many good television viewers like you that Giscard is so good on television."

Fabius does not flinch. Mitterrand gets more and more worked up: "I acknowledge that he's marvelous at explaining how nothing is ever his fault. Prices went up in September? It's the beef, by Jove. [Barthes notes Mitterrand's use of "by Jove."] In October, it's melons. In November, it's gasoline, electricity, the railways, and rents. How could prices not go up? Brilliant." His face is disfigured by a malicious grin. His voice grows husky: "And we are wonder-struck at being initiated so easily into the mysteries of the economy, at being allowed to follow this erudite guide into the minutiae of high finance." He is shouting now: "Oh yes, oh yes, it's the beef! Those damn melons! The treacherous railways! Long live Giscard!"

The guests are petrified, but Fabius, lighting a cigarette, replies: "A bit over the top."

Mitterrand's smile becomes charming again, his voice returns to normal, and, without anyone knowing whether he is replying to Fabius or attempting to reassure his other guests, he says: "I was joking, of course. Although, not entirely. But let's be honest: it takes a high degree of intelligence to do such a good job convincing people that governing is about not being responsible for anything."

Jack Lang slips away.

Barthes thinks that what he's up against here is a very good specimen of the manic-obsessive: this man wants power, and in his adversary he has crystallized all the rancor he might feel for a destiny that has denied him power for too long. It's as if he is already raging about his next defeat, and at the same time one senses he is ready to do anything except give up. Perhaps he doesn't believe in his victory, but it is in his nature to fight for it nevertheless. Or maybe life made him like that. Defeat is undoubtedly the best teacher. Suddenly filled by a faint melancholy, Barthes lights a cigarette as a smokescreen. But defeat can also make a man get stuck in a rut. Barthes wonders what this little man really wants. His determination can't be questioned, but isn't he trapped in a system? 1965, 1974, 1978 . . . Each one a sort of glorious defeat, for which he personally is not blamed. So he feels empowered to persevere in his raison d'être, and his raison d'être, of course, is politics. But perhaps it is also defeat.

Fabius speaks up again: "Giscard is a brilliant orator, and you know it. Not only that, but his style is tailor-made for TV. That's what it means to be modern."

Mitterrand, faux-conciliatory: "But of course, my dear Laurent, I've been sure of that for quite some time. I was already an admirer of his presentational gifts when he used to speak at the National Assembly. Back then, I remarked that he was the best orator I'd heard since . . . Pierre Cot. Yes, a radical who was a minister during the Popular Front era. But I digress. Monsieur Fabius is so young, he barely remembers the Programme Commun, so as for the Popular Front . . . [Timid laughter around the table.] But, if you insist, let us return to Giscard, that beacon of eloquence! The clarity of his discourse, the fluency of his delivery, studded with pauses that made his listeners feel they were allowed to think, like slow-motion replays on televised sport, even the way he holds his head . . . it all readied Giscard for invading our television screens. No doubt he put in a great deal of graft to supplement his natural abilities. The age of the amateur is over! But he got his reward. He makes the television breathe."

Fabius is still unimpressed. "Well, it seems to work rather well. People listen to him, and there are even some who vote for him."

Mitterrand replies, as if to himself: "I wonder, though. You talk about a modern style. I think he's old-fashioned. Heartfelt, literary rhetoric is mocked these days. [Barthes hears the echo of the 1974 debate, still an open wound after his defeat.] And rightly so, more often than not. [Oh, how this admission must have pained him! Oh, how hard Mitterrand must have worked on his self-control to reach this point!] The affectations of language offend the ear like makeup offends the eye."

Fabius waits, Barthes waits, everyone waits. Mitterrand is used to people waiting for him; he takes his time before continuing: "But not just rhetoric—rhetoric and a half. The rhetoric of the technocrat is already worn out. Yesterday it was precious. Now it's ridiculous. Who said recently: 'I am suffering with my balance of payments'?"

Jack Lang comes back to sit down, and asks: "Wasn't it Rocard?"

Mitterrand lets his irritation show again: "No, it was Giscard." He glares at the bespectacled young man who ruined his punch line, then goes on regardless: "One wants to palpate him like a doctor. Suffering with a headache? Suffering with heartburn, backache, stomachache? Everyone knows how those things feel. But suffering with his balance of payments? Where is that, between the sixth and seventh ribs? Some unknown gland? One of those little bones in the coccyx? Giscard isn't over the line yet."

The guests no longer know if they should laugh or not. In doubt, they hold off.

Mitterrand goes on, staring out the window: "He has common sense and he's a reasonable technician. He knows and feels politics like no one else."

Barthes understands the compliment's ambiguity: for someone like Mitterrand, it is obviously the highest praise, but—via a schizophrenia inherent in politics, making use of a very rich polysemy—the term "politics" also suggests something disparaging, even insulting, in his mouth.

Mitterrand is unstoppable now: "But his generation is being

wiped out along with economism. Margot, who dried his eyes, is starting to get bored."

Barthes wonders if Mitterrand might be drunk.

Fabius, who seems increasingly amused, tells his boss: "Watch out. He's still moving, and he knows how to aim straight. Remember his jibe: 'You do not have a monopoly on the heart.'"

The guests stop breathing.

Unexpectedly, Mitterrand's response is almost composed: "And I don't claim to! My opinions concern the public man. I reserve judgment on the private man, whom I don't know." Having made this necessary concession and thus demonstrated his spirit of fair play, he is able to conclude: "But we were talking about technique, weren't we? And it has become so important to him that he is no longer capable of the unexpected. The difficult moment in life—his, yours, mine, the life of anyone ambitious—is when you see the writing on the wall telling you that you are starting to repeat yourself."

Hearing this, Barthes plunges his nose into his glass. He feels nervous laughter welling up inside him, but he contains it by reciting this saying to himself: "Every man laughs for himself."

Reflexivity. Always reflexivity.

PART II

BOLOGNA

.

47

4:16 p.m.

"Fuck me, it's hot!" Simon Herzog and Jacques Bayard wander the jagged streets of Bologna, the Red City, seeking refuge under its intersecting arches in the hope of a second's respite from the blazing sun that in the summer of 1980 is beating down once again on northern Italy. Spray-painted on a wall, they read: *Vogliamo tutto! Prendiamoci la città!* Three years earlier, in this exact spot, carabinieri killed a student, triggering genuine mass protests that the minister of the interior chose to put down by sending in the tanks: like Czechoslovakia in 1977, but in Italy. Today, everything's calm: the armored cars have returned to their burrows, and the entire city seems to be having a siesta.

"Is that it? Where are we?"

"Show me the map."

"But you've got it!"

"No, I gave it back to you!"

Via Guerrazzi, in the heart of the student quarter of the oldest university city on the continent. Simon Herzog and Jacques Bayard enter an old Bolognan palace, now the headquarters of the DAMS: Discipline Arte Musica e Spettacolo. From what they are able to decipher from the obscure headings on the noticeboard, it is here, each week, that Professor Eco gave his biannual course. But the professor is not there; a porter explains in perfect French that classes are over ("I knew it was stupid to go to a university during the summer!" says Simon to Bayard) but that he will in all probability be at a café: "He usually goes to the Drogheria Calzolari or the Osteria del Sole. *Ma*, the Drogheria closes earlier. So it depends how thirsty he is, *il professore*."

The two men cross the sublime Piazza Maggiore, with its unfinished fourteenth-century basilica, half in white marble, half in ocher stone, and its fountain of Neptune surrounded by fat, obscene nereids who touch their breasts while straddling demonic-looking dolphins. They find the Osteria del Sole in a tiny alleyway, already packed with students. On the wall outside they read: *Lavovare meno—lavovare tutti!* Having a bit of Latin, Simon is able to decipher: "Work less—work for all." Bayard thinks: "Lazy-ass whiners everywhere, workers nowhere."

In the entrance hall is a huge poster of a sun drawn in the style of an alchemist's sign. Here, you can drink wine pretty cheaply and bring your own food. Simon orders two glasses of Sangiovese while Bayard asks after Umberto Eco. Everyone seems to know him but, as they say: *Non ora, non qui.* The two Frenchmen decide to stay for a while anyway, sheltered from the oppressive heat, in case Eco turns up.

At the back of the L-shaped room a group of students is noisily celebrating a young woman's birthday; her friends have given her a toaster, which she shows off gratefully. There are some old people, too, but Simon notices that they are all sitting at the bar, near the entrance, and he realizes that's so they don't have to make a trip to order a drink, because there is no waiter service in the café. Behind the bar, an old, severe-looking woman dressed in black, her gray hair tied neatly in a bun, directs operations. Simon guesses that she is the manager's mother, so he scans the room and soon spots him: a tall, gangling man playing cards at a table. From the way he grumbles and his exaggerated air of unpleasantness, Simon guesses that he works here and, given that he is not actually working, since he's playing cards (Simon doesn't recognize the type of cards; it looks like some kind of tarot deck), that must be him, the boss. From time to time his mother calls out to him: "Luciano! Luciano!" He responds with grunts.

In the corner of the L is a door that leads to a small internal courtyard, which functions as a terrace; Simon and Bayard see some couples kissing there and three conspiratorial young men in scarves. Simon also detects a few foreigners, their non-Italianness betrayed in one way or another by their clothes, body language, or facial expressions. The events of the previous months have left him a little paranoid and he imagines he can see Bulgarians everywhere.

The atmosphere is not particularly conducive to paranoia, however. People unwrap little cakes stuffed with bacon and pesto, or nibble on artichokes. Everyone smokes, of course. Simon does not spot the young conspirators in the little courtyard exchange a packet under the table. Bayard orders another glass of wine. Soon, one of the students at the back of the room walks over to offer them a glass of Prosecco and a slice of apple cake. His name is Enzo, he is extremely talkative, and he, too, speaks French. He invites them to join his friends, who are arguing joyfully about politics, to judge by the yells of *"fascisti," "communisti," "coalizione," "combinazione,"* and *"corruzione."* Simon asks about the meaning of *pitchi,* which keeps cropping up in their conversation. A short, olive-skinned brunette stops mid-sentence to explain to them in French that this is how "PC"—the initials of the Communist Party—is pronounced in Italian. She tells him that all the political parties are corrupt, even the Communists, who are *notabili* ready to play along with the bosses and cut deals with the Christian Democrats. Thankfully, the Red Brigades overturned the *compromesso storico* by kidnapping Aldo Moro. Fair enough, they killed him, but that's the fault of the pope and that *porco* Andreotti, who refused to negotiate.

Luciano, who heard her talking to the Frenchmen, waves his arms and shouts over to her: *"Ma, che dici! Le Brigate Rosse sono degli assassini!* They killed him and they tossed him in the boot of the *macchina*, like *un cane!*"

The girl swivels to face him: "*Il cane sei tu!* They're at war. They wanted to swap him for their comrades, political prisoners. They waited fifty-five days for the government to agree to talk with them, nearly two whole months! The government refused. Not a single prisoner, Andreotti said! Moro begged them: my friends, save me, I'm innocent, you must *negoziare*! And all his friends, they said: that's not him, he's been drugged, he's been coerced, he's changed! That's not the Aldo I knew, they said, *'sti figli di putana!*"

And she pretends to spit before downing the contents of her glass, then she turns back to Simon with a smile, while Luciano returns to his *tarocchino*, mumbling incomprehensibly.

Her name is Bianca. She has very dark eyes and very white teeth. She is Neapolitan. She is studying political science. She would like to be a journalist, but not for the bourgeois press. Simon nods and smiles idiotically. He gets a few brownie points when he says he's working on his thesis at Vincennes. Bianca claps her hands: three years ago, a huge conference took place here, in Bologna, with the great French intellectuals, Guattari, Sartre, and that young guy in a white shirt, Lévy . . . She interviewed Sartre and Simone de Beauvoir for *Lotta Continua*. Sartre said, she recites from memory, one finger in the air: "I cannot accept that a young activist could be murdered in the streets of a city governed by the Communist Party." And, fellow traveler that he was, he declared: "I am on the side of the young activist." It was *magnifico*! She remembers that Guattari was welcomed like a rock star; in the streets, it was madness, you'd have thought he was John Lennon. One day, he took part in a protest march, he met Bernard-Henri Lévy, so he made him leave the procession, because the students were really excited and 'cause the philosopher in the *camicia bianca*, he was going to get beaten up. Bianca bursts out laughing and pours herself more Prosecco.

But Enzo, who is chatting with Bayard, gets involved in the

conversation: "The *Brigate Rosse? Ma*, left-wing terrorists . . . they're still terrorists, *no?*"

Bianca flares up again: "*Ma che terroristi?* Activists who use violence as a means of action, *ecco!*"

Enzo laughs bitterly: "*Sì*, and Moro was a capitalist *lacchè, io so.* He was just a *strumento* in a suit and tie in the hands of Agnelli and the Americans. *Ma*, behind the tie, there was an *uomo*. Ah, if he hadn't written those letters, to his wife, to his grandson . . . we'd only have seen the *strumento*, probably, and not the *uomo*. That's why his friends panicked: they can say that he wrote those words under coercion, but everyone knows that's not true: they weren't dictated by a *carceriere*, they came from the bottom of the heart of a *pover'uomo* who was going to die. And you're agreeing with his friends who abandoned him: you want to forget his letters so you can forget that your Red Brigade friends killed a *vecchietto* who loved his grandson. *Va bene!*"

Bianca's eyes are shining. After a diatribe like that, her only option is to go for broke, with added lyricism if possible, but not too much because she knows that all politicized lyricism tends to sound religious, so she says: "His grandson will get over it. He'll go to the best schools, he'll never go hungry, he'll get an internship at UNESCO, at NATO, at the UN, in Rome, in Geneva, in New York! Have you ever been to Naples? Have you seen the Neapolitan children who live in houses that the government—the government run by Andreotti and your friend Moro—have allowed to collapse? How many women and children have been abandoned by the Christian Democrats' corrupted policies?"

Enzo snorts as he fills Bianca's glass: "So two wrongs make a right, *giusto?*"

At this instant, one of the three young men stands up and tosses his napkin on the floor. With the lower part of his face covered by his scarf, he walks up to the table of card players, waves a pistol at the bar owner, and shoots him in the leg.

Luciano crumples to the floor, groaning.

Bayard is not armed, and in the scramble that follows he

cannot reach the young man, who walks out of the bar, escorted by his two friends, the smoking gun in his hand. And in the blink of an eye, the gang has disappeared. Inside, it is not exactly a scene of panic, even if the old woman behind the bar has rushed over to her son, screaming, but young and old alike are all yelling at the tops of their voices. Luciano pushes his mother away. Enzo shouts at Bianca, with venomous irony: *"Brava, brava! Continua a difenderli i tuoi amici brigatisti? Bisognava punire Luciano, vero? Questo sporco capitalista proprietario di bar. È un vero covo di fascisti, giusto?"* Bianca goes over to help Luciano, lying on the floor, and replies to Enzo, in Italian, that it almost certainly wasn't the Red Brigades, that there are hundreds of far-left or far-right factions who practice *gambizzazione* with shots from a P38. Luciano tells his mother: *"Basta, mamma!"* The poor woman lets loose a long sob of anguish. Bianca does not see why the Red Brigades would have attacked Luciano. While she tries to stanch the bleeding with a dishcloth, Enzo points out that her being unsure whether to attribute this attack to the far left or far right indicates a slight problem. Someone says they should call the police, but Luciano groans categorically: *niente polizia*. Bayard leans down over the wound: the bullet hole is above the knee, in the thigh, and the amount of blood loss suggests that it missed the femoral artery. Bianca replies to Enzo, in French, so that Simon realizes she is also speaking to him: "You know perfectly well that's how it is—the strategy of tension. It's been like that since the Piazza Fontana." Simon asks what she's talking about. Enzo replies that in Milan, in '69, a bomb in a bank on the Piazza Fontana killed fifteen people. Bianca adds that during the investigation, the police killed an anarcho-syndicalist by throwing him through the police station window. "They said it was the anarchists, but afterward we realized it was the far right, working with the state, who planted the bomb in order to accuse the far left and justify their fascist policies. That is the *strategia della tensione*. It's been going on for ten years. Even the pope is involved." Enzo confirms: "Yeah, that's true. A Pole!" Bayard asks:

"And these, er, kneecappings, do they happen a lot?" Bianca thinks while she improvises a tourniquet with her belt. "No, not really. Probably not even once a week."

And so, as Luciano does not seem to be at death's door, the customers disperse into the night, and Simon and Bayard head toward the Drogheria Calzolari, guided by Enzo and Bianca, who have no desire to go home.

7:42 p.m.
The two Frenchmen move through the streets of Bologna as in a dream. The city is a theater of shadows, furtive silhouettes dancing a strange ballet to a mysterious choreography: students appear suddenly and disappear again behind pillars; junkies and prostitutes loiter under vaulted porches; carabinieri run silently in the background. Simon looks up. Two handsome medieval towers stand over the gate that used to open on the road to byzantine Ravenna, but the second tower leans like the one in Pisa, only more steeply. This is the Severed Tower, the *Torre Mezza*, placed when it was taller and more menacing by Dante in the last ring of Hell: "As when one sees the tower called *Garisenda* from underneath its leaning side, and then a cloud passes over and it seems to lean the more." The star of the Red Brigades decorates the red brick walls. In the distance police whistles can be heard, and partisans chanting. A beggar accosts Bayard to ask him for a cigarette and tells him that there must be a revolution, but Bayard doesn't understand and walks obstinately on, even though the succession of arches, street after street of them, seems endless to him. Daedalus and Icarus in the country of Italian communism, thinks Simon, seeing the electoral posters stuck to the stone walls and wooden beams. And, of course, among this crowd of ghosts there are the cats, who, as everywhere in Italy, are the city's true inhabitants.

The window of the Drogheria Calzolari shines in the greasy night. Inside, professors and students drink wine and nibble *antipasti*. The boss says he's about to close, but the lively atmosphere suggests the opposite. Enzo and Bianca order a bottle of Manaresi.

A bearded man is telling a funny story; everyone laughs, except for one man in gloves and another holding a bag; Enzo translates for the two Frenchmen: "There's this *uomo*, he goes home, at night, he's completely drunk, but on the way, he meets a nun, with her robe and her hood. So he throws himself at her, and he beats her up. And once he's given her a good kicking, he picks her up and says: '*Ma*, Batman, I thought you were tougher than that!'" Enzo laughs, and so does Simon. Bayard hesitates.

The bearded guy is talking with a young woman in glasses and a man that Bayard immediately identifies as a professor because he looks like a student, but older. When the bearded guy finishes his glass, he pours himself another from the bottle on the counter, but does not fill the young woman's and the professor's empty glasses. Bayard reads the label: Villa Antinori. He asks the waiter if it's any good. It's a white from Tuscany, no, it's not very good, replies the waiter in excellent French. His name is Stefano and he is studying political science. "Here, everyone's a student and everyone's political!" he tells Bayard, and adds a toast: *"Alla sinistra!"* Bayard clinks glasses with him and repeats: *"Alla sinistra!"* The bar owner looks worried and says: *"Piano col vino, Stefano!"* Stefano laughs and tells Bayard: "Pay no attention to him, he's my father."

The man in gloves demands the release of the philosopher Toni Negri and denounces Gladio, that far-right organization funded by the CIA. *"Negri complice delle Brigate Rosse, è altrettanto assurdo che Trotski complice di Stalin!"*

Bianca is outraged: *"Gli stalinisti stanno a Bologna!"*

Enzo goes up to a young woman and tries to guess what she's studying. He gets it right first time. (Political science.)

Bianca explains to Simon that the Communist Party is very strong in Italy: it has 500,000 members and, unlike in France, it did not hand over its weapons in '44, hence the phenomenal number of German P38s in circulation in the country. And Bologna the Red is a bit like the Italian Communist Party's shop window, with its Communist mayor who works for Amendola, the current administration's representative. "The right wing," says Bianca, wrinkling her nose in contempt. "That historic compromise bullshit, that's him." Bayard sees Simon hanging on her every word, and raises his glass of red toward him: "So, lefty, you like Bologna, eh? Isn't this better than your dump in Vincennes?" Bianca repeats, eyes shining: "Vincennes . . . Deleuze!" Bayard asks the waiter, Stefano, if he knows Umberto Eco.

Just then, a hippie in sandals enters, walks straight over to the bearded guy, and taps him on the shoulder. The bearded guy turns around. The hippie solemnly unzips his trousers and pisses on him. The bearded guy reels back, horrified, and everyone starts yelling. There is general confusion, and the hippie is ushered toward the exit by the boss's son. People crowd around the bearded guy, who moans: *"Ma io non parlo mai di politica!"* The hippie, before leaving, shouts at him: *"Appunto!"*

Stefano comes back behind the counter and points out the bearded man to Bayard: "That's Umberto."

The man with the bag leaves, forgetting it on the floor by the bar, but thankfully the other customers catch him and hand it back. The man, embarrassed, apologizes strangely, says thank you, then disappears into the night.

Bayard approaches the bearded man, who is symbolically wiping his trousers, because the piss has already soaked into the cloth, and takes out his card: "Monsieur Eco? French police." Eco becomes agitated: "Police? *Ma*, you should have arrested the hippie, then!" Then, considering the clientele of left-wing students that fill the Drogheria, he decides not to pursue this line of attack. Bayard explains why he is here: Barthes asked a young man to contact him if anything happened, but the young man died, with Eco's name on his lips. Eco seems sincerely surprised. "I knew Roland well, but we weren't close friends. It's a terrible tragedy, of course, *ma* it was an accident, no?"

Bayard realizes he is going to have to be patient again, so he finishes his drink, lights a cigarette, looks at the man in gloves waving his arms around as he talks about *materialismo storico*. Enzo is hitting on the young student while playing with her hair, Simon and Bianca are toasting "desiring autonomy," and Bayard says: "Think about it. There must be a reason why Barthes expressly asked him to contact you."

He then listens to Eco failing to answer his question: "Roland's great semiological lesson that has stayed with me is pointing to any event in the universe and explaining that it signifies something. He always repeated that the semiologist, walking in the street, detects meaning where others see events. He knew that we say something in the way that we dress, hold our glass, walk . . . You, for example, I can tell that you fought in the Algerian War and . . ."

"All right! I know how it works," grumbles Bayard.

"Ah? *Bene.* And, at the same time, what he loved in literature is that one is not obliged to settle on a particular meaning, *ma* one can play with the meaning. *Capisce?* It's *geniale.* That's why he was so fond of Japan: at last, a world where he didn't know any of the codes. No possibility of cheating, but no ideological or political issues, just aesthetic ones, or maybe anthropological. But perhaps not even anthropological. The pleasure of interpretation, pure, open, free of referents. He said to me: 'Above all, Umberto, we must kill the referent!' Ha ha! *Ma attenzione*, that doesn't mean that the signified does not exist, *eh*! The signified is in everything. [He takes a swig of white wine.] Everything. But that does not mean either that there is an infinity of interpretations. It's the Kabbalists who think like that! There are two currents: the Kabbalists, who think the Torah can be interpreted in every possible way to produce new things, and Saint Augustine. Saint Augustine knew that the text of the Bible was a *foresta infinita di sensi*—'infinita sensuum silva,' as Saint Jerome said—but that it could always be submitted to a rule of falsification, in order to exclude what the context made it impossible to read, no matter what hermeneutic violence it was subjected to. You see? It is impossible to say if one interpretation is valid, or if it is the best one, but it is possible to say if the text refuses an interpretation incompatible with its own contextuality. In other words, you can't just say whatever you want about it. *Insomma*, Barthes was an Augustinian, not a Kabbalist."

And while Eco drones on at him, in the hubbub of conversations and the clinking of glasses, amid the bottles arranged on the shelves, while the students' young, supple, firm bodies exude their belief in the future, Bayard watches the man in gloves haranguing his listeners about some unknown subject. And he wonders why a man would wear gloves in eighty-five-degree heat.

The professor to whom Eco was telling jokes cuts in, in accentless French: "The problem, and you know this, Umberto, is that Barthes did not study signs, in the Saussurian sense, but symbols, at a push, and mostly clues. Interpreting a clue is not unique to semiology, it is the vocation of *all* science: physics, chemistry, anthropology, geography, economics, philology . . . Barthes was not a semiologist, Umberto, he didn't understand what semiology was, because he didn't understand the specificity of the sign, which, unlike the clue (which is merely a fortuitous trace picked up by a receiver), must be deliberately sent by a sender. Fair enough, he was quite an inspired generalist, but at the end of the day he was just an old-fashioned critic, exactly like Picard and the others he was fighting against."

"*Ma no*, you're wrong, Georges. The interpretation of clues is not *all* science, but the semiological moment of all science and the essence of semiology itself. Roland's *Mythologies* were brilliant semiological analyses because daily life is subject to a continual bombardment of messages that do not always manifest a direct intentionality but, due to their ideological finality, mostly tend to be presented under an apparent 'naturalness' of the real."

"Oh, really? I don't see why you insist on labeling as semiology what is ultimately just a general epistemology."

"*Ma*, that's exactly it. Semiology offers instruments to recognize what science does, which is, first and foremost, learning to see the world as a collection of signifying events."

"In that case, you might as well come out and say that semiology is the mother of all sciences!"

Umberto spreads out his hands, palms open, and a broad smile splits his beard: *"Ecco!"*

There is the pop, pop, pop of bottles being uncorked. Simon gallantly lights Bianca's cigarette. Enzo tries to kiss his young student, who shies away, laughing. Stefano fills everyone's glasses.

Bayard sees the man in gloves put down his glass without finishing it and disappear into the street. The store is arranged in such a way, with a closed counter denying access to the whole back half of the room, that Bayard deduces there is no customer toilet. So, by the look of things, the man in gloves does not want to do what the hippie did, and has gone outside to piss. Bayard has a few seconds to come to a decision. He grabs a coffee spoon from the counter and walks after him.

He has not gone very far: there is no lack of dark alleyways in this part of town. He is facing the wall, in the midst of relieving himself, when Bayard grabs him by the hair, yanks him backward, and pins him to the ground, yelling into his face: "You keep your gloves on to piss? What's up, don't like getting your hands dirty?" The man is of average build, but he is too stupefied to fight back or even cry out, so he simply stares wide-eyed in terror at his assailant. Bayard immobilizes him by pressing his knee into the man's chest and grabs his hands. Feeling something soft under the leather of the left-hand glove, he tears it off and discovers two missing phalanges, on the pinkie and ring fingers.

"So . . . you like cutting wood, too, huh?"

He crushes his head against the damp cobblestones.

"Where is the meeting?"

The man makes some incomprehensible gurgling noises, so Bayard lessens the pressure and hears: *"Non lo so! Non lo so!"*

Perhaps infected by the climate of violence that permeates the city, Bayard does not seem in the mood to show much patience. He takes the little spoon from his jacket pocket and wedges it deeply under the man's eye. The man starts to screech like a frightened bird. Behind him, he hears Simon running up and shouting: "Jacques! Jacques! What are you doing?" Simon pulls at his shoulders, but Bayard is much too strong to be moved. "Jacques! Fucking hell! What's wrong with you?"

The cop digs the spoon into the eye socket.

He does not repeat his question.

He wants to cause distress and despair at maximum intensity, at maximum speed, taking advantage of the element of surprise. His aim is efficiency, as it was in Algeria. Less than a minute ago, the man in gloves thought he was going to have a nice, relaxed evening and now some French guy has appeared out of nowhere and is trying to enucleate him while he pisses all over himself.

When he feels the terrorized man is ready to do anything to save his eye and his life, Bayard finally consents to make his question more specific.

"The Logos Club, you little shit! Where is it?" And the man with the missing fingers stammers: *"Archiginnasio! Archiginnasio!"* Bayard does not understand. "Archi what?" And behind him, he hears a voice that is not Simon's: "The Palazzo dell'Archiginnasio is the headquarters of the old university, behind the Piazza Maggiore. It was built by Antonio Morandi, known as *Il Terribilia, perché . . .*"

Bayard, without turning around, recognizes the voice of Eco, who demands: *"Ma, perché* are you torturing this *pover'uomo?"*

Bayard explains: "There is a meeting of the Logos Club tonight, here in Bologna." The man in gloves emits a hoarse wheezing sound.

Simon asks: "But how do you know that?"

"Our services obtained this information."

"'Our' services? The Renseignements Généraux, you mean?"

Simon thinks about Bianca, who has stayed behind in the Drogheria, and would like to make it clear to everyone within earshot that he does not work for the French secret services but, to spare himself the bother of putting his growing identity crisis into words, he remains silent. He also realizes that they did not come to Bologna simply to interrogate Eco. And he notes that Eco does not ask what the Logos Club is, so he decides to ask the question himself: "What do you know about the Logos Club, Monsieur Eco?"

Eco strokes his beard, clears his throat, lights a cigarette.

"The Athenian city was founded on three pillars: the gymnasium, the theater, and the school of rhetoric. The trace of this tripartition remains today in a society obsessed with spectacle that promotes three categories of individuals to the rank of celebrity: athletes, actors (or singers: the ancient theater made no distinction between the two), and politicians. Of these three, the third, up to now, has always been dominant (even if, with Ronald Reagan, we see that some overlap is possible), because it involves the mastery of man's most powerful weapon: language.

"From antiquity until the present day, the mastery of language has always been at the root of all politics, even during the feudal period, which might look as though it was dominated by the laws of physical force and military superiority. Machiavelli explains to the Prince that one governs not by force but by fear, and they are not the same thing: fear is the product of speech about force. *Allora*, whoever has mastery of speech, through its capacity to provoke fear and love, is virtually the master of the world, *eh*!

"It was on the basis of this supposition, and also to counter Christianity's growing influence, that a sect of heretics founded the Logi Consilium in the third century A.D.

"Thereafter, the Logi Consilium spread through Italy, then through France, where it took the name the Logos Club in the eighteenth century, during the revolution.

"It developed as a highly compartmentalized secret society,

structured like a pyramid, with its leaders—a body of ten members known as the sophists—presided over by a Protagoras Magnus, practicing their rhetorical talents, which they used essentially in the service of their political ambitions. Certain popes—Clement the Sixth, Pius the Second—are suspected of having been leaders of the organization. It has also been said that Shakespeare, Las Casas, Roberto Bellarmino (the inquisitor who led the trial of Galileo, *sapete?*), La Boétie, Castiglione, Bossuet, Cardinal de Retz, Christina of Sweden, Casanova, Diderot, Beaumarchais, de Sade, Danton, Talleyrand, Baudelaire, Zola, Rasputin, Jaurès, Mussolini, Gandhi, Churchill, and Malaparte were all members of the Logos Club."

Simon remarks that this list is not restricted to politicians.

Eco explains: "In fact, there are two main currents within the Logos Club: the *immanentistes*, who consider the pleasure of the oratory duel an end in itself, and the *fonctionnalistes*, who believe rhetoric is a means to an end. Functionalism itself can be divided into two subcurrents: the Machiavellians and the Ciceronians. Officially, the former seek simply to persuade, and the latter to convince—the latter thus have more moral motivations—but in reality, the distinction is blurred because the goal for both factions is to acquire or conserve power, so . . ."

Bayard asks him: "And you?"

Eco: "Me? I'm Italian, *allora* . . ."

Simon: "Like Machiavelli. But also like Cicero."

Eco laughs: "*Si, vero.* Anyway, I would be more of an immanentist, I think."

Bayard asks the man in gloves for the password. He has recovered from his fright a little and protests: "*Ma*, it's a secret!"

Behind Bayard, Enzo, Bianca, Stefano, and half the wine merchant's clientele, drawn by the noise, have come to see what is going on. All of them listened to Umberto Eco's little lecture.

Simon asks: "Is it an important meeting?" The man in gloves replies that tonight the standard will be extremely high because there is a rumor that a sophist may attend, maybe even the Great

Protagoras himself. Bayard asks Eco to accompany them, but Eco refuses: "I know those meetings. I went to the Logos Club when I was young, you know! I even went up onstage and, as you can see, I didn't lose a finger." He proudly shows them his hands. The man in gloves represses a grimace of bitterness. "But I didn't have time for my research, so I stopped going to meetings. I lost my rank a long time ago. I would be curious to see how good today's duelists are, *ma* I am going back to Milan tomorrow. I have a train at eleven a.m. and I have to finish preparing a lecture on the ekphrasis of Quattrocento bas-reliefs."

Bayard cannot force him, but in the least threatening tone he can manage, he says: "We still have questions to ask you, Monsieur Eco. About the seventh function of language."

Eco looks at Bayard. He looks at Simon, Bianca, the man in gloves, Enzo and his new friend, his French colleague, Stefano and his father, who has also come out, and his gaze scans all the other customers who have crowded into the alleyway.

"*Va bene.* Meet me at the station tomorrow. Ten o'clock in the second-class waiting room."

Then he goes back to the store to buy some tomatoes and cans of tuna and finally disappears into the night with his little plastic bag and his professor's satchel.

Simon says: "We're going to need a translator."

Bayard: "Fingerless here can do it."

Simon: "He's not looking his best. I'm afraid he won't do a very good job."

Bayard: "All right, then, you can bring your girlfriend."

Enzo: "I want to come too!"

The Drogheria customers: "We want to come too!"

The man in gloves, still lying on the ground, waves his mutilated hand: "*Ma*, it's a private function! I can't get everyone in."

Bayard gives him a slap. "What? That's not very Communist! Come on, let's go."

And in the hot Bologna night a little troop sets off toward

the old university. From a distance, the procession looks a bit like a Fellini film, but it's hard to tell whether it's *La Dolce Vita* or *La Strada*.

12:07 a.m.
Outside the entrance of the Archiginnasio is a small crowd and a bouncer who looks like all bouncers except that he wears Gucci sunglasses, a Prada watch, a Versace suit, and an Armani tie.

The man in gloves speaks to the bouncer, flanked by Simon and Bayard. He says: *"Siamo qui per il Logos Club. Il codice è fifty cents."*

The bouncer, suspicious, asks: *"Quanti siete?"*

The man in gloves turns around and counts: "Uh . . . *Dodici.*"

The bouncer suppresses a smirk and says that won't be possible.

So Enzo moves forward and says: *"Ascolta amico, alcuni di noi sono venuti da lontano per la riunione di stasera. Alcuni di noi sono venuti dalla Francia, capisci?"*

The bouncer doesn't bat an eyelid. He does not seem overly impressed by the notion of a French branch of the Logos Club.

"Rischi di provocare un incidente diplomatico. Tra di noi ci sono persone di rango elevato."

The bouncer gives the group the once-over and says all he sees is a bunch of losers. He says: *"Basta!"*

Enzo does not give up: *"Sei cattolico?"* The bouncer lifts up his sunglasses. *"Dovresti sapere che l'abito non fa il Monaco. Che diresti tu di qualcuno che per ignoranza chiudesse la sua porta al Messia? Como lo giudicheresti?"* How would he judge the man who, in ignorance, closed the door to Christ?

The bouncer pulls a face. Enzo can tell he's on the fence. The man spends several seconds considering the matter, thinks about the rumor of the Great Protagoras arriving incognito, then, finally, points to the twelve of them: *"Va bene. Voi dodici, venite."*

The group enters the palace and climbs a stone staircase decorated with coats of arms. The man in gloves leads them to the

Teatro Anatomico. Simon asks him why the code word *fifty cents*? He explains that, in Latin, the initials of the Logos Club signify 50 and 100. Like that, it's easy to remember.

They enter a magnificent room constructed entirely in wood, designed as a circular amphitheater, decorated with wooden statues of famous anatomists and doctors, with a white marble slab at its center where corpses used to be dissected. At the back of the room, two statues of flayed men, both in wood, support a tray holding a statue of a woman in a thick dress that Bayard supposes to be an allegory of medicine but who if she had her eyes blindfolded could also be justice incarnate.

The tiered seating is already mostly full; the judges preside beneath the flayed men; a vague murmur of conversation fills the room as the spectators continue to arrive. Bianca, excited, tugs at Simon's sleeve: "Look! It's Antonioni! Have you seen *L'Avventura*? It is so *magnifico*! Oh, he came with Monica Vitti! *Che bella!* And look over there, that man on the jury, the one in the middle? That's 'Bifo,' the head of Radio Alice, an independent station that's really popular in Bologna. It was his programs that sparked the civil war, three years ago, and he's the one who introduced us to Deleuze, Guattari, Foucault. And look there! That's Paolo Fabbri and Omar Calabrese, two of Eco's colleagues, they're semioticians like him, and they're really famous too. And there! Verdiglione. Another semiotician, but he's a psychoanalyst too. And there! That's Romano Prodi, a former minister of industry, *ditchi* of course. What's he doing here? Does he still believe in the historic compromise, *quel buffone*?"

Bayard says to Simon: "And there, look." He points out Luciano, sitting on the benches with his old mother, chin resting on a crutch, smoking a cigarette. And, at the other end of the room, the three young guys in scarves who shot at him. All of them are acting as if nothing happened. The young guys don't seem too worried. What a strange country, thinks Bayard.

It is gone midnight. The session begins: a voice rings out. It's

Bifo who speaks first, the man from Radio Alice who set Bologna ablaze in '77. He quotes a Petrarch *canzone* that Machiavelli used in the conclusion of *The Prince*: *"Vertú contra furore / prenderà l'arme, et fia 'l combatter corto: / ché l'antico valore / ne gli italici cor' non è ancor morto."*

Virtue against fury shall advance the fight,
And it i' th' combat soon shall put to flight:
For the old Roman valor is not dead,
Nor in th' Italians' breasts extinguished.

Bianca's eyes flame blackly. The man in gloves sticks out his chest, fists on hips. Enzo puts his arm around the waist of the young student he picked up at the Drogheria. Stefano whistles enthusiastically. The melody of a patriotic anthem rises inside the circular amphitheater. Bayard is searching the dark recesses for someone, but he doesn't know who. Simon does not notice the man with the bag from the Drogheria amid the audience because he is absorbed by Bianca's copper skin and the sight of her quivering breasts afforded by her low neckline.

Bifo draws the first subject, a line by Gramsci that Bianca translates for them:

"The crisis consists precisely in the fact that the old is dying and the new cannot be born."

Simon thinks about this phrase. Bayard scans the room indifferently. He observes Luciano with his crutch and his mother. He observes Antonioni and Monica Vitti. He does not see Sollers and BHL hidden in a nook. In his head, Simon problematizes: "precisely" what? His mind syllogizes: we are in crisis. We are blocked. The Giscards govern the world. Enzo kisses his student on the mouth. What to do?

The two candidates stand either side of the dissecting table, below the audience, as at the center of an arena. Standing, it is easier for them to turn around and address the whole room.

Surrounded by all the wood of the anatomical theater, the marble table glows supernaturally white.

Behind Bifo, framing the pulpit (a real pulpit, as in a church) that is usually reserved for the professor, the flayed men stand watch, guardians of an imaginary door.

The first candidate—a young man with an Apulian accent, open-shirted, big silver belt buckle—begins.

If the dominant class has lost *consentement*—in other words if it is no longer *dirigeante* but merely *dominante* and the only power it holds is of *coercition*—this signifies precisely that the great masses are detached from traditional ideologies, that they no longer believe in what they believed before . . .

Bifo looks around the room. His gaze lingers for a moment on Bianca.

And it is precisely this interregnum that encourages the birth of what Gramsci calls *a great variety of morbid symptoms.*

Bayard watches Bifo watching Bianca. In the shadows, Sollers points out Bayard to BHL. In order to pass incognito, BHL is wearing a black shirt.

The young duelist rotates slowly, declaiming to the whole room. We know exactly what morbid phenomenon Gramsci was alluding to. Don't we? It is the same one that menaces us today. He leaves a pause. He shouts: *"Fascismo!"*

By leading his audience to conjure the idea before he pronounces the word, it is as if, at this instant, he delivers the thought of all his listeners telepathically, creating a sort of collective mental communion by the power of suggestion. The idea of fascism crosses the room like a silent wave. The young duelist has at least achieved one essential objective: setting the agenda of the debate. And, into the bargain, dramatizing it as intensely as possible: the fascist danger, the still fertile womb, etc.

The man with the bag holds it tight against his knees.

Sollers's cigarette, thrust into his ivory cigarette holder, shines in the darkness.

And yet there is a difference between the situation today and Gramsci's era. Today we no longer live under the threat of fascism. Fascism is already established in the heart of the government. It writhes there like larvae. Fascism is no longer the catastrophic consequence of a state in crisis and a dominant class that has lost control of the masses. It is no longer the sanction of the ruling class but its insidious recourse, its extension, designed to contain the advance of progressive forces. This is no longer a fascism supported openly but a slinking, shadowy, ashamed fascism, a fascism not of soldiers but shifty politicians, not a party of youth but a fascism of old people, a fascism of secret, dubious sects made up of aging spies in the pay of racist bosses who want to preserve the status quo but who are suffocating Italy inside a deadly cocoon. It is the cousin who makes embarrassing jokes during dinner but who we still invite to family meals. It is no longer Mussolini, it is the Freemasons of Propaganda Due.

There are boos from the audience. The young Apulian need only wrap up now: Incapable of imposing itself completely, but sufficiently established in every echelon of the state machinery to prevent any change in government (he wisely says nothing about the historic compromise), fascism in its larval form is no longer the menace hovering over a never-ending crisis, but is the very condition of that crisis's permanence. The crisis that has mired Italy for years will be resolved only when fascism is eradicated from the state. And for that, he says, raising his fist, *"la lotta continua!"*

Applause.

Although his opponent will offer a strong defense of the *négrienne* idea that the crisis is no longer a passing or possibly cyclical moment, the product of a dysfunctional or exhausted system, but the necessary engine of a mutant, polymorphic capitalism obliged to keep moving forward in order to regenerate, to find new markets and keep the workforce under pressure, citing as evidence the election of Thatcher and the imminent election of Reagan, he will be defeated by two votes to one. In the audience's opinion, the two duelists will have put on a high-quality show, justifying their rank of dialectician (the fourth of the seven levels). But the young Apulian will certainly have drawn some advantage from speaking against fascism.

It's the same thing for the next duel: *"Cattolicesimo e marxismo."* (A great Italian classic.)

The first duelist talks about Saint Francis of Assisi, about mendicant orders, about Pasolini's *The Gospel According to Saint Matthew*, about worker priests, about liberation theology in South America, about Christ driving the money changers from the temple, and concludes by making Jesus the first authentic Marxist-Leninist.

Uproar in the amphitheater. Bianca applauds noisily. The scarf gang lights a joint. Stefano uncorks a bottle that he brought with him just in case.

The second duelist can talk all he likes about the opium of the people, about Franco and the Spanish Civil War, about Pius XII and Hitler, about the collusion between the Vatican and the Mafia, about the Inquisition, about the Counter-Reformation, about the Crusades as a perfect example of an imperialist war, about the trials of Jan Hus, Bruno, and Galileo. But it's hopeless. The audience is impassioned. Everyone gets to their feet and starts singing "Bella Ciao," even though this has no connection with anything. With the crowd fully behind him, the first duelist wins by three votes to zero, but I wonder if Bifo was entirely convinced. Bianca sings her heart out. Simon watches her in profile as she sings, fascinated by the supple, mobile features of her radiant face. (He thinks she looks like Claudia Cardinale.) Enzo and the student sing. Luciano and his mother sing. Antonioni and Monica Vitti sing. Sollers sings. Bayard and BHL try to figure out the words.

The next duel pits a young woman against an older man; the question is about soccer and the class struggle; Bianca explains to Simon that the country has been rocked by *"Totonero,"* a match-fixing scandal involving the players of Juventus, Lazio, Perugia . . . and also Bologna.

Once more, against all expectations, it is the young woman

who wins by defending the idea that the players are proletarians like other workers and that the club bosses are stealing their hard work.

Bianca explains to Simon that the national team's young striker, Paolo Rossi, was suspended for three years following the match-fixing scandal, meaning that he will not be able to play in the World Cup in Spain. Tough shit for him, says Bianca, he refused a transfer to Napoli. Simon asks why. Bianca sighs. Napoli is too poor; it can't compete with the biggest clubs. No great player will ever go to Napoli.

Strange country, thinks Simon.

The night wears on, and the time is come for the digital duel. The silence of the statues—Gallienus, Hippocrates, the Italian anatomists, the flayed men, and the woman on the tray—contrasts with the agitation of the living. People smoke, drink, chat, eat picnics.

Bifo summons the duelists. A dialectician is challenging a peripatetician.

A man takes his place next to the dissecting table. It's Antonioni. Simon observes Monica Vitti, wrapped up in a delicately patterned gauze scarf, as she stares lovingly at the great director.

And facing him, stiff-backed and severe with her immaculate bun, Luciano's mother walks down the steps to the dissecting table.

Simon and Bayard look at each other. They look at Enzo and Bianca: they also seem surprised.

Bifo draws the subject: *"Gli intellettuali e il potere."* Intellectuals and power.

It is the prerogative of the lower-ranked player to begin—the dialectician.

In order for the subject to be discussed, it is up to the first duelist to problematize it. In this case, that's easy to work out: Are intellectuals the enemies or the allies of those in power? It's simply a question of choosing. For or against? Antonioni decides to criticize the caste to which he belongs, the caste that fills the amphitheater. Intellectuals as accomplices with those in power. *Così sia.*

Intellectuals: functionaries of the superstructures that participate in the construction of the hegemony. So, Gramsci again: all men are intellectuals, true, but not all men serve the function of intellectuals in society, which consists in working for the spontaneous consent of the masses. Whether "organic" or "traditional," the intellectual always belongs to an "economic-corporative" logic. Organic or traditional, he is always in the service of those in power, present, past, or future.

The salvation of the intellectual, according to Gramsci? Becoming one with the Party. Antonioni laughs sardonically. But the Communist Party itself is so corrupt! How could it provide redemption for anyone these days? *Compromesso storico, sto cazzo!* Compromise leads to compromised principles.

The subversive intellectual? *Ma fammi il piacere!* He recites a phrase from another man's film: "Think about what Suetonius did for the Caesars! You start with the ambition to denounce something and you end up an accomplice."

Theatrical bow.

Prolonged applause.

It's the old lady's turn to speak.

"Io so."

She, too, begins with a quotation, but she chooses Pasolini. His now-legendary "J'accuse," published in the *Corriere della Sera* in 1974.

"I know the names of those responsible for the massacre of Milan in 1969. I know the names of those responsible for the massacres of Brescia and Bologna in 1974. I know the names of important people who, with the aid of the CIA, Greek colonels, and the Mafia, launched an anti-Communist crusade, then tried to pretend they were anti-fascists. I know the names of those who, between two Masses, gave instructions and assured the protection of old generals, young neo-fascists, and ordinary criminals. I know the names of the serious and important people behind comic characters or behind drab characters. I know the names of serious and important people behind the tragic young people who have offered themselves as hired killers. I know all these names and I know all the crimes—the attacks on institutions and massacres—of which they are guilty."

The old woman growls and her trembling voice rings out in the Archiginnasio.

"I know. But I have no proof. Not even any clues. I know because I am an intellectual, a writer, who strives to follow everything that happens, to read everything that is written on this subject, to imagine all that is unknown or shrouded in silence; who puts together disparate facts, gathering the fragmentary, disordered pieces of an entire, coherent political situation, who restores logic where randomness, madness, and mystery seem to reign."

Less than a year after that article, Pasolini was found murdered, beaten to death on a beach in Ostia.

Gramsci dead in prison. Negri imprisoned. The world changes because intellectuals and those in power are at war with one another. The powerful win almost every battle, and the intellectuals pay with their lives or their freedom for having stood up to the powerful, and they bite the dust. But not always. And when an intellectual triumphs over the powerful, even posthumously, then the world changes. A man earns the name of intellectual when he gives voice to the voiceless.

Antonioni, whose physical integrity is at stake, does not let her finish. He cites Foucault, who says we must "put an end to spokespeople." Spokespeople do not speak for the others, but in their place.

So the old woman responds straight away, insulting Foucault as *senza coglioni*: didn't he refuse to intervene, here, in the parricide scandal that shook the whole country three years ago, just after publishing his book on the parricide of Pierre Rivière? What is the point of an intellectual if he doesn't intervene in a matter that corresponds precisely to his field of expertise?

In the shadows, Sollers and BHL chuckle, although BHL wonders what Sollers's field of expertise might be.

In response, Antonioni says that Foucault, more than anyone else, has exposed the vanity of this posture, this way the intellectual has of (he quotes Foucault again) "giving a bit of seriousness to minor, unimportant disputes." Foucault defines himself as a researcher, not an intellectual. He belongs to the long-term goals of research, not to the agitation of polemic. He said: "Aren't intellectuals hoping to give themselves greater importance through ideological struggle than they actually have?"

The old woman gasps. She spells it out: Every intellectual, if he correctly carries out the work of heuristic study for which he is qualified and that ought to be his vocation, even if he is in the service of those in power, works against the powerful because, as Lenin said (she turns around theatrically, her gaze sweeping the entire audience), the truth is always revolutionary. *"La verità è sempre rivoluzionaria!"*

Take Machiavelli. He wrote *The Prince* for Lorenzo de Medici: he could hardly have been more of a courtesan. And yet . . . this work, often regarded as the height of political cynicism, is a definitive Marxist manifesto: "Because the aims of the people are more honest than those of the nobles, the nobles wishing to oppress the people, and the people wishing not to be oppressed." In reality, he did not write *The Prince* for the Duke of Florence, because it has been published everywhere. By publishing *The Prince*, he reveals truths that would have remained hidden and reserved exclusively for the purposes of the powerful: so—it's a subversive act, a revolutionary act. He delivers the secrets of the Prince to the people. The arcana of political pragmatism stripped of fallacious divine or moral justifications. A decisive act in the liberation of humankind, as all acts of deconsecration are. Through his will to reveal, explain, expose, the intellectual makes war on the sacred. In this, he is always a liberator.

Antonioni knows his classics. Machiavelli, he replies, had so little concept of the proletariat that he couldn't even consider its condition, its needs, its aspirations. Hence he *also* wrote: "And when neither their property nor their honor is taken from them, the majority of men live content." In his gilded cage, he was incapable of imagining that the overwhelming majority of humankind was (and still is) absolutely lacking in property and honor, and could therefore not have them taken from them . . .

The old woman says that this is the very beauty of the true intellectual: he does not need to want to be revolutionary in order to be revolutionary. He does not need to love or even know the people in order to serve them. He is naturally, necessarily Communist.

Antonioni snorts contemptuously that she will have to explain that to Heidegger.

The old woman says that he would do better to reread Malaparte.

Antonioni talks about the concept of *cattivo maestro*, the bad master.

The old woman says that if there is a need to make clear with an adjective that the *maestro* is bad, that is because the *maestro* is essentially good.

It is clear there will be no knockout in this bout, so Bifo whistles to signal the end of the duel.

The two adversaries stare at each other. Their features are hardened, their jaws tensed, they are sweating, but the old woman's bun is still immaculate.

The audience is divided, indecisive.

Bifo's two fellow judges vote, one for Antonioni, the other for Luciano's mother.

Everyone waits for Bifo's decision. Bianca squeezes Simon's hand in hers. Sollers salivates slightly.

Bifo votes for the old woman.

Monica Vitti turns pale.

Sollers smiles.

Antonioni does not flinch.

He places his hand on the dissecting table. One of the judges gets to his feet: a tall and very thin man, armed with a small, blue-bladed hatchet.

When the hatchet chops off Antonioni's finger, the echo of the severed bone mingles with that of the blade hitting marble and the director's scream.

Monica Vitti bandages his hand with her gauze scarf while the judge respectfully picks up the finger and hands it to the actress.

Bifo proclaims loudly: *"Onore agli arringatori."* The audience choruses: Honor to the duelists.

Luciano's mother returns to sit down next to her son.

As at the end of a movie when the lights have not yet come back up, when the return to the real world is experienced as a slow, hazy awakening, when the images are still dancing behind our eyes, several minutes pass before the first spectators, stretching their numb legs, stand up and leave the room.

The anatomical theater empties slowly. Bifo and his fellow judges gather pages of notes into cardboard folders then retire ceremoniously. The session of the Logos Club dissolves into the night.

Bayard asks the man in gloves if Bifo is the Great Protagoras. He shakes his head like a child. Bifo is a tribune (level six), but not a sophist (level seven, the highest). The man in gloves thought it was Antonioni, who, it was said, used to be a sophist in the 1960s.

Sollers and BHL slip out discreetly. Bayard does not see them leave, because in the bottleneck near the door, they are hidden behind the man with the bag. He must make a decision. He decides to follow Antonioni. Turning back, he says out loud to Simon, in front of everyone: "Tomorrow, ten o'clock at the station. Don't be late!"

3:22 a.m.

The amphitheater is almost empty. The crowd from the Drogheria has gone. Simon wants to leave last, just to be sure. He watches the man in gloves walk out. He watches Enzo and the young student leaving together. He notes with satisfaction that Bianca has not moved. He might even suppose that she is waiting for him. They are the last ones. They stand up, walk slowly toward the door. But just as they are about to exit the room, they stop. Gallienus, Hippocrates, and the others observe them. The flayed men are absolutely motionless. Desire, alcohol, the intoxication of being away from home, the warm welcome that French people so often receive when they travel abroad . . . all these things give Simon a boldness—albeit a very shy boldness!—that he knows he would never have had in Paris.

Simon takes Bianca's hand.

Or maybe it's the other way around?

Bianca takes Simon's hand and they walk down the steps to the stage. She turns in a circle and the statues flash past her eyes like a ghostly slide show, like *images-mouvements*.

Does Simon realize at this precise moment that life is role-play, in which it is up to us to play our part as best we can, or does the spirit of Deleuze suddenly breathe life into his young, supple, slim body, with his smooth skin and short nails?

He puts his hands on Bianca's shoulders and slips off her low-cut top. Suddenly inspired, he whispers into her ear, as if to himself: "I desire the landscape that is enveloped in this woman, a landscape I do not know but that I can feel, and until I have unfolded that landscape, I will not be happy . . ."

Bianca shivers with pleasure. Simon whispers to her with an authority that he has never felt before: "Let's construct an assemblage."

She gives him her mouth.

He tips her back and lays her on the dissecting table. She takes off her skirt, spreads her legs, and tells him: "Fuck me like a machine." And while her breasts spill out, Simon begins to flow into her assemblage. His tongue-machine slides inside her like a coin in a slot, and Bianca's mouth, which also has multiple uses, expels air like a bellows, a powerful, rhythmic breathing whose echo—"*Si! Si!*"—reverberates in the pulsing blood in Simon's cock. Bianca moans, Simon gets hard, Simon licks Bianca, Bianca touches her breasts, the flayed men get hard, Gallienus starts to jerk off under his robe, and Hippocrates under his toga. "*Si! Si!*" Bianca grabs Simon's dick, which is hot and hard as if it's just come out of a forge, and connects it to her mouth-machine. Simon declaims as if to himself, quoting Artaud in an oddly detached voice: "The body under the skin is an overheated factory." The Bianca factory automatically lubricates her *devenir-sexe*. Their mingled moans ring out through the deserted anatomical theater.

Well, not entirely deserted: the man in gloves has come back to check out the two youngsters. Simon sees him, crouching in a shadowy angle of the tiered seating. Bianca sees him while she is sucking Simon. The man in gloves sees Bianca's dark eyes shine as they observe him, even as she goes down on Simon.

Outside, the Bologna night finally begins to cool. Bayard lights a cigarette while he waits for Antonioni, who is dignified but dazed, to decide to move. At this stage of the investigation, he isn't sure whether the Logos Club is just a bunch of harmless lunatics or something more dangerous, implicated in the deaths of Barthes and the gigolo, connected to Giscard, the Bulgarians, and the Japanese. A church bell strikes four times. Antonioni starts to walk, followed by Monica Vitti, the two of them followed by Bayard. They silently traverse arcades lined with chic boutiques.

Arched on the dissecting table, Bianca whispers to Simon, loud enough for the man in gloves to hear: "*Scopami come una macchina.*" Simon stretches over her, fits his cock into the mouth of her vulva, which is, he notes with pleasure, producing a constant flow of fluid, and when he finally thrusts inside her, he feels like pure liquid in its free state, unimpeded, sliding on the voluptuous Neapolitan's writhing body.

After going up to the top of Via Farini, outside the Basilica of Santo Stefano of the Seven Churches (constructed during the interminable Middle Ages), Antonioni sits on a stone post. He is holding his mutilated hand in his other hand, and his head hangs low. Standing at a distance under the arcades, Bayard can tell he is crying. Monica Vitti walks up to him. Nothing appears to indicate that Antonioni knows she is there, just behind him, but he knows, all the same, and Bayard knows that he knows. Monica Vitti raises her hand, but it remains suspended in the air, hesitant, immobile above the lowered head, like the sketch of a fragile and undeserved halo. Behind his column, Bayard lights a cigarette. Antonioni sniffs. Monica Vitti looks like a dream in stone.

Bianca struggles more and more under the weight of Simon's body, which she grips convulsively, crying out: *"La mia macchina miracolante!"* as Simon's dick pumps inside her like a piston. From his hiding place, the man in gloves hallucinates the hybridization of a locomotive and a wild horse. The anatomical theater swells with their union, a muffled, irregular growl testifying to the fact that desiring machines continually break down as they run, but run only when they are breaking down. "The product is always an offshoot of production, implanting itself upon it like a graft, and the machine parts are the fuel that makes it run."

Bayard has had time to light another cigarette, and then another. Monica Vitti at last decides to put her hand on Antonioni's head. The director is now sobbing openly. She strokes his hair with an ambiguous tenderness. Antonioni weeps and weeps. He can't stop. She lowers her beautiful gray eyes to the director's neck and Bayard is too far away to distinguish the expression on her face clearly. He tries to squint through the darkness but when he finally thinks he can see the compassion that his logical mind supposes, Monica Vitti turns her gaze away, lifting her eyes toward the massive edifice of the basilica. Perhaps she is already elsewhere. A cat's yowling can be heard in the distance. Bayard decides it is time to go to bed.

On the dissecting table, Bianca is now the iron horse atop Simon, who lies on the marble slab, all his muscles tensed to give more depth to the Italian girl's thrusts. "There is only one kind of production: the production of the real." Bianca slides up and down

Simon, faster and faster and harder, until they reach the point of impact, when the two desiring machines collide in an atomic explosion and become, finally, that body without organs: "For desiring machines are the fundamental category of the economy of desire; they produce a body without organs all by themselves, and make no distinction between agents and their own parts . . ." Deleuze's phrases flash through the young man's mind just as his body convulses, as Bianca's bolts and breaks down, then collapses on top of him, exhausted, their sweat mingling.

The bodies relax, shaken by aftershocks.

"Thus fantasy is never individual: it is group fantasy."

The man in gloves has not yet managed to leave. He, too, is exhausted, but it is not a pleasant form of exhaustion. His ghost fingers hurt him.

"The schizophrenic deliberately seeks out the very limit of capitalism: he is its inherent tendency brought to fulfilment, its surplus product, its proletariat, and its exterminating angel."

Bianca explains the Deleuzian *schizo* to Simon as she rolls a joint. Outside, the first notes of birdsong can be heard. The conversation goes on until morning. "No, the masses were not deceived; they wanted fascism at that moment, in those circumstances . . ." The man in gloves ends up falling asleep in a row between seats.

8:42 a.m.

The two young people at last leave their wooden friends and go out into the already hot air of the Piazza Maggiore. They skirt the fountain of Neptune, his demonic dolphins, his obscene nymphs. Simon is giddy with fatigue, alcohol, pleasure, and cannabis. Less than twenty-four hours after his arrival in Italy, he thinks to himself that it is not going too badly so far. Bianca accompanies him to the station. Together, they walk up Via dell'Independenza, the city center's main artery, past the still drowsy stores. Dogs sniff at trash cans. People come out, suitcases in hand: it is the start of a holiday, and everyone is going to the train station.

Everyone is going to the train station. It is 9:00 a.m., August 2, 1980. The July people are coming home, the August people preparing to leave.

Bianca rolls a joint. Simon thinks he should change his shirt. He stops outside an Armani shop and wonders if he could claim that on expenses.

At the end of the long avenue is the massive Porta Galliera, in appearance half byzantine house, half medieval arch, which Simon would like to pass under, though he doesn't really know why, and then, as it's not yet time for the meeting at the train station, he leads Bianca toward some stone steps by a park, they stop in front of a strange fountain embedded in the wall of the staircase, and they take turns smoking the joint as they contemplate the sculpture of a naked woman grappling with a horse, an octopus, and some other sea creatures that they are unable to identify. Simon feels lightly stoned. He smiles at the statue, thinking about Stendhal, which leads him to Barthes: "We always fail to talk about what we love . . ."

Bologna Central swarms with vacationers in shorts and bawling brats. Simon lets himself be guided by Bianca, who leads him to the waiting room, where they find Eco and Bayard, who has brought his little suitcase from the hotel where they checked in but in Simon's case didn't sleep. A small child, running after his little brother, charges into Simon, almost knocking him off balance. He hears Eco explaining to Bayard: "That is tantamount to saying that Little Red Riding Hood is not in a position to conceive of a universe where the Yalta Conference took place or where Reagan will succeed Carter."

Despite the look Bayard shoots him, which he decodes as a cry for help, Simon does not dare interrupt the great academic, so he looks around and thinks he spots Enzo in the crowd, with his family. Eco says to Bayard: "So anyway, for Little Red Riding Hood, judging a possible world where wolves don't speak, the 'actual' world would be hers, the one where wolves do speak." Simon feels a vague rising anxiety, which he puts down to the joint. He thinks he sees Stefano with a young woman, moving off toward the tracks. "We can read the events described in *The Divine Comedy* as 'credible' in comparison with the medieval encyclopedia and legendary in comparison with ours." Simon feels as if Eco's words are ricocheting inside his head. He thinks he sees Luciano and his mother carrying a large bag overflowing with provisions. To reassure himself, he checks that Bianca is standing next to him. He has a vision of a German tourist, very blond, with a Tyrolean-style hat, a large camera on a strap around her neck, leather shorts, and knee-length socks, walking behind her. In the hubbub of Italian voices echoing under the roof of the station, Simon strains to isolate Eco's French phrases: "On the other hand, if, reading a historical novel, we find a King Runcibald of France, the comparison with the world zero of the historical encyclopedia makes us feel uneasy in a way that presages the readjustment of cooperative attention: obviously, this is not a historical novel, but a fantasy novel."

Just as Simon finally decides to greet the two men, he thinks he might be able to deceive the Italian semiologist, but he sees that Bayard has immediately understood that he is—as he realized himself, standing by the statue—*lightly stoned*.

Eco addresses him as if he had been there since the start of the conversation: "When reading a novel, what does it signify to recognize that what is happening is 'truer' than what happens in real life?" Simon thinks that in a novel, Bayard would bite his lip or shrug.

Then Eco finally stops talking and, for a second, no one breaks the silence.

Simon thinks he sees Bayard biting his lip.

He thinks he sees the man in gloves walking behind him.

"What do you know about the seventh function of language?" In a haze, Simon doesn't realize at first that it's not Bayard who asks this, but Eco. Bayard turns toward him. Simon notices that he is still holding hands with Bianca. Eco gazes at the girl with lightly lustful eyes. (Everything seems light.) Simon tries to pull himself together: "We have good reason to believe that Barthes and three other people were killed because of a document relating to the seventh function of language." Simon hears his own voice but feels as if Bayard is speaking.

Eco listens with interest to the story of a lost manuscript for which people are being killed. He sees a man walk past holding a bouquet of roses. His mind wanders for a second, and a vision of a poisoned monk flashes through it.

In the middle of the crowd, Simon thinks he recognizes the man with the bag from the night before. The man sits in the waiting room and slides the bag under his seat. It looks full to bursting.

It is 10:00 a.m.

Simon does not want to insult Eco by reminding him that there are only six functions of language in Jakobson's theory; Eco knows this perfectly well but, according to him, it is not entirely correct.

Simon concedes that there is a mention of a "magic or incantatory function," but reminds Eco that it was not considered serious enough to be kept in Jakobson's classification.

Eco does not claim that the "magic" function exists, strictly speaking, and yet one can probably find something inspired by it in works that followed Jakobson's.

Austin, an English philosopher, did indeed theorize the existence of another function of language, which he called "performative," and which could be summarized in the formula "When saying is doing."

It consists in the capacity that certain pronouncements have to produce (Eco says "realize") what they pronounce through the very fact of their pronouncement. For example, when the minister says, "I now pronounce you husband and wife," or when the monarch declares, "Arise, Sir So-and-so," or when the judge says, "I sentence you . . . ," or when the president of the National

Assembly says, "I declare the assembly open," or simply when you say to someone, "I promise . . . ," it is the very fact of pronouncing these phrases that makes what they pronounce come into being.

In one way, this is the principle of the magical formula, Jakobson's "magic function."

A clock on the wall shows 10:02.

Bayard lets Simon take charge of the conversation.

Simon knows Austin's theories, but does not see anything in them worth killing people for.

Eco says that Austin's theory is not limited to those few cases but is extended to more complex linguistic situations, when a pronouncement is not intended merely to affirm something but seeks to provoke an action—which is either produced or not by the simple fact that this pronouncement is made. For example, if someone says to you "it's hot in here," it can be a simple observation about the temperature, but generally you would understand that he's counting on the effect of his remark being that you will open the window. Likewise, when someone asks, "Do you have the time?," he expects not a simple yes/no answer but that you should tell him what time it is.

According to Austin, speaking is a *locutionary act* since it consists in saying something but can also be an *illocutionary* or *perlocutionary act*, which surpasses the purely verbal exchange because it *does* something, in the sense that it produces actions. The use of language enables us to remark something, but also to *perform* something.

Bayard has no idea where Eco is going with this, and Simon is not too sure either.

The man with the bag has left, but Simon thinks he can glimpse the bag under the seat. (But was it that big before?) Simon thinks the man must have forgotten it again; there are some pretty absentminded people around. He looks for him in the crowd but doesn't see him.

The wall clock shows 10:05.

Eco continues: "Now, let us imagine that the performative function is not limited to these few cases. Let us imagine a function of language that enables someone, in a much more extensive fashion, to convince anyone else to do anything at all in any situation."

10:06.

"Whoever had the knowledge and the mastery of such a function would be virtually the master of the world. His power would be limitless. He could win every election, whip up crowds, provoke revolutions, seduce any woman, sell any kind of product imaginable, build empires, swindle the entire world, obtain anything he wanted in any circumstances."

10:07.

Bayard and Simon are beginning to understand.

Bianca says: "He could dethrone the Great Protagoras and take control of the Logos Club."

Eco replies, with an easygoing smile: *"Eh, penso di si."*

Simon says: "But since Jakobson didn't talk about that function of language . . ."

Eco: "Maybe he did, *in fin dei conti*? Maybe there is an unpublished version of *Essays in General Linguistics* in which this function is detailed?"

10:08.

Bayard thinks out loud: "And Barthes found himself in possession of this document?"

Simon: "And someone killed him to steal it?"

Bayard: "Not only for that. To prevent him from using it."

Eco: "If the seventh function exists and it really is a kind of performative function, it would lose a large part of its power were it known by everyone. Knowledge of a manipulative mechanism doesn't necessarily protect us from it—look at advertising, public relations: most people know how they work, what methods they use—but, all the same, it does weaken it . . ."

Bayard: "And whoever stole it wants it for his own exclusive use."

Bianca: "Well, one thing's for sure: Antonioni didn't steal it."

Simon realizes that he has been staring at the black bag forgotten under the seat for the past five minutes. It looks enormous. He has the impression that it has tripled in volume. It must weigh ninety pounds now. Either that or he's still really high.

Eco: "If someone wanted to appropriate the seventh function for himself alone, he would have to ensure that no copies existed."

Bayard: "There was a copy at Barthes's apartment . . ."

Simon: "And Hamed was a walking copy; he carried it around inside him." He has the impression that the gold-colored buckle on the bag is an eye, staring at him as if he were Cain in the tomb.

Eco: "But it's also probable that the thief himself would make a copy and hide it somewhere."

Bianca: "If this document is really so valuable, he can't take the risk of losing it . . ."

Simon: "And he has to take the risk of making a copy and entrusting it to someone . . ." He thinks he sees a curl of smoke float out of the bag.

Eco: "My friends, I'm going to have to leave you! My train leaves in five minutes."

Bayard looks at the clock. It is 10:12 a.m. "I thought your train was at eleven?"

"Yes, but in the end I decided to take the one before. This way, I'll be in *Milano* earlier!"

Bayard asks: "Where can we find this Austin?"

Eco: "He's dead. *Ma*, he had a student who has continued to work on all those questions of the performative, the illocutionary, the perlocutionary, and so on . . . He's an American philosopher, his name is John Searle."

Bayard: "And where can we find this John Searle?"

Eco: "*Ma* . . . in America!"

10:14. The great semiologist goes off to catch his train.

Bayard looks at the departures board.

10:17. Umberto Eco's train leaves Bologna Central. Bayard lights a cigarette.

10:18. Bayard tells Simon that they are going to catch the eleven o'clock train to Milan, from where they must fly to Paris. Simon and Bianca say goodbye. Bayard goes to buy the tickets.

10:19. Simon and Bianca smooch in the middle of the crowded waiting room. The kiss goes on for a while and, like boys often do, Simon keeps his eyes open while he kisses Bianca. A woman's voice announces the arrival of the Ancona-Basel train.

10:21. While he is kissing Bianca, Simon glimpses a young blonde. She is maybe thirty feet away. She turns around and smiles at him. He jumps.

It's Anastasia.

Simon thinks the grass must really have been powerful stuff or maybe he's just tired, but no: that figure, that smile, that hair . . . it really is Anastasia. The nurse from the hospital in Paris, here, in Bologna. Before Simon can emerge from his stupor and call her name, she walks out of the station. He says to Bianca, "Wait here for me!" and he runs after the nurse, just to be sure.

Thankfully, Bianca does not obey him but follows him instead. This is what will save her life.

10:23. Anastasia has already crossed the traffic circle outside the station but she stops and turns around again, as if she is waiting for Simon.

10:24. At the station exit, Simon looks around for her and spots her at the edge of the old town's ring road, so he walks quickly across the flower beds in the middle of the traffic circle. Bianca follows him, about ten feet behind.

10:25. The train station explodes.

10:25 a.m.
Simon is thrown to the ground. His head hits the grass. The rumble of an earthquake spreads above him in a series of waves. Lying in the grass, breathless, covered in dust, stung by a dense rain of debris, deafened by the noise of the explosion, disoriented, Simon experiences the collapse of the building behind him as in

a dream where you are falling endlessly or when you are drunk and the earth sways beneath your feet. It seems that the flower bed is a flying saucer whirling all over the place. When the background finally starts to slow down, he tries to come back down to earth. He looks around for Anastasia, but his field of vision is obstructed by an advertising billboard (for Fanta) and he can't move his head. But his hearing gradually returns and he hears voices screaming in Italian and, in the distance, the first sirens.

He feels someone moving his body. It is Anastasia, turning him onto his back and examining him. Simon sees her beautiful Slavic face against the dazzlingly blue Bologna sky. She asks him if he's injured but he is incapable of responding because he has no idea and because the words remain trapped in his throat. Anastasia takes his head in her hands and tells him (her accent returning): "Look at me. There's nothing wrrrong with you. Everrrything's fine." Simon manages to sit up.

The entire left-hand side of the station has been pulverized. All that remains of the waiting room is a heap of stones and beams. A long, formless groan rises from the bowels of the devastated building, its twisted skeleton visible where the roof has been blown away.

Simon glimpses Bianca's body close to the flower bed. He crawls over to her and lifts up her head. She is groggy but alive. She coughs. She has a gash on her forehead and blood is streaming down her face. She whispers: *"Cosa è successo?"* In a reassuring reflex, her hand fumbles in the little handbag that still hangs from her shoulder and lies on her bloodstained dress. She takes out a cigarette and asks Simon: *"Accendimela, per favore."*

And Bayard? Simon searches for him among the wounded, the terrified survivors, the policemen arriving in Fiats, and the medics jumping out of the first ambulances like parachutists. But in this confused ballet of hysterical marionettes, he can no longer recognize anyone.

And then, suddenly, he sees him, Bayard, the French cop,

emerging from the rubble, covered in dust, looking massive and powerful and giving off a slow-burning, righteous anger, carrying an unconscious young man on his back. Amid the scene of warlike chaos, this ghostly apparition leaves a deep mark on Simon, who thinks of Jean Valjean in *Les Misérables*.

Bianca whispers: *"Sono sicura che si tratta di Gladio . . ."*

Simon spots a shape like a dead animal on the ground, and realizes it is a human leg.

"Between the desiring machines and the body without organs, an apparent conflict arises."

Simon shakes his head. He contemplates the first bodies being evacuated on stretchers, alive and dead alike, all lying still with their arms hanging down and dragging along the ground.

"Each machine connection, each machine production, each machine noise has become unbearable to the body without organs."

He turns to Anastasia and finally thinks to ask her the question that he imagines will answer many others: "Who do you work for?"

Anastasia spends a few seconds thinking about this, then replies, in a professional tone he has never heard her use before: "Not for the Bulgarians."

And, despite the fact that she is a nurse, she slips away, without offering to help the paramedics or look after the wounded. She runs toward the ring road, crosses, and disappears under the arcades.

At that very moment, Bayard reaches Simon, as if the whole thing had been meticulously choreographed, like a play, thinks Simon, whose paranoia has not exactly been eased by the combination of the bomb and the joints.

Holding up the two tickets to Milan, Bayard says: "We'll rent a car. I don't think there'll be any trains today."

Simon borrows Bianca's cigarette and lifts it to his own lips. Around him, everything is chaos. He closes his eyes and inhales the smoke. The presence of Bianca, stretched out on the pavement, reminds him of the dissecting table, the flayed men, Antonioni's finger, and Deleuze. A smell of burning floats in the air.

"Beneath its organs, it senses there are larvae and loathsome worms, and a God at work messing it all up or strangling it by organizing it."

PART III

ITHACA

■

48

Althusser is in a panic. He's searched through all his papers, but he cannot find the precious document that was entrusted to him and which he hid in a junk-mail envelope, left in plain sight on his desk. Although he never read the document, he's a nervous wreck because he knows it is of the utmost importance that he return it to the people who gave it to him for safekeeping, and that this is his responsibility. He rummages around in his waste-paper basket, empties his drawers, takes his books one by one from the shelves and hurls them onto the floor in a rage. He feels filled with a dark anger at himself, mixed with an embryonic suspicion, when he decides to shout: "Hélène! Hélène!" She runs up to him, worried. Does she, by any chance, know where . . . an envelope . . . opened . . . junk mail . . . a bank or a pizzeria . . . he can't remember . . . Hélène, in a natural voice, says: "Oh yes, I remember, that old envelope . . . I threw it away."

Time stops for Althusser. He doesn't ask her to repeat it. What's the point? He heard her perfectly well. But still, there's hope: "The trash . . . ?" I emptied it last night, and the garbage-men took it away this morning. A long groan howls deep inside the philosopher while he tenses his muscles. He looks at his wife, dear old Hélène, who has put up with him for so many years, and he knows that he loves her, he admires her, he feels sorry for her, he blames himself, he knows what he put her through with his caprices, his infidelities, his immature behavior, his childlike need for his wife to support him in his choice of mistresses, and his manic-depressive fits ("hypomania," they call it), but this, this is too much, this is much, much more than he can tolerate—yes, him, the immature impostor—and he throws himself at his wife, screaming like a wild beast, and grabs her throat with his hands, which tighten around it like a vise, and Hélène, taken by surprise, stares at him wide-eyed but does not try to defend herself, putting her hands on his but not really struggling. Maybe she knew all along that it would have to end like this, or maybe she just wanted to put an end to it one way or another, and this way was as good as any, or maybe Althusser is just too fast, too violent. Maybe she wanted to live and recalled, at that instant, one or two phrases written by Althusser, this man she loved—"one does not abandon a concept like a dog," perhaps—but Althusser strangles his wife like a dog, except that he is the dog, ferocious, selfish, irresponsible, maniacal. When he loosens his grip, she is dead. A bit of tongue—a "poor little bit of tongue," he will say—sticks out of her mouth and her bulging eyes stare at her murderer or the ceiling or the void of her existence.

Althusser has killed his wife, but there will be no trial because he will be judged to have been temporarily insane at the time. Yes, he was angry. But why didn't he say anything to his wife? If Althusser is a "victim of himself," it's because he didn't disobey the person who asked him to remain silent. You should have said something, you jerk, at least to your wife. A lie is far too precious a thing to be misused. He should at least have told her: "Don't touch this envelope, it's extremely valuable, it contains a highly important document that X or Y [he could have lied here] gave me to look after." Instead of which, Hélène is dead. Judged insane, Althusser will have his case dismissed. He will be committed for a few years, then will leave his apartment on Rue d'Ulm and move to the Twentieth Arrondissement, where he will write that very strange autobiography, *The Future Lasts*

Forever, which contains this crazy phrase, placed inside parentheses: "Mao even granted me an interview, but for reasons of 'French politics,' I made the stupid mistake, *the biggest of my life*, of not turning up for it . . ." (The italics are mine.)

49

"Italy! That place is unbelievable!" D'Ornano paces the presidential office, lifting his hands above his head. "What the hell is going on in Bologna? Is that connected to our case? Were our men targeted?"

Poniatowski rummages around in the drinks cabinet. "Hard to say. It could be just coincidence. It could be the far left or the far right. It could also have been ordered by the government. You never know with the Italians." He opens a can of tomato juice.

Sitting behind his desk, Giscard closes the copy of *L'Express* that he was leafing through and puts his hands together in silence.

D'Ornano (tapping his foot): "Coincidence, my ass! If—and I mean *if*—a group, of whatever kind, or a government, or an agency, or a service, or an organization possesses the means *and* the determination to set off a bomb that kills eighty-five people just to hamper our investigation, then I think we have a problem. The Americans have a problem. The English have a problem. The Russians have a problem. Unless it's them, obviously."

Giscard asks: "It seems like the kind of thing they'd do, Michel, don't you think?"

Poniatowski unearths some celery salt. "Random killing with as many civilian victims as possible? I have to say that's more the far right's style. And anyway, according to Bayard's report, there was that Russian agent who saved the kid's life."

D'Ornano (startled): "The nurse? She might just as easily have planted the bomb."

Poniatowski (opening a bottle of vodka): "Why would she show herself in the station, then?"

D'Ornano (pointing at Poniatowski as though he were personally responsible): "We checked. She never worked at Salpêtrière."

Poniatowski (stirring his Bloody Mary): "It's more or less proven that Barthes no longer had the document by the time he got to the hospital. In all probability, things went like this: he comes out of the lunch with Mitterrand, gets knocked over by a laundry van—driven by the first Bulgarian. A man posing as a doctor pretends to examine him and steals his papers and his keys. Everything suggests that the document was with his papers."

D'Ornano: "In that case, what happened at the hospital?"

Poniatowski: "Witnesses saw two intruders whose description matches the two Bulgarians who killed the gigolo."

D'Ornano (trying to keep count of the number of Bulgarians involved): "But since he didn't have the document anymore?"

Poniatowski: "They probably came back to finish the job."

D'Ornano, who is soon out of breath, stops pacing and, as if his attention has been suddenly drawn to something, starts examining a corner of Delacroix's painting.

Giscard (picking up the biography of JFK and stroking the cover): "Let's assume that it was our men who were targeted in Bologna."

Poniatowski (adding Tabasco): "That would prove they're on the right track."

D'Ornano: "Meaning?"

Poniatowski: "If it was really our men they were trying to eliminate, it must have been to prevent them from discovering something."

Giscard: "This . . . club?"

Poniatowski: "Or something else."

D'Ornano: "So we should send them to the USA?"

Giscard (sighing): "Doesn't he have a phone, this American?"

Poniatowski: "The kid says it'll be a chance to 'get down to brass tacks.' "

D'Ornano: "You don't say! So that little twat wants to go on a trip paid for by the Republic?"

Giscard (perplexed, as if chewing on something): "Given the available evidence, wouldn't it be just as useful to send them to Sofia?"

Poniatowski: "Bayard's a good cop, but he's no James Bond. Maybe we could send a Service Action team?"

D'Ornano: "To do what? Bump off some Bulgarians?"

Giscard: "I'd rather keep the Ministry of Defense out of all this."

Poniatowski (grinding his teeth): "Besides, we don't want to risk a diplomatic crisis with the USSR."

D'Ornano (trying to change the subject): "Talking of crisis, what's happening in Tehran?"

Giscard (starting to leaf through *L'Express* again): "The shah is dead, the mullahs are dancing."

Poniatowski (pouring himself a neat vodka): "Carter is screwed. Khomeini will never free the hostages."

Silence.

In *L'Express*, Raymond Aron writes: "It is better to let laws become dormant when, rightly or wrongly, they are refused by the morals of the day." Giscard thinks: "How wise."

Poniatowski kneels in front of the refrigerator.

D'Ornano: "Uh, and the philosopher who killed his wife?"

Poniatowski: "Who cares? He's a Commie. We shut him up in an asylum."

Silence. Poniatowski gets some ice cubes from the icebox.

Giscard (in a belligerent voice): "This case must not have any influence on the campaign."

Poniatowski (who understands that Giscard has returned to the subject at hand): "We can't find the Bulgarian driver or the fake doctor anywhere."

Giscard (tapping his index finger against his leather desk blotter): "I don't care about the driver. I don't care about the doctor. I don't care about this . . . Logos Club. I want the document. On my desk."

50

When Baudrillard learned that under the weight of more than 30,000 visitors the metallic structure of the Centre Georges-Pompidou, opened by Giscard in 1977 on Rue Beaubourg and immediately nicknamed "The Refinery" or "Our Lady of the Pipes," risked "folding," he grew as excited as a child, like the rascal of French Theory that he is, and wrote a little book entitled *The Beaubourg Effect: Implosion and Deterrence*.

"That the mass (of visitors) magnetized by the structure should become a destructive variable for the structure itself—this, if the designers intended it (though how could we hope for that?), if they planned, in this way, the possibility of putting an end, in a single blow, to the architecture and culture . . . then Beaubourg constitutes the most audacious object and the most successful happening of the century."

Slimane knows the Marais quarter well, and in particular Rue Beaubourg, where students line up as soon as the library opens. He knows it because he's seen all this when coming out of clubs, exhausted by the night's excesses and wondering how two worlds could coexist in parallel like this without ever touching.

But today, he is in the line. He smokes, his Walkman's earphones stuck in his ears, trapped between two students with their noses in books. Discreetly, he tries to read the titles. The student in front is reading a book by Michel de Certeau entitled *The Practice of Everyday Life*. The other, behind him, Cioran's *The Trouble with Being Born*.

Slimane listens to "Walking on the Moon" by the Police.

The line advances very slowly. Someone says it'll be another hour before they get in.

"MAKE BEAUBOURG FOLD! The new watchword of the revolution. No need to burn it. No need to protest it. Come on! It's the best way of destroying it. Beaubourg's success is no longer a mystery: people go there for that very reason; they rush to enter this building, whose fragility already exudes catas-trophe, with the single aim of making it fold."

Slimane has not read Baudrillard but when his turn comes he goes through the turnstile, unaware that he is participating in this post-Situationist undertaking.

He crosses a sort of press room where people are looking at microfiche on viewers, and takes an escalator up to the reading room, which resembles a huge textile workshop, except that the workers are not cutting out and assembling shirts using sewing machines but reading books and making notes in little notebooks.

Slimane also spots youngsters who've come to cruise and tramps who've come to sleep.

What impresses Slimane is the silence, but also the height of the ceiling: half factory, half cathedral.

Behind a large glass wall, an immense TV screen shows im-ages from Soviet television. Soon, the images switch to an Ameri-can channel. Spectators of various ages are sprawled in red chairs. It smells a bit. Slimane does not hang around here, but begins striding through the aisles of shelves.

Baudrillard writes: "The people want to accept everything, swipe everything, eat everything, touch everything. Looking, de-ciphering, studying doesn't move them. The one mass affect is that of touching, or manipulating. The organizers (and the art-ists, and the intellectuals) are alarmed by this uncontrollable im-pulse, for they reckoned only with the apprenticeship of the masses to the *spectacle* of culture."

Inside, outside, on the square, on the ceiling, there are wind-socks everywhere. If he survives this adventure, Slimane, like everyone else, will associate the identity of Beaubourg—this big, futuristic ocean liner—with the image of the windsock.

"They never anticipated this active, destructive fascination—this original and brutal response to the gift of an incompre-hensible culture, this attraction which has all the semblance of housebreaking or the sacking of a shrine."

Slimane glances randomly at titles. *Have You Read René Char?* by Georges Mounin. *Racine and Shakespeare* by Stendhal. *Promise at Dawn* by Gary. *The Historical Novel* by Georg Lukács. *Under the Volcano. Paradise Lost. Pantagruel* (that one rings a bell).

He passes Jakobson without seeing it.

He bumps into a guy with a mustache.

"Oh, sorry."

Perhaps it's time to give some substance to this Bulgarian so he doesn't end up like his partner, an anonymous soldier fallen in a secret war where the whys are clear but the wherefores remain hazy.

Let's suppose his name is Nikolai. In any case, his real name will remain unknown. Along with his partner, he followed the investigators' leads, which brought them to the gigolos. They killed two of them. He still doesn't know if he ought to kill this one, too. Today, he is unarmed. He has come without his umbrella. The specter of Baudrillard whispers in his ear: *"Panic in slow motion, without external movement."* He asks: "What arrre you looking for?" Slimane, who has been suspicious of strangers since the deaths of his two friends, rears back and replies: "Nothing." Nikolai smiles at him: "That's like everrrything: difficult to find."

51

We are in a Parisian hospital again, but this time no one can enter the room—because this is Sainte-Anne, the psychiatric hospital, and Althusser is sedated. Régis Debray, Etienne Balibar, and Jacques Derrida stand guard outside the door and discuss how best to protect their old mentor. Peyrefitte, the minister of justice, is also a former student of the École Normale Supérieure, but that doesn't seem to incline him to magnanimity, because he is already demanding in the press that the case go to trial. On the other hand, the three men must listen patiently to the denials of good Dr. Diatkine, who has been Althusser's psychiatrist for years, and who regards it as absolutely unthinkable—more than that—physically, "technically" impossible (I quote) that Althusser could have strangled his wife.

Foucault turns up. If you were a professor at the ENS between 1948 and 1980, then among your students and/or colleagues, you'd have had Derrida, Foucault, Debray, Balibar, Lacan. And BHL, too. That's how it is in France.

Foucault asks for the latest news, and they tell him what Althusser has been repeating endlessly: "I killed Hélène. What happens next?"

Foucault leads Derrida aside and asks him if he's done what was asked of him. Derrida nods. Debray watches them on the sly.

Foucault says he shouldn't have done such a thing, and that he refused when he was asked. (Professional rivalry obliges him to rub in the fact that he was asked *before* Derrida. Asked what? It's still too early to say. But he refused because one shouldn't deceive a friend, even what is known as "an old friend," with all those implications of weariness and only partly repressed bitterness.)

Derrida says they must move forward. That there are interests at play. Political.

Foucault rolls his eyes.

BHL arrives. He is politely shown the door. Naturally, he will find a way back in.

Meanwhile, Althusser sleeps. His former students hope for his sake that he is not dreaming.

52

"Tennis clay-court vision satellite broadcast on grass you see that's how it is you have to hit back each phrase hard straight away second ball net cord topspin volley backhand forehand winner borg connors vilas mcenroe . . ."

Sollers and Kristeva are sitting at a table in a refreshment area in the Jardin du Luxembourg, and Kristeva is nibbling tentatively at a *crêpe au sucre*, while Sollers monologues tirelessly and drinks his *café crème*.

He says:

"In Christ's case, there's one pretty special thing—that he said he's coming back."

Or:

"As Baudelaire said: I took a long time to become infallible."

Kristeva stares at the skin of milk floating on the surface of the coffee.

"Apocalypse in Hebrew is *gala*, which means 'to discover.'"

Kristeva arches her back to hold back the nausea rising in her chest.

"If the God of the Bible had said I am everywhere, we'd know about it . . ."

Kristeva tries to reason with herself. She reminds herself silently: "The sign is not the thing, but still . . ."

An editor they know, Gitane in his mouth, limping slightly as he takes a small child for a walk, comes over to say hello. He asks Sollers what he's working on "at the moment," and naturally Sollers is only too happy to tell him: "A novel full of portraits and characters . . . hundreds of notes taken in real-life situations . . . about the war of the sexes . . . I can't imagine any novel being more informed, more multilayered, more corrosive and lighthearted than this . . ."

Still mesmerized by the film of milk, Kristeva suppresses a retch. As a psychoanalyst, she makes her own diagnosis: she wants to spit herself out.

"A philosophical novel, even metaphysical, with a cold, lyrical realism."

Infantile regression linked to a traumatic shock. But she is Kristeva: mistress of *herself*. She *controls* herself.

Sollers spews his torrent of words over the editor, who frowns to make clear his intense attentiveness, while the small child tugs at his sleeve: "The highly symptomatic turning point of the second half of the twentieth century will be described in its secret and concrete ramifications. One could draw a chemical table of it: the negative feminine bodies (and why), the positive bodies (and how)."

Kristeva reaches slowly toward the cup. Slips a finger into the handle. Brings the beige liquid to her lips.

"The philosophers will be shown in their private limitations, the women in their hysteria and their calculations, but also as being free (in both senses)."

Kristeva closes her eyes as she swallows. She hears her husband quote Casanova: "If pleasure exists, and if it can be experienced only in life, then life is a joy."

The editor hops about: "Excellent! Very good! Good!"

The child looks up, surprised.

Sollers is just warming up, and moves on to the plot: "Here, the bigots look miserable, the sociopaths and *sociomanes* denounce superficiality, the spectacular industry becomes trapped or desperately wants to distort the fact, the Devil is annoyed because pleasure should be destructive and life a calamity."

The coffee streams into Kristeva like a river of lukewarm lava. She *feels* the skin in her mouth, in her throat.

The editor wants to commission a book from Sollers when he has finished this one.

For the thousandth time Sollers recounts an anecdote about himself and Francis Ponge. The editor listens politely. Ah, these great writers! Always banging on about their obsessions, always shaping their material . . .

Kristeva thinks that phobia does not disappear but slides under the tongue, under language itself, that the object of the phobia is a proto-writing and, conversely, all use of words, inasmuch as it is writing, is a language of fear. "The writer: a phobic who succeeds in making life a metaphor in order not to die of fear but to come back to life in the signs," she thinks.

The editor asks: "What's the latest on Althusser?" Suddenly, Sollers falls silent. "After Barthes, it's so awful. What a year!" Sollers looks away when he replies: "Yes, the world is mad. What can you do? But that is the fate of sad souls." He doesn't see Kristeva's eyes open like two black holes. The editor takes his leave and walks off with the child, who makes little yapping noises.

Sollers stands silently. Kristeva visualizes the mouthful of coffee forming a sort of stagnant pool in her stomach. The danger has passed, but the skin is still there. The nausea remains at the bottom of the cup. Sollers says: "I have a talent for differences." Kristeva drains the cup in a single gulp.

They walk toward the large pond where children play with wooden boats that their parents rent by the hour for a few francs.

Kristeva asks for the latest on Louis. Sollers replies that the dogs are standing guard but that Bernard was able to see him. "In a total daze. Apparently, when they found him, he kept repeating: 'I killed Hélène. What happens next?' Can you imagine? What . . . happens . . . next? Extraordinary, isn't it?" Sollers savors the anecdote greedily. Kristeva brings him back to more practical concerns. Sollers tries to reassure her: the chaos of the apartment means that if the copy wasn't destroyed, it has at least been lost forever. At worst, it will end up in a cardboard box and some Chinese people will find it, two hundred years from now, with no idea what it is, and they'll use it to light their opium pipe.

"Your father was wrong. No copy, next time."

"There were no consequences, and there won't be a next time."

"There is always a next time, my squirrel."

Kristeva thinks about Barthes. Sollers says: "I knew him better than anyone."

Kristeva replies coldly: "But I killed him."

Sollers quotes Empedocles: "The blood around the heart is men's thought." But as he is unable to last more than a few seconds without bringing the conversation back to himself, he grits his teeth and whispers: "His death will not be in vain. I will be what I will be."

Then he takes up his monologue again, as if nothing happened: "Of course the message has no importance anymore . . . ah, ah, this little affair is far from clear, oh, oh . . . the public, by definition, has no memory it is blank it is virgin forest . . . You and I, we are like fish in air . . . What does it matter if Debord is wrong about me, even going so far as to compare me with Cocteau? . . . Who are we, to begin with, and in the end?"

Kristeva sighs. She leads him toward the chess players.

Sollers is like a child—his short-term memory lasts only three minutes—so he becomes absorbed in a game between an old man and a young man, both wearing baseball caps with logos featuring a team from New York. While the young guy launches an attack clearly designed to neuter his opponent's ability to castle, the writer whispers into his wife's ear: "Look at that old guy, he's as cunning as a fox, ha ha. But if they look for me, they will find me, ha ha."

They hear the *poc-poc* of tennis balls on nearby courts.

It is Kristeva's turn to drag her husband by the sleeve because it is nearly time.

They walk through a forest of swings and arrive at a little puppet theater. They sit on wooden benches, surrounded by children.

The man who sits just behind them is badly dressed and has a mustache.

He pulls at his crumpled jacket.

He traps his umbrella between his legs.

He lights a cigarette.

He leans toward Kristeva and whispers something in her ear. Sollers turns and exclaims joyfully: "Hello there, Sergei!" Kristeva corrects him curtly: "His name is Nikolai." Sollers takes a cigarette from a blue tortoiseshell case and asks the Bulgarian for a light. The child sitting next to him watches curiously. Sollers sticks out his tongue. The curtain opens, and the puppet Guignol appears. "Hello, children!" "Hello, Guignol!" Nikolai explains to Kristeva, in Bulgarian, that he has been tailing Hamed's friend. He searched his house (without making a mess, this time) and he is absolutely certain: there is no copy. But there is something odd: for some time now, he's been spending his days at the library.

As Sollers does not speak Bulgarian, he watches the play while he waits for them. The conflict is between Guignol and two others: an unshaven burglar, and a gendarme who rolls his *r*'s like Sergei. The story revolves around a simple dispute that is the pretext for multiple action scenes involving violence perpetrated with a stick. Essentially, Guignol must recover the Marquise's necklace, stolen by the thief. Sollers immediately suspects the Marquise of having given it to the thief of her own free will in exchange for sexual favors.

Kristeva asks what kind of books Slimane has been reading.

Guignol asks the children if the thief went thataway.

Nikolai replies that most of the books he saw Slimane consulting were about linguistics and philosophy, but that, in his opinion, the gigolo is not really sure what he is looking for.

The children cry out: "Yeeeeeessssss!"

Kristeva thinks the main point is that he is looking for something. When she tries to repeat this to Sollers, he cries out: "Yeeeesss!"

Nikolai specifies: mostly Anglophone authors. Chomsky, Austin, Searle, and also a Russian, Jakobson, two Germans, Bühler and Popper, and one Frenchman, Benveniste.

The list speaks for itself as far as Kristeva is concerned.

The thief asks the children to betray Guignol.

The children shout: "Nooooooo!" Sollers, facetiously, says "Yeeesss!" but his answer is drowned out by the children's cries.

Nikolai becomes even more specific: Slimane only leafed through some of the books, but he read Austin with particular care.

Kristeva deduces from this that he is seeking to contact Searle.

The thief sneaks up behind Guignol, armed with a stick. The children try to warn Guignol: "Watch out! Watch out!" But each time Guignol turns around, the thief hides. Guignol asks the children if the thief is nearby. The children try to tell him, but he acts like he's deaf, pretending not to understand, which makes them hysterical. They scream, and Sollers screams with them: "Behind you! Behind you!"

Guignol is hit by the stick. Anxious silence in the theater. He looks as if he's been knocked out, but in fact he's just pretending. Phew.

Kristeva thinks.

A cunning trick allows Guignol to knock out the thief. For good measure, he rains blows on him with the stick. (In the real world, thinks Nikolai, no one would survive head trauma like that.)

The gendarme arrests the thief and congratulates Guignol.

The children clap until their hands are sore. In the end, we don't know if Guignol has handed over the necklace or kept it for himself.

Kristeva puts a hand on her husband's shoulder and shouts into his ear: "I have to go to the USA."

Guignol waves: "Goodbye, children!"

The children and Sollers: "Goodbye, Guignol!"

The gendarme: "Goodbye, childrrren!"

Sollers, turning around: "Bye, Sergei."

Nikolai: "Goodbye, Monsieur Krrristeva."

Kristeva to Sollers: "I'm going to Ithaca."

53

Slimane also wakes up in a bed that is not his own, but other than him the bed is empty, containing only the outline of a body, as if drawn in chalk on the still-warm sheets. Rather than a bed, he is lying on a mattress placed on the floor in a dark, windowless, almost completely bare room. From the other side of the door, he can hear men's voices mixed with the sound of classical music. He remembers exactly where he is and he knows that music. (It's Mahler.) He opens the door and, without bothering to get dressed, goes into the living room.

It is a very long and narrow room, with a long bay window overlooking Paris (toward Boulogne and Saint-Cloud). We are on the ninth floor. Around a low table, Michel Foucault, wrapped in a black kimono, is explaining the mysteries of elephant sexuality to two young men in underpants, one of whom has his portrait reproduced in three photographs hung on a pillar next to the sofa.

Or more exactly, Slimane thinks he understands, how elephant sexuality was perceived and described in seventeenth-century France.

The two young men smoke cigarettes that Slimane knows are stuffed with opium, because this is their technique to cushion the comedown. Curiously, Foucault has never had to resort to this, such is his tolerance for all drugs: he can be at his typewriter at nine in the morning after spending the whole of the previous night on LSD. The young men look less on form. All the same, they greet Slimane, hollow-voiced. Foucault offers him coffee, but just then there is a loud noise in the kitchen and a third young man appears, looking distressed, holding a bit of plastic. This is Mathieu Lindon, who has just broken the coffeepot. The two others cannot suppress a tubercular giggle. Foucault, in a debonair way, suggests tea. Slimane sits down and begins buttering a *biscotte* while the tall bald man in his black kimono returns to his lecture on elephants.

For François de Sales, bishop of Geneva in the seventeenth century and author of *Introduction to the Devout Life*, the elephant is a model of chastity: faithful and temperate, he has only one partner, with whom he mates once every three years for a period of five days, away from prying eyes, before they wash each other at length in order to purify themselves. Handsome Hervé, in his underpants, grumbles from behind his cigarette about the truth behind this elephant fable: the horror of Catholic morality, on which he spits—at least symbolically, as he is short on saliva, so he just coughs on it instead. Foucault, in his kimono, becomes animated: "Exactly! What is very interesting here is that even in Pliny we find the same analysis of the elephant's morals. So if we trace the genealogy of this moral, as Nietzsche would say, we realize that its roots reach deep into an epoch prior to Christianity, or at least into an epoch where its development was still largely embryonic." Foucault looks jubilant. "You see, we talk about Christianity as if it were a single thing . . . But Christianity and paganism do not constitute clearly defined and distinct entities. One mustn't think of impenetrable blocks that appear out of nowhere and disappear just as suddenly, without influencing each other, interpenetrating, metamorphosing."

Mathieu Lindon, who is still standing holding the handle of the broken coffeepot, asks: "But, uh, Michel, what's your point exactly?"

Foucault gives Lindon one of his dazzling smiles: "In fact, paganism can't be regarded as a single entity, but the same is even more true of Christianity! We need to reevaluate our methods, you understand?"

Slimane bites into his *biscotte* and says: "Hey, Michel, you know that conference at Cornell, are you still going? Where is that place, exactly?"

Foucault, always happy to answer questions, no matter what they might be, and unsurprised that Slimane should be interested in his conference, replies that Cornell is a large American university situated in a small city in the northern United States named Ithaca, like Ulysses's island. He doesn't know why he accepted the invitation, because it's a conference on language, the "linguistic turn" as they say over there, and he hasn't worked in that field for a long time (*The Order of Things* came out in 1966) but anyway he said yes and he doesn't like to go back on his word, so he'll be there. (In fact, he knows perfectly well why he accepted: he adores the United States.)

When Slimane has finished chewing his *biscotte*, he drinks a mouthful of the scorchingly hot tea, lights a cigarette, clears his throat, and asks: "Do you think I could come with you?"

54

"No, darling, you can't come with me. It's a conference for academics only and you hate it when people call you Monsieur Kristeva."

Sollers's smile cannot conceal the wound to his ego that, alas, may never heal.

Can you imagine Montaigne or Pascal or Voltaire doing a postgraduate degree?

Why do those pathetic Americans obstinately refuse to take any notice of him, this giant among giants, who will be read and reread in 2043?

Can you imagine Chateaubriand, Stendhal, Balzac, Hugo? Will I one day have to ask permission to think?

The funniest thing is that they're inviting Derrida, obviously. But aren't you aware, my dear Yankee friends, that your idol, this man you revere because he writes *différance* with an *a* (the world decomposes, the world dissolves), wrote his masterpiece, *Dissemination* (the world *disseminates*), as an homage to his own *Nombres*, which no one in New York or California has ever bothered to translate! Seriously, it's just priceless!

Sollers laughs and pats his stomach. Ho ho ho! Without him, no Derrida! Ah, if only the world knew . . . Ah, if only the Americans knew . . .

Kristeva listens patiently to this speech, which she knows by heart.

"Can you imagine Flaubert, Baudelaire, Lautréamont, Rimbaud, Mallarmé, Claudel, Proust, Breton, Artaud, taking a *post-graduate degree*?" Sollers abruptly stops talking and pretends to think, but Kristeva knows what he is going to say next: "It's true that Céline wrote a doctoral thesis, but it was for a medical degree, although in literary terms it was superb." (Subtext: He has read Céline's medical thesis. How many academics can say as much?)

Then he rubs against his wife, sliding his head under her arm, and says in a dopey voice:

"But why do *you* want to go, my beloved squirrel?"

"You know why. Because Searle will be there."

"And all the others!" Sollers explodes.

Kristeva lights a cigarette. She examines the embroidered motif on the cushion she is leaning against, a reproduction of the unicorn from Cluny's tapestry, which she and Sollers bought together back in the old days, at the Singapore airport. Her legs are folded under her, her hair is in a ponytail, and she caresses the potted plant next to the sofa as she says in an undertone, articulating exaggeratedly with her very faint accent: "Yes . . . the otherrrs."

To contain his nervousness, Sollers recites his little personal rosary:

"Foucault: too irritable, jealous, vehement. Deleuze? Too dark. Althusser? Too sick (ha ha!). Derrida? Too hidden in his successive envelopments (ha ha). Hate Lacan. Don't see any harm in the Communists looking after security at Vincennes. (Vincennes: a place for monitoring the fanatics.)"

The truth, Kristeva knows, is that Sollers is afraid of not ending up published in the Pléiade collection, that one sure sign of having made it.

For now, the misunderstood genius strives to vilify the Americans, with their "gay and lesbian studies," their totalitarian feminism, their fascination for "deconstruction" or for Lacanian psychoanalysis, when it's obvious that they've never even heard of Molière!

And their women!

"American women? Mostly unbearable: money, complaints, family sagas, pseudo-psychological infection. Thankfully, in New York, there are Latino and Chinese girls, and quite a few Europeans, too." But at Cornell! Pfft.

Kristeva drinks a jasmine tea while she leafs through an English-language psychoanalysis journal.

Sollers paces around the large living-room table, livid, shoulders hunched forward like a bull: "Foucault, Foucault, that's all they think about."

Then he suddenly lifts his head and thrusts out his chest, like a sprinter on the finishing line: "Oh, screw it, what do I care? I know how it works: you have to travel, give speeches, speak Anglo-American like a good slave, participate in tedious conferences, 'work together,' water down your thoughts, seem human."

Putting her cup down, Kristeva speaks to him gently: "You'll have your revenge, my love."

Sollers, feverish now, starts talking about himself in the second person while touching his wrist: "You have a facility for elocution; it is flagrant, annoying (they'd prefer it if you stuttered, but never mind) . . ."

Kristeva takes his hand.

Sollers smiles at her and says: "Sometimes you need a little encouragement."

Kristeva smiles back at him and says: "Come on, let's read some Joseph de Maistre."

55

Quai des Orfèvres. Bayard types up his report while Simon reads a Chomsky book on generative grammar, which he has to admit he doesn't really understand.

Each time he comes to the edge of the page, Bayard uses his right hand to move the lever that sends the typewriter cylinder flying back across to the other side while, with his left, he grabs his cup of coffee, drinks a mouthful, takes a drag on his cigarette and puts it back on the edge of a yellow ashtray bearing the Pastis 51 logo. *Crac tac tac tac, tac tac tac, crac tac tac tac,* and so on.

But the *tac-tac* sound stops abruptly. Bayard sits up on his padded imitation leather chair, turns toward Simon, and asks:

"Actually, where's it from, that name? Kristeva?"

56

Serge Moati is stuffing his face with slices of Savane marble cake when Mitterrand arrives. Fabius, in slippers, opens the door of his mansion in the Panthéon to let him in. Lang, Badinter, Attali, Debray, all wait patiently, drinking coffee. Mitterrand tosses his scarf to Fabius, moaning: "Your friend Mauroy? I'm going to give him a good beating!" He's in a bad mood, no doubt about it. The young conspirators realize that this meeting is not going to be much fun. Mitterrand bares his teeth: "Rocard! Rocard!" No one says a word. "They messed up Metz and now suddenly they're desperate to sign me up for the presidential election so they can be rid of me!" His young lieutenants sigh. Moati chews his Savane in slow motion. The young adviser with the birdlike face risks saying, "President . . ." but Mitterrand turns on him, cold-eyed, furious, poking his finger into his chest as he moves toward him: "Shut your mouth, Attali . . ." And Attali retreats all the way to the wall as the would-be candidate goes on: "They all want me to fail but I can thwart their strategy easily: all I have to do is not accept it! Let that idiot Rocard get a good hiding from that imbecile Giscard. Rocard, Giscard . . . it'll be the war of the morons! Magnificent! Sublime! The Deuxième Gauche? Fiddlesticks, Debray! French fiddlesticks! Robert, get a pen, I'm going to dictate a press release. I abdicate! I fold. Ha! How do you like that?" He moans: "Fail! What does that mean, to fail?"

No one dares respond, not even Fabius, who does occasionally stand up to his boss but who wouldn't dare get involved in a subject as sticky as this. Anyway, the question was purely rhetorical.

Mitterrand must record his statement of principle. He has prepared his little speech: it is dreary, formulaic . . . it's just crap. It talks about stasis and the dangers of not changing. No passion, no message, no inspiration, just hollow, bombastic phrases. The cold anger of the eternal loser, palpable on the screen. The recording takes place in gloomy silence. Fabius's toes writhe nervously inside his slippers. Moati chews his Savane like it's cement. Debray and Badinter look blankly at each other. Attali watches through the window as a traffic cop puts a parking ticket on Moati's R5. Even Jack Lang looks perplexed.

Mitterrand grits his teeth. He wears the mask he has worn all his life, walled up inside that morgue where he always goes to conceal the anger gnawing at him. He gets to his feet, picks up his scarf, and leaves without saying goodbye to anyone.

The silence drags on for a few minutes longer.

Moati, pale: "Well, that's it, then . . . We'd better call a spin doctor. It's our only hope."

Lang, behind him, mutters: "No, there is another one."

57

"I don't understand how he could have missed it the first time. He knew he was looking for a document about that Russian linguist, Jakobson. He sees a book about Jakobson on the desk and he doesn't even glance at it?"

Yes, it has to be said, that does seem *implausible*.

"And just by chance, he's there exactly when we arrive at Barthes's place, when he'd had weeks to go back to the apartment, 'cause he had the key."

Simon listens to Bayard while the Boeing 747 crawls over to the runway. Giscard, that horrible bourgeois fascist, finally agreed to pay for their airfare, but was still too mean to book them on Concorde.

The investigation into the Bulgarians led them to Kristeva.

Now Kristeva has gone to the United States.

So . . . it's hot dogs and cable TV for our heroes.

Naturally, there is a kid crying in their row.

A stewardess comes over and asks Bayard to extinguish his cigarette because smoking is prohibited during takeoff and landing.

Simon has brought Umberto Eco's *Lector in Fabula* to read on the journey. Bayard asks him if he's learning anything interesting from his book, and by interesting he means useful for the investigation, though maybe that's not all he means, actually. Simon reads out loud: "I live (I mean: I who write, I have the intention of being alive in the only world I know), but at the moment when I create a theory of possible narrative worlds, I decide (based on the world of which I have direct physical experience) to reduce this world to a semiotic experience in order to compare it to narrative worlds."

Simon gets a hot flush while the stewardess moves her arms to mime the safety instructions. (The kid stops crying; he is fascinated by this traffic-cop choreography.)

Officially, Kristeva has gone to Cornell University, in Ithaca, New York, for a conference whose title and subject Bayard has not even attempted to understand. All he needs to know is that John Searle, the American philosopher mentioned by Eco, is also among the guests. The aim is not to kidnap the Bulgarian woman in an Eichmann-style raid. If Giscard had wanted to arrest Barthes's murderer (because everything suggests she is involved), he would have prevented her from leaving the country. The aim is to understand what's going on. Isn't that always the way?

For Little Red Riding Hood, the real world is the one where wolves speak.

And to recover that bloody document.

Bayard tries to understand: Is the seventh function a set of instructions? A magic spell? A chimera provoking hysteria in all those little political and intellectual cabals who see in it the ultimate jackpot for whoever can get their hands on it?

In the seat next to his, separated by the aisle, the kid takes out a cube with multicolored sides that he starts twisting in different directions.

When it comes down to it, Simon wonders, what is the fundamental difference between himself and Little Red Riding Hood or Sherlock Holmes?

He hears Bayard thinking aloud, or maybe he's talking to him: "Let's assume that the seventh function of language really is this performative function. It enables whoever masters it to convince anyone to do anything in any circumstances . . . okay. Apparently, the document fits into a single page. Let's say it's written on both sides, in small letters. How can the instructions for something so powerful fit into such a tiny space? All user manuals, for a dishwasher or a TV or my 504, are pages and pages long."

Simon grinds his teeth. Yes, it's hard to understand. No, there is no explanation. If he had even the tiniest intuition of what that document contains, he would already have been elected president and have slept with every woman he wanted.

While he is speaking, Bayard keeps his eyes fixed on the kid's toy. From what he can observe, the cube is subdivided into smaller cubes that must be arranged by color using vertical and horizontal rotations. The kid is going at it frenetically.

In *Lector in Fabula*, Eco writes about the status of fictional characters that he calls "supernumeraries" because they add to the people in the real world. Ronald Reagan and Napoleon are part of the real world, but Sherlock Holmes is not. But then what meaning can there be in an assertion such as "Sherlock Holmes is not married" or "Hamlet is mad"? Is it possible to regard a supernumerary as a real person?

Eco quotes Volli, an Italian semiologist who said: "I exist; Madame Bovary doesn't." Simon feels increasingly anxious.

Bayard gets up to go to the toilets. Not that he really needs to piss, but he can see that Simon is absorbed by his book, so he may as well stretch his legs, particularly as he's already knocked back all those little bottles of booze.

Walking to the back of the plane, he bumps into Foucault, who is mid-conversation with a young Arab man with headphones around his neck.

He saw the conference schedule and Foucault's presence here should not surprise him because he knew the philosopher was invited, but all the same he cannot suppress a slight start. Foucault flashes him his predatory smile.

"Don't you know Slimane, Superintendent? He was a good

friend of Hamed's. You haven't cleared up the circumstances of his death, I suppose? Just another queer, eh? Or is it because he was an Arab? Does that count double?"

When Bayard returns to his seat, he finds Simon asleep, head hanging forward, in that uncomfortable position typical of people who try to sleep while sitting. It was another phrase of Eco's, quoting his mother-in-law, that finished him off: "What would have happened if my son-in-law had not married my daughter?"

Simon dreams. Bayard daydreams. Foucault takes Slimane to the bar upstairs, to talk to him about his lecture on sexual dreams in Ancient Greece.

They order two whiskeys from the stewardess, who smiles almost as much as the philosopher.

According to Artemidorus, our sexual dreams are like prophecies. You have to establish parallels between the sexual relations experienced in dreams and the social relations experienced in reality. For example, dreaming that you sleep with a slave is a good sign: insofar as the slave is your property, that means your estate is going to increase. With a married woman? Bad sign: you mustn't touch another man's property. With your mother, it depends. According to Foucault, we have greatly exaggerated the importance the Greeks attributed to Oedipus. In any case, the point of view is that of the free, active male. Penetrating (man, woman, slave, family member) is good. Being penetrated is bad. The worst, the most unnatural (just after sexual relations with gods, animals, and corpses), is lesbians practicing penetration.

"Each to his own criteria, all is normative!" Foucault laughs, orders two more whiskeys, and leads Slimane to the toilets, where the gigolo graciously lets him do what he wants (though he refuses to take off his Walkman).

We have no way of knowing what Simon dreams about, because we are not inside his head, are we?

Bayard notes Foucault and Slimane climbing the stairs to go to the bar on the plane's upper deck. Driven by intuition rather than reason, he goes back to examine their empty seats. There are some books in the pocket in front of Foucault's seat and some magazines on Slimane's seat. Bayard opens the overhead compartment and grabs the luggage that he supposes must belong to the two men. He sits in Foucault's seat and goes through the philosopher's bag and the gigolo's backpack. Papers, books, a spare T-shirt, cassettes. No obvious sign of a document, but Bayard realizes it probably won't have "The Seventh Function of Language" written on it in bold, so he takes the two bags and walks over to his own seat to wake Simon.

By the time Simon has emerged from his dream, grasped the situation, expressed his surprise at Foucault's presence on the plane, become indignant at what Bayard is asking him to do, and in spite of this agreed to rummage through things that do not belong to him, a good twenty minutes have passed, so that when Simon is finally in a position to guarantee to Bayard that there is not, in Foucault's or in Slimane's belongings, anything that might bear any resemblance at all to the seventh function of language, the two men see Foucault coming down the stairs.

He is going to return to his seat and is bound to realize, sooner or later, that his things have disappeared.

Without any need to confer, the two men react like old teammates. Simon steps over Bayard and goes to meet Foucault in the aisle, while Bayard slips into the parallel aisle to walk back to the tail of the airplane and come around in the other direction to Foucault's row.

Simon stands in front of Foucault, who waits for him to move out of the way. But as Simon doesn't budge an inch, Foucault looks at him and, from behind his thick-lensed glasses, recognizes the young man.

"Well . . . if it isn't Alcibiades!"

"Monsieur Foucault, what a surprise! . . . It's an honor! I adore your work . . . What are you working on at the moment? . . . Still sex?"

Foucault narrows his eyes.

Bayard walks down the far aisle but is blocked by a stewardess pushing a drinks cart. She calmly serves cups of tea and glasses of red wine to the passengers while trying to sell them duty-free, and Bayard hops up and down behind her.

Simon doesn't listen to Foucault's reply because he is concentrating on his next question. Behind Foucault, Slimane grows impatient. "Can we move forward?" Simon grabs his opportunity: "Oh, you're with someone? *Enchanté, enchanté!* So does he call you Alcibiades too? Ha ha . . . uh . . . So have you been to the United States before?"

At a pinch, Bayard could push past the stewardess, but there is no way he could get around the cart, and he still has another three rows to go.

Simon asks: "Have you read Peyrefitte? What a load of crap, huh? We miss you at Vincennes, you know."

Gently but firmly, Foucault takes Simon by the shoulders and makes a sort of tango move, pivoting with him, so that Simon finds himself between Foucault and Slimane, which effectively means that Foucault has got past him and that nothing but a few paces now separates him from his seat.

Finally, Bayard comes level with the toilets at the back of the plane, where he is able to cross to the opposite aisle. He reaches Foucault's seat, but the philosopher is moving toward him and he is going to see him putting the bags back in the overhead compartment.

Simon, who does not need glasses and is well aware of the situation, has seen Bayard before Foucault has, so he cries out: "Herculine Barbin!"

The passengers jump. Foucault turns around. Bayard opens the compartment, shoves the two bags in, and closes it again. Foucault stares at Simon. Simon smiles stupidly and says: "We're all Herculine Barbins, don't you think, Monsieur Foucault?"

Bayard moves past Foucault, apologizing, as if he is just returning from the toilets. Foucault watches Bayard pass, then shrugs, and at last everyone returns to his own seat.

"Who's that, Herculine Whatsisname?"

"A nineteenth-century hermaphrodite who had a very unfortunate life. Foucault edited his memoirs. He turned it into a slightly personal thing, used it to denounce the normative assignments of biopower, which force us to choose our sex and our sexuality by recognizing only two possibilities, man or woman, in both cases heterosexual, unlike the Greeks, for example, who were much more relaxed about the question, even if they had their own norms, which were . . ."

"Okay, got it."

"Who's the young guy with Foucault?"

The rest of the journey passes without any problems. Bayard lights a cigarette. The stewardess comes over to remind him that smoking is prohibited during landing, so the superintendent falls back on his emergency miniatures.

We know that the young guy with Foucault is called Slimane; we don't know his surname. But when they reach American soil, Simon and Bayard see him deep in discussion with several policemen at passport control because his visa is not valid, or rather, because he does not have a visa at all. Bayard wonders how he was allowed to take off from Roissy. Foucault tries to intervene on his behalf, but it's no good: American policemen are not in the habit of joking around with foreigners. Slimane tells Foucault not to wait for him, and not to worry—he'll be fine. Then Simon and Bayard lose sight of them and get on a suburban train.

They do not arrive by ship like Céline in *Journey to the End of the Night*, but emerge from underground at Madison Square Garden, and their sudden entrance into central Manhattan is no less of a shock: the two stunned men stare at the skyscrapers lining the sidewalks to vanishing point and the smear of light on Eighth Avenue, filled at once with a feeling of unreality and a no less powerful feeling of familiarity. Simon, who used to read *Strange*, expects to see Spider-Man leaping over the yellow taxis and red lights. (But Spider-Man is a "supernumerary," so this is impossible.) A busy-looking native stops spontaneously to ask if they need help and this completes the two Parisians' disorientation, so un-used are they to such solicitude. In the New York night, they walk up Eighth Avenue until they reach the Port Authority Bus Terminal, opposite the gigantic building that houses *The New York Times*, as the massive gothic letters on the façade un-equivocally indicate. Then they get on a bus to Ithaca. Goodbye to the skyscraper wonderland.

As the journey lasts five hours and everyone is tired, Bayard takes a small, multicolored cube out of his bag and starts to play with it. Simon cannot believe it: "You nicked that kid's Rubik's Cube?" Bayard finishes his first row as the bus emerges from the Lincoln Tunnel.

58

"Shift into overdrive in the linguistic turn"
Cornell University, Ithaca, fall 1980
(CONFERENCE ORGANIZER: **Jonathan D. Culler**)

LIST OF TALKS:
Noam Chomsky
  Degenerative grammar
Hélène Cixous
  Les larmes de l'hibiscus
Jacques Derrida
  A Sec Solo
Michel Foucault
  Jeux de polysémie dans l'onirocritique d'Artémidore
Félix Guattari
  Le régime signifiant despotique
Luce Irigaray
  Phallogocentrisme et métaphysique de la substance
Roman Jakobson
  Stayin' Alive, structurally speaking

Fredric Jameson

The Political Unconscious: Narrative as a socially symbolic act

Julia Kristeva

Le langage, cette inconnue

Sylvère Lotringer

Italy: Autonomia—Post-political politics

Jean-François Lyotard

PoMo de bouche: la parole post-moderne

Paul de Man

Cerisy sur le gâteau: la déconstruction en France

Jeffrey Mehlman

Blanchot, the laundry man

Avital Ronell

"Because a man speaks, he thinks he's able to speak about language."—Goethe & the metaspeakers

Richard Rorty

Wittgenstein vs Heidegger: Clash of the continents?

Edward Said

Exile on Main Street

John Searle

Fake or feint: performing the F words in fictional works

Gayatri Spivak

Should the subaltern shut up sometimes?

Morris J. Zapp

Fishing for supplement in a deconstructive world

59

"Deleuze isn't coming, right?"

"No, but Anti-Oedipus is playing tonight. I'm so excited!"

"Have you heard the new single?"

"Yeah, it's awesome. So L.A.!"

Kristeva is sitting on the grass between two boys. Stroking their hair, she says: "I love America. You are so ingenuous, boys."

One of them tries to kiss her neck. She pushes him away, laughing. The other whispers in her ear: "You mean 'genuine,' right?" Kristeva giggles. She feels a shiver of electricity run down her squirrelish body. Facing them, another student finishes rolling and lights a joint. The pleasant smell of the grass spreads through the air. Kristeva takes a few hits. Her head spins a little bit. She pontificates soberly: "As Spinoza said, each negation is a definition." The three young pre–New Wave post-hippies laugh and exclaim rapturously: "Wow, say that again! What did Spinoza say?"

On campus, students come and go, some looking busy, others less so, crossing the wide lawn between Gothic, Victorian, and Neoclassical buildings. A sort of bell tower overlooks the scene, itself perched on top of a hill that rises above a lake and some gorges. We may be in the middle of nowhere, but at least we're in the middle. Kristeva bites into a club sandwich because the baguette, which she loves so much, has not yet reached the remote Tompkins County, in deepest New York State, halfway between New York City and Toronto, former territory of the Cayuga tribe, which was part of the Iroquois Confederation, and home to the small city of Ithaca, home in turn to the prestigious Cornell University. She frowns and says: "Unless it's the other way around . . ."

They are joined by a fourth young man, who comes out of the hotel-management school carrying an aluminum packet in one hand and *Of Grammatology* in the other (but he doesn't dare ask Kristeva if she knows Derrida). He's brought muffins, oven fresh, that he made himself. Kristeva is happy to take part in this improvised picnic, getting tipsy on tequila. (Unsurprisingly, the bottle is hidden inside a paper bag.)

She watches the students walk past, carrying books or hockey sticks or guitar cases under their arms.

An old man with a receding hairline, his abundant hair

brushed back as if he once had a thick bush on his head, mumbles to himself under a tree. His hands, which shake in front of him, look like branches.

A young, short-haired woman, who looks a bit like a cross between Cruella in *101 Dalmatians* and Vanessa Redgrave, appears to be the only member of an invisible protest march. She shouts slogans that Kristeva does not understand. She seems very angry.

A group of young guys is playing with an American football. One recites Shakespeare while the others drink red wine from the bottle. (Not wrapped in paper, the rebels.) They throw the ball to one another, taking care to get a good spiral. The one with the bottle fails to catch the ball in his other hand (which is holding a cigarette), so the others make fun of him. They already seem pretty drunk.

Kristeva looks at the bush-man with the receding hairline; he looks back at her and they hold each other's gaze, just for an instant, but a touch too long for it to be insignificant.

The angry young woman stands in front of Kristeva and says: "I know who you are. Go home, bitch." Kristeva's friends stare wide-eyed at each other, burst out laughing, then reply excitedly: "Are you stoned? Who the fuck do you think you are?" The woman walks away and Kristeva watches as she recommences her solitary protest. She is fairly certain she has never seen her before in her life.

Another group of young people bear down on the football players, and the atmosphere changes immediately; from where she is sitting, Kristeva can tell that the two groups are openly hostile to each other.

A church bell rings.

The new group noisily calls out to the first group. From what Kristeva can hear, they are calling them "French suckers." Kristeva does not understand at first if this is a prepositional apposition (suckers who also happen to be French) or a genitive construction (they practice fellatio on French people), but given that the group in question seems Anglo-Saxon (because she thinks she spotted that they knew some of the rules of American football), she thinks the second hypothesis is the more likely.

Whatever, the first group responds with insults of the same kind ("you analytic pricks!") and the situation would no doubt have degenerated had not a man in his sixties intervened to separate them, shouting (in French, surprisingly): "Calm down, you lunatics!" As if to impress her with his grasp of the situation, one of Kristeva's young admirers then whispers to her: "That's Paul de Man. He's French, isn't he?" Kristeva replies: "No, he's Belgian."

Under his tree, the bush-man mutters: "The sound shape of language . . ."

The one-woman protest march screams at the top of her lungs, as if she were supporting one of the two teams: "We don't need Derrida, we have Jimi Hendrix!"

Distracted by Cruella Redgrave's disconcerting slogan, Paul de Man does not hear the man approach him from behind until a voice says: "Turn around, man. And face your enemy." A guy in a tweed suit is standing there, his jacket too big for his skinny body, the sleeves too short for his long arms, his hair side-parted with a lock of hair hanging over his forehead; he looks like a supporting actor in a Sydney Pollack film, except for his eyes, which are so piercing you feel as if they are x-raying you.

This is John Searle.

The bush-man observes Kristeva as she observes the scene. Attentive, concentrated, Kristeva lets her cigarette burn down to her fingertips. The bush-man's eyes move from Searle to Kristeva, and from Kristeva to Searle.

Paul de Man tries to appear simultaneously ironic and conciliatory, and he is only half-convincing in this role of a man at ease. "Peace, my friend!" he says. "Put your sword down and help me separate those kids." Which, for reasons unknown, serves to annoy Searle, who advances toward Paul de Man. Everyone thinks that he is about to hit him. Kristeva squeezes one young man's arm, and he takes advantage of the situation to hold her hand. Paul de Man remains immobile, paralyzed, fascinated by the menacing body coming toward him and the idea of a fist's impact, but when he moves to protect himself or—who knows?—maybe even attack, a third voice rings out, its falsely jovial intonation barely concealing a faintly hysterical anxiety: "Dear Paul! Dear John! Welcome to Cornell! I'm so glad you could come!"

This is Jonathan Culler, the young researcher who has organized the conference. He rushes over to hold out his hand to Searle, who shakes it with bad grace; his hand is limp and his expression malicious as he stares at Paul de Man. In French, he says to the Belgian: "Take your Derrida boys and piss off. Now." Paul de Man leads the little group away, and the incident is over. The young man hugs Kristeva as if they'd escaped from great danger, or at least as if they'd lived through a moment of great intensity together, and perhaps Kristeva feels something similar—in any case, she doesn't push him away.

The sound of a car engine roars through the dusk. A Lotus Esprit comes to a sudden halt with a screech of tires. A spry man in his forties gets out, cigar between his lips, bucket hat on his head, silk pocket handkerchief, and heads straight for Kristeva. "Hey, chica!" He kisses her hand. She turns to her young admirers and points at the newcomer: "Boys, allow me to introduce Morris Zapp, a specialist in structuralism, poststructuralism, New Criticism, and lots of other things."

Morris Zapp smiles and adds, in a tone sufficiently detached that one does not immediately suspect him of vanity (but in French, all the same): "The first professor in the world with a six-figure salary!"

The young men say "Wow" as they smoke their joint.

Kristeva laughs her clear laugh and asks: "Have you prepared your presentation on Volvos?"

Morris Zapp puts on an apologetic tone: "You know . . . I don't think the world is ready." He glances over at Searle and Culler, who are talking together on the lawn. He doesn't hear Searle explain to Culler that all the speakers at the conference are crap except for him and Chomsky, but he decides not to go over and say hello to them anyway, and tells Kristeva: "Well, I'll see you later. I have to check in at the Hilton."

"You're not sleeping on campus?"

"What? My God, certainly not!"

Kristeva laughs. And yet Telluride House, which is where all Cornell's visiting speakers are put up, has an impeccable reputation. In some people's eyes, Morris Zapp has elevated the academic career to the ranks of the fine arts. Watching him get back in his Lotus, rev the engine, almost crash into the bus from New York, and tear off up the hill at top speed, she thinks that those people are not wrong.

Then she spots Simon Herzog and Superintendent Bayard getting off the bus, and her face falls.

She pays no further attention to the bush-man, still watching her from under his tree, but he in turn does not notice that he is being watched by a skinny young North African man. The old man with the receding hairline wears a pinstriped suit in thick cloth that looks like it belongs in a Kafka novel, and a woolen tie. He mumbles something under his tree. No one hears it, but even if they had, very few would understand it because it's in Russian. The young Arab puts his Walkman headphones back over his ears. Kristeva walks along the grass, looking up at the stars. After five hours on the bus, Bayard has succeeded in doing only one side of the Rubik's Cube. Simon stands there, amazed by the beauty of the campus, and can't help thinking about Vincennes, which in comparison is a total dump.

60

"In the beginning, there was philosophy and science and until the eighteenth century they walked hand in hand, basically so they could fight against the Church's obscurantism, and then, gradually, from the nineteenth century on, with Romanticism and all that stuff, they started to get into the spirit of the Enlightenment, and philosophers in Germany and France (but not in England) started saying: science cannot penetrate the secret of life; science cannot penetrate the secret of the human soul; only philosophy can do that. And suddenly, continental philosophy was not only hostile to science but also to its principles: clarity, intellectual rigor, the culture of proof. It became increasingly esoteric, increasingly freestyle, increasingly spiritualist (except for the Marxists), increasingly vitalist (with Bergson, for example).

"And all this culminated in Heidegger: a reactionary philosopher, in the full meaning of the term, who decided that philosophy had been heading the wrong way for centuries and that it had to return to the primordial question, which is the question of Being, so he wrote *Being and Time*, where he says he's going to search for Being. Except he never found it, ha ha, but anyway. So it was he who really inspired this fashion for nebulous philosophers full of complicated neologisms, convoluted reasoning, dubious analogies, and risky metaphors, leading to Derrida, who's the heir to all that stuff now.

"Meanwhile the English and the Americans stayed faithful to a more scientific idea of philosophy. This is called analytic philosophy, and Searle is the leader of that movement."

[Anonymous student, interviewed on campus.]

61

Let's be honest: the food is excellent in the United States, and especially so at the cafeteria in Cornell reserved for the professors, which even if it's self-service is more like a restaurant in terms of culinary quality.

It is lunchtime, and most of the conference's speakers are scattered through the refectory in a geopolitical pattern that Bayard and Simon have not yet figured out. The room consists of tables that can seat six to eight, none of them fully occupied. But—Simon and Bayard can scent this in the air—there are clearly various camps.

"I wish I could get a rundown on the different forces here," says Bayard to Simon, choosing a double rib steak with mashed potato, plantains, and *boudin blanc*. The black chef, who overheard him, responds in French: "You see the table near the door? That's where the analytics sit. They're in enemy territory, and they're outnumbered, so they're sticking together." There is Searle, Chomsky, and Cruella Redgrave, whose real name is Camille Paglia, a specialist in the history of sexuality and a direct rival of Foucault, whom she detests with all her being. "On the other side, near the window, there's a *belle brochette*, as you say in France: Lyotard, Guattari, Cixous, and Foucault in the middle—you know him, of course, the tall bald guy who's talking, right? Kristeva is over there, with Morris Zapp and Sylvère Lotringer, the boss of the magazine *Sémiotext(e)*. In the corner, on his own, the old guy with the wool tie and the weird hair, I don't know who that is. [Strange-looking man, thinks Bayard.] And the young lady with the violet hair behind him? I don't know her, either." His Puerto Rican sous-chef glances over and remarks tonelessly: "Probably Heideggerians."

A professional reflex rather than any genuine interest prompts Bayard to ask how serious the rivalries between the professors are. In reply, the black chef just points at Chomsky's table, where a young, mousy man is passing. Searle calls out to him:

"Hey, Jeffrey, you need to translate that asshole's latest piece of crap for me."

"Hey, John, I'm not your bitch. Do it yourself, okay?"

"Fine, dickhead. My French is good enough for that shit."

The black chef and his Puerto Rican assistant burst out laughing and high-five each other. Bayard didn't understand the dialogue, but he gets the idea. Behind him in the line, an impatient voice grumbles: "Can you move along, please?" Simon and Bayard recognize the young Arab who was on the plane with Foucault. He is holding a tray of chicken curry, purple potatoes, hardboiled eggs, and celery purée, but he does not have official accreditation so is held back at the checkout. Foucault, seeing this, starts to intervene, but Slimane signals that everything is fine, and after brief negotiations he is allowed through with his tray.

Bayard sits down next to Simon at the solitary old man's table.

Then he sees Derrida arrive, recognizing him in spite of never having seen him before: head pulled into his shoulders, square-jawed, thin-lipped, eagle-nosed, wearing a corduroy suit, the top buttons of his shirt undone, silver hair springing up from his head like flames. He helps himself to couscous and red wine. He is accompanied by Paul de Man. The people at Searle's table stop speaking, and so does Foucault. Cixous gestures to him but he doesn't see her: his eyes have immediately sought and found Searle. A moment's indecision, his meal tray in hand, then he goes over to join his friends. Cixous kisses him on both cheeks, Guattari pats him on the back, Foucault shakes his hand while looking surly (the consequence of an old article by Derrida, "Cogito and the History of Madness," in which, roughly speaking, he suggested that Foucault had completely misunderstood Descartes). The young woman with violet hair also goes over to say hello: her name is Avital Ronell, she is a Goethe specialist and a great admirer of deconstruction.

Bayard observes the body language and facial expressions. He eats his *boudin* in silence while Simon talks about the program of events that lies on the table between them: "Have you seen? There's a symposium on Jakobson. Shall we go?"

Bayard lights a cigarette. He almost feels like saying yes.

62

"The analytic philosophers are real drudges. They're Guillermo Vilas, you know? They're so boring. They spend hours defining their terms. For each argument, they never fail to write the premise, and then the premise of the premise, and so on. They're fucking logicians. Essentially, they take twenty pages to explain stuff that could easily be summarized in ten lines. Weirdly, they often make exactly that criticism of the continentals, while also having a go at them for their unbridled whimsy, for not being rigorous, for not defining their terms, for writing literature rather than philosophy, for lacking the crucial mathematical spirit, for being poets, basically, guys who aren't serious, who are like crazy mystics (even though they're all atheists, ha!). But anyway, the continentals are more like McEnroe. At least they're never boring."

[Anonymous student, interviewed on campus.]

63

Simon is generally considered to have a reasonably good grasp of English, but oddly, what is considered reasonable in France, in terms of mastery of a foreign language, always seems to prove woefully inadequate in reality.

So Simon understands only about one word in three of Morris Zapp's speech. In his defense, it has to be said that the subject—deconstruction—is not one he's very familiar with, and involves some difficult, or at least obscure, concepts. But still, he was hoping to find it enlightening.

Bayard did not go with him, and Simon is pleased: he would have been unbearable.

Given that the content of the speech largely escapes him, he seeks meaning elsewhere: in Morris Zapp's ironic inflections, in the audience's knowing laughter (each member wishing to seal his rightful sense of belonging to the here-and-now of this

amphitheater—"another amphitheater," thinks Simon, succumb-
ing to an unhealthy structuralist-paranoiac reflex to search for
recurrent *motifs*), in the questions of the listeners, which are never
really about the matter at hand but rather attempts if not to
challenge the master, at least to position the questioner, in relation to the other listeners, as a serious thinker blessed with acute
critical faculties and superior intellectual capacities (in a word, to
distinguish the questioner, as Bourdieu would say). From the
tone of each question, Simon can guess the asker's situation: undergrad, postgrad, professor, specialist, rival . . . He can easily
detect the bores, the wallflowers, the asslickers, the snobs, and—
most numerous of all—those who forget to ask their question,
so busy are they reeling off their interminable monologues, in-
toxicated by the sound of their own voices, driven by that imperious need to offer their opinion. Clearly, something existential
is going on in this puppet theater.

But finally he does seize upon a passage that holds his attention: "The root of critical error is a naïve confusion of literature
with life." This intrigues him, so he asks his neighbor, an Englishman in his forties, if he might be able to provide a sort of simultaneous translation, or at least summarize what's being said, and
as the Englishman, like half the campus and three-quarters
of those at the conference, has very good French, he explains to
Simon that according to Morris Zapp's theory there is, at the
source of literary criticism, an original methodological error of
confusing life with literature (Simon redoubles his attention)
whereas it is not the same thing, it does not *function* in the same
way. "Life is transparent, literature opaque," the Englishman
tells him. (That's arguable, thinks Simon.) "Life is an open system, literature a closed system. Life is made of things, literature
of words. Life is what it seems to be: when you are afraid of flying,
it is a question of fear. When you try to date a girl, it is a question
of sex. But in *Hamlet*, even the most stupid critic realizes that it is
not about a man who wants to kill his uncle—it is about something else."

This reassures Simon slightly, as he doesn't have the faintest idea what his adventures could be *about*.

Apart from language, obviously. Ahem.

Morris Zapp continues his speech in an increasingly Derridean mode; now he affirms that understanding a message involves decoding it, because language is a code. And "all decoding is a new encoding." So, broadly speaking, we can never be sure of anything, because no one can be sure that he is using words in exactly the same sense as the person he is talking to (even when they are speaking the same language).

Sounds about right, thinks Simon.

And Morris Zapp employs this startling metaphor, translated by the Englishman: "Conversation is essentially a game of tennis played with a ball of modeling clay that changes shape each time it crosses the net."

Simon feels the earth deconstruct beneath his feet. He leaves the lecture smoking a cigarette, and bumps into Slimane.

The young Arab is waiting for the lecture to end so he can talk to Morris Zapp. Simon asks him what he wants to ask. Slimane replies that he is not in the habit of asking anyone anything.

64

"Yeah, well, obviously, the paradox is that so-called continental philosophy is now much more successful in the U.S. than it is in Europe. Here, Derrida, Deleuze, and Foucault are absolute stars on campus, while in France they're not studied by literature students and they're snubbed by philosophy students. Here, we study them in English. For English departments, French Theory was a revolutionary weapon that enabled them to go from being the fifth wheel of the social sciences to being the one discipline that subsumes all the others, because since French Theory is founded on the assumption that language is at the base of everything, then the study of language involves studying philosophy, sociology, psychology . . . That's the famous linguistic turn. Suddenly, the philosophers got upset, and they started working on language too—your Searles, your Chomskys, they spend a good part of their time denigrating the French, with demands for clarity ('what is clear in conception is clear in articulation') and demystifications, objections along the lines of 'nothing new under the sun, Condillac said it all already, Anaxagoras used to repeat the same thing, they all cribbed Nietzsche, et cetera.' They feel as if their thunder's being stolen by clowns, buffoons, and charlatans. It's to be expected that they're angry about it. But you have to admit, Foucault is a lot sexier than Chomsky."

[Anonymous student, interviewed on campus.]

65

It's late. The day has been punctuated with seminars. The public has come out in force and listened attentively. Now, briefly, the excitement on campus dies down again. Here and there the laughter of drunken students can be heard in the night.

Slimane is alone, lying in the room he shares with Foucault, listening to his Walkman, when there is a knock at the door. "Sir? There's a phone call for you."

Slimane ventures out carefully into the corridor. He has already received some initial offers; maybe a potential buyer wants to raise his bid? He picks up the receiver from the telephone on the wall.

It's Foucault on the line, in a panic. He struggles to say: "Come and get me. It's starting again. *I've lost my English.*"

How Foucault has managed to find a gay club—S&M into the bargain—in this godforsaken hole, Slimane has no idea. He gets in a taxi and is driven to an establishment named the White Sink, located in the suburbs near the lower part of town. The clientele wear leather trousers and Village People baseball caps. To Slimane, the atmosphere seems fairly pleasant at first.

A bodybuilder with a riding crop offers to buy him a drink, but he declines politely and goes off to inspect the back rooms. He finds Foucault on LSD (Slimane recognizes the symptoms immediately), crouching on the floor—half-naked, with wide red welts on his body, in a total daze—in the middle of three or four Americans who seem to be questioning him anxiously. All he can do is repeat, in French: "I've lost my English! No one understands me! Get me out of here!"

The taxi driver refuses to take Foucault, either because he's afraid he will throw up on his seats or because he hates queers, so Slimane holds him up, supporting him under the shoulders, and they walk back to the campus hotel.

Ithaca is a small city of 30,000 inhabitants (a figure doubled by the students on campus), but it is very spread out. They have to trek a long way through the deserted streets, past endless rows of more or less identical wooden houses, each with its sofa or rocking chair on the porch, a few empty beer bottles on low tables, overflowing ashtrays. (Americans still smoke in 1980.) Every hundred yards there is a wooden church. The two men cross several streams. Foucault sees squirrels everywhere.

A police car slows down next to them. Slimane can make out the cops' suspicious faces behind the torchlight that shines in his eyes. He says something in French, sounding cheerful. Foucault makes a gurgling noise. Slimane knows that to a trained eye the man leaning on him does not look merely drunk but completely high. He just hopes that Foucault has no LSD on him. The policemen hesitate. Then drive away without taking any further action.

Finally they arrive downtown. Slimane buys Foucault a waffle in a diner run by Mormons. Foucault yells out: "Fuck Reagan!"

It takes them an hour or more to climb up the hill. Thankfully Slimane has the idea of cutting through the cemetery. During the walk, Foucault repeats: "A nice club sandwich with a Coke . . ."

In the hotel corridors Foucault has a panic attack because he saw *The Shining* just before he left France. Slimane tucks him in. Foucault demands a good-night kiss, and falls asleep dreaming of Greco-Roman wrestlers.

66

"I'm not saying this because I'm Iranian, but Foucault talks a load of crap. Chomsky is right."

[Anonymous student, interviewed on campus.]

67

Simon makes friends with a young Jewish feminist lesbian, coming out of Cixous's conference on women's writing. Her name is Judith, her family is from Hungary, she is doing a PhD in philosophy, and it so happens that she is interested in the performative function of language and suspects the patriarchal powers that be of resorting to some sneaky form of the performative in order to naturalize the cultural construction that is the model of the heteronormative monogamous couple: in plain English, according to Judith, all it takes is for the white heterosexual male to declare that something *is* in order for it *to be*.

Performative utterances are not restricted to knighting people; they also encompass the rhetorical ruse of transforming the result of an age-old balance of power.

And above all: "natural." Yes, nature—that's the enemy. The reactionaries' argumentative *coup de grâce* "against nature," the vaguely modernized variation on what used to be known as "against God's will." (Even in the USA, God is a little tired by 1980, but the forces of reaction are stronger than ever.)

Judith: "Nature is pain, sickness, cruelty, barbarism, and death. *Nature is murder.*" She laughs, parodying the pro-lifers' slogan.

Simon agrees in his own way: "Baudelaire hated nature."

She has a squarish face, a neat student haircut, and the look of a teacher's pet from Sciences Po, except that she is a radical feminist who is not far from thinking, like Monique Wittig, that a lesbian is not a woman, since a woman is defined as the *supplement* of a man, to whom she is, *by definition*, subject. In a sense, the myth of Adam and Eve is the original performative function: from the moment it was decreed that the woman came after the man, that she was created from the man's rib, and that she committed the sin of biting into the apple, that it was all her fault, the slut, and that she fully deserved to give birth in terrible pain, she was, basically, screwed. What next? Would she refuse to look after the kids?

Bayard arrives: he missed the Cixous seminar, preferring to go to see the ice hockey team train so he could, he says, drink in the campus atmosphere. He is holding a half-empty beer and a packet of chips. Judith looks at Bayard with curiosity but, contrary to what Simon might have expected, without any apparent animosity.

"Lesbians aren't women, and they screw you and your phallogocentrism." Judith laughs. Simon laughs with her. Bayard asks: "What's all this about?"

68

"Take off those black glasses. You can see perfectly well that it's not sunny. The weather is foul."

In spite of his reputation, Foucault is pretty groggy after his exploits last night. He dips a huge pecan cookie in a remarkably drinkable double espresso. Slimane sits with him, eating a bacon cheeseburger with blue cheese.

The restaurant is at the top of the hill, at the campus entrance, on the other side of the gorge spanned by a bridge where depressed students commit suicide from time to time. They are not really sure if they're in a bar or a tearoom. To find out, the ever-curious Foucault orders a beer despite his throbbing head, but Slimane cancels it. The waitress, probably used to the caprices of visiting professors and other campus stars, shrugs and turns on her heel, reciting mechanically: "No problem, guys. Let me know if you need anything, okay? I'm Candy, by the way." Foucault mutters: "Hello, Candy. You're so sweet." The waitress does not catch this, which is probably *for the best*, thinks Foucault, noting in passing that his English has returned.

He feels something touch his shoulder. He looks up and, from behind his glasses, recognizes Kristeva. She is holding a steaming paper cup the size of a thermos flask. "How are you, Michel? It's been a long time." Foucault composes himself instantly. After rearranging his features, he takes off his glasses and offers Kristeva his famous toothy smile. "Julia, you look radiant." As if they saw each other just the night before, he asks her: "What are you drinking?"

Kristeva laughs: "Some godawful tea. The Americans have no idea how to make tea. Once you've been in China, you know . . ."

In order to conceal even a hint of the state he's in, Foucault says quickly: "How did your conference go? I wasn't able to make it."

"Oh, you know . . . nothing revolutionary." She pauses. Foucault hears his stomach rumble. "I keep the revolutions for special occasions."

Foucault pretends to laugh, then excuses himself. "The coffee here makes me want to piss." He gets up and walks as calmly as possible toward the toilets, where liquid will gush from every orifice.

Kristeva takes his seat. Slimane looks at her but does not say a word. She noticed Foucault's paleness, and she knows he won't return from the bathroom until he thinks he can fool her about his physical state, so she guesses she has two or three minutes to play with.

"I am told that you have in your possession something that may find a buyer here."

"You must be mistaken, madame."

"On the contrary, I think it is you who is about to make a mistake. A mistake that would be regrettable, for everyone."

"I don't understand what you're talking about, madame."

"Nevertheless, I am prepared to purchase it myself, for a substantial compensation, but what I want, more than anything, is a guarantee."

"What sort of guarantee, madame?"

"The assurance that no one else will benefit from this acquisition."

"And how do you imagine you will obtain this guarantee, madame?"

"That's for you to say, Slimane."

Slimane notes the use of his first name.

"Listen to me carefully, you stupid bitch. This isn't Paris, and your two lapdogs aren't with you now. Talk to me again and I'll bleed you like a pig and throw your body in the lake."

Foucault returns from the toilets. He has obviously splashed water on his face, but his bearing is impeccable. The illusion would be perfect, thinks Kristeva, were it not for a waxy look in his eyes. You would swear he was ready to give a talk—and in fact that is exactly what he is going to do, just as long as he can remember what time his lecture is supposed to take place.

Kristeva excuses herself as she gives him back his seat. "It was a pleasure to meet you, Slimane." She doesn't offer him her hand because she knows he won't take it. He won't drink from bottles that have already been opened. He will not use the salt cellar on the table. He will avoid all physical contact of any kind whatsoever. He's deeply suspicious, that one, and he's right to be. Without Nikolai, things are going to be a bit more complicated. But nothing, she thinks, that she can't deal with.

69

"Deconstructing a speech consists in showing how it undermines the philosophy to which it lays claim, or the hierarchy of oppositions to which it appeals, by identifying within the text the rhetorical operations that confer on its contents a presumed foundation, its key idea or premise."

[Jonathan Culler, organizer of the conference Shift into Overdrive in the Linguistic Turn.]

70

"We are, so to speak, in the golden age of the philosophy of language."

Searle is making his speech, and all of American academia knows it is going to be an all-out attack on Derrida to avenge the honor of his master, Austin, whose reputation the American logician believes was seriously damaged by the French deconstructionist.

Simon and Bayard are in the room, but they don't understand anything, or not much anyway, because the talk is in English. It mentions "speech acts," and they get that part. Simon gets "illocutionary" and "perlocutionary." But what does "utterance" mean?

Derrida didn't come, but he has sent emissaries, who will report back on the speech's contents: his faithful lieutenant Paul de Man, his translator Gayatri Spivak, his friend Hélène Cixous . . . In truth, everyone is there, except for Foucault, who did not feel like leaving his room. Maybe he is relying on Slimane to give him a summary, or maybe he just doesn't care.

Bayard spots Kristeva, along with all the people he saw in the cafeteria, including the old man in the wool tie.

Searle repeats several times that it is not necessary to restate this or that, that he will not insult his esteemed audience by explaining such and such a point, that there is no need to dwell here on what is so blindingly obvious, etc.

In spite of this, Simon gathers that Searle thinks you must be really, really stupid to confound "iterability" with "permanence," written language with spoken language, a serious discourse with a fake discourse. Essentially, Searle's message is: *Fuck Derrida*.

Jeffrey Mehlman leans down to whisper into Morris Zapp's ear: "I had failed to note that the charmingly spiky Searle had the philosophical temperament of a cop." Zapp laughs. Students in the row behind shush him.

When the speech is over, a student asks a question: Does Searle think that the dispute between himself and Derrida (because, even though he took care not to name his adversary, everyone realizes the Frenchman was the subject and the target of his ire— murmurs of approval in the lecture hall) is emblematic of the confrontation between two great philosophical traditions (analytic and continental)?

Searle responds in tones of suppressed anger: "I think it would be a mistake to believe so. The confrontation never quite takes place." The understanding of Austin and his theory of speech acts by "some so-called continental philosophers" has been so confused, so approximate, so filled with errors and misinterpretations, "as I just demonstrated," that it is pointless to dwell on the subject any longer. And Searle adds, like a severe clergyman: "Stop wasting your time on those lunacies, young man. This is not the way serious philosophy works. Thank you for your attention."

Then, contemptuously ignoring the tumult in the lecture hall, he stands up and leaves.

But while the audience starts to scatter, Bayard spots Slimane walking after the philosopher. "Herzog, look! Seems like the Arab has some questions about the perlocutionary function . . ." Simon mechanically notes the latent racism and anti-intellectualism. But it has to be said, behind the petit-bourgeois reactionary sarcasm of Bayard's question, the cop does have a point: What exactly *does* Slimane want with Searle?

71

"'Let there be light.' And there was light."

[Dead Sea Scrolls, the second century B.C., the oldest occurrence of the performative function yet found in the Judeo-Christian world.]

72

Even as he presses the elevator button, Simon knows he is about to go up to heaven. The doors open at the floor for Romance Studies and Simon enters a labyrinth of floor-to-ceiling bookshelves lit by dull, flickering neon lamps. The sun never sets on Cornell's library, open twenty-four hours a day.

All the books Simon could desire are there, and all the others, too. He is like a kid in a candy store, and all he has to do if he wants to fill his pockets is complete a form. Simon's fingertips brush the books' spines as if he were caressing ears of wheat in a field that was about to become his property. This, he thinks, is true communism: what's yours is mine, and vice versa.

At this hour of the night, however, the library is in all likelihood deserted.

Simon strides along the Structuralism aisle. Look—a book about Japan by Lévi-Strauss?

He stops at the Surrealism aisle and thrills at the sight of such wonders: *Connaissance de la Mort* by Roger Vitrac . . . *Dark Spring* by Unica Zürn . . . *La Papesse du Diable*, attributed to Desnos . . . rare books by Crevel in French and English . . . unpublished works by Annie Le Brun and Radovan Ivsic . . .

A creak. Simon freezes. The sound of footsteps. Instinctively—because he feels as if his presence in the middle of the night in a university library must be, if not illegal, at least, as the Americans say, *inappropriate*—he hides behind the volumes on sex on the Surrealist Studies bookshelf.

He sees Searle walk past Tzara's collected letters.

He hears him talking to someone in an adjacent aisle. Simon delicately withdraws the folder containing twelve photocopied issues of *Révolution Surréaliste* to get a better view and, through the crack, recognizes Slimane's slender figure.

Searle is whispering too quietly, but Simon distinctly hears Slimane tell him: "You've got twenty-four hours. After that, I sell to the highest bidder." Then he puts his Walkman back on and returns toward the elevator.

But Searle does not walk back with him. He leafs distractedly through a few books. Who can say what he's thinking? Simon has a feeling of déjà-vu, but he drives it from his mind.

Trying to put *Révolution Surréaliste* back in its place, Simon accidentally knocks a copy of *Grand Jeu* to the floor. Searle pricks up his ears, like a pointer. Simon decides to slip away as discreetly as possible, and silently zigzags through the bookshelves as he hears the philosopher of language behind him picking *Grand Jeu* off the floor. He imagines him sniffing the magazine. Hearing footsteps, he quickens his pace. He crosses the Psychoanalysis aisle and enters the Nouveau Roman aisle, but this is a dead end. He turns around and jumps when he sees Searle moving toward him, a paper knife in one hand, *Grand Jeu* in the other. Automatically, he grabs a book to defend himself (*The Ravishing of Lol V. Stein*: he's not going to get far with that, he thinks, tossing it on the floor and grabbing another, *The Flanders Road*: yes, that's better); Searle does not raise his arm in a *Psycho* fashion, but Simon feels certain that he is going to have to protect his vital organs from the blade, when he hears the doors of the elevator open.

Nestled in their cul-de-sac, Simon and Searle see a young woman in boots and a man with a bull-like body pass them in the direction of the photocopier. Searle puts the paper knife in his pocket, Simon lowers his Claude Simon, and, moved by the same sense of curiosity, the two men observe the couple through the complete works of Nathalie Sarraute. They hear the photocopier's hum and see its blue light, but soon the bull-man wraps himself around the young woman as she leans against the machine. She lets loose an imperceptible sigh and, without looking at him, puts her hand on his crotch. (Simon thinks of Othello's handkerchief.) Her skin is very white and her fingers are very long. The bull-man unbuttons her dress and it falls to her feet. She is not wearing any undergarments, and her body is like a Raphael painting: her breasts are heavy, her waist slender, her hips wide, her shoulders sturdy, and her pussy shaved. Her black, square-cut hair gives her triangular face the look of a Carthaginian princess. Searle and Simon stare wide-eyed as she kneels down to take the bull-man's cock in her mouth. They want to see if the man's cock is bull-sized too. Simon puts down *The Flanders Road*. The bull picks up and flips over the young woman and thrusts inside her as she rears back, pulling apart her buttocks with her own hands as he holds her in place by the scruff of her neck. He does what it is in a bull's nature to do: he charges into her, first slowly and heavily, then with a growing ferocity, and they hear the photocopier banging against the wall until it is lifted from the floor and the girl emits a long yowl that echoes through the aisles of what they think is the deserted library.

Simon cannot tear his eyes from this Jupiterian coupling, and yet he must. But he has qualms about interrupting such a magnificent fucking session. With a violent effort of will, his sense of self-preservation forces him to knock all the Duras books from the shelf in front of him. They tumble to the floor with a noise that immobilizes everyone in the room. The carnal moans cease instantly. Simon looks Searle straight in the eye. He slowly walks around him, and the philosopher does not move a muscle. When he emerges into the central aisle, he turns toward the photocopier. The bull-man glares at him, prick in the air. The young woman carefully picks up her dress, while staring defiantly at Simon, and puts it over one leg, then the other, then turns her back to the bull-man so he can zip her up. Simon realizes that she never took her boots off. He flees down the emergency staircase.

Outside, on the campus lawn, he spots Kristeva's young friends, who to judge from the empty bottles and chip bags strewn over the grass around them have not moved in the past three days. At their invitation, he sits down with them, helps himself to a beer, and gratefully accepts the joint they hand him. Simon knows that he is out of danger (if there ever was any danger—is he sure he saw that paper knife?) but the fear in his chest has not subsided. There is something else.

In Bologna, he had sex with Bianca in a seventeenth-century amphitheater and narrowly escaped death in the bombed train station. Here, he has almost been stabbed in a library at night by a linguistics philosopher and has witnessed a decidedly mytho-logical doggy-style sex scene on a photocopier. He met Giscard in the Élysée Palace, bumped into Foucault in a gay sauna, took part in a car chase that ended with an attempt on his life, saw a man kill another man with a poisoned umbrella, discovered a secret society where people had their fingers cut off if they lost a debate, and crossed the Atlantic in pursuit of a mysterious docu-ment. In the course of a few months he has lived through more extraordinary events than he expected to witness in his entire lifetime . . . Simon knows how to spot the novelistic when he sees it. He thinks again about Umberto Eco's supernumeraries. He takes a drag on the joint.

"What's up, man?"

Simon passes around the joint. The film of the past few months flashes through his mind, and he is powerless to stop it. As it is his job, he analyzes it for its narrative structures, its additives, its adversaries, its allegorical significance. A sex scene (actor), an attack (bomb) in Bologna. An attack (paper knife), a sex scene (spectator) at Cornell. (Chiasmus.) A car chase. A rewriting of the final duel in *Hamlet*. The recurrent library motif (but why does he think of Beaubourg?) The pairs of characters: the two Bulgarians, the two Japanese, Sollers and Kristeva, Searle and Derrida, Anastasia and Bianca . . . And, most of all, the im-plausibilities: Why would the third Bulgarian wait until they realized there was a copy of the manuscript at Barthes's apartment before going there to search for it? How did Anastasia, supposedly a Russian spy, manage to be assigned so quickly to the hospital ward where Barthes was being kept? Why did Giscard not have Kristeva arrested and tortured by one of his henchmen until she talked, rather than sending him and Bayard to the USA to keep an eye on her? Why would the document be written in French, rather than Russian or English? Who translated it?

Simon takes his head in his hands and utters a groan.

"I think I'm trapped in a fucking novel," he says.

"What?"

"I think I'm trapped in a novel."

The student he says this to lies back, blows cigarette smoke toward the sky, watches the stars speed past in the ether, drinks a mouthful of beer from the bottle, leans on one elbow, lets a long silence linger in the American night, and says: "Sounds cool, man. Enjoy the trip."

73

"And so the paranoiac participates in this powerlessness of the deterritorialized sign that assails him from all sides in the slippery atmosphere, but in his majestic feeling of anger he accedes all the more to the overarching power of the signifier as the master of the network that spreads through the atmosphere."

[Guattari, spoken at the Cornell conference, 1980.]

74

"Come on, hurry up, it's time for the talk on Jakobson."

"Nah, it's okay, I've had my fill."

"You're fucking kidding? That's really annoying—you told

me you'd go. There'll be lots of people there. We'll learn stuff . . .
Put that Rubik's Cube down!"

Click click. Bayard nonchalantly twists and turns the multicolored rows. He has almost completed two of the six faces.

"All right, but Derrida's on later, we mustn't miss that."

"Why not? What makes that knob any more interesting than
the others?"

"He's one of the most interesting thinkers *in the world*. But
that's not the point, you moron. He's seriously embroiled with
Searle in a row over Austin's theory."

Click click.

"Austin's theory is the performative function, remember?
The illocutionary and the perlocutionary. Saying is doing? How
to do stuff by talking? How to make people do stuff simply
by talking to them? For example, if I had stronger perlocutionary powers, or if you were less of an idiot, all I'd have to say is
'Derrida conference' and you'd jump up straight away and we'd
already have our places booked. It's obvious that if the seventh
function is anywhere around here, Derrida won't be far away."

"Why is everyone looking for Jakobson's seventh function if
Austin's functions are freely available?"

"Austin's work is purely descriptive. It explains how it works,
but not what to do to make it work. Austin describes the mecha-
nisms in operation when you make a promise or a threat or when
you address someone with the intention of making them act in
one way or another, but he doesn't tell you how to make your
listener believe you and take you seriously or act how you want
him to. He just notes that a speech act can succeed or fail, and he
sets out certain conditions for success: for example, in France,
you must be mayor or deputy mayor for the phrase 'I now pronounce you husband and wife' to function. (But that is for pure
performative utterances.) He doesn't tell you how to succeed for
sure. It's not a user manual, it's just an analysis—you understand
the subtle difference?"

Click click.

"And Jakobson's work isn't just descriptive?"

"Well, yeah, it is, actually, but this seventh function . . . we'd have to assume it's not."

Click click.

"Fuck, it's not working."

Bayard cannot quite finish off the second face.

He feels Simon's accusing gaze on him.

"All right. What time is it on?"

"Don't be late!"

Click click. Bayard changes his strategy and, instead of trying to complete a second face, attempts to build a crown around the first face. While he manipulates his cube with growing dexterity, he thinks that he has not really grasped the difference between the illocutionary and the perlocutionary.

Simon is on his way to the conference on Jakobson, which he is excited to attend, with or without Bayard, but as he is crossing the campus lawn, he's arrested by a burst of throaty but crystal-clear laughter, and when he turns around he spots the young woman from the photocopier. The Carthaginian princess in leather boots, now fully clothed. She is chatting to a small Asian girl and a tall Egyptian girl (or maybe she's Lebanese, thinks Simon, who instinctively noted her Arab features and the little cross hanging from her neck; maybe a Maronite, but more likely a Copt, in his opinion). (What clue is he basing this assessment on? It's a mystery.)

The three young women head cheerfully toward the upper town.

Simon decides to follow them.

They pass a science building where the brain of the serial killer and supposed genius Edward Rulloff is preserved in formaldehyde.

They pass the hotel-management school, with its pleasant odor of baking bread.

They pass the veterinary school. Concentrating fully on following the girls, Simon does not see Searle entering the building with a large bag of dog biscuits. Or perhaps he does see him without bothering to decode this information.

They pass the Romance Studies building.

They cross the bridge over the gorge that separates campus from town.

They sit at a table in a bar named after the serial killer. Simon discreetly takes a seat at the bar.

He hears the princess in boots say to her friends: "Jealousy doesn't interest me, and competition even less . . . I'm tired of men who are afraid of what they want . . ."

Simon lights a cigarette.

"I always say that I don't love Borges . . . But to what extent, at every moment, I shoot myself in the foot . . ."

He orders a beer and opens the *Ithaca Journal*.

"I'm not afraid to say that I'm made for powerful physical love."

The three young women burst out laughing.

The conversation moves on to the mythological and sexist reading of the constellations and to the way Greek heroines are perpetually sidelined (Simon checks them off in his head: Ariadne, Phaedra, Penelope, Hera, Circe, Europa . . .).

So he, too, ends up missing the conference on Jakobson's living structures, because he preferred to spy on a black-haired young woman eating a hamburger with two friends.

75

There is electricity in the air. Everyone is there: Kristeva, Zapp, Foucault, Slimane, Searle. The lecture hall is packed, overflowing; it's impossible to move without standing on a student's or a professor's toes. There's a loud murmur among the audience, as at the theater, and the master arrives: Derrida, onstage, it's happening now.

He smiles at Cixous in the front row, makes a brief sign of

friendship to his translator Gayatri Spivak, spots his friends and his enemies. Spots Searle.

Simon is there, with Bayard. They are sitting next to Judith, the young lesbian feminist.

"The word of reconciliation is the speech act through which by speaking a word we make a start, we offer reconciliation by addressing the other person; which means that, at least before this word, there was war, suffering, trauma, a wound . . ."

Simon spots the Carthaginian princess, which has the immediate effect of muddling his powers of concentration, so much so that he does not manage to decode the subtext of Derrida's opening words, which suggest he is going to be placatory.

And in fact, Derrida comes calmly and methodically to Austin's theory, developing some objections to it, in strictly academic terms and in what appears to be the most objective manner possible.

The theory of speech acts, which posits that the word is *also* an act—in other words that the speaker acts at the same time as he speaks—implies a presupposition that Derrida disputes: intentionality. Namely: that the speaker's intentions preexist his speech and are perfectly clear to him as well as to his receiver (assuming that the receiver is clearly identified).

If I say, "It's late," it is because I want to go home. But what if I actually wanted to stay? If I wanted the other person to keep me there? To prevent me from leaving? If I wanted the other person to reassure me by saying: "No, it's not that late."

When I write, do I really know what I want to write? Isn't it the case that the text reveals itself as it is formulated? (Does it ever really reveal itself?)

And when I do know what I want to say, does my receiver receive it exactly as I think it (as I think I thought it)? Does what he understands of what I say correspond exactly to what I think I wanted to tell him?

It's clear that these opening remarks deal a serious blow to the theory of speech acts. These modest objections make it perilous to evaluate the illocutionary (and especially the perlocutionary) power in terms of success or failure, as Austin does (in lieu of truth or falsehood, as the philological tradition has done until now).

Hearing me say "It's late," my receivers believed that I wanted to go home and they offer to accompany me. Success? But what if, in fact, I wanted to stay? If someone or something deep inside me wanted to stay, without me even being aware of it?

"In fact, in what sense does Reagan claim to be Reagan, president of the United States? Who will ever know him, strictly speaking? Him?"

The audience laughs. Everyone is at maximum attentiveness. They have forgotten the *context*.

It is now that Derrida chooses to strike.

"But what would happen if in promising 'Sarl' to criticize him I went beyond what his Unconscious desires, for reasons we'll analyze, and do everything I can to provoke him? Would my 'promise' be a promise or a threat?"

In a whisper, Bayard asks Judith why Derrida pronounces it "Sarl." Judith explains that he is mocking Searle: in French, as far as she understands, "Sarl" signifies "Société à responsabilité limitée," a private limited company. Bayard thinks this is quite funny.

Derrida goes on:

"What is the unity or identity of the speaker? Is he responsible for speech acts dictated to him by his unconscious? Because I have mine, too, which might want to give pleasure to Sarl inasmuch as he wants to be criticized, or cause him pain by not criticizing him, or give him pleasure by not criticizing him, or cause him pain by criticizing him, to promise him a threat or to threaten him with a promise, or offer myself up for criticism by taking pleasure in saying things that are obviously false, enjoying my weakness or loving exhibitionism more than anything, et cetera."

The whole audience turns toward Searle, of course, who, as

if he had anticipated this moment, is sitting in the exact center of the tiered seating. The lone man in the middle of the crowd: it's like a scene from Hitchcock. His face remains impassive under this barrage of scrutiny. He looks like he's been killed and stuffed.

And besides, when I make phrases, is it really me who is speaking? How can anyone ever say anything original, personal, *unique to him*, when by definition language obliges us to draw from a well of preexisting words? When we are influenced by so many external forces: our times, the books we read, our sociocultural determinisms, our linguistic "tics" so precious that they form our identity, the speeches we are constantly bombarded with in every possible and imaginable form.

Who has never caught a friend, a parent, a colleague or a father-in-law repeating an argument they have read in a newspaper or heard on the television almost word for word, as if he were speaking for himself, as if he had *appropriated* that speech, as if he were the source of those thoughts rather than a sponge for them, rehashing the same formulas, the same rhetoric, the same presuppositions, the same indignant inflections, the same knowing tone, as if he were not simply the medium through which a newspaper's prerecorded voice repeated the words of a politician who himself had read them in a book whose author, and so on . . . the medium through which the nomadic, sourceless voice of a ghostly speaker expresses itself, communicates, in the sense of two places communicating via a *passage*.

Repeating what he has read in a newspaper . . . to what extent can the conversation with your father-in-law be considered a *citation*?

Derrida has returned seamlessly to the central thread of his argument. Now he touches on his other principal argument: citationality, or rather, iterability. (Simon is not sure he's really grasped the distinction.)

To be *understood*, at least partially, by our receiver, we must use the same language. We must *repeat* (*reiterate*) words that have already been used, otherwise our receiver will not be able to understand them. So we are always, fatally, in some form of citation. We use the words of others. Now, as with Chinese whispers, it is more than probable—it is inevitable—that through repetitions each and every one of us will employ the words of others, in a slightly different sense to those others.

Derrida's *pied-noir* voice becomes more formal and bombastic:

"Even that which will ensure the functioning of the mark (psychic, oral, graphic, whatever) beyond this moment, namely the possibility of being repeated, even that begins, divides, expropriates the fullness or the intrinsically 'ideal' presence of intention, of the desire to express, and *a fortiori* the harmony between meaning and saying."

Judith, Simon, the young black-haired woman, Cixous, Guattari, Slimane, everyone in the lecture hall, even Bayard, is hanging on his every word when he says:

"Limiting even that which authorizes, transgressing the code or law that it constitutes, iterability irreducibly inscribes alteration in the repetition."

And he adds, imperiously:

"The accident is never an accident."

76

"Even in what Sarl calls 'real life,' the possibility of parasitic contamination is already there—that 'real life' of which he is so assured, with a confidence that is almost, not quite, inimitable, of knowing what it is, where it begins and where it ends; as if the meaning of those words ('real life') could immediately create unanimity, without the slightest risk of parasitical contamination, as if literature, theater, lying, infidelity, hypocrisy, infelicity, parasitical contamination, the simulation of real life did not form part of real life!"

[Words spoken by Derrida at the Cornell conference, 1980, or dreamed by Simon Herzog.]

77

They are bent over like slaves in antiquity pushing blocks of stone, but these are students puffing and panting as they roll barrels of beer across the floor. It is going to be a long evening and they will need reserves. The Seal and Serpent Society is an old fraternity founded in 1905, one of the most prestigious and therefore, in American terminology, one of the most "popular." Lots of people are expected because we are celebrating the end of the conference tonight. All the guest speakers are invited and this is the last chance for the students to see the stars until their next visit. In the entrance to the fraternity's Victorian lodge, someone has written on a sheet: "Uncontrolled skid in the linguistic turn. Welcome." Though entry is theoretically reserved for undergrads, tonight the lodge is hosting people of all ages. Of course, this doesn't mean that it is open to just anyone: there are always those who come in and those who remain outside the door, in accordance with universal social and/or symbolic criteria.

Slimane is unlikely to forget this, being regularly refused entry in France, and it looks as though it's going to be the same old story here when a pair of students acting as bouncers bar his way. But, without anyone knowing how he does it, or in what language, he talks to them briefly and passes through, his Walkman around his neck, watched enviously by the outcasts in acrylic turtleneck sweaters.

The first person he sees, inside, is telling an audience of young people: "Heraclitus contains everything that is in Derrida and more." It's Cruella Redgrave alias Camille Paglia. She holds a mojito in one hand and in the other a cigarette holder, with a black cigarette exhaling a sweet perfume. Next to her Chomsky is talking with a student from El Salvador, who explains that the Revolutionary Democratic Front has just been decapitated by his country's paramilitaries and government forces. In fact, there is no remaining left-wing opposition, which seems to greatly worry Chomsky, who sucks nervously at a joint.

Perhaps because he is used to back rooms, Slimane goes down to look around in the basement, where Black Sabbath's "Die Young" is playing. He finds bunches of well-dressed and already drunk students, lap dancing haphazardly. Foucault is there too, in a black leather jacket, without his sunglasses (so he can taste the fog of life, thinks Slimane, who knows him well). He gives him a friendly wave and points to a student in a skirt who is entwined around a metal pole like a stripper. Slimane notes that she is not wearing a bra but is wearing white knickers that match her white Nike sneakers, each with a large red swoosh (like Starsky and Hutch's car, but with the colors reversed).

Kristeva, who is dancing with Paul de Man, spots Slimane. De Man asks her what she's thinking about. She replies: "We are in the catacombs of the first Christians." But her eyes do not leave the gigolo.

He looks as though he's searching for someone. He climbs upstairs. Bumps into Morris Zapp on the staircase, who winks at him. The stereo plays "Misunderstanding" by Genesis. He grabs a paper cup of tequila. Behind bedroom doors, he hears students fucking or vomiting. Some doors are open and inside the rooms he sees them smoking, drinking beers, sitting cross-legged on single beds, talking about sex, politics, literature. Behind one closed door he thinks he recognizes Searle's voice, and some strange growling noises.

In the large entrance hall, Simon and Bayard are talking to Judith, who sips a Bloody Mary through a straw. Bayard sees Slimane. Simon sees the Carthaginian princess, who comes in with her two friends, the short Asian girl and the tall Egyptian. A male student yells: "Cordelia!" The princess turns around. Hugs, kisses, effusive greetings. The student immediately trots off to fetch her a gin and tonic. Judith tells Bayard and Simon (who is not listening): "The power can be understood by considering the model of divine power, according to which making an utterance is equivalent to creating the utterance." Foucault comes up from the basement with Hélène Cixous, grabs a Malibu and

O.J., and disappears upstairs. Seeing this, Judith quotes Foucault: "Discourse is not life; its time is not our time." Bayard nods. Some boys gather around Cordelia and her friends, who seem very popular. Judith quotes Lacan, who said somewhere: "The name is the time of the object." Bayard wonders if one might as easily say "the time is the name of the object," or "the time is the object of the name," or maybe "the object is the name of the time," or even "the object is the time of the name," or simply "the name is the object of the time," but he grabs another beer, takes a hit of the joint that's being passed around, and nearly cries out: "But you already have the right to vote, get divorced, and have an abortion!" Cixous would like to talk to Derrida, but he is hemmed in by a dense mob of transfixed admirers. Slimane avoids Kristeva. Bayard asks Judith: "What do *you* want?" Cixous hears Bayard and joins the conversation: "Let's get a room!" Sylvère Lotringer, the founder of the magazine *Sémiotext(e)*, holds an orchid and talks to Derrida's translators Jeffrey Mehlman and Gayatri Spivak, who shouts: "Gramsci is my brother!" Slimane talks with Jean-François Lyotard about the economics of lust or a postmodern transaction. Pink Floyd sing: "Hey! Teacher! Leave them kids alone!"

Cixous tells Judith, Bayard, and Simon that the new history that's coming is beyond the male imagination, and for good reason, it will deprive them of their conceptual crutches and begin by ruining their illusion machine, but Simon is no longer listening. He observes Cordelia's group like a general sizing up the enemy army: six people, three boys and three girls. Approaching her would have been extremely difficult anyway, but in this grouping it now seems particularly inconceivable.

All the same, he starts to move toward them.

"White, physically attractive, with a skirt and fake jewelry, I employ all the codes of my sex and my age," he thinks, attempting to enter the girl's head. Passing close, he hears her say, in French, in a tone of perfectly erotic worldliness: "Couples are like birds, inseparable, abundant, uselessly beating their wings outside the cage." He detects no accent. An American says something to her in English that Simon doesn't understand. She replies, first in English (also accentless, as far as he can tell), then in French, throwing back her throat: "I've never been able to have affairs, only novels." Simon goes off to grab a drink, maybe two. (He hears Gayatri Spivak say to Slimane: "We were taught to say yes to the enemy.")

Bayard takes advantage of his absence to ask Judith to explain the difference between the illocutionary and the perlocutionary. Judith tells him that the illocutionary act of discourse is *itself the thing that it performs*, whereas the perlocutionary act provokes certain effects that are *not to be confused with* the act of discourse. "For example, if I ask you: 'Do you think there are any free rooms upstairs?,' the objective illocutionary reality contained in the question is that I'm hitting on you. *By* asking that question, I hit on you. But the perlocutionary stakes are played at another level: knowing that I am hitting on you, are you interested in my proposition? The *illocutionary* act will be performed with success if you understand my invitation. But the *perlocutionary* act will be fulfilled only if you follow me to a room. It's a subtle difference, isn't it? And it's not always stable, in fact."

Bayard stammers something incomprehensible, but the fact of his stammering indicates that he has understood. Cixous smiles her Sphinx-like smile and says: "So let's *perform*!" Bayard follows the two women, who pick up a six-pack and climb the stairs, where Chomsky and Camille Paglia are making out. In the corridor, they pass a Latin American student wearing a D&G-branded silk shirt, who Judith buys some little pills from. As he isn't aware of that particular brand, Bayard asks Judith what the initials stand for and Judith tells him it's not a brand but the initials of "Deleuze & Guattari." The same two letters feature on the pills.

Down below, an American guy tells Cordelia: "You are the muse!"

Cordelia pouts disdainfully, and Simon guesses she has

practiced this expression to show off her voluptuous lips: "That's not enough."

This is the moment Simon chooses to approach her, in front of all her friends, with the resolve of an Acapulco diver. Feigning a cool spontaneity, as if he just happened to be passing, he says that having overheard her remark he *couldn't help* responding: "Well, sure, who wants to be an object?" Silence. He reads in Cordelia's eyes: "Okay, now you have my attention." He knows he must not only show himself to be urbane and cultivated but must pique her curiosity, provoke her without shocking her, demonstrate his spirit in order to arouse hers, mix lightheartedness with profundity while avoiding pedantry and pretentiousness, indulge the comedy of social life but suggest that neither of them is fooled by it, and, naturally, immediately eroticize the relationship.

"You are made for powerful physical love and you love the iterability of photocopiers, right? A sublimated fantasy is nothing other than a fantasy fulfilled. Anyone who claims the opposite is a liar, a priest and an exploiter of the people." He hands her one of the two glasses he is holding. "You like gin and tonic?"

The stereo plays "Sexy Eyes" by Dr. Hook. Cordelia takes the glass.

She raises it for a toast and says: "We are lies of trust." Simon lifts his glass and drinks it almost in a single gulp. He knows he has passed the first test.

Instinctively, he scans the room and spots Slimane, leaning with one hand on the banister of the staircase, on the half-landing, surveying the crowd in the hall, making a V-for-victory sign with his free hand, then using both hands to draw a sort of cross, the hand forming the horizontal bar slightly above the midpoint of the vertical hand. Simon tries to make out who he is addressing the sign to, but all he can see are students and professors drinking and dancing and flirting to Kim Wilde's "Kids in America," and he senses that something is wrong, though he can't tell what. And the increasingly tight group forming around Derrida: it is him Slimane is looking at.

He does not see Kristeva or the old man with the bush hair and the wool tie, but they are there, all the same, and if he could see them, if they weren't hidden in different but equally concealed positions, he would see that both had their eyes fixed on Slimane and he would know that both had intercepted the sign Slimane was making with his hands and he would guess that both had guessed that the sign was addressed to Derrida, hidden, too, behind his admirers.

Nor does he see the man with the bull's neck who fucked Cordelia on the photocopier, but he is there too, staring at her with his bull's eyes.

He searches for Bayard in the crowd but doesn't find him, for the very good reason that Bayard is in a bedroom upstairs, beer in hand, unidentified chemical substance coursing through his veins, discussing pornography and feminism with his new friends.

He hears Cordelia say: "The Church, in the goodness of its heart, did at least ask the council of Mâcon in 585 if a woman had a soul . . . ," so to please her, he adds: ". . . and was very careful not to find a response."

The tall Egyptian girl quotes a line of Wordsworth whose provenance Simon does not manage to pinpoint. The short Asian girl explains to an Italian man from Brooklyn that she is writing her thesis on the queer in Racine.

Someone says: "Everyone knows that psychoanalysts don't even talk anymore, and they don't do much interpreting either."

Camille Paglia screams: "French go home! Lacan is a tyrant who must be driven from our shores."

Morris Zapp laughs and yells across the hall: "You're damn right, General Custer!"

Gayatri Spivak thinks: "You're not Aristotle's granddaughter, you know."

In the bedroom, Judith asks Bayard: "So where do you work, actually?" Bayard, taken by surprise, replies dumbly, immediately hoping that Cixous does not pick up on it: "I do research . . . at Vincennes." But Cixous, of course, raises an eyebrow, so he looks her in the eye and says: "In law." Cixous raises her other eyebrow. Not only has she never seen Bayard at Vincennes, but the university has no law department. To create a diversion, Bayard puts a hand under her blouse and squeezes a breast through her bra. Cixous suppresses a look of surprise but decides not to react, then Judith puts a hand on her other breast.

An undergrad named Donna has joined Cordelia's group, and the Carthaginian princess asks her: "How's Greek life so far?" In fact, Donna and her sorority sisters are planning to stage a bacchanal. Cordelia is excited and amused by the idea. Simon thinks that Slimane must have been arranging to meet Derrida. Maybe the sign he made was not a V for victory, but the time of the meeting. Two o'clock, but where? Had it been a church, Slimane would have made a standard sign of the cross, rather than that bizarre gesture. He asks: "Is there a cemetery nearby?" Young Donna claps her hands: "Oh yeah! That's a great idea! Let's go to the cemetery!" Simon is about to say that that was not what he meant, but Cordelia and her friends seem so thrilled by the proposal that in the end he says nothing.

Donna says she'll go and fetch the stuff. The stereo plays "Call Me" by Blondie.

It is already almost one o'clock.

He hears someone say: "The interpretative priest, the soothsayer, is one of the despot-god's bureaucrats, you see? Here's another aspect of the priest's treachery, damn it: the interpretation goes on forever and never finds anything to interpret that is not itself already an interpretation!" It's Guattari, clearly quite drunk, hitting on an innocent postgrad from Illinois.

He has to tell Bayard.

The stereo sends Debbie Harry's voice ricocheting from the walls: "When you're ready, we can share the wine."

Donna returns with a toiletry bag and says they can go now.

Simon rushes upstairs to tell Bayard to meet them at the cemetery at two o'clock. He opens all the doors, finding all kinds of stoned students, some more active than others. He finds

Foucault jerking off in front of a poster of Mick Jagger, finds Andy Warhol writing poems (in fact, it's Jonathan Culler filling out pay stubs), finds a greenhouse with marijuana plants growing up to the ceiling, even finds some well-behaved students watching baseball on a sports channel while they smoke crack, then finally locates Bayard.

"Oh? Sorry!"

He quickly closes the door, but he has time to see Bayard wedged between the legs of a woman he is unable to identify while Judith fucks him with a strap-on, yelling: "I am a man and I fuck you! Now you feel my performative, don't you?"

Impressed by this vision, he doesn't have the presence of mind to leave a message and rushes downstairs to join Cordelia's group.

He passes Kristeva on the stairs, but pays no attention to her.

He is well aware that he is not following the emergency protocol, but his attraction to Cordelia's white skin is too strong. After all, he'll be at the meeting place, he thinks, legitimizing a plan he knows full well is driven only by the logic of his desire.

Kristeva knocks on the door with the strange growling noises behind it. Searle opens it. She does not go in, but whispers something to him. Then she heads for the room she saw Bayard go into with his two friends.

The cemetery in Ithaca is on a wooded hillside, and the gravestones look as if they have been scattered randomly between the trees. The only sources of light are the moon and the city. The group gathers around the tomb of a woman who died very young. Donna explains that she is going to recite the secrets of the Sibyl, but that they must prepare the "birth ceremony of the new man," and that they need a volunteer. Cordelia volunteers Simon. He would like to ask for more details, but when she starts undressing him, he lets her do it. Around them, a dozen people have come to watch the spectacle, and this seems like a crowd to Simon. When he is completely naked, she lays him down in the grass, at the foot of the gravestone, and whispers in his ear: "Relax. We're going to kill the former man."

Everyone has been drinking, everyone is extremely disinhibited, so all this *could* happen *in reality*, thinks Simon.

Donna hands the toiletry bag to Cordelia, who takes out a cutthroat razor and solemnly opens it. As Simon hears Donna mention the radical feminist Valerie Solanas in her introduction, he does not feel entirely reassured. But Cordelia also takes out a can of shaving foam and sprays it over his crotch before carefully shaving off his pubic hair. A symbol of symbolic castration, Simon thinks, following the operation attentively, all the more so when he feels Cordelia's fingers delicately moving his penis.

"In the beginning, no matter what they say, there was only a goddess. One goddess, and one only."

All the same, he would have preferred it if Bayard were there.

But Bayard is smoking a cigarette in the dark, naked, stretched out on the carpet of a student bedroom, between the naked bodies of his two friends, one of whom has fallen asleep, her arm across his chest, her hand holding the other woman's.

"In the beginning, no matter what they think, women were all and one. The only power was female, spontaneous, and plural."

Bayard asks Judith why she is interested in him. Judith, nestled against his shoulder, meows and replies, in her Jewish Midwestern accent: "Because you didn't seem to fit in here."

"The goddess said: 'I came, that is just and good.'"

There is a knock at the door and someone comes in. Bayard sits up and recognizes Kristeva, who says: "You should get dressed."

"The very first goddess, the very first female powers. Humanity by, on, in her. The ground, the atmosphere, water, fire. Language."

A church bell tolls twice.

"Thus the day came when the little prankster appeared. He didn't look like much but was self-confident. He said: 'I am God, I am the son of man, they need a father to pray to. They will know how to be faithful to me: I know how to communicate.'"

The cemetery is only about a hundred yards away. The sounds of the party echo over the tombs, giving the ritualistic ceremony a decidedly anachronistic soundtrack: the stereo plays ABBA's "Gimme! Gimme! Gimme! (A Man After Midnight)."

"Thus man imposed the image, the rules, and the veneration of all human bodies endowed with a dick."

Simon turns his face away to hide his embarrassment and his arousal, and it is then that he makes out, about thirty yards away, two figures meeting under a tree. He sees the slimmer figure pass the earphones of his Walkman to the stockier figure, who is carrying a sports bag in one hand. He realizes that Derrida is checking the merchandise, and that the merchandise is a cassette recording of the seventh function of language.

"The real is out of control. The real fabricates stories, legends, and creatures."

He watches as Derrida—only a few yards away, beneath a tree, amid the gravestones of Ithaca's cemetery—listens to the seventh function of language.

"On horseback on a tomb, we will feed our sons with their fathers' entrails."

Simon wants to intervene, but cannot move a single muscle in his body in order to stand up, nor even the muscle of his tongue (which he knows is the most powerful) in order to articulate a word, particularly as the stage following the symbolic castration is that of the symbolic rebirth, and that the dawning of the new man is here symbolized by fellatio. When Cordelia takes him in her mouth and he feels the heat of the Carthaginian princess's mucus membranes spreading through every particle of him, he knows that as far as the mission is concerned the game is up.

"We form with our mouths the breath and the power of the Sorority. We are one and many, we are a female legion . . ."

The exchange will take place, and he will do nothing to prevent it.

But throwing his head back, he sees at the top of the hill, illuminated by the lights of the campus, an unreal vision (and that unreality itself terrifies him more than the vision's possible reality): a man with two huge, ferocious dogs on a leash.

In spite of the darkness, he knows it is Searle. The dogs bark. The startled spectators look over at them. Donna interrupts her prayer. Cordelia stops sucking Simon's cock.

Searle makes a noise with his mouth and unleashes the two dogs, which rush at Slimane and Derrida. Simon gets up and runs to help them, but suddenly he feels a powerful grip on his arm: it's the bull-necked man, the one who fucked Cordelia on the photocopier, who pulls him back and then punches him in the face. Simon, sprawled on the ground, naked and helpless, sees the two dogs leap on the philosopher and the gigolo, who fall backward.

Growls and screams.

The bull-necked man is completely indifferent to the drama being played out behind him and clearly wants to rip Simon to pieces. Simon hears insults in English, and understands that the fellow expected some exclusivity in his carnal relations with Cordelia. Meanwhile, the dogs are about to tear Slimane and Derrida limb from limb.

The mingled cries of men and beasts have petrified the apprentice Bacchae and their friends. Derrida rolls between gravestones, propelled by the slope and the fury of the dog pursuing him. Slimane is younger and tougher, and has blocked the animal's jaw with his forearm, but the pressure bearing down on his muscles and bones is so powerful that he will faint any second, and then nothing can stop the beast devouring him. Suddenly, though, he hears a squeal and sees Bayard appear out of nowhere to dig his fingers into the dog's head, gouging out its eyes. The dog makes a horrible yelping noise and runs away, stumbling blindly into gravestones as it goes.

Then Bayard hurtles down the hill to help Derrida, who is still rolling.

He grabs the second dog's head to break its neck, but the dog turns on him, knocking him off balance. He immobilizes the hind legs, but the beast's gaping mouth is only four inches from his face, so Bayard plunges a hand into his jacket pocket and takes out the Rubik's Cube, the six faces perfectly assembled, and stuffs it down the dog's throat, all the way to the esophagus. The dog makes a vile gurgling noise, smashes its head against trees, rolls in the grass, goes into convulsions, and finally lies still, choked to death on the toy.

Bayard crawls over to the human form lying next to it. He hears a horrible liquid noise. Derrida is bleeding profusely. The dog literally went for his jugular.

While Bayard is busy killing dogs and Simon is engaged in a full and frank discussion with the bull-man, Searle has rushed over to Slimane, who is still lying on the ground. Now that he understands where the seventh function was hidden, he naturally wants to take the Walkman. He turns over Slimane, who groans with pain, puts his hand on the tape player, and presses eject.

But the cassette holder is empty.

Searle roars like a rabid dog.

From behind a tree, a third man appears. He has a wool tie and a haircut that matches his surroundings. He has perhaps been hiding there since the beginning.

In any case, he is holding a cassette.

And he has unspooled its length of tape.

With his other hand, he thumbs the wheel of a lighter.

Searle, horrified, cries out: "Roman, don't do that!"

The old man in the wool tie brings the Zippo's flame to the tape, which is instantly set alight. From a distance, it is just a little green glimmer in the great dark night.

Searle screams as though someone has just torn his heart out.

Bayard turns around. So does the bull-man. Simon can at last escape. He moves toward the bush-man like a sleepwalker (he is still naked) and asks, hollow-voiced: "Who are you?"

The old man readjusts his tie and says simply: "Roman Jakobson, linguist."

Simon's blood turns to ice.

Down the hill, Bayard is not sure he heard correctly. "What? What did he say? Simon!"

267

The last scraps of tape crackle before being transformed into ash.

Cordelia has hurried over to Derrida. She tears her dress to make a bandage for his neck. She is hoping she can stop the bleeding.

"Simon?"

Simon makes no reply, but silently answers Bayard's silent question: Why didn't he tell him that Jakobson was alive? You never asked.

The truth is that Simon never imagined that the man who was there at the birth of Structuralism, the man who gave Lévi-Strauss the idea for Structuralism when they met in New York in 1941, the Russian formalist from the Prague School, one of the most important pioneers of linguistics after Saussure, could still be alive. For Simon, he belonged to another age. The age of Lévi-Strauss, not Barthes. He laughs at the stupidity of this reasoning: Barthes is dead, but Lévi-Strauss is alive, so why not Jakobson?

Jakobson crosses the few yards between him and Derrida, taking care not to trip on a stone or a clod of earth.

The philosopher is lying with his head on Cordelia's knees. Jakobson takes his hand and says: "Thank you, my friend." Derrida articulates feebly: "I would have listened to the tape, of course. But I would have kept the secret." He lifts his eyes to the weeping Cordelia: "Smile for me as I will have smiled for you until the end, my child. Always prefer life and constantly affirm survival . . ."

And with these words, Derrida dies.

Searle and Slimane have disappeared. So has the sports bag.

78

"Is it not pathetic, naïve, and downright childish to come before the dead to ask for their forgiveness?"

Never before has the little cemetery of Ris-Orangis been trodden by so many feet. Lost in the Parisian suburb, beside the Route Nationale 7 highway, bordered by blocks of brutalist council flats, the place is crushed under the weight of a silence only large crowds can produce.

In front of the coffin, above the hole in the ground, Michel Foucault gives the funeral oration.

"Out of a fervor born of friendship or gratitude, out of approval, too, we could be content to cite, to accompany the other, more or less directly, to let him speak, to efface ourselves before him . . . But through this excessive concern for fidelity, we will end up saying nothing, and sharing nothing."

Derrida will not be buried in the Jewish section but with the Catholics, so that when the time comes his wife will be able to join him.

In the front row, Sartre listens to Foucault, his expression serious, head bowed, standing next to Etienne Balibar. He isn't coughing anymore. He looks like a ghost.

"Jacques Derrida is his name, but he can no longer hear it or bear it."

Bayard asks Simon if that's Simone de Beauvoir next to Sartre.

Foucault does Foucault: "How can we believe in the contemporary? Even if we seem to belong to the same era, whether in terms of historic dates or social horizons, et cetera, it would be easy to show that their time remains infinitely heterogeneous? And, truth be told, unrelated."

Avital Ronell cries softly. Cixous leans on Jean-Luc Nancy and stares down expressionlessly into the hole. Deleuze and Guattari meditate on serial singularities.

The three little public housing blocks with their cracked paintwork, their rusted balconies, watch over the cemetery like sentinels, or like teeth planted in the sea.

In June 1979, at the "Estates General of Philosophy," organized in the main lecture hall of the Sorbonne, Derrida and BHL literally got into a fistfight, but BHL is present at the funeral of the man he will soon call, or is already calling, "my old master."

Foucault goes on: "Contrary to popular wisdom, the individual 'subjects' who live in the most important zones are not authoritarian 'superegos'; they do not possess a power, supposing that Power can be possessed."

Sollers and Kristeva have come too, of course. Derrida had participated in *Tel Quel*, at the beginning. *Dissemination* had been published in the "Tel Quel" collection, but he had broken with the magazine, though no one knew what part personal feelings played in the separation and what part politics. However, in December 1977, when Derrida was arrested in Prague, trapped by the Communist regime that planted drugs in his luggage, he received and accepted Sollers's support.

Bayard has still not received the order to arrest Sollers or Kristeva. Apart from the Bulgarian connection he has no proof that they were involved in Barthes's death. But above all, he has no proof, even if he is almost certain, that they have the seventh function.

It was Kristeva who told Bayard about the meeting at the cemetery in Ithaca, and he thinks she told Searle, too. Bayard's theory is that she wished to sabotage the transaction by bringing together all those involved, thus multiplying the potential disruptions, because she didn't know or refused to believe that Derrida, in concert with Jakobson, was working toward the destruction of the copy. Jakobson always believed his discovery should not be made public. To this end, he helped Derrida raise the money to buy the cassette from Slimane.

While Foucault continues his oration, a woman materializes behind Simon and Bayard.

Simon recognizes Anastasia's perfume.

She whispers something to them and, instinctively, the two men do not turn around.

Foucault: "For what was earlier called 'following the death,' 'on the occasion of the death,' we have a whole series of typical solutions. The worst ones, or the worst in each of them, are either base or derisory, and yet so common: still to maneuver, to speculate, to try to profit or derive some benefit, whether subtle or sublime, to draw from the dead a supplementary force to be turned against the living, to denounce or insult them more or less directly, to authorize and legitimate oneself, to raise oneself to the very heights where we presume death has placed the other beyond all suspicion."

Anastasia: "There will soon be a major event organized by the Logos Club. The Great Protagoras has been challenged. He is going to defend his title. That will mean a huge meeting. But only accredited people will be able to attend."

Foucault: "In its classical form, the funeral oration had a good side, especially when it permitted one to call out directly to the dead, sometimes very informally. This is of course a supplementary fiction, for it is always the dead in me, always the others standing around the coffin whom I call out to. But because of its caricatured excess, the overstatement of this rhetoric at least pointed out that we ought not to remain among ourselves."

Bayard asks where the meeting will take place. Anastasia replies that it will be in Venice, in a secret venue that has probably not yet been chosen because the "organization" she works for has not been able to locate it.

Foucault: "The interactions of the living must be interrupted, the veil must be torn toward the other, the other dead in us, though other still, and the religious promises of an afterlife could indeed still grant this 'as if.'"

Anastasia: "Whoever challenges the Great Protagoras is the one who stole the seventh function. You have the motive."

Neither Searle nor Slimane has been found. But they are not the prime suspects. Slimane wanted to sell it. Searle wanted to buy it. Jakobson helped Derrida outbid him, but Kristeva did everything she could to sink the transaction and Derrida is dead. The two men are still on the run, and one of them has the money, but—as far as Bayard's employer is concerned—that is not what matters.

What we need, Bayard thinks, is to catch them red-handed.

Simon asks how they can obtain accreditation. Anastasia

replies that they must be at least level six (tribune), and that there will be a big qualification tournament organized especially.

"The Novel is a death; it transforms life into destiny, a memory into a useful act, duration into an oriented and meaningful time."

Bayard asks Simon why Foucault is talking about the novel.

Simon replies that it must be a quotation but he is wondering the same thing, and it is making him decidedly anxious.

79

Leaning over the bridge, Searle can barely make out the water at the bottom of the gorge, but he can hear it flowing in the darkness. It is night in Ithaca and the wind snakes through the corridor of vegetation formed by Cascadilla Creek. Pouring over its bed of stones and moss, the creek follows its course through the steep-sided valley, indifferent to the tragedies of humankind.

A pair of students holds hands as they cross the bridge. There are not many people around at this time of night. No one pays Searle any notice.

If only he'd known. If only he could have . . .

But it's too late now to rewrite history.

Without a word, the philosopher steps over the railing, gets his balance on the parapet, glances down into the void, looks up at the stars one last time, lets go, and falls.

Barely even a spray of water: just a small splash. The brief sparkle of foam in the blackness.

The creek is not deep enough to cushion the impact, but the rapids take the body toward the falls and Cayuga Lake, where a long time ago fish were caught by Native Americans who probably—though who knows?—knew very little about the illocutionary and the perlocutionary.

PART IV

VENICE

∎

80

"I am forty-four years old. That means I have outlived Alexander, dead at thirty-two, Mozart, dead at thirty-five, Jarry, thirty-four, Lautréamont, twenty-four, Lord Byron, thirty-six, Rimbaud, thirty-seven, and throughout the long life that remains to me, I will overtake all the great dead men, all the giants who dominated their eras, and so, if God spares me, I will pass Napoleon, Caesar, Georges Bataille, Raymond Roussel . . . But no! . . . I will die young . . . I can feel it . . . I won't be around for long . . . I won't end up like Roland . . . sixty-four years old . . . Pathetic . . . When it comes down to it, we did him a favor . . . No, no . . . I wouldn't make a good retiree . . . Not that such a thing is even possible . . . I'd rather burn up . . . The flame that burns twice as bright . . ."

81

Sollers does not like the Lido, but he has fled the Carnival crowds and, in memory of Thomas Mann and Visconti, taken refuge at the Grand Hôtel des Bains, where *Death in Venice*'s highly languorous action takes place. He imagined he'd be able to meditate at his ease there, facing the Adriatic, but for now he is at the bar, hitting on the waitress as he knocks back a whiskey. At the far end of the empty room, a pianist plays Ravel halfheartedly. It should be pointed out that it is midafternoon in midwinter and, while there is no cholera outbreak, the weather is not particularly conducive for swimming.

"And what is your name, my dear child? No, don't tell me! I am going to baptize you Margherita, like Lord Byron's mistress. She was married to a baker, did you know that? La Fornarina... fiery temperament and marble thighs... She had your eyes, of course. They went horse-riding on the beach: madly romantic, don't you think? A little kitsch perhaps, yes, you're right... Would you like me to teach you to ride later?"

Sollers thinks of that passage in *Childe Harold*: "The spouseless Adriatic mourns her lord..." The doge can no longer marry the sea, the lion no longer inspires fear: it's about castration, he thinks. "And the *Bucentaur* lies rotting unrestored, neglected garment of her widowhood!" But he immediately drives away these dark thoughts. He shakes his empty glass to order a second whiskey. "On the rocks." The waitress smiles politely. *"Prego."*

Sollers sighs cheerfully. "Ah, how I wish I could say, like Goethe: 'I am perhaps known only to one man in Venice, and he won't be meeting me anytime soon.' But I'm very well known in my country, my dear child, that is my misfortune. Do you know France? I'll take you. What a great writer he was, that Goethe. But what's the matter? You're blushing. Ah, Julia, there you are! Margherita, allow me to present my wife."

Kristeva entered the bar discreetly, like a cat. "You're exhausting yourself in vain, darling. This young woman doesn't understand a quarter of what you're saying. Isn't that right, miss?"

The young woman smiles again. *"Prego?"*

Sollers puffs up his chest: "Well, what does it matter? When, like me, one inspires devotion at first sight, one does not need (thank God!) to be *understood*."

Kristeva does not tell him about Bourdieu, whom he hates because the sociologist threatens his entire system of representation, with which he still manages to play the swaggering dandy.

She doesn't tell him either that he shouldn't drink too much before this week's meeting. For a long time, she has chosen to treat him simultaneously as a child *and* as an adult. She doesn't bother explaining certain things to him, *but* expects him to raise himself to the level she believes she has a right to demand.

The pianist plays a particularly dissonant chord. A bad omen? But Sollers believes in his lucky star. Perhaps he will go for a swim? Kristeva notices that he has already put his sandals on.

82

Two hundred galleys, two dozen galliots (those half-galleys), and six gigantic galleasses (the B-52s of their age) speed across the Mediterranean in pursuit of the Turkish fleet.

Sebastiano Venier, the irascible captain of the Venetian fleet, rages to himself: among his Spanish, Genevan, Savoyard, Neapolitan, and papal allies he thinks he is the only one who wants this battle. But he is wrong.

While the Spanish crown, in the person of Philip II, is generally uninterested in the Mediterranean, fully occupied as it is by the conquest of the New World, young Don John of Austria, the hotheaded commander of the Holy League's fleet, illegitimate son of Charles V, the Holy Roman Emperor, and hence half-brother to the king, is seeking in this war the honor that his bastardy denies him elsewhere.

Sebastiano Venier wants to preserve the vital interests of La Serenissima, but Don John of Austria, fighting for his own glory, is his best ally, and he doesn't know it.

83

Sollers contemplates the portrait of Saint Anthony in the Gesuati church and thinks that he looks like him. (Does Sollers look like

Saint Anthony or Saint Anthony look like Sollers? I don't know which way around he considers it.) He lights a blessing candle to himself and goes out for a walk in the city's Dorsoduro quarter, which he loves so much.

Outside the Accademia, he sees Simon Herzog and Superintendent Bayard in the line.

"Dear Superintendent, what a surprise to see you here! What brings you to Venice? Ah yes, I've heard about the exploits of your young protégé. I can't wait to see the next round. Yes, yes, you see, no point in keeping secrets, is there? Is this your first time in Venice? And you'll go to the museum for some culture, I suppose. Say hello to Giorgione's *Tempest* from me; it's the only painting there worth the hassle of all those Japanese tourists. Have you noticed how they snap at everything without even looking?"

Sollers points to two Japanese men in the line, and Simon makes an imperceptible gesture of surprise. He recognizes them from the Fuego that saved his life in Paris. They are indeed armed with the latest Minoltas and are photographing everything that moves.

"Forget the Piazza San Marco. Forget Harry's Bar. Here, you are in the heart of the city; in other words, in the heart of the world: the Dorsoduro . . . Venice is a convenient scapegoat, don't you think? Ha ha . . . Anyway, you must absolutely go to the Campo Santo Stefano; just cross the Grand Canal . . . You'll see the statue of Niccolò Tommaseo there, a political writer, therefore not of interest, known to the Venetians as Cagalibri: the book-shitter. Because of the statue. It really looks like he's shitting books. Ha. But above all you must see the Giudecca, on the other bank. You can admire the churches designed by the great Palladio, all in a row. You don't know Palladio? A man who did not like things to be too easy . . . like you, perhaps? He was in charge of constructing an edifice *opposite* the Piazza San Marco. Can you imagine? What a *challenge*, as our American friends, who have never understood art, would say . . . they've never understood women either, for that matter, but that's another story . . . Anyway, there you have it: rising up from the water, San Giorgio Maggiore. And, top of the list, the Redentore, a Neoclassical masterpiece: on one side, Byzantium and the flamboyant Gothic of the past; on the other, Ancient Greece resurrected eternally by the Renaissance and the Counter-Reformation. Go and see it, it's only a hundred yards away! If you hurry, you'll get there for the sunset . . ."

Then a cry rings out in the line. "Thief! Thief!" A tourist runs after a pickpocket. Instinctively, Sollers puts his hand in his inside jacket pocket.

But he pulls himself together instantly: "Ha, did you see? A Frenchman, obviously . . . The French are always easily taken in. Be careful, though. The Italians are a great people, but like all great peoples they're bandits . . . I should leave you, I'll be late for Mass . . ."

And Sollers walks away, his sandals slapping against the Venetian cobbles.

Simon says to Bayard: "Did you see?"

"Yes, I saw."

"He has it on him."

"Yes."

"So why not take him now?"

"First we have to check it works. That's why you're here, remember."

An undetectable smile of pride flickers on Simon's face. Another round. He has forgotten the Japanese men behind him.

84

Two hundred galleys pass through the Straits of Corfu and head toward the Gulf of Corinth. Among them is *La Marchesa*, commanded by the Genovese Francesco San-Freda, carrying Captain Diego of Urbino and his dice-playing men, among them the son of a debt-ridden dentist also here to seek glory as well as riches, a Castilian hidalgo, an adventurer, a penniless sword-wielding nobleman: the young Miguel de Cervantes.

85

On the fringes of the Carnival, private parties proliferate in Venice's palazzos, and the one currently being held in the Ca' Rezzonico is among the most popular and the most private.

Drawn by the voices coming from the building, envious passersby and vaporetto passengers look up toward the ball-room, where they can glimpse or imagine the trompe-l'oeil art-works, the massive chandeliers in multicolored glass, and the magnificent eighteenth-century frescoes decorating the ceiling, but invitations are strictly by name only.

Logos Club parties are not exactly announced in the news-paper.

And yet the party does take place, in the heart of the Floating City. A hundred people rush in, their faces uncovered. (Evening wear is required, but this is not a masked ball.)

At first glance, there is nothing to distinguish this party from any other chic gathering. But listen closely and you will hear the difference. The conversations are of exordiums, perorations, propositions, altercations, refutations. (As Barthes said: "The pas-sion for classification always appears byzantine for those who do not participate in it.") Anacoluthon, catachresis, enthymeme, and metabole. (As Sollers would say: "But of course.") "I do not believe *Res* and *Verba* should be translated simply by Things and Words. *Res*, says Quintilian, are *quae significantur*, and *Verba: quae significant*; in other words, in terms of discourse, the signi-fied and the signifier." Of course.

The guests also talk of past and future duels. Many are veter-ans with severed fingers or young guns of the debates, and most have memories of glorious or tragic campaigns, which they like to dwell on below Tiepolo's paintings.

"I didn't even know the author of the citation!"

"And then, he came out with a line by Guy Mollet! That killed me."

"I was there for the legendary duel between Jean-Jacques Servan-Schreiber and Mendès France. I don't even remember the subject now."

"*I* was there for the one between Lecanuet and Emmanuel Berl. Surreal."

"You French people are so dialectical . . ."

"So, I draw a subject . . . botany! I thought I was screwed, and then I remembered my grandfather in his allotment. Grandpa saved my finger!"

"And then he says: 'We must stop seeing atheists everywhere. Spinoza was a great mystic.' What an idiot!"

"*Picasso contra Dalí. Categoría historia del arte, un clásico. Me gusta más Picasso pero escogí a Dalí.*"

"And the guy starts talking about soccer. I don't know a thing about it, but he won't stop going on about the Reds and a cauldron . . ."

"Oh no, I haven't been in a duel for two years. I'm back down to being a rhetorician. I don't have the time or the energy anymore, with the kids, work . . ."

"I was ready to give up when suddenly, a miracle: he comes out with *the* biggest pile of crap, the worst thing he could have said . . ."

"*C'è un solo dio ed il suo nome è Cicerone.*"

"I went to Harry's Bar (in memory of Hemingway, like everyone else). Fifteen thousand lire for a Bellini, seriously?"

"*Heidegger, Heidegger . . . Sehe ich aus wie Heidegger?*"

Suddenly, a frisson spreads across the room from the staircase. The crowds open to welcome a new arrival. Simon enters, accompanied by Bayard. The guests gather around, and at the same time they appear almost intimidated. So this is the young prodigy everyone is talking about, who has risen from nowhere to the rank of peripatetician incredibly quickly: four promotions in three consecutive sessions, in Paris, when progress like that usually takes years. And perhaps five, soon. He is wearing a charcoal Armani suit, a grayish pink shirt, and a black tie with violet pinstripes. As for Bayard, he didn't think it was worth bothering to change out of his usual crumpled suit.

Around the prodigy, people grow bolder and soon they are pressing him to talk about his Parisian exploits: with what ease, by way of warming up, he first crushed a rhetorician on a subject of domestic politics ("In the end, is an election always won at the center?") by citing Lenin's *What Is to Be Done?*

How he brushed aside an orator on a fairly technical philosophy question ("Is legal violence still violence?") by recourse to Saint-Just ("No one can reign innocently" and, above all: "A king must reign or die.")

How he battled a pugnacious dialectician over a Shelley quotation ("He hath awaken'd from the dream of life") by delicately manipulating Calderon and Shakespeare, but also, with exquisite refinement, *Frankenstein*.

With what elegance he dueled a peripatetician over a line by Leibniz ("Education can do anything: it can make bears dance") by allowing himself the luxury of a demonstration founded almost entirely on quotations from de Sade.

Bayard lights a cigarette while looking through the window at the gondolas on the Grand Canal.

Simon answers his admirers with good grace. An old Venetian in a three-piece suit hands him a glass of champagne:

"Maestro, you know Casanova, *naturalmente*? In the account of his famous duel with the Polish count, he writes: 'The first advice one gives someone who is taking part in a duel is to convince one's adversary as quickly as possible of the impossibility of harming you.' *Cosa ne pensa?*"

(Simon takes a sip of champagne and smiles at an old lady, who bats her eyelashes.)

"Was it a duel with swords?"

"*No, alla pistola.*"

"In the case of a duel with pistols, I think the advice is valid."
Simon laughs. "For an oratory duel, the principles are a little
different."

"*Come mai?* Dare I, *maestro*, ask why?"

"Well . . . I, for example, like to strike at my opponent's
speech code. Which implies letting him come at you. I allow
him to reveal himself, *capisce*? An oratory duel is more like a duel
with swords. You reveal yourself, you close your guard, you de-
robe, you feint, you cut, you disengage, you parry, you riposte . . ."

"*Uno spadaccino, si. Ma*, is the pistol not *migliore*?"

Bayard elbows the young prodigy. Simon is aware that it is
not wise, on the eve of a duel at this level, to obligingly provide
anyone that asks with strategic instructions, but the reflex is too
strong. He just can't help *teaching*.

"In my opinion, there are two main approaches. The semiological and the rhetorical, you see?"

"*Si, si . . . credo di si, ma . . .* Could you explain *un poco, maestro*?"

"Well, it's very simple. Semiology enables us to understand,
analyze, decode; it's defensive, it's Borg. Rhetoric is designed to
persuade, to convince, to conquer; it's offensive, it's McEnroe."

"Ah *si. Ma* Borg, he wins, *no*?"

"Of course! You can win with either; they're just different
styles of play. With semiology, you decode your opponent's rhetoric, you grasp his things, and you rub his nose in it. Semiology's
like Borg: it is enough to get the ball over the net one time more
than your opponent. Rhetoric is aces, volleys, winners down the
line, but semiology is returns, passing shots, topspin lobs."

"And it's *migliore*?"

"Well, no, not necessarily. But that's my style. It's what I
know how to do, so that's how I play. I'm not a brilliant lawyer or
a preacher or a political orator or a messiah or a vacuum-cleaner
salesman. I'm an academic, and my job is analyzing, decoding,
criticizing, and interpreting. That's my game. I'm Borg. I'm Vilas.
I'm José Luis Clerc. Ahem."

"*Ma*, your opponent, who's that?"

"Well . . . McEnroe, Roscoe Tanner, Gerulaitis . . ."

"And Connors?"

"Ah yeah, Connors, shit."

"*Perchè* shit? What's so special about Connors?"

"He's really good."

It is difficult, just now, to assess how much irony there is in Simon's last reply, because in February 1981 Connors has not beaten Borg in eight consecutive meetings, his last victory in a Grand Slam is almost three years back (U.S. Open 1978, against Borg), and people are starting to think he is finished. (They don't know that he will win Wimbledon and the U.S. Open the following year.)

Whatever, Simon becomes serious again and asks: "I suppose he won his duel?"

"Casanova? *Si*, he hit the Pole in the stomach and *quasi* killed him, but he also took a bullet to the thumb, and almost had to have his left hand *amputato*."

"Ah . . . really?"

"*Si*, the surgeon told Casanova that gangrene would set in. So Casanova asked if it was already there. And the surgeon said no, so Casanova, he said, '*Va bene*, let's just wait and see when it's there.' And the surgeon, he said *allora*, they'll have to cut the whole arm off. You know what Casanova said to that? '*Ma*, what would I do with an arm without my hand?' Ha ha!"

"Ha ha. Uh . . . *bene*."

Simon politely takes his leave and goes off to find a Bellini. Bayard stuffs himself with canapés and observes the guests as they watch his partner with curiosity, admiration, and even a little fear. Simon accepts a cigarette from a woman in a lamé dress. The way the evening is unfolding confirms what he came to establish: that the reputation he has acquired in a few Parisian sessions has definitely reached Venice.

He has come to care for his *ethos*, but he doesn't want to get home too late. At no point has he attempted to find out if his adversary is in the room, while that person may have been observing him attentively the whole time, leaning on the precious wooden furniture, nervously stubbing out his cigarettes on the Brustolon statuettes.

As Bayard is being hit on by the woman in the lamé dress (who wants to know his role in the prodigy's rise), Simon decides to go home alone. And no doubt overly absorbed by the dress's plunging neckline, a little stunned, perhaps, by the beauty of the setting and by the intensive cultural tourism that Simon has inflicted on him since their arrival, Bayard pays no attention, or, at least, doesn't object.

It is not especially late and Simon is slightly tipsy; the party continues in the streets of Venice, but there is something wrong. Sensing a presence: what does that mean? Intuition is a convenient concept for dispensing with explanations, like God. One does not "sense" anything at all. One sees, hears, calculates, and decodes. Intelligence-reflex. Simon keeps seeing the same mask, and another one, and another one. (But there are so many masks, and so many turns.) He hears footsteps behind him in the deserted backstreets. "Instinctively," he takes a detour and inevitably he gets lost. He has the impression that the footsteps are growing closer. (Although that doesn't take into account an extremely precise and complex psychic mechanism, *impression* is a more solid concept than *intuition*.) His meanderings bring him to Campo San Bartolomeo, at the foot of the Rialto, where street musicians are having some sort of contest, and he knows that he is not far from his hotel—a few hundred yards at most, as the crow flies—but the twists and turns of the Venetian backstreets render this figure meaningless, and with every attempt he comes up against the dark water of a secondary canal. Rio della Fava, Rio del Piombo, Rio di San Lio . . .

Those young people leaning on the stone well, drinking beer and nibbling *cicchetti* . . . Hasn't he already passed this *osteria*?

This backstreet is narrowing, but that does not mean that there is no passage after the bend it must inevitably form. Or after the next bend.

Lap, glimmer, *rio*.

Shit, no bridge.

When Simon turns around, three Venetian masks bar his way. They don't say a word, but their intentions are clear because each is armed with a blunt object that Simon mechanically notes: a cheap statuette of a winged lion as found in the stalls of the Rialto; an empty bottle of Limoncello held by its neck; and a long and heavy pair of glassblower's tongs (it is far from obvious that this last one should be called a "blunt" object).

He recognizes the masks because, at the Ca' Rezzonico, he examined Longhi's paintings of Carnival: the *capitano* with the large aquiline nose, the plague doctor's long white beak, and the *larva*, which serves as a mask for the *bauta*, with the tricorn and the black cape. But the man who wears this last mask is in jeans and sneakers, like the two others. Simon deduces from this that they are just some young thugs hired to beat him up. Their wish to remain unidentified makes him think that they do not want to kill him, so that's something at least. Unless the masks are worn simply to hide their faces from potential witnesses.

The plague doctor approaches silently, bottle in hand, and Simon, once again, as in Ithaca when the dog attacked Derrida, is fascinated by this bizarre, *unreal* pantomime. He hears bursts of laughter from customers at an *osteria*, very close by: he knows it is only a few yards away, but the uneven echoes of the street musicians and the ambient agitation of the Venetian night immediately persuade him that if he calls for help (he tries to remember how to say "Help" in Italian), no one will pay any attention.

While he retreats, Simon thinks: in the hypothesis where he is truly a character from a novel (a hypothesis strengthened by the situation, the masks, the picturesque blunt objects: a novel by an author unafraid of tackling clichés, he thinks), what would he really risk? A novel is not a dream: you can die in a novel. Then again, the central character is not normally killed. Except, perhaps, at the end of the story.

But if it *was* the end of the story, how would he know? How can he know what page of his life he is on? How can any of us know when we have reached our last page?

And what if he wasn't the central character? Doesn't everyone believe himself the hero of his own existence?

From a conceptual point of view, Simon is not sure he is sufficiently equipped to correctly grasp the problem of life and death from the perspective of novelistic ontology, so he decides to return, while there is still time—i.e., before the masked man moving toward him smashes him in the face with the empty bottle—to a more pragmatic approach.

Theoretically, his only way out is the *rio* behind him, but this is February, the water must be ice-cold, and he fears it would be too easy afterward for one of the thugs to grab a gondola oar (there are gondolas parked every ten yards) and—while he was floundering in the canal—to pummel him like a tuna, like in Aeschylus's *The Persians*, like the Greeks at the Battle of Salamis.

Thought is faster than action, and he has time to think all this before the white beak finally lifts his bottle. But just as he is about to bring it down on Simon, the bottle falls from his hand. Or rather someone tears it from his hand. The white beak turns around and, where his two accomplices were, he sees two Japanese men in black suits. The *bauta* and the *capitano* are lying on the ground. The white beak stares dumbly, arms hanging, at a scene he cannot understand. He is duly hit over the head with his own bottle in a succession of precise, muted movements. His assailant's expertise is such that the bottle does not break, and his suit barely picks up a wrinkle.

The three men on the ground groan softly. The three men standing do not make any sound at all.

If a novelist is presiding over his fate, Simon wonders why this author has chosen these two mysterious guardian angels to watch over him. The second Japanese man approaches, greets him with a discreet bow, and replies to the unasked question: "Any friend of Roland Barthes is a friend of ours." Then they both vanish into the night like ninjas.

Simon considers this explanation to be rather minimal, but he realizes he will have to be content with it, so he heads back to the hotel, where he will finally be able to get some sleep.

86

In Rome, in Madrid, in Constantinople, and perhaps even in Venice, people are wondering. What is the aim of this formidable armada? What territories do the Christians want to retake or conquer? Do they want to retake Cyprus? Do they want to start a thirteenth crusade? But as yet no one knows that Famagusta has fallen, and the screams of the tortured Bragadin have not yet been heard. Only Don John of Austria and Sebastiano Venier have the intuition that the battle may represent an end in itself, and that what is at stake is the total destruction of the enemy army.

87

While they wait for the duel, Bayard continues to go for walks with Simon to clear his head. Their wanderings bring them to the foot of the equestrian statue of Colleone, and while Bayard admires the statue, fascinated by the strength of the bronze, by the dexterity of Verrocchio's chisel, and by what he imagines of the life of the *condottiere*, a severe warrior, powerful and authoritarian, Simon enters the San Zanipolo basilica, where he sees Sollers praying before a mural fresco.

Simon is suspicious, and startled by the coincidence. But then again, Venice is a small city and there is really nothing so exceptional about bumping into the same person twice at a tourist site when you are a tourist yourself.

All the same, as he does not particularly want to talk to him, Simon pushes on discreetly into the nave, contemplates the tombs of the doges (and among them, that of Sebastiano Venier, the hero of the Battle of Lepanto), admires Bellini's paintings, and, in the Chapel of the Rosary, those of Veronese.

When he is sure that Sollers has left, he approaches the fresco.

There is a sort of urn surrounded by two little winged lions and, above them, an engraving representing the torture of an elderly bald man with a long beard and prominent, sinewy muscles, who is being carved up.

Below, a plaque with Latin inscriptions that Simon deciphers with difficulty: Marcantonio Bragadin, governor of Cyprus, was horribly martyred by the Turks for having heroically defended a siege that lasted from September 1570 to July 1571 in the fortress of Famagusta. (And also for having shown his conqueror a lack of respect upon surrender, but the marble plaque does not say this. Apparently he arrogantly refused to free the customary hostage in exchange for the liberation of Christian commanders, and he showed no interest in the fate of Turkish prisoners that the *pasha* accused him of having let his men massacre.)

So anyway, they cut off his ears and his nose, and left him to become infected and start rotting for a week. Then, when he refused to convert (he still had enough strength to spit insults at his torturers), they weighed him down with sacks full of earth and rocks and dragged him from battery to battery, mocked and beaten by the Turkish soldiers.

And his torment did not end there: they hoisted him onto the yardarm of a galley so all the Christian slaves could behold the vision of their defeat and of the Turkish anger. And for an hour, the Turks yelled at him: "Behold! Can you see your squadron? Behold the great Christ! Can you see your rescuers on their way?"

Finally, he was tied naked to a column and flayed alive.

Then his corpse was stuffed and taken through the streets of the town on the back of an ox, before being sent to Constantinople.

But it is his skin inside the urn, a pathetic relic. How did it get here? The Latin inscription does not say.

Why was Sollers praying before this wall? Simon has no idea.

88

"I am not under orders to receive Venetian scum."

Obviously, the Tuscan captain who says this to the chief admiral, Sebastiano Venier, gets into deep trouble; aware that he has gone too far and knowing the old Venetian's reputation for severity, he resisted arrest and it all ended in mutiny, with the captain gravely injured then hanged as an example.

But he was under Spanish command, which implies that Venier did not have the right to decide his punishment and, above all, to summarily execute him. When Don John learns this, he seriously considers whether Venier should himself be hanged to teach him due respect for hierarchy, but the *provveditore* Barbarigo, second-in-command of the Venetian fleet, convinces him not to do anything that might compromise the entire operation.

The fleet continues on its way to the Gulf of Lepanto.

89

Tatko,

We have safely arrived in Venice and Philippe is going to compete.

The city is very lively because they are trying to revive the Carnival. There are people in masks and lots of things to see in the streets. And, contrary to what we were told, Venice does not stink. On the downside, there are armies of Japanese tourists, but that's no different from Paris.

Philippe doesn't seem too worried. You know him—he always has that unshakable optimism that sometimes verges on irresponsibility but, all in all, is a strength.

I know you don't understand why your daughter let him take her place, but you must admit that in a situation like this—in other words, with a jury composed exclusively of men—a man will always have a better chance of winning than a woman of equal skill.

When I was very young, you taught me that a woman was not

only a man's equal, but was even superior to him, and I believed you.
I still believe you, but we cannot ignore this sociological reality (I
have been afraid of it for some time now) known as male domination.

It is said that in the whole history of the Logos Club, only four
women have ever attained the rank of sophist: Catherine de Medici,
Emilie du Châtelet, Marilyn Monroe, and Indira Gandhi (and we
can still hope that she will become one again). That is not very
many. And none, of course, has ever been the Great Protagoras.

But if Philippe wins the title, things will change for everyone: for
him, as he'll become one of the most influential men on the planet.
For you, benefiting from his secret power, who will no longer have
to fear Andropov or the Russians, and will be in a position to change
the face of your country. (I would like to be able to say "our" country,
but you wanted me to be French, and in that respect at least, my
dear Papa, I exceeded your expectations.) And for your only daughter,
who will gain another form of power and will reign supreme over
French intellectual life.

Don't judge Philippe too severely: recklessness is a form of cour-
age and you know what he has agreed to risk. You always taught
me to respect the journey from thought to act, even if the person
making it treats it as a game. Without a tendency to melancholy,
there is no psyche, and I know that Philippe lacks that, which perhaps
makes him a poor player that struts and frets his hour upon the stage,
as Shakespeare says, but that is probably what I like about him.

All my love, dear Papa,
Your loving daughter,
Julenka

PS: Did you receive the Jean Ferrat album I sent you?

90

"*Ma si*, it is a little approximate, *vero*."

Simon and Bayard have just bumped into Umberto Eco on

Piazza San Marco. It really does seem as if everyone has come to Venice. Simon's paranoia now interprets any apparent coincidence as a sign that his entire life may be nothing but a fictional narrative; this muddles his analytical faculties and prevents him from thinking about the possible and likely reasons for Eco's presence, here and now.

On the lagoon, a motley variety of boats maneuver in joyous disorder, to a soundtrack of colliding hulls, cannonades, and the roaring of extras.

"It's a reconstruction of the Battle of Lepanto." Eco has to shout to be heard over the noise of the cannonade and the cheers of the crowd.

For this second edition since its rebirth the year before, the Carnival is offering, among other colorful spectacles, a historical reconstruction: the Holy League, led by the Venetian fleet, alongside the Invincible Armada and the papal armies, affronting the Turks of Selim II, known as "Selim the Sot," the son of Suleiman the Magnificent.

"*Ma*, you see that large vessel? It's a replica of the *Bucintoro*, the ship on board which the doge, every year, on the Feast of the Ascension, would celebrate the *sposalizio del mare*, the marriage with the sea, by throwing a gold ring into the Adriatic. It was a ceremonial ship not at all intended to go to war. They took it out for official engagements, but it never left the lagoon and it has no business being here, because we are supposed to be in the Gulf of Lepanto on October 7, 1571."

Simon is not really listening. He walks toward the dock, fascinated by this ballet of counterfeit galleys and painted skiffs. But when he is about to pass between the two columns that look like the uprights of an invisible door, Eco stops him: "*Aspetta!*"

Venetians never pass between the *colonne di San Marco*; they say it brings bad luck because it was here that the Republic would execute its prisoners before hanging their corpses by the feet.

At the top of the columns, Simon sees the winged lion of Venice and Saint Theodore flooring a crocodile. He mutters,

"I'm not Venetian," crosses the invisible threshold, and advances to the water's edge.

And he sees. Not the slightly kitsch "son et lumière" show and the boats disguised as warships with their actors in their Sunday best. But the collision of armies: the six galleasses rising from the sea like floating fortresses, destroying everything around them; the two hundred galleys divided between the left wing, yellow banner, commanded by the Venetian *provveditore-generale* Agostino Barbarigo, who is shot in the eye with an arrow and dies at the start of the battle; the right wing, green banner, led by the timorous Genovese Gian Andrea Doria, transfixed by the agile maneuvers of the elusive Euldj Ali (Ali the convert, Ali the one-eyed, Ali the renegade, a Calabrian by birth who became the Bey of Algiers); in the center, blue banner, the high commander, Don John of Austria, for Spain, with Colonna, commander of the pope's galleys, and seventy-five-year-old Sebastiano Venier, severe of face and white of beard, future doge of Venice, to whom John no longer says a word, at whom he never even glances since the incident with the Spanish captain. In the rearguard, in case things go badly, is the Marquis of Santa Cruz, white banner. Facing them, the Turkish fleet, commanded by Sufi Ali Pasha, *kapudan pasha*, with his janissaries and his corsairs.

And on board the galley *La Marchesa*, sick with fever, midshipman Miguel de Cervantes, who has been ordered to remain lying down in the hold but who wants to fight and begs his captain, because what will people say of him if he doesn't take part in the greatest naval battle of all time?

So the captain agrees, and when the galleys ram into each other and collide, when the men fire their arquebuses at point-blank range and start to board the enemy ship, he fights like a dog, and in the fury of the sea and in the storm of war he chops up Turks like tuna but is shot in the chest and in the left hand. He continues to fight. Soon there will be no doubt that the Christians have won their victory—the head of the *kapudan pasha* is mounted on top of the mast on the admiral's ship—but

Miguel de Cervantes, the brave midshipman under the orders of his captain, Diego of Urbino, has lost the use of his left hand in the battle, or maybe the surgeons did a bad job.

Either way, from now on he will be known as the "one-armed man of Lepanto," and some will mock his handicap. Incensed and wounded in body and soul, he will make this clarification in his preface to the second volume of *Don Quixote*: "As if the loss of my hand had been brought about in some tavern, and not on the grandest occasion the past or present has seen, or the future can hope to see."

Amid the crowd of tourists and masks, Simon, too, feels feverish, and when he feels a tap on his shoulder, he half expects to see the doge, Alvise Mocenigo, burst into view along with the Council of Ten, who are out in force, and the three state inquisitors, to celebrate this dazzling victory of the Venetian lion and Christianity, but it is simply Umberto Eco, who smiles pleasantly and says to him: "There are some who went off in search of unicorns, but found only rhinoceroses."

91

Bayard lines up outside La Fenice, the Venetian opera house, and when his turn comes and his name is found on the list, he feels that universal relief of getting past an official barrier (something he'd forgotten in his line of work), but the guard asks him in what capacity he is invited and Bayard explains that he is accompanying Simon Herzog, one of the competitors. But the guard insists: *"In qualità di che?"* And Bayard doesn't know how to respond, so he says: "Uh, coach?"

The guard lets him in and he takes his place in a gold-painted theater box furnished with crimson chairs.

On the stage, a young woman confronts an old man over a quotation from *Macbeth*: *"Let every man be master of his time."* The two opponents speak English and Bayard does not use the headphones providing simultaneous translation that are available to the audience, but he has the impression that the young woman is getting the upper hand. ("Time is on my side," she says graciously. And she will indeed be declared the victor.)

The room is full. People have come from all over Europe to attend the great qualifying tournament: tribunes are challenged by duelists of lower ranks, the vast majority peripateticians, but also some dialecticians and even a few orators ready to risk three fingers in a single match to be granted the right to witness *the* meeting.

Everyone knows that the Great Protagoras has been challenged and that only tribunes, accompanied by a person of their choice, will be invited to the match (along with the sophists, naturally, who comprise the jury). The duel will take place tomorrow in a secret venue that will be communicated only to authorized persons at the end of tonight's tournament. Officially, no one knows the identity of the challenger, but there are several rumors in circulation.

Flicking through his Michelin guide, Bayard discovers that La Fenice is a theater that has regularly been burned down and rebuilt since its opening. Hence, presumably, that name: Phoenix.

On the stage, a brilliant Russian stupidly loses a finger over a mistake in quotation: a Mark Twain phrase is attributed to Malraux, allowing his opponent, a wily Spaniard, to turn the tables on him. The audience goes "ooohh" at the moment of the *tchack*.

The door opens behind Bayard, making him jump. "Well, well, my dear superintendent. You look like you just saw Stendhal in person!" It's Sollers, with his cigarette holder, come to pay a visit to his box. "Interesting event, isn't it? The cream of Venetian society and, my word, everyone of any culture in Europe. There are even a few Americans, I've been told. I wonder if Hemingway was ever part of the Logos Club. He wrote a book that took place in Venice, you know? The story of an old colonel who masturbates a young woman in a gondola with his wounded hand. Not bad at all. You know Verdi created *La Traviata* here?

But also *Ernani*, based on Victor Hugo's play . . ." Sollers stares out at the stage, where a sturdy little Italian is battling a pipe-smoking Englishman, and he adds dreamily: "*Hernani* amputated of its H." Then he withdraws, clicking his heels like an Austro-Hungarian officer, with a slight bow, and goes back to his own box, which Bayard tries to spot, in order to see if Kristeva is there.

Onstage, a presenter in a dinner jacket announces the next duel, "*Signore, Signori* . . . ," and Bayard puts on his headphones: "Duelists from every land . . . he comes to us from Paris . . . his victories speak for themselves . . . no friendly matches . . . four digital duels . . . four victories, all unanimous . . . enough for him to have made a name for himself . . . I ask you to welcome . . . the Decoder of Vincennes."

Simon makes his entrance, dressed in a well-tailored Cerruti suit.

Along with the rest of the spectators, Bayard applauds nervously.

Simon smiles and waves to the audience, all his senses alert, while the subject is drawn.

"*Classico e Barocco.*" The Classical and the Baroque: an art history subject? Why not, since we're in Venice?

Instantly, ideas rush through Simon's head, but it is too early to sort through them. First he must concentrate on something else. During the handshake with his adversary, he keeps his hand in his for a few seconds and reads the following about the man who faces him:

- a southern Italian, to judge by his bronzed complexion;
- small in height, so a drive to dominate;
- energetic handshake: a man of contact;
- paunchy: eats lots of meals with sauces;
- looks at the crowd, not at his opponent: a politician's reflex;
- not very well dressed for an Italian: a slightly worn and

mismatched suit, the hems of his trouser legs a little too short, and yet his black shoes are polished: a cheap-skate or a demagogue;

- a luxury watch on his wrist, a recent model, so not an heirloom, obviously too expensive for his standing: strong probability of passive corruption (which confirms the Mezzogiorno hypothesis);

- a wedding ring, plus a signet ring: a wife and a mistress who gave him the signet ring, which he probably wore before his marriage (otherwise he'd have to justify its appearance to his wife, whereas this way he could claim it was a family heirloom), so a long-term mistress, whom he didn't want to marry but couldn't resolve to leave.

Naturally, all these deductions are merely suppositions, and Simon cannot be sure that each one is correct. Simon thinks: "This isn't a Sherlock Holmes story." But when the clues point to a collection of converging presumptions, Simon decides to trust them.

His conclusion is that he is facing a politician, probably a Christian Democrat, a Napoli or Cagliari supporter, a man without strong convictions, a skilled social climber, but someone who is loath to make decisions.

So he decides at the start of the game to try something to destabilize him: he makes a show of giving up his right to go first, always granted to the lower-ranked player, and generously offers to leave the initiative to his honorable opponent, which in concrete terms means that he is leaving him to choose which of the two terms of the subject he wants to defend. After all, in ten-nis, one can choose to receive rather than serve.

His opponent is absolutely not obliged to accept. But Simon's gamble is as follows: the Italian will not want his refusal to be taken the wrong way; he will not want people to see in it a sort of contempt, ill grace, rigidity, or, worst of all, fear.

The Italian must be a player, not a spoilsport. He cannot begin by refusing to pick up the gauntlet, even if the gauntlet that has been thrown down looks more like a baited hook. He accepts.

Based on that, Simon has no doubt about which position he will choose to defend. In Venice, any politician will praise the Baroque.

So that when the Italian begins to remind his audience of the origin of the word *Barocco* (which, in the form *barroco*, refers to an irregular pearl in Portuguese), Simon believes himself at least one step ahead.

To start with, the Italian is rather scholarly, rather sluggish, because Simon has unsettled him by handing him the initiative and also, perhaps, because he is not a specialist in art history. But he has not reached the rank of tribune by chance. Gradually, he pulls himself together and grows in confidence.

The Baroque is that aesthetic trend that sees the world as a theater and life as a dream, an illusion, a mirror of bright colors and broken lines. *Circe and the Peacock*: metamorphoses, ostentation. The Baroque prefers curves to straight lines. The Baroque likes asymmetry, trompe-l'oeil, extravagance.

Simon has put his headphones on, but he hears the Italian cite Montaigne in French in the line: "I do not paint its being, I paint its passage."

The Baroque is elusive, it moves from country to country, from century to century, the sixteenth in Italy, the Council of Trent, the Counter-Reformation, the first half of the seventeenth century in France, Scarron, Saint-Amant, second half of the seventeenth century, return to Italy, Bavaria, eighteenth century, Prague, St. Petersburg, South America, Rococo . . . There is no unity to the Baroque, no essence of fixed things, no permanence. The Baroque is movement. Bernini, Borromini. Tiepolo, Monteverdi.

The Italian lists generalities in good taste.

Then, suddenly, by who knows what mechanism, what path, what detour in the human mind, he finds his guiding principle, the one he can ride like a surfer on a wave of rhetoric and paradox: *"Il Barocco è la Peste."*

The Baroque is the Plague.

The quintessence of the Baroque is to be found here, in Venice. In the bulbs of the San Marco basilica, in the arabesques of the façades, in the grotesque palaces that reach out toward the lagoon, and, of course, in the Carnival.

And why? The Italian knows his local history. From 1348 to 1632, the plague comes and goes and comes again, tirelessly delivering its message: *Vanitas vanitatum.* In 1462, 1485, the plague strikes and ravages the Republic. In 1506, *omnia vanita*, it returns. In 1576, it takes Titian. Life is a carnival. The doctors have masks with long white beaks.

The history of Venice is essentially a long dialogue with the plague.

The Serenissima's response was Veronese (*Christ Arresting the Plague*), Tintoretto (*St. Roch Curing the Plague*), and, at the point of the Dogana, Baldassare Longhena's church without a façade: the Salute, of which the German art critic Wittkower would say: "an absolute triumph in terms of sculptural form, baroque monumentality, and the richness of the light within it."

In the audience, Sollers takes notes.

Octagonal, no façade, filled with emptiness.

The strange stone wheels of the Salute are like rolls of foam petrified by the Medusa. The perpetual movement is a response to the vanity of the world.

The Baroque is the Plague, and therefore it is Venice.

Pretty good, thinks Simon.

Swept along by his own momentum, the Italian goes on: what is the *Classique*? Where have we ever seen the "Classical"? Is Versailles Classical? The Classical is always postponed. We always name something as Classical after the event. People talk about it, but no one has ever seen it.

They wanted to transpose the political absolutism of Louis

299

XIV's reign into an aesthetic current based on order, unity, harmony, in opposition to the period of instability of the Fronde, which had preceded it.

Simon thinks that, all things considered, this southern peasant with his too-short trousers knows quite a bit about history, art, and art history.

He hears the simultaneous translation in his headphones: "But there are no classical authors . . . in the present . . . The label *classical* . . . is just a sort of medal . . . awarded by school textbooks."

The Italian concludes: The Baroque is here. The Classical does not exist.

Prolonged applause.

Bayard nervously lights a cigarette.

Simon leans on his lectern.

He had a choice between preparing his speech while the other man was speaking or listening attentively so he could turn his words against him, and he preferred the second, more aggressive option.

"To say that classicism does not exist is to say that Venice does not exist."

A war of annihilation, then. Like Lepanto.

By using the word *classicism*, he knows that he is committing an anachronism but he doesn't care because "Baroque" and "Classical" are ideas forged in retrospect, inherently anachronistic, summoned to support unstable, debatable realities.

"And it is all the more curious that these words should be pronounced *here*, in La Fenice, this neoclassical pearl."

Simon uses the word *pearl* deliberately. He already has his plan of attack.

"It also means wiping the Giudecca and San Giorgio from the map rather quickly." He turns to his adversary. "Did Palladio never exist? Are his neoclassical churches just baroque dreams? My honorable opponent sees the Baroque everywhere, and that is his right, but . . ."

Without any discussion, then, the two adversaries have come to an agreement on the subject's central problem: Venice. Is Venice baroque or classical? It is Venice that will decide the tie.

Simon turns to the audience again and declaims: "Order and beauty, luxury, peace and pleasure: Is there a more appropriate line to describe Venice? And is there a better definition of classicism?" And Barthes, to follow Baudelaire: "Classics. Culture (the more culture there is, the greater and more diverse the pleasure). Intelligence. Irony. Delicacy. Euphoria. Mastery. Safety: the art of living." Simon: "Venice!"

The Classical exists and its home is here, in Venice. Step one.

Step two: Show that your opponent has not understood the subject.

"My honorable adversary must have misheard: it is not Baroque or Classical, but Baroque *and* Classical. Why oppose them? They are the yin and the yang that comprise Venice and the universe, like the Apollonian and the Dionysian, like the sublime and the grotesque, reason and passion, Racine and Shakespeare." (Simon does not dwell on this last example, as Stendhal quite obviously preferred Shakespeare—as he does, for that matter.)

"It is not a question of playing Palladio against the bulbs of the San Marco basilica. Look. Palladio's Redentore?" Simon peers toward the back of the theater as though visualizing the bank of the Giudecca. "On one side, Byzantium and the flamboyant Gothic of the past (if I may put it like that); on the other, Ancient Greece resurrected eternally by the Renaissance and the Counter-Reformation." Nothing ever goes to waste for a duelist. Sollers smiles as he looks at Kristeva, who recognizes his words, and he makes smoke rings of contentment, tapping his fingers on the gilded wood of his box.

"Take Corneille's *Le Cid*. A quasi-picaresque baroque tragicomedy when it was written, later reclassified (after much debate) as classical tragedy when genre fantasies went out of fashion. Order, unities, framework? Doesn't matter. Two plays in one, and yet the same play: baroque one day, classical the next."

Simon has other interesting examples—Lautréamont, for instance, champion of the darkest romanticism, who transforms into Isidore Ducasse, perverse defender of mutant classicism in his incredible *Poésies*—but he does not want to digress: "Two great rhetorical traditions: Atticism and Asianism. On one side, the West's rigorous clarity, Boileau's 'Whatever is well conceived is clearly said'; on the other, the lyrical flights and ornaments, the abundance of tropes of the sensual, tangled East."

Simon knows perfectly well that Atticism and Asianism are concepts without any concrete geographical foundation, at most transhistorical metaphors. But by this point he knows that the judges know he knows this, so he has no need to make it clear.

"And at the confluence of the two? Venice, the crossroads of the universe! Venice, amalgam of Sea and Earth, earth on sea, lines and curves, Heaven and Hell, the lion and the crocodile, San Marco and Casanova, sun and mist, movement *and* eternity!"

Simon takes one last pause before closing his peroration resoundingly: "Baroque and Classical? The proof: Venice."

Prolonged applause.

The Italian wants to strike back without delay, but Simon has deprived him of his synthesis, so he is forced to play against his nature. He says, in French, which Simon admires but interprets as evidence of his annoyance: "But Venice is the sea! My opponent's poor attempt at dialectics makes no difference. The liquid element is the *barocco*. The solid, the fixed, the rigid, is the *classico*. Venice *è il mare!*" So Simon remembers what he has learned during his stay here: the *Bucentaur*, the ring thrown into the sea, and Eco's stories: "No, Venice is the husband of the sea; that is not the same thing."

"The city of masks! Of mirrored glass! Of sparkling mosaics! The city sinking into the lagoon! Venice is made of water, sand, and mud!"

"And stone. Lots of marble."

"The marble is baroque! It is striated with veins, full of internal layers, and it breaks all the time."

"No, marble is classical. In France, we say *gravé dans le marbre*."

"The Carnival! Casanova! Cagliostro!"

"Yes, in the collective unconscious Casanova is the king of baroque *par excellence*. But he is the last. We bury a bygone world in an apotheosis."

"*Ma*, that is the identity of Venice: an eternal agony. The eighteenth century is Venice."

Simon senses that he is losing ground, that he cannot maintain this paradox of solid, straight-lined Venice much longer, but he refuses to give up: "No, the Venice of strength, glory, dominance, is the Venice of the sixteenth century, before its disappearance, its decomposition. The Baroque that you defend is what is killing it."

The Italian sees his chance and takes it: "But decomposition *is* Venice! Its identity is precisely its inevitable advancement toward death."

"But Venice must have a future! The Baroque that you describe is the rope that supports the hanged man."

"Another baroque image. First you argue, then you condemn, but everything brings you back to the Baroque. Which proves that it is the spirit of the Baroque that forms the grandeur of the city."

In terms of purely logical demonstration, Simon senses that he has begun an argument where his opponent has the upper hand. But, thankfully, rhetoric is not all about logic, so he plays the *pathos* card: Venice must live.

"Perhaps the Baroque is that poison that kills her but renders her more beautiful in death." (Avoid making concessions, Simon thinks.) "But take *The Merchant of Venice*: where does salvation come from? Women who live on an island: on earth!"

The Italian exclaims triumphantly: "Portia? Who disguises herself as a man? *Ma*, that's *totalmente barocco*! It is even the triumph of the Baroque over the obtuse rationalism of Shylock, over law, behind which Shylock shelters to claim his pound of flesh. That inflexible interpretation of the letter of the law is the very expression, dare I say, of a *proto-classical neurosis*."

Simon can feel that the audience appreciates the audacity of this phrase, but at the same time he can see that his adversary is rambling a bit about Shylock, and this is a good thing because he is beginning to be seriously perturbed by the theme under discussion: his doubts and paranoia about the solidity of his own existence are returning to haunt his mind when he needs all his concentration. He rushes to move his pawns toward Shakespeare ("life is a poor player that struts and frets his hour upon the stage": Why does this line from *Macbeth* come to him now? *Where* does it come from? Simon forces himself to push the question away for later consideration): "Portia is precisely that mélange of baroque madness and classical genius that enables her to defeat Shylock not, like the other characters, by recourse to feelings but with firm, unassailable legal arguments, with an exemplary rationality, founded on Shylock's own demonstration, which she throws back at him: 'A pound of that same merchant's flesh is thine; the court awards it, and the law doth give it . . . [but] *this bond doth give thee here no jot of blood.*' At this moment, Antonio is saved by a piece of legal trickery: a *baroque* gesture, admittedly, but a *classical* baroque."

Simon can feel the public's approval. The Italian knows he has lost the initiative again, so he strives to dismantle what he calls Simon's "specious and pathetic convolutions" and, in doing so, makes a small mistake of his own. To denounce Simon's dubious leaps of logic, he asks: "*Ma*, who decided that the law was a classical value?," when it was he himself who had presupposed it in his previous argument. But Simon, too tired or too distracted, misses his opportunity to point out the contradiction and the Italian is able to go on: "Are we not reaching the limits of my opponent's system?"

And he puts his boot on Simon's neck: "What my honorable adversary is doing is very simple: he is forcing his analogies."

So Simon is attacked where he normally excels—in the area of metadiscourse—and he feels that if he lets that happen, he risks being beaten at his own game, so he clings to his argument: "Your defense of Venice is booby-trapped. You had to reinvent it with an alliance, and that alliance is Portia: that cocktail of trickery and pragmatism. When Venice risks losing itself behind its masks, Portia brings from her island her baroque madness *and* her classical common sense."

Simon is finding it harder and harder to concentrate; he thinks about the "prestiges" of the seventeenth century, of Cervantes fighting at Lepanto, of his course on James Bond at Vincennes, of the dissecting table at the anatomical theater in Bologna, of the cemetery in Ithaca and a thousand things at the same time, and he understands that he can only triumph if he overcomes, in a *mise en abyme* that he would savor in other circumstances, this baroque vertigo that is taking hold of him.

He decides to bring an end to the discussion of Shakespeare, which he thinks he has safely negotiated, and condense all his mental energy into changing the subject, to turn his adversary away from the metadiscursive approach he had begun, where, for the first time, Simon does not feel at ease.

"One word, again: *Serenissima.*"

With this, he obliges his opponent to react and by interrupting the rhetorical sequence that he was about to build, to wrestle the initiative away from him again. The Italian ripostes: *"Repubblica e barocco!"*

At this stage of the improvisation, Simon plays for time and says everything that comes to mind: "That depends. A thousand years of doges. Stable institutions. Firm authority. Churches everywhere: God is not baroque, as Einstein said. Napoleon, on the contrary [and Simon deliberately invokes the man who was the gravedigger of the Venetian Republic]: an absolute monarch, but he moved all the time. Very baroque, but also very classical, in his way."

The Italian tries to respond, but Simon cuts in: "Ah, it's true, I forgot: the Classical does not exist! In that case, what have we been talking about for the last half hour?" The audience stops breathing. His opponent reels slightly under the force of this uppercut.

Heads spinning from the effort and the nervous tension, the two men are now debating in a way that can only be described as anarchic. Behind them, the three judges, appreciating that they have each given the best of themselves, decide to put an end to the duel.

Simon suppresses a smile of relief and turns toward them. He realizes that these three judges must be sophists (because normally the jury is composed of members of higher ranks than the duelists). All three wear Venetian masks, like the men who attacked Simon, and he understands the advantage of organizing these meetings during Carnival: that way, one can preserve one's anonymity with complete discretion.

The judges vote amid oppressive silence.

The first votes for Simon.

The second for his opponent.

So the verdict rests in the hands of the last judge. Simon stares at the sort of cutting board, stained red by the fingers of the previous competitors. He hears a murmur in the theater as the audience watches the third judge vote, and he dares not look up. For once, he is unable to *interpret* that murmur.

No one has picked up the machete lying on the table.

The third judge voted for him.

His opponent breaks down. He will not lose his finger, because Logos Club rules dictate that only the challenger risks his digital capital, but his rank was very important to him and he is clearly upset at the prospect of demotion.

The audience cheers as Simon is promoted to the rank of tribune. But above all, he is formally given an invitation for two people at the next day's summit meeting. Simon verifies the time and the place, waves to the audience one last time, and joins Bayard in his box, while the theater begins to empty out.

In the box, Bayard reads the information on the invitation card and lights a cigarette, at least his twelfth of the evening. An Englishman pokes his head in to congratulate the victor: "Good game. That guy was tough."

Simon looks at his hands, which are trembling slightly, and says: "I wonder if the sophists are much better."

92

Behind Sollers is *Paradise*: Tintoretto's gigantic canvas, which also, in its time, won a competition—to decorate the Chamber of the Great Council in the Doge's Palace.

At the base of the picture is a huge platform where there are seated not three but ten members of the jury: the full complement of sophists.

In front of them, three-quarters turned to the audience, the Great Protagoras in person, and Sollers, leaning on a lectern.

The ten judges and the two duelists wear Venetian masks, but Simon and Bayard had no trouble recognizing Sollers. Besides, they already spotted Kristeva in the audience.

Unlike in La Fenice, the audience here is standing, gathered in this immense room designed in the fourteenth century to host more than a thousand nobles: 175 feet long, with a ceiling that makes viewers wonder how it is held up without a single column, inlaid with innumerable old master paintings.

The room's effect on the audience is such that a sort of fearful hubbub can be heard. Everyone whispers respectfully under the gaze of Tintoretto and Veronese.

One of the judges stands up, formally announces the start of the meeting in Italian, and draws the subject from one of the urns in front of him.

"On forcène doucement."

One fanatics gently?

The subject seems like it ought to be French, but when Bayard turns to Simon, his partner makes a gesture that suggests he has no clue either.

A wave of perplexity moves through the 175 feet of the room. The non-Francophone spectators check that their simultaneous translation machine is tuned to the right channel.

If Sollers had a second's hesitation behind his mask, he doesn't let it show. In any case, Kristeva, who is standing in the audience, does not bat an eyelid.

Sollers has five minutes to understand the subject, to problematize it, to come up with a thesis, and to back it up with coherent and—if possible—spectacular arguments.

In the meantime, Bayard asks the people around him: What is this incomprehensible subject?

A handsome, well-dressed old man with a silk pocket handkerchief that matches his scarf explains: "*Ma*, the Frenchman is challenging *il Grande Protagoras*. Surely he can't expect 'for or against the death penalty,' *vero?*"

Bayard is willing to agree with this, but he asks why the subject is in French.

The old man replies: "An act of courtesy by the *Grande Protagoras*. I've heard he speaks every language on earth."

"He isn't French?"

"Ma no, è italiano, eh!"

Bayard watches the Great Protagoras calmly smoking his pipe while scribbling a few notes. His figure, his appearance, the shape of his jaw (because the mask covers only his eyes) . . . all of this is vaguely familiar.

When the five minutes are up, Sollers stands tall behind his lectern, eyes the audience, makes a little dance step punctuated by a complete rotation, as if he wanted to verify the presence of the Ten behind his back, bows more or less soberly to his opponent, and begins his speech, a speech he already knows will remain in the annals as *the* speech made by Sollers in his duel with the Great Protagoras.

"*Forcène . . . forcène . . . Fort . . . Scène . . . Fors . . . Seine . . . Faure (Félix) . . . Cène.* President Félix Faure died of a blow job and a heart attack, which caused him to enter history but exit the stage. As a prolegomenon . . . A little appetizer . . . An introduction (ha ha!) . . ."

Simon thinks that Sollers is attempting a boldly Lacanian approach.

Bayard observes Kristeva out of the corner of his eye. Her expression betrays nothing but absolute attentiveness.

"*La force. Et la scène. La force sur scène.* [Strength. And the stage. Strength onstage.] Rodrigue, basically. *Forêt sur Seine.* (Val-de-Marne. Apparently they still nail crows to the doors there.) To squeeze or not to squeeze the Commander's peepee? *That is the question.*"

Bayard gives Simon a questioning look. He replies in a whisper that Sollers has apparently chosen an audacious tactic of replacing logical connections with analogical connections, or rather juxtapositions of ideas, even sequences of images, rather than pure reasoning.

Bayard tries to understand: "Is it baroque?"

Simon is surprised: "Er, yes, I suppose it is."

Sollers goes on: "*Fors scène: hors la scène. Obscène.* [Save for the stage: offstage. Obscene.] It's all there. The rest is of no interest, naturally. The thundering article on 'Sollers the obscene' by Marcelin Pleynet? Without hesitation. Well, well, what? Oh there, oh! Gently ... From where ... seed ... From where does the seed come? From up above, of course! [He points to the ceiling and Veronese's paintings.] Art is the seed of God. [He points to the wall behind him.] Tintoretto is his prophet ... *D'ailleurs, il tinte aux rets* ... [What's more, he rings the net ...] Blessed is the age when the bell and thread will once again replace the hammer and sickle ... After all, are these not the two tools of the fisherman?"

Does Bayard detect a faint wrinkle of concern on Kristeva's Slavic face?

"If the fish could put their heads above the water, they would perceive that their world is not the only world ..."

Simon is beginning to find Sollers's strategy *extremely* audacious.

Bayard whispers in his ear: "A bit too Hollywood, isn't it?"

The old man with the pocket handkerchief mutters: "He's got *coglioni*, this *francese*. At the same time, if he's going to use them, it's now or never."

Bayard asks him to elaborate.

The old man replies: "Clearly, he has not understood the subject any more than we have, *vero*? So he is trying to *flamber à l'esbroufe*—to bullshit his way through it, *no*? It's brave."

Sollers rests an elbow on the lectern, which obliges him to lean down lopsidedly. Curiously, however, this unnatural pose makes him look relatively relaxed.

"*Je suis venu j'ai vu j'ai vomu.*" I came, I saw, I vomited.

Sollers's speech accelerates, becomes more fluid, almost musical: "God is really close without mystery gently oiled gently hand of *mysfère* glove of hell . . ." Then he says something that Simon and even Bayard find surprising: "The belief in tickle-wickle on the organ enables the corpse to be maintained as the sole fundamental value." After uttering these words, Sollers licks his lips lasciviously. Bayard can now observe clear signs of tension on Kristeva's face.

Bayard lets himself be rocked by the rhythm, like a river carrying little logs that occasionally knock against a fragile boat.

". . . the whole soul of Christ did it enjoy bliss in its passion it seems not for several reasons is it not impossible to suffer and to enjoy at the same time since pain and joy are opposites Aristotle notes it does not deep sadness prevent delectation however the opposite is true . . ."

Sollers is salivating more and more but he goes on: "I change form name revelation nickname I am the same I mutate sometimes palace sometimes hut pharaoh dove or sheep transfiguration transubstantiation ascension . . ."

Then he comes to his peroration—the audience can tell, even if they cannot follow it: "I will be what I will be that means take care of what I am as much as I am in I am don't forget that I am what follows if I am tomorrow I will be what I am at the point where I would be . . ."

Bayard exclaims to Simon: "Is that it, the seventh function of language?"

Simon feels his paranoia rise again, thinking that a character like Sollers cannot really exist.

Sollers concludes, abruptly: "I am the opposite of the Nazi-Soviet."

Universal stupefaction.

Even the Great Protagoras looks gobsmacked. He hums and haws, a little embarrassed. Then he takes the stand, because it's his turn.

Simon and Bayard recognize Umberto Eco's voice.

"I don't know where to start, after that. My honorable opponent has, how to say it, fired on all cylinders, *si?*"

Eco turns to Sollers and politely bows, readjusting the nose of his mask.

"Perhaps I might make a little etymological remark, to begin with? You will no doubt have noted, dear audience, honorable members of the jury, that the verb *forcener* no longer exists in modern French, its only surviving trace being the substantive *forcené*, which signifies a mad individual who behaves violently.

"Now, this definition of *forcené* might lead us into error. Originally—if I may make a little orthographical remark—*forcener* was written with an *s*, not a *c*, because it came from the Latin *sensus*, 'sense' (*'animal quod sensu caret'*): *forsener*, then, is literally to be out of one's senses, in other words, to be mad, but to begin with there was no connotation of force.

"That said, this connotation must have appeared gradually, with the orthographic renovation that suggested a false etymology and, I would say, that from the sixteenth century onward this spelling was attested to in Middle French.

"*Allora*, the question that I would have discussed, if my honorable opponent had raised it, is this: Is '*forcener doucement*' an oxymoron? Is this an association of two contradictory terms?

"*No*, if one considers the true etymology of *forcener*.

"*Si*, if one accepts the connotation of force in the false etymology.

"*Si*, but . . . are *gentle* and *strong* necessarily opposed? A force can be exercised gently, for example when you are taken by the current of a river, or when you gently squeeze a loved one's hand . . ."

The singsong accent resonates through the large room, but everyone has grasped the violence of the attack: beneath his debonair appearance, Eco has calmly underlined the insufficiencies in Sollers's speech by conjuring, alone, a discussion that his opponent was unable to even begin.

"But none of that tells us what it's about, *no?*

"I will be more modest than my opponent, who attempted some very ambitious and, I think, pardon me, somewhat fanciful interpretations of this expression. For my part, I will simply try to explain it to you: he who '*forcène doucement*' is the poet, *ecco*. It is the *furor poeticus*. I am not sure who uttered that phrase, but I would say it is a sixteenth-century French poet, a disciple of Jean Dorat, a member of the Pléiade, because one can clearly sense here the Neoplatonic influence.

"For Plato, you know, poetry is not an art, not a technique, but a divine inspiration. The poet is inhabited by the god, in a trancelike state: that is what Socrates explains to Ion in his famous dialogue. So the poet is mad, but it is a gentle madness, a creative madness, not a destructive madness.

"I do not know the author of this citation, but I think it is perhaps Ronsard or Du Bellay, both of them disciples of a school where, *giustamente*, '*on forcène doucement.*'

"*Allora*, we can discuss the question of divine inspiration, if you like? I don't know, because I didn't really understand what my honorable opponent wanted to discuss."

Silence in the room. Sollers realizes that it is his turn to speak. He hesitates.

Simon mechanically analyzes Eco's strategy, which can be summarized very simply: do the opposite of Sollers. This implies adopting an ultramodest *ethos* and a very sober and minimalist level of development. The refusal of all fanciful interpretations and a very literal explanation. By falling back on his proverbial erudition, Eco simply explained without making an argument, as if to underline the impossibility of discussion in the face of his opponent's frenzied logorrhea. He uses rigor and humility to highlight his megalomaniacal adversary's mental disorder.

Sollers starts to speak again, less confidently: "I talk about philosophy because the action of literature now is to show that the philosophical discourse can be integrated into the position of the literary subject, if only so that its experience be taken all the way to the transcendental horizon."

But Eco does not reply.

Sollers, panic-stricken, blurts out: "Aragon wrote a thundering article about me! About my genius! And Elsa Triolet! I have their autographs!"

Embarrassed silence.

One of the ten sophists makes a gesture and two guards, stationed at the room's entrance, seize the dazed Sollers, who rolls his eyes and yells: "Tickle-wickle! Ho ho ho! No no no!"

Bayard asks why there has not been a vote. The old man replies that in certain cases, unanimity is obvious.

The two guards lay the loser on the marble floor in front of the platform and one of the sophists advances, a large pair of pruning shears in his hands.

The guards strip Sollers from the waist down as he screams beneath Tintoretto's *Paradise*. Some of the other sophists leave their seats to help control him. In the confusion, his mask comes off.

Only the first few rows of the audience see what happens at the foot of the platform but everyone, all the way to the back, knows.

The sophist with the doctor's beak wedges Sollers's balls between the two blades of the shears, firmly grips the handles, and presses them together. Snip.

Kristeva shudders.

Sollers makes an unidentifiable noise, a sort of throat-clack followed by a long caterwaul that ricochets off the paintings and reverberates throughout the room.

The sophist with the doctor's beak picks up the two balls and drops them in a second urn, which Simon and Bayard now realize was put there for that very purpose.

Pale-faced, Simon asks his neighbor: "Isn't the penalty normally a finger?"

The man replies that it is when one challenges a duelist of a rank just above yours, but Sollers wanted to cut corners. He had never participated in a single duel and he directly challenged the Great Protagoras. "In that case, the price is higher."

While the attendants attempt to give first aid to Sollers, who squirms and makes horrible moaning noises, Kristeva takes the urn containing the testicles and leaves the room.

Bayard and Simon follow her.

She quickly crosses Piazza San Marco, cradling the urn in her arms. The night is still young and the square is packed with tourists, stilt-walkers, fire-eaters, actors in eighteenth-century costumes pretending to duel with swords. Simon and Bayard push their way through the crowds so as not to lose her. She rushes down narrow alleyways, crosses bridges, does not turn around once. A man dressed as Harlequin grabs her by the waist to kiss her, but she emits a piercing cry, escapes his clutches like a small wild animal, and runs away carrying her urn. Crosses the Rialto. Bayard and Simon are not certain that she knows where she is going. From far off, in the sky, they hear fireworks exploding. Kristeva trips on a step and almost drops the urn. Her breath hangs in the air. It's cold, and she has left her coat at the Doge's Palace.

All the same, she does make it somewhere: to the basilica Santa Maria Gloriosa dei Frari, home, in her husband's own words, to "the glorious heart of the Serenissima," with Titian's tomb and his red *Assumption*. At this time of night, the basilica is closed. But she doesn't want to go inside.

It is chance that has brought her here.

She advances over the little bridge that straddles the Rio dei Frari and stops in the middle. She puts the urn on the stone ledge. Simon and Bayard are just behind her, but they dare not set foot on the bridge, nor climb the handful of steps to join her.

Kristeva listens to the murmur of the city, and her dark eyes stare down at the little waves formed by the nocturnal breeze. A fine rain wets her short hair.

From within her blouse, she takes a sheet of paper folded in four.

Bayard feels an urge to throw himself at her and tear the document from her hands, but Simon holds him back. She turns toward them and narrows her eyes, as though she has only just noticed their presence, as though she has only just learned of their existence, and glares at them with hatred, a cold look that petrifies Bayard, while she unfolds the page.

It is too dark to see what is written on it, but Simon thinks he can make out a few cramped letters. And there is definitely writing on both sides.

Slowly, calmly, Kristeva starts to rip it up.

As she does this, the increasingly small scraps fly off over the canal.

In the end, nothing remains but the black wind and the delicate sound of rain.

93

"But in your opinion, did she know or didn't she?"

Bayard tries to understand.

Simon is perplexed.

It seems possible that Sollers failed to realize that the seventh function didn't work. But Kristeva?

"Difficult to say. I'd have had to read the document."

Why would she have betrayed her husband? And, from another perspective, why not use the function herself to compete?

Bayard says to Simon: "Maybe she was like us. Maybe she wanted to see if it worked before she tried it?"

Simon watches the crowd of tourists leaving Venice as if in slow motion. Bayard and he are waiting for the vaporetto with their little suitcases and, as Carnival is coming to an end, the line is long, with hordes of tourists heading to the train station and the airport. A vaporetto arrives, but it's not the right one; they must wait a little longer.

Simon is pensive, and asks Bayard: "What is reality, for you?"

As Bayard obviously has no idea what he's talking about, Simon tries to be more specific: "How do you know that you're not in a novel? How do you know you are not living inside a work of fiction? How do you know that you're *real*?"

Bayard looks at Simon with genuine curiosity and replies indulgently: "Are you stupid or what? Reality is what we live, that's all."

Their vaporetto arrives, and as it draws alongside, Bayard pats Simon's shoulder: "Don't ask yourself so many questions, son."

The vessel is boarded in a disorderly scramble, the vaporetto guys herding the stupid tourists who climb on board so clumsily, with their bags and their children.

When it is Simon's turn to get in the boat, the head-count man brings down a metal barrier just behind his back. Stuck on the dock, Bayard tries to protest, but the Italian replies indifferently: *"Tutto esaurito."*

Bayard tells Simon to wait for him at the next stop. Simon waves goodbye, as a joke.

The vaporetto moves away. Bayard lights a cigarette. Behind him, he hears raised voices. He turns around and sees two Japanese men yelling at each other. Intrigued, he goes over to them. One of the Japanese men says to him, in French: "Your friend has just been abducted."

It takes Bayard a second or two to process this information.

A second or two, no more, then he switches into cop mode and asks the only question a cop must ask: "Why?"

The second Japanese man says: "Because he won, the day before yesterday."

The Italian he beat is a very powerful Neapolitan politician, and he did not take defeat well. Bayard knows about the assault after the party at the Ca' Rezzonico. The Japanese men explain: the Neapolitan sent some henchmen to beat Simon up so he couldn't compete, because he was afraid of him. Now that he has lost the duel, he wants vengeance.

Bayard watches the vanishing vaporetto. He quickly analyzes the situation, then looks around: he sees the bronze statue of a sort of general with a thick mustache, he sees the façade of the Hotel Danieli, he sees boats moored at the dock. He sees a gondolier on his gondola, waiting for the tourists.

He jumps in the gondola, along with the Japanese men. The gondolier does not seem overly surprised and welcomes them by singing to himself in Italian, but Bayard tells him:

"Follow that vaporetto!"

The gondolier pretends not to understand, so Bayard takes out a wad of lire and the gondolier starts to scull.

The vaporetto is a good three hundred yards ahead, and in 1981 there are no mobile phones.

The gondolier is surprised. It's strange, he says: that vaporetto is not going the right way. It's headed toward the island of Murano.

The vaporetto has been hijacked.

On board, Simon has not realized what is happening, since almost all the passengers are tourists with no idea where they should be going, and apart from two or three Italians who protest to the driver, no one notices that they are headed the wrong way. Besides, Italians complaining loudly is nothing new; the passengers simply think it is part of the local color. The vaporetto docks at Murano.

In the distance, Bayard's gondola is attempting to catch up. Bayard and the Japanese men exhort the gondolier to go faster, and they yell Simon's name to warn him, but they are too far away and Simon has no reason to pay them any attention.

But he does suddenly feel the point of a knife in his back and hears a voice behind him say: *"Prego."* He understands that he must get off the boat. He obeys. The tourists, in a rush to catch their plane, do not see the knife, and the vaporetto is on its way again.

Simon stands on the dock. He feels almost certain that the men behind him are the same three who attacked him in masks the other night.

They enter one of the glassblowers' workshops that open directly onto the docks. Inside, a craftsman is kneading a piece of molten glass just removed from the oven, and Simon watches, fascinated, as the bubble of glass is blown, stretched, modeled, taking shape with only a few touches of a plunger as a little rearing horse.

Next to the oven stands a balding, paunchy man in a mismatched suit. Simon recognizes him; his opponent from La Fenice.

"Benvenuto!"

Simon faces the Neapolitan, surrounded by the three thugs. The glassblower continues shaping his little horses unperturbed.

"Bravo! Bravo! I wanted to congratulate you personally before you leave. Palladio—that was well played. Easy, but well played. And Portia. It didn't convince me, but it convinced the jury, *vero?* Ah, Shakespeare . . . I should have mentioned Visconti . . . Have you seen *Senso?* The story of a foreigner in Venice. It doesn't end well."

The Neapolitan approaches the glassblower, who is busy shaping the hoofs of a second little horse. He takes out a cigar, which he lights with the incandescent glass, then turns to Simon with an evil grin.

"Ma, I can't let you leave without giving you something to remember me by. How do you say it? To each his due, yes?" One of the henchmen immobilizes Simon with an arm around his neck. Simon tries to free himself, but the second punches him in the chest, winding him, and the third grabs his right arm.

The three men push him forward and pull his arm over the glassblower's workbench. The little glass horses fall and smash on the floor. The glassblower takes a step back but does not seem surprised. Their eyes meet, and Simon sees in this man's expression that he knows exactly what is expected of him and he is in no position to refuse. Simon starts to panic. He struggles and yells, but his yelling is pure reflex, because he is certain that he cannot expect any help. He doesn't know that reinforcements are on their way, that Bayard and the Japanese are arriving in a gondola and that they have promised the gondolier they will triple his fee if he gets them there in record time.

The glassblower asks: *"Che dito?"*

Bayard and the Japanese use their suitcases as oars to make the boat move faster and the gondolier puts his all into it because, without knowing what exactly is at stake, he has gathered that it is serious.

The Neapolitan asks Simon: "Which finger? Do you have a preference?"

Simon kicks like a horse, but the three men hold his arm firmly on the workbench. He no longer wonders if he is a character in a novel; his reactions are pure survival instinct, and he tries desperately to free himself, but in vain.

The gondola finally reaches land and Bayard throws all his lire at the gondolier and jumps onto the dock, along with the Japanese, but there is a whole line of glassblowers' workshops and they have no idea where Simon was taken. So they rush into each of them randomly, calling out to the craftsmen and salesmen and tourists, but no one has seen Simon.

The Neapolitan takes a drag on his cigar and orders: *"Tutta la mano."*

The glassblower changes his tongs for a bigger pair and seizes Simon's wrist in the cast-iron jaws.

Bayard and the Japanese burst into a workshop, where they have to describe the young Frenchman to Italians who do not understand them because they are talking too fast, so Bayard leaves the workshop and goes into the one next door, but there, too, no one has seen the Frenchman. Bayard knows perfectly well that rushing around in a panic is no way to carry out an investigation but he has a policeman's intuition of urgency, even though he is not aware of exactly what is happening, and he runs from one workshop to the next, and from one shop to the next.

But it's too late: the glassblower again closes the cast-iron jaws around Simon's wrist and crushes the flesh, the ligaments, and the bones, until the latter break with a sinister cracking noise and his right hand is detached from his arm in a fountain of blood.

The Neapolitan contemplates his mutilated adversary as he collapses, and seems to hesitate briefly.

Has he obtained sufficient compensation, yes or no?

He takes a drag on his cigar, blows a few smoke rings, and says: "Let's go."

Simon's screaming alerts Bayard and the Japanese, who find him at last lying inanimate on the floor of the glassblower's workshop, bleeding profusely, surrounded by little broken horses.

Bayard knows there is not a second to lose. He is searching for the hand but he can't find it. He looks all over the floor, but there is nothing but fragments of little glass horses that crack under his soles. If nothing is done in the next few minutes, he realizes, Simon will bleed to death.

So one of the Japanese men takes a sort of spatula from the still-hot oven and presses it to the wound. The cauterized flesh emits a hideous whistling noise. The pain wakes Simon, who screams deliriously. The smell of burned flesh reaches the shop next door, intriguing the customers, oblivious to the drama unfolding in the glassblower's workshop.

Bayard thinks that cauterizing the wound has made any kind of hand transplant impossible and that Simon will remain one-handed for the rest of his life, but the Japanese man who performed the operation, as if reading his thoughts, shows him the oven, so that he will have no regrets: inside, like a Rodin sculpture, the curled-up fingers crackle and glow at the end of the charred hand.

PART V

PARIS

■

94

"I don't believe it! That bitch Thatcher let Bobby Sands die!"

Simon hops about angrily as he watches Patrick Poivre d'Arvor announce, on the Channel 2 news, the death of the Irish activist after sixty-six days of hunger strike.

Bayard comes out of his kitchen and glances at the TV. He remarks: "Yeah, but you can't really stop someone committing suicide, can you?"

Simon yells at him: "Can you hear yourself, you stupid pig? He was twenty-seven!"

Bayard tries to argue his point: "He belonged to a terrorist organization. The IRA kill people, don't they?"

Simon almost chokes: "That's exactly what Laval said about the Resistance! I wouldn't have wanted a cop like you checking my papers in 1940!"

Bayard decides that it is better not to reply to this, so he pours his guest another glass of port, puts a bowl of cocktail sausages on the coffee table, and goes back into the kitchen.

PPDA talks about the assassination of a Spanish general and presents a report on Spaniards nostalgic for the Franco years, barely three months after the attempted coup d'état in the Madrid parliament.

Simon turns back to the magazine that he bought before

coming here and which he began to read on the metro. It was the front-page headline that had made him curious: "Referendum: The Top 42 Intellectuals." The magazine asked five hundred "cultural personalities" (Simon pulls a face) to name the three most important French intellectuals alive today. First comes Lévi-Strauss; second: Sartre; third: Foucault. After that, Lacan, Beauvoir, Yourcenar, Braudel . . .

Simon looks for Derrida in the rankings, forgetting that he is dead. (He imagines he would have been on the podium, though no one will ever know.)

BHL is tenth.

Michaux, Beckett, Aragon, Cioran, Ionesco, Duras . . .

Sollers, twenty-fourth. As there is a rundown of the votes and Sollers is also one of the voters, Simon notes that he voted for Kristeva while Kristeva voted for him. (Same reciprocal deal with BHL.)

Simon nabs a cocktail sausage and shouts at Bayard: "So, have you heard any news about Sollers?"

Bayard comes out of the kitchen, holding a dish towel: "He's out of the hospital. Kristeva stayed at his bedside throughout his convalescence. From what I've heard, he's leading a normal life again. According to my information, he had his balls buried on an island cemetery in Venice. He says he'll go back twice a year to pay tribute to them—once for each ball."

Bayard hesitates before adding, gently, without looking at Simon: "He looks like he's recovering quite well."

Althusser, twenty-fifth: the murder of his wife hasn't made much of a dent in his credibility, Simon thinks.

"Hey, that smells good, what is it?"

Bayard goes back into the kitchen: "Eat some olives while you're waiting."

PPDA (who voted for Aron, Gracq, and d'Ormesson) says: "In Washington, where they are celebrating the rise in the dollar: five francs forty . . ."

Bayard pokes his head in: "Were you talking to me?"

Simon grumbles incoherently; Bayard returns to his kitchen. PPDA's program ends with the weather forecast, given by Alain Gillot-Pétré, who predicts some sunshine at last to brighten this freezing May (54 degrees in Paris, 48 in Besançon).

After the ads, the screen turns blue, bombastic music featuring brass and cymbals plays, and a message announces the great presidential election debate.

Then the blue screen gives way to the two journalists who will chair the debate. It is May 5, 1981.

Simon shouts: "Jacques, come on! It's starting."

Bayard joins Simon in the living room with beers and Apéricubes. He pops open two bottles while the journalist chosen by Giscard, Jean Boissonnat—Europe 1 commentator, gray three-piece suit, stripy tie, face of a man who will flee to Switzerland if the Socialists win—explains how the evening will unfold.

Beside him, Michèle Cotta—RTL journalist, black helmet hair, fluorescent lipstick, fuchsia blouse, and mauve waistcoat—pretends to take notes while smiling nervously.

Simon, who does not listen to RTL, asks who the pink Russian doll is. Bayard sniggers stupidly.

Giscard explains that he would like this debate to be constructive.

Simon tries to unwrap one of the ham-flavored cream-cheese cubes with his teeth, but can't manage it and becomes annoyed. Bayard takes the Apéricube from Simon's hand and removes the foil wrapper for him.

Giscard and Mitterrand taunt each other over their embarrassing allies: Chirac, who, at the time, is considered a representative of the hard Right, ultraconservative, borderline fascist (18 percent), and Marchais, the Communist candidate during the Brezhnev era of decomposing Stalinism (15 percent). Both finalists need their respective support in order to be elected to the second round.

Giscard points out that if he was reelected he would not need to dissolve the National Assembly, whereas his opponent would either govern with the Communists or be a president without a majority: "One cannot lead the people blindfolded. This is an important country and its people must know where they are going." Simon notes that Giscard has problems conjugating the verb *dissoudre* (dissolve) and says to Bayard that Polytechnique graduates are illiterates. Reflexively, Bayard replies: "Send the Commies to Moscow!" Giscard says to Mitterrand: "You cannot say to the French people: 'I want to deliver major change, but it could be with anyone . . . even including the current Assembly.' In that case, don't dissolve it."

As Giscard hammers away at his point about parliamentary instability, because he cannot imagine that the Socialists could possibly win a majority in the Assembly, Mitterrand replies, rather formally: "I wish to win the presidential election, I believe I will win it, and when I have won it, I will do all that must be done within the law to win the legislative elections. And if you imagine that, from next Monday, that will not be France's state of mind, its formidable desire for change, then it is because you do not understand anything that is happening in this country." And while Bayard curses the Bolshevik vermin, Simon mechanically notes the coded message: Mitterrand is obviously not speaking to Giscard, but to all those who detest Giscard.

But they have been discussing the parliamentary majority for half an hour now, with Giscard's game plan being to constantly suggest the bogeyman of Communist ministers, and Simon thinks it is getting rather boring, when suddenly Mitterrand—who's been on the defensive up to that point—finally decides to launch a counterattack: "As for your anti-Communist outpourings, let me just say that they merit a few corrections. After all, it's a bit too easy. [Pause.] You realize, there is a large number of Communist workers. [Pause.] Following your line of logic, you have to ask: What purpose do they serve? They serve to produce, to work, to pay taxes, they serve to die in wars, they serve to do everything. But they can never serve to make a majority in France?"

Simon, who was about to stuff another cocktail sausage into his mouth, stops with the sausage in midair. And while the journalists home in on another boring question, he realizes, just like Giscard, that perhaps the debate has shifted. Because Giscard finds himself on the defensive and changes his tone, aware as he is of what's at stake now, in an era when the equation *Worker = Communist* is not even questioned: "But . . . I am not attacking the Communist electorate, not at all. In seven years, Monsieur Mitterrand, I have never said a single disobliging word about the French working class. Never! I respect it in its work, in its activities, even in its political expression."

Simon laughs mockingly: "Oh yes, of course, every year you wolf down merguez at the Fête de l'Humanité. Between safaris with Bokassa, you like to toast the union metalworkers. Ha ha, yeah, right!"

Bayard glances at his watch and goes back into the kitchen to check the cooking while the journalists question Giscard on his record as president. According to him, it's very good. Mitterrand puts his large glasses back on to demonstrate that, on the contrary, it is absolutely dreadful. Giscard responds by citing Rivarol: "It is a huge advantage to have done nothing. But one should not abuse it." And he maintains the pressure where it hurts. "It is true that you have been minister of words since 1965. Since 1974, I have governed France." Simon gets annoyed: "Yeah, and we've all seen how!" But he knows it is a difficult argument to counter. From the kitchen, Bayard replies: "It's true that compared with ours the Soviet economy is booming!"

Mitterrand decides to twist the knife: "You have a tendency to repeat your old refrain from seven years ago: 'the man of the past.' It is rather awkward that, in the meantime, you have become the passive man."

Bayard laughs: "He still hasn't got over it, has he, eh? That 'man of the past' gibe. Seven years he's been brooding on that."

Simon says nothing because he agrees: it's not a bad comeback, but it does have the feel of something too obviously prepared in advance. At least it has the effect of relaxing Mitterrand, though, like an ice-skater who has just pulled off a triple axel.

There follows a good battle over the French and global economies, and at least the viewers feel that the candidates have earned their keep. Bayard finally serves his main course: a lamb tagine. Simon is wide-eyed: "Whoa, who taught you to cook?" Giscard paints a horrifying picture of a future France under socialism. Bayard says to Simon: "I met my first wife in Algeria. You can play the smart-ass with your semiology, but you don't know everything about my life." Mitterrand reminds Giscard that it was de Gaulle who initiated mass nationalizations in 1945. Bayard opens a bottle of red, a 1976 Côte-de-Beaune. Simon tastes the tagine: "But this is really good!" Mitterrand keeps taking off his glasses and putting them back on. Bayard explains: "Seventy-six was a very good year for Burgundies." Mitterrand declares: "Portugal nationalized its banks, and it is not a socialist country." Simon and Bayard savor the tagine and the Côte-de-Beaune. Bayard deliberately chose a meal that would not necessitate a knife, the stewed meat being tender enough to be cut with the side of a fork. Simon knows that Bayard knows that he knows this, but the two men ignore it. Neither is keen to mention Murano.

While this is going on, Mitterrand shows his teeth. "The bureaucracy is down to you. You are the one in government. If you make all these speeches complaining now of all the administration's misdeeds, where do you think the blame lies? You are governing, so you are responsible! You beat your chest three days before an election—of course you do, I understand perfectly why you do it, but why should I believe that in the next seven years you would do anything differently from what you have done during the last seven?"

Simon notes the shrewd use of the conditional but, absorbed by the delicious tagine and by more bitter memories, his concentration wavers.

Surprised by this sudden aggression, Giscard tries to parry it with his customary disdain: "Please, let us maintain an appropriate tone." But now Mitterrand is ready to let rip: "I intend to express myself exactly as I wish."

And he hits home: "One and a half million unemployed."

Giscard tries to correct him: "Job seekers."

But Mitterrand is no longer in a mood to let anything go: "I am well aware of how you can split hairs."

He goes on: "You have had both inflation and unemployment, but what's more—this is the flaw, this is the sickness that risks being fatal for our society: sixty percent of the unemployed are women . . . most of them are young people . . . it is a tragic attack on the dignity of man and woman . . ."

To start with, Simon does not pay attention. Mitterrand speaks faster and faster, he is more and more aggressive, more and more precise, more and more eloquent.

Giscard is on the ropes, but he is not about to give up without a fight. He suppresses his country squire accent and calls out his Socialist opponent: "The rise in the minimum wage—how much?" Small businesses will not survive it. All the more so since the Socialist program is irresponsible enough to plan to lower social thresholds and extend employees' rights in companies with fewer than ten employees.

The bourgeois from Chamalières has no intention of surrendering.

The two men trade blows.

But Giscard makes a mistake when he asks Mitterrand to tell him the exchange rate of the deutsche mark: "Today's."

Mitterrand replies: "Here, I am not your student and you are not president of the Republic."

Simon drains his glass of wine thoughtfully: there is something self-fulfilling, something of the performative, in that phrase . . .

Bayard goes off to fetch the cheese.

Giscard says: "I am against the suppression of family tax benefits . . . I am in favor of a return to a system of flat-rate taxation . . ." He reels off a whole series of measures with the precision of the good Polytechnique graduate that he is, but it's too late: he has lost.

The debate goes on though, fierce and technical, over nuclear power, the neutron bomb, the Common Market, East-West relations, the defense budget . . .

Mitterrand: "Is Monsieur Giscard d'Estaing trying to say that the Socialists would be bad French people, unwilling to defend their country?"

Giscard, off screen: "Not at all."

Mitterrand, not looking at him: "If he didn't mean that, then his speech was pointless."

Simon is troubled. He grabs a beer from the coffee table, wedges it under his armpit, and tries to remove the cap, but the bottle slips out and falls onto the floor. Bayard waits for Simon to explode with rage because he knows how much his friend hates it when daily life reminds him that he is disabled, so he wipes up the beer that has spilled onto the floorboards and is quick to say: "No big deal!"

But Simon looks strangely perplexed. He points to Mitterrand and says: "Look at him. Notice anything?"

"What?"

"Have you listened to him since the beginning? Don't you think he's been good?"

"Well, yeah, he's better than he was seven years ago, that's for sure."

"No, it's more than that. He's *abnormally* good."

"What do you mean?"

"It's subtle, but since the end of the first half hour, he's been maneuvering Giscard, and I can't work out how he's doing it. It's like an invisible strategy: I can sense it, but I can't understand it."

"You're not saying . . ."

"Watch."

Bayard watches as Giscard busts a gut to show that the Socialists are irresponsible fools who must not under any circumstances be trusted with military hardware and the nuclear deterrent: "When it comes to defense, on the contrary . . . you have never voted with the government on defense, and you have voted against every bill relating to defense. Those bills were presented outside of the budgetary discussion and so it would be perfectly imaginable that either your party or your . . . or you yourself, aware of the very high stakes of national security, would make a nonpartisan vote on military bills. I note that you did not vote for any of the three military bills . . . notably that of January 24, 1963 . . ."

Mitterrand doesn't even bother responding and Michèle Cotta moves on to another subject, so an irritated Giscard insists: "This is very important!" Michèle Cotta protests politely: "Absolutely! Of course, Monsieur President!" And she moves on to African politics. Boissonat is visibly thinking about something else. No one cares. No one is listening to him anymore. It looks as if Mitterrand has completely demolished him.

Bayard begins to understand.

Giscard continues to sink.

Simon spells out his conclusion: "Mitterrand has the seventh function of language."

Bayard tries to assemble the pieces of the puzzle while Mitterrand and Giscard debate French military intervention in Zaire.

"But, Simon, we saw in Venice that the function didn't work."

Mitterrand gives Giscard the coup de grâce on the Kolwezi affair: "So basically, you could have repatriated them earlier . . . if you'd thought about it."

Simon points at the TV set:

"*That* works!"

95

It is raining in Paris, the celebrations have begun at the Bastille, but the Socialist leaders are still at party headquarters, in Rue de Solférino, where an electric joy courses through the ranks of activists. Victory is always an achievement in politics, an end as well as a beginning; that is why the excitement it causes is a mix of euphoria and vertigo. What's more, the alcohol is flowing freely and, already, the canapés are piling up. "What a night!" says Mitterrand.

Jack Lang shakes hands, kisses cheeks, hugs everyone who crosses his path. He smiles at Fabius, who cried like a baby when the results were announced. In the street, people are singing and shouting in the rain. It is a waking dream and a historic moment. On a personal level, he knows that he will be minister of culture. Moati waves his arms around like a conductor. Badinter and Debray dance a sort of minuet. Jospin and Quilès drink to the memory of Jean Jaurès. Young men and women climb on the railings in Rue de Solférino. Camera flashes crackle like thousands of little lightning streaks in the great storm of history. Lang doesn't know which way to turn anymore. Someone hails him: "Monsieur Lang!"

He turns around and sees Bayard and Simon.

Lang is surprised. He immediately realizes that these two have not come to join the celebrations.

Bayard speaks first: "Would you mind giving us a few moments of your time?" He presents his card. Lang registers the red, white, and blue stripes.

"What's this about?"

"It's about Roland Barthes."

The sound of the dead critic's name is like an invisible hand slapping Lang in the face.

"Uh, listen . . . Not really, I don't think this is the right time. Later in the week, perhaps? Just see my secretary and she can make an appointment for you. Now, if you'll excuse me . . ."

But Bayard holds him back by the arm: "I insist."

Pierre Joxe, who is passing, asks: "Is there a problem, Jack?"

Lang looks over at the policemen guarding the gates. Until tonight, the police have been in the service of their opponents, but now he is in a position to ask them to escort these two gentlemen outside.

In the street, the crowd is chanting "The Internationale," punctuated by a chorus of car horns.

Simon rolls up the right sleeve of his jacket and says: "Please. It won't take long."

Lang stares at the stump. Joxe says to him: "Jack?"

"Everything's fine, Pierre. I'll be back in a minute."

He finds an unoccupied ground-floor office, just off the entrance hall. The light switch doesn't work, but the glow of the streetlamps comes through the window, so the three men remain in this gloom. None has any desire to sit down.

Simon takes over: "Monsieur Lang, how did you come into possession of the seventh function?"

Lang sighs. Simon and Bayard wait. Mitterrand is president. Lang can tell them now. And in all probability, Simon thinks, Lang *wants* to tell them.

He organized a lunch with Barthes because he knew that Barthes was in possession of Jakobson's manuscript.

"How?" asks Simon.

"How what?" says Lang. "How did Barthes come into possession of the manuscript or how did I know that he had?"

Simon is calm, but he knows that Bayard often has a hard time containing his impatience. As he doesn't want his policeman friend to threaten to gouge out Jack Lang's eyeballs with a coffee spoon, he says softly: "Both."

Jack Lang does not know how Barthes came into possession of the manuscript, but in any case his extraordinary network of contacts in cultural circles enabled Lang to become aware of this fact. It was Debray, after talking about it with Derrida, who convinced him of the document's importance. So they decided to organize the lunch with Barthes in order to steal it from him. During the meal, Lang discreetly pilfered the sheet of paper that was in Barthes's jacket pocket and gave it to Debray, who was waiting, hidden, in the entrance hall. Debray ran off to hand the document to Derrida, who fabricated a false function based on the original text, which Debray took back to Lang, who slipped it into Barthes's pocket before lunch was over. The timing of the operation was extremely precise; Derrida had to write the false function in record time, based on the real one, so that it would be credible but would not actually work.

Simon is amazed: "But what was the point? Barthes knew the text. He would have realized straight away."

Lang explains: "We banked on the assumption that if we were aware of the existence of this document, we weren't the only ones, and that it would be bound to arouse keen interest."

Bayard interrupts him: "You anticipated that Sollers and Kristeva would steal it from him?"

Simon replies on Lang's behalf: "No, they thought Giscard would try to get hold of it. And they weren't wrong, were they, as that was precisely the mission he gave you? Except that, contrary to what they had supposed, when Barthes was knocked over by the laundry van, Giscard wasn't yet aware of the seventh function's existence." He turns to Lang: "Seems his network of cultural informers was not as efficient as yours . . ."

Lang cannot conceal a faint smile of vanity: "In fact, the whole operation was based on what I must say was a fairly audacious gamble: that Barthes would have the false document stolen from him before he noticed the substitution, so that the thieves would believe they had the real seventh function and, additionally, so that we would remain beyond suspicion."

Bayard: "And that's exactly what happened. Except that it wasn't Giscard, but Sollers and Kristeva who were behind the theft."

Lang: "Ultimately, that didn't make much difference to us. It would have been nice to play a trick on Giscard, to make him think he had a secret weapon. But the essential thing was that we had the seventh function—the real one."

Bayard asks: "But why was Barthes killed?"

Lang had never expected things to go that far. They had had no intention whatsoever of killing anyone. It was immaterial to them that others should possess and even use the seventh function, as long as it wasn't Giscard.

Simon understands. Mitterrand's objective was purely short-term: to beat Giscard in the debate. But Sollers, in a way, was aiming higher. He wanted to take Eco's title as the Great Protagoras of the Logos Club, and for that he needed the seventh function, which would have given him a decisive rhetorical advantage. But in order to preserve the position once it was his, he would have to make sure that no one else got to know about it, in case they challenged him. Hence the Bulgarian assassins hired by Kristeva to track down all the copies: it was imperative that the seventh function remain the exclusive property of Sollers, and Sollers alone. So Barthes had to die, as did all those who had been in possession of the document and who might either use it or disseminate it.

Simon asks if Mitterrand had approved Operation Seventh Function.

Lang does not reply in so many words, but the answer is obvious, so he doesn't attempt to deny it: "Mitterrand was not convinced that it would work until the very last minute. It took him a little while to master the function. But when it came down to it, he crushed Giscard." The future minister of culture smiles wolfishly.

"And Derrida?"

"Derrida wanted Giscard to lose. Like Jakobson, he would have preferred no one to possess the seventh function, but he was not in any position to prevent Mitterrand from getting it, and he liked the idea of the false function. He asked me to make the president promise to keep the seventh function for his exclusive use and not share it with anyone." Lang smiles again. "A promise that the president, I feel absolutely certain, will have no trouble keeping."

"What about you?" Bayard asks. "Did you see it?"

"No. Mitterrand asked us, Debray and me, not to open it. I

wouldn't have had time anyway, because as soon as I took it from Barthes, I gave it to Debray."

Jack Lang remembers the scene: he had to watch over the cooking of the fish, help keep the conversation ticking over, and steal the function without anyone noticing.

"As for Debray, I don't know if he obeyed the presidential order, but he didn't have much time either. Knowing how loyal he is, I would bet that he followed instructions."

"So, theoretically," says Bayard, sounding dubious, "Mitterrand is the last person still alive who knows the function?"

"Along with Jakobson himself, obviously."

Simon says nothing.

Outside, the people chant: "To the Bastille! To the Bastille!"

The door opens and Moati's head appears. "Are you coming? The concerts have started. Apparently, the Bastille is packed!"

"I'll be there in a minute."

Lang would like to rejoin his friends, but Simon still has one more question: "The false document forged by Derrida . . . was it intended to mess up whoever used it?"

Lang considers this: "I'm not sure . . . The most important thing was that it seem plausible. It was already quite a feat on Derrida's part to write a credible imitation in such a short space of time."

Bayard thinks back to Sollers's performance in Venice and says to Simon: "Anyway, Sollers was a bit messed up to start with, wasn't he?"

With all the courtesy he can muster, Lang asks permission to leave, now that he has satisfied their curiosity.

The three men exit the dark office and go back to the celebrations. Outside the former Gare d'Orsay, egged on by passersby, a man staggers around repeatedly yelling: "Giscard the loser! Let's dance the Carmagnole!" Lang asks Simon and Bayard if they would like to accompany him to the Bastille. On the way, they bump into Gaston Defferre, the future minister of the interior.

Lang makes the introductions. Defferre says to Bayard: "I need men like you. Let's meet this week."

The rain is bucketing down, but it does not dampen the euphoria of the crowds in the Bastille. Even though it is already night, people shout: "Mitterrand, sunlight! Mitterrand, sunlight!"

Bayard asks Lang if he thinks Kristeva and Sollers will be troubled by the long arm of the law. Lang pulls a face: "Quite frankly, I doubt it. The seventh function is now a state secret. The president has no interest in stirring this up. Anyway, Sollers has already paid a heavy price for his ambitions, don't you think? I met him several times, you know. A charming man. He had the insolence of a courtier."

Lang smiles his charming smile. Bayard shakes his hand, and the soon-to-be minister of culture can at last go off to join his comrades in celebrating their victory.

Simon contemplates the human tide that fills the square.

He says: "What a waste."

Bayard is surprised: "What do you mean, what a waste? You're going to be able to retire at sixty now—isn't that what you want? You'll have your thirty-five-hour workweek, your extra week's vacation every year, your nationalizations, your abolition of the death penalty . . . Aren't you happy?"

"Barthes, Hamed, his friend Saïd, the Bulgarian on the Pont-Neuf, the Bulgarian in the DS, Derrida, Searle . . . They all died for nothing. They died so Sollers could have his balls chopped off in Venice because he had the wrong document. Right from the beginning, we were chasing a mirage."

"Well, not entirely. The sheet in Barthes's apartment, the one inside the Jakobson book, that was a copy of the original. If we hadn't intercepted the Bulgarian, he'd have given it to Kristeva, who would have realized there'd been a substitution when she compared the two texts. And Slimane's cassette: that was a recording of the original too. It was important it didn't fall into the wrong hands." (*Shit,* thinks Bayard, *stop talking about hands!*)

"But Derrida wanted to destroy it."

"But if Searle had got his hands on it"—*seriously, what the fuck is wrong with me?*—"who knows what would have happened?"

"They know in Murano."

An oppressive silence, despite the singing crowd. Bayard doesn't know what to say. He remembers a film he saw when he was a kid—*The Vikings*, with Tony Curtis as a one-armed man who kills the two-armed Kirk Douglas—but he is not sure that Simon would appreciate this reference.

There was nothing wrong with their investigation, no matter what anyone thinks. They tracked down Barthes's murderers. How could they have guessed that they didn't have the real document? No, Simon is right: they were barking up the wrong tree from the very start.

Bayard says: "Without this investigation, you wouldn't have become what you are."

"Disabled?" sneers Simon.

"When I first met you, you were a little library rat, you looked like a hippie virgin, and now look at you! You're wearing a decent suit, you meet loads of girls, you're the rising star of the Logos Club . . ."

"And I lost my right hand."

A series of performers appears on the huge stage in the Bastille. Among a group of kissing, dancing young people, blond hair blowing in the wind (this is the first time he has seen her with her hair down), Simon recognizes Anastasia.

What were the odds of him bumping into her again, tonight, in this crowd? The thought flashes through Simon's mind that either he is being manipulated by a really bad novelist or Anastasia is some sort of superspy.

Onstage, the group Téléphone are playing their hit, "Ça (C'est Vraiment Toi)."

Their eyes meet and, as she dances with a long-haired guy, Anastasia gives him a little wave.

Bayard has seen her too; he tells Simon that it's time for him to go home.

"You're not staying?"

"It's not my victory. You know I voted for the other baldy. Anyway, I'm too old for all this." He gives a vague wave at the groups of people jumping up and down in time with the music, getting drunk, smoking joints, and making out.

"Oh, give me a break, granddad—you weren't saying that at Cornell when you were high as a kite, screwing God knows who with your friend Judith up your ass!"

Bayard does not take the bait:

"Anyway, I've got cabinets full of files that I need to shred before your friends get their . . . get hold of them."

"What if Defferre offers you a job?"

"I'm a *fonctionnaire*. I'm paid to serve the government."

"I see. Your patriotism does you honor."

"Shut your mouth, you little twerp."

The two men laugh. Simon asks Bayard if he isn't curious to at least hear Anastasia's side of the story. Bayard puts out his left hand to shake and tells him, watching the young Russian woman dance: "You can tell me later."

And Bayard vanishes into the crowd.

When Simon turns around, Anastasia is standing in front of him, covered in sweat and rain. There is a brief moment of awkwardness. Simon notices that she is looking at the space where his missing hand should be. To create a diversion, he asks her: "So, what do they think about Mitterrand's victory in Moscow?" She smiles. "Brezhnev, you know . . ." She hands him a half-empty can of beer. "Andropov is the coming man."

"And what does the coming man think of his Bulgarian counterpart?"

"Kristeva's father? We knew he was working for his daughter. But we couldn't work out why they wanted the function. It's thanks to you that I was able to discover the existence of the Logos Club."

"What will happen to him now, Kristeva Senior?"

"Times have changed. This isn't '68 anymore. I have not received any orders. Not for the father or for the daughter. As for the agent who tried to kill you, we last saw him in Istanbul, but after that we lost track of him."

The rain falls harder. Onstage, Jacques Higelin sings "Champagne."

In a pained voice, Simon asks her: "Why weren't you in Venice?"

Anastasia ties up her hair and takes a cigarette from a soft packet, but is unable to light it. Simon leads her to a sheltered place, under a tree, above the Port de l'Arsenal. "I was following another trail." She had discovered that Sollers had entrusted a copy of the seventh function to Althusser. She didn't know it was a false document, so she searched everywhere in Althusser's apartment while he was in an asylum—and that required a great deal of work because there were tons of books and papers, the document could have been hidden anywhere, and she had to be extremely methodical. But she didn't find it.

Simon says: "That's a shame."

Behind them, onstage, they catch a glimpse of Rocard and Juquin, hand in hand, singing "The Internationale," echoed by the entire crowd. Anastasia mumbles the words in Russian. Simon wonders if the Left can actually be in power, in real life. Or, more precisely, he wonders if, in real life, it is possible to change one's life. But before he is drawn, once again, down the rabbit hole of his ontological reflections, he hears Anastasia whisper to him: "I'm going back to Moscow tomorrow; tonight, I'm not on duty." And, as if by magic, she takes a bottle of champagne from her bag. Simon has no idea how or where she got it, but who cares? They take turns drinking from the bottle, and Simon kisses Anastasia, wondering if she is about to slice open his carotid artery with a hairpin or if he will fall to the ground, poisoned by her toxic lipstick. But Anastasia lets him kiss her, and she isn't wearing lipstick. With the rain and the celebrations in the background, the scene is like something from a Hollywood film, but Simon decides not to dwell on this.

The crowd yells: "Mitterrand! Mitterrand!" (But the new president is not there.)

Simon goes up to a street vendor who has drinks in his cooler, including, for tonight only, champagne. So he buys another bottle and uncorks it with one hand, while Anastasia smiles at him, her eyes shining from the alcohol and her hair, unpinned again, falling over her shoulders.

They clink their bottles together and Anastasia shouts over the clamor of the storm:

"To socialism!"

Everyone around them cheers.

And Simon replies, as a flash of lightning streaks across the Paris sky:

"The real kind!"

96

The French Open men's final, 1981. Borg is crushing his opponent yet again, this time the Czechoslovakian Ivan Lendl; he takes the first set 6–1. All the heads in the crowd turn to follow the ball, except for Simon's, because his thoughts are elsewhere.

Maybe Bayard doesn't care, but he wants to know; he wants proof that he is not a character in a novel, that he lives in the real world. (What is it, the real? "You know it when you bump into it," Lacan said. And Simon looks at his stump.)

The second set is tougher. The players send clouds of dust into the air when they slide around on the dry court.

Simon is alone in his box until a young North African–looking man joins him. The young man sits on the seat next to his. It's Slimane.

They greet each other. Lendl snatches the second set.

It is the first set Borg has lost in the entire tournament.

"Nice box."

"An advertising agency rents it, the one that did Mitterrand's campaign. They want to recruit me."

"Are you interested?"

"I think we can call each other *tu*."

"I'm sorry about your hand."

"If Borg wins, it'll be his sixth Roland-Garros title. Hard to believe, isn't it?"

"Looks like he's got a good chance."

It's true: Borg will pull away quite quickly in the third set.

"Thank you for coming."

"I was passing through Paris anyway. Was it your cop friend who told you?"

"So you live in the U.S. now?"

"Yeah, I got my green card."

"In six months?"

"There's always a way."

"Even with the American government?"

"Yep, even with them."

"What did you do, after Cornell?"

"I ran off with the money."

"I know that bit."

"I went to New York. To start with, I enrolled at Columbia University and took a few courses."

"In the middle of the academic year? Is that possible?"

"Yeah, sure, you just have to convince a secretary."

Borg breaks Lendl for the second time in the set.

"I heard about your victories in the Logos Club. Congratulations."

"Actually, that reminds me: isn't there an American branch?"

"Yes, but it's still embryonic. I'm not sure there's even a single tribune in the whole country. There's a peripatetician in Philadelphia, I think, one or two in Boston, maybe, and a few dialecticians scattered over the West Coast."

Simon doesn't ask him if he's planning to join.

Borg takes the third set 6–2.

"Got any plans?"

"I'd like to get into politics."

"In the U.S.? You think you can get American nationality?"

"Why not?"

"But you want to, uh, stand for election?"

"Well, I need to improve my English first, and I need to be naturalized. After that, it's not just a question of winning debates to become a candidate; you have to—what's the expression?—do the hard yards. Maybe I'll be able to aim for the Democratic primaries in 2020, who knows. Not before that, though, ha ha."

Precisely because Slimane sounds as if he's joking, Simon wonders if he isn't serious.

"No, but listen, I met a student at Columbia. I have a feeling he can go far, if I help him."

"What do you mean by 'far'?"

"I think I can make him a senator."

"To what end?"

"Just because. He's a black guy from Hawaii."

"Hmm, I see. A suitable test for your new powers."

"It's not exactly a power."

"I know."

Lendl hits a forehand that speeds ten feet past Borg.

Simon remarks: "That doesn't happen very often to Borg. He's good, this Czech guy."

He is delaying the moment when he will touch upon the real reason he wanted to talk with Slimane, even though the ex-gigolo knows exactly what he has in mind.

"I listened to it over and over on my Walkman, but it's not enough just to learn it by heart, you know."

"So it's a method? A secret weapon?"

"It's more like a key, or a path, than a method. It's true that Jakobson called it the 'performative function,' but 'performative' is just an image."

Slimane watches Borg play his two-handed backhand.

"It's a technique, I guess."

"In the Greek sense?"

Slimane smiles.

"A *technè*, sure, if you like. *Praxis, poiesis* . . . I learned all that stuff, you know."

"And you feel unbeatable?"

"Yeah, but that doesn't mean I am. I think I could be beaten."

"Without the function?"

Slimane smiles.

"We'll see. But I still have plenty to learn. And I have to train. Convincing a customs official or a secretary is one thing, winning elections is something else. I've still got a long way to go."

Simon wonders how great Mitterrand's mastery of the technique is, and whether the Socialist president could lose an election or if he's destined to be reelected until his death.

In the meantime, Lendl fights against the Swedish machine and wins the fourth set. The spectators shiver: this is the first time in ages that Borg has been taken to the fifth set at Roland-Garros. In fact, he hadn't lost a single set here since 1979 and his final against Victor Pecci. As for his last defeat in Paris, that goes all the way back to 1976, against Panatta.

Borg hits a double fault, offering Lendl a break point.

"I don't know what's more improbable," says Simon. "A sixth victory for Borg . . . or him losing."

Borg responds with an ace. Lendl shouts something in Czech.

Simon realizes that he wants Borg to win, and that in this desire there is probably a bit of superstition, a bit of conservatism, a fear of change, but it would also be a victory for plausibility: the undisputed world number one ahead of Connors and McEnroe, Borg crushed all his opponents to reach the final, whereas Lendl, fifth in the world, almost lost against José Luis Clerc in the semifinal and even against Andres Gomez in the second round. The order of things . . .

"Actually, have you heard from Foucault?"

"Yeah, we write to each other regularly. He's putting me up while I'm in Paris. He's still working on his history of sexuality."

"And, uh, the seventh function . . . he's not interested in that? At least, as a subject of study?"

"He abandoned linguistics a while ago, you know. Maybe he'll come back to it one day. But in any case, he's too tactful to bring it up."

"Ah. I see."

"Oh, no, I wasn't saying that about you."

Borg breaks Lendl.

Simon and Slimane stop talking for a while to follow the match.

Slimane thinks about Hamed.

"And that bitch Kristeva?"

"She's fine. You know what happened to Sollers?"

An evil grin lights up Slimane's face.

The two men sense vaguely that one day they will go head to head for the position of Great Protagoras, but they are not going to admit that to each other today. Simon has carefully avoided mentioning Umberto Eco.

Lendl breaks back.

The outcome is increasingly uncertain.

"So what about your plans?"

Simon laughs grimly, holding up his stump.

"Well, it's going to be difficult to win Roland-Garros."

"I bet you could take the Trans-Siberian, though."

Simon smiles at the allusion to Cendrars, another one-armed intellectual, and wonders when Slimane acquired this literary knowledge.

Lendl doesn't want to lose, but Borg is so strong.

And yet.

The unthinkable happens.

Lendl breaks Borg again.

He serves for the match.

The young Czechoslovak trembles under the weight of expectation.

But he wins.

Borg the invincible is beaten. Lendl raises his arms to the sky.

Slimane applauds, along with the rest of the spectators.

When Simon sees Lendl lift the cup, he no longer knows what to think.

EPILOGUE

NAPLES

■

97

Simon stands outside the entrance of Galleria Umberto I, and from this position he can perceive its proud and happy union of glass and marble, but he remains on the threshold. The gallery is a landmark, not a destination. He stares at the map he has unfolded, puzzling over why Via Roma cannot be found. He has the feeling that his map is wrong.

He should be standing on Via Roma. Instead of which, he is on Via Toleda.

Behind him, on the opposite pavement, an old shoeshine guy watches him curiously.

Simon knows the shoeshine guy is waiting to see how he will manage to fold his map back up with only one hand.

The old man has a wooden crate, on which he has created a sort of makeshift rack on which customers can wedge their shoes. Simon notes the slope for the heel.

The two men look at each other.

Perplexity reigns on both sides of this Neapolitan street.

Simon does not know exactly where he is. He begins folding the map, slowly but dexterously, never taking his eyes off the old shoeshine guy.

But suddenly the old man points at a spot directly above

Simon, who senses that something abnormal is happening because the man's glum expression changes to one of stupefaction.

Simon looks up just in time to see the pediment above the gallery entrance, a bas-relief representing two cherubs flanking a coat of arms, or something like that, come loose from the façade.

The shoeshine guy tries to yell something, a warning (*"Statte accuorto!"*) to prevent the tragedy, or at least to participate in it in some way, but no sound emerges from his toothless mouth.

But Simon has changed a lot. He is no longer a library rat about to be crushed by half a ton of white stone, but a one-handed man ranked quite high in the hierarchy of the Logos Club who has cheated death at least three times. Instead of stepping back, as our instinct would prompt us, he has the counter-intuitive reflex of pressing his body against the building's wall, so that the huge block of stone smashes the pavement next to his feet without injuring him.

The shoeshine guy cannot believe it. Simon looks down at the rubble, he looks over at the old man, he looks around him at the petrified pedestrians.

He points at the poor shoeshine guy, but it is not him, of course, he addresses when he declares, aggressively: "If you want to kill me, you're going to have to try a bit harder than that!" Or maybe the novelist wanted to send him a message? In that case, he'll have to express himself a bit more clearly, thinks Simon angrily.

98

"It's last year's earthquake; it made all the buildings fragile. They could collapse at any moment."

Simon listens to Bianca explaining why he almost got his skull caved in by a huge chunk of marble.

"*San Gennaro*—Saint January—stopped the lava during an eruption of Vesuvius and he has been Naples's protector ever since. Every year, the bishop takes a bit of his dried blood in a glass vial and he keeps turning it upside down until the blood becomes liquid. If the blood dissolves, Naples will be spared misfortune. And what happened last year, do you think?"

"The blood didn't dissolve."

"And then the Camorra embezzled millions that the European Commission gave the city because they're in control of the reconstruction contracts. So of course, they didn't do anything, or they did such shoddy work that it's just as dangerous as before. There are accidents all the time. Neapolitans are used to them."

Simon and Bianca are sipping coffee on the terrace of the Gambrinus, a very touristy literary café and pastry shop that Simon chose for this meeting. He nibbles a rum baba.

Bianca explains that the expression "See Naples and die" (*vedi Napoli e poi muori*; in Latin, *videre Neapolim et Mori*) is in fact a play on words: Mori is a small town near Naples.

She also tells him the history of the pizza: one day, Queen Margherita, married to the king of Italy, Umberto I, discovered this popular meal and made it famous throughout Italy. In tribute, a pizza was named after her, the one containing the colors of the national flag: green (basil), white (mozzarella), and red (tomato).

Up to now, she has not asked a single question about his hand.

A white Fiat double-parks near them.

Bianca becomes more and more animated. She starts talking politics. She tells Simon again about the hatred she feels for bourgeois people who hoard all the wealth and starve the people. "Can you believe it, Simon? Some of those bourgeois bastards spend hundreds of thousands of lire just to buy a handbag. A handbag, Simon!"

Two young men get out of the white Fiat and sit on the terrace. They are joined by a third, a biker who parks his Triumph on the pavement. Bianca can't see them because they are behind her back. It is the scarf gang from Bologna.

If Simon is surprised to see them here, he doesn't show it.

Bianca sobs with rage, thinking about the excesses of the Italian middle classes. She heaps insults on Reagan. She is suspicious of Mitterrand because, on that side of the Alps as on this one, the socialists are always traitors. Bettino Craxi is a piece of shit. They all deserve to die, and she would happily execute them herself given the chance. The world seems infinitely dark to her, thinks Simon, who cannot really claim she is wrong.

The three young men have ordered beers and lit cigarettes when another character arrives, already known to Simon: his Venice opponent, the man who mutilated him, flanked by two bodyguards.

Simon leans over his rum baba, hiding his face. The man shakes hands like a VIP, a local elected official or a high-ranking Camorra member (the distinction is often not very clear, here). He disappears inside the café.

Bianca spits on Forlani and his Pentapartito government. Simon worries that she is having a nervous breakdown. Attempting to calm her, he utters some soothing words—"come on, not everything's that bad, think about Nicaragua . . ."—and moves his hand under the table to rest on her knee, but through the fabric of Bianca's trouser leg he touches something hard that is not flesh.

Bianca, startled, abruptly pulls her leg beneath her chair. She immediately stops sobbing. She stares at Simon, defiant and imploring at the same time. There is rage, anger, and love in her tears.

Simon says nothing. So, that's how it is: a happy ending. The one-handed man and the one-legged girl. And, as in all good stories, some guilt to drag around with him: if Bianca lost her leg at Bologna Central, it was his fault. If she had never met him, she would have two legs and would still be able to wear skirts.

But then again, they would also not form this touching handicapped couple. Will they marry and make lots of little Leftists?

Except that this is not the final scene that *he* had in mind.

Yes, while visiting Naples, he wanted to see Bianca, the young woman he fucked on a dissecting table in Bologna, but right now he has other plans.

Simon makes an imperceptible nod to one of the young men in scarves.

The three of them stand up, put their scarves over their mouths, and enter the café.

Simon and Bianca exchange a long look, communicating an infinity of messages, stories, and emotions, of the past, the present, and, already, the conditional past (the worst of all, the tense of regrets).

The sound of two gunshots. Screams and confusion.

The gang emerge, pushing Simon's opponent forward. One of the three has his P38 wedged in the lower back of the important Camorra member. Another sweeps the terrace with his, threatening the shocked clientele.

As he passes Simon, the third gang member puts something on the table, which Simon covers with his napkin.

They shove the Camorra guy in the back of the Fiat and speed off.

There is panic in the café. Simon listens to the screams from inside and understands that the two bodyguards are injured. Each one has a bullet in his leg, as planned.

Simon says to the frightened-looking Bianca: "Come with me."

He leads her over to the third man's motorbike and hands her the napkin, inside which is a key. He says to Bianca: "Drive."

Bianca protests: she's ridden a scooter before, but never a bike as powerful as this one.

Lifting his right arm, Simon says, scowling: "Well, I can't either."

So Bianca straddles the Triumph, Simon kickstarts it and sits behind her, arms around her waist, and she twists the handle to accelerate, sending the bike flying forward. Bianca asks which direction she should take and Simon replies: "Pozzuoli."

99

It is like a lunar landscape, somewhere between a spaghetti western and a science fiction film.

At the center of an immense crater coated with whitish clay, the three gang members surround the paunchy VIP, who is kneeling next to a boiling mud pit.

Around them, geysers of sulfur burst from the bowels of the earth. The air is thick with the stench of rotten eggs.

Simon's first thought was to go to the Sibyl's cave in Cumae, where no one would have come to find them, but he decided against that because it was too kitsch, too obviously symbolic, and he's getting tired of symbols. Except it is not that easy to get away from them: as they tread the cracked earth, Bianca tells him that the Romans believed the Solfatara, this dormant volcano, to be the gates of Hell. Okay . . .

"*Salve!* What do we do with him, *compagno?*"

Bianca, who had not recognized the three men at the Gambrinus, asks wide-eyed:

"You hired the Red Brigades from Bologna?"

"I thought they weren't *necessarily* the Red Brigades; isn't that what you insisted to your friend Enzo?"

"No one hired us."

"*Non siamo dei mercenari.*"

"No, it's true, they did this for free. I convinced them."

"To kidnap this guy?"

"*Si tratta di un uomo politico corrotto di Napoli.*"

"He hands out building permits from the mayor's office. Thanks to the permits he sold the Camorra, hundreds of people died during the *terremoto*, crushed by the rotten buildings the Camorra had constructed."

Simon approaches the man and rubs his stump against the man's face. "Not only that, but he's a bad loser." The man shakes his head like an animal. "*Strunz! Si mmuort!*"

The three Red Brigades members suggest ransoming him in

exchange for a revolutionary hostage. The French-speaker among them turns to Simon: "*Ma*, it's not certain that anyone will want to pay for a pig like him, ha ha!" The three men laugh, and Bianca, too, though she wants him to die, even if she doesn't say so.

An Aldo Moro–style uncertainty: Simon likes that. He wants vengeance, but he also likes the idea of leaving it to chance. He grabs the Camorra man's chin in his left hand and squeezes it like a vise. "You understand the alternatives? Either your body is found in the boot of a Renault 4L or you can go home and continue being a bastard. But don't you dare set foot in the Logos Club again." He remembers their duel in Venice, the only one in which he ever truly felt in danger. "Anyway, how does a peasant like you end up so cultivated? You find time to go to the theater when you're not too busy organizing crimes?" But he immediately regrets this question, loaded as it is with politically incorrect prejudices.

He releases the man's chin, which immediately starts wagging. He speaks very rapidly in Italian. Simon asks Bianca: "What's he on about?"

"He's offering your friends lots of money to kill you."

Simon laughs. He knows the kneeling man's persuasive talents better than anyone, but he also knows that between a Mafia bureaucrat with Christian Democrat connections and Red Brigades members in their early twenties, there can be no possible dialogue. He could spend all day and all night talking without persuading them of anything.

His opponent must realize the same thing because, with a suppleness and speed one would never suspect in someone so corpulent, he leaps at the nearest brigade member and tries to wrestle his P38 from him. But the gang are young, fit men; the man is smashed over the head with the butt of a gun and crumples to the ground. The three brigade members aim their guns at him while yelling insults.

And so this is how the story will end. They'll shoot him here and now for that stupid escape attempt, thinks Simon.

A gunshot goes off.

But it is one of the brigade members who collapses.

Silence falls again on the volcano.

Everyone breathes in the sulfurous vapors that saturate the air.

Nobody tries to hide, because Simon had the brilliant idea of bringing the man to this completely exposed place: in the middle of a volcanic crater more than two thousand feet in circumference. In other words, there is not a single tree, not a single bush behind which they can take shelter. Simon scans his surroundings for any potential hiding place and spots a well and a small building made of smoking stones (ancient steam rooms representing the gates of Purgatory and Hell), but they are out of reach.

Two men in suits advance toward them. One carries a pistol, the other a rifle. Simon thinks he recognizes a German Mauser. The two brigade members who are still alive raise their hands, because they know their P38s are useless at this distance. Bianca stares at the corpse, a bullet in the head.

The Camorra has sent a team to rescue the corrupt politician. The *sistema* does not let its creatures get stolen from it that easily. And Simon is confident that it is equally punctilious when it comes to avenging an attack on its interests, which means that in all likelihood he will be executed on the spot along with what remains of the gang. As for Bianca, she must suffer the same fate, as the "system" has never been easygoing when it comes to witnesses either.

He has the confirmation of this when the politician gets to his feet, puffing like a seal, and slaps him, first, followed by the two brigade members, and lastly Bianca. Thus their fates are sealed. The politician growls at the two henchmen: *"Acceritele."*

Simon thinks of the Japanese men in Venice. So, won't there be any deus ex machina to save him this time? In his last moments, Simon renews his dialogue with that transcendent authority he used to imagine: if he were trapped in a novel, what narrative economy would require him to die at the end? Simon goes over several narratological reasons, all of which he considers questionable. He thinks of what Bayard would say. "Remember Tony Curtis in *The Vikings*." Hmm, yeah. He thinks of what Jacques would do: neutralize one of the armed men, then take out the second one using the first one's gun, probably. But Bayard isn't here, and Simon isn't Bayard.

The Camorra henchman points the rifle at his chest.

Simon understands that he should expect nothing from any transcendent authority. He senses that the novelist, if he exists, is not his friend.

His executioner is not much older than the brigade members. But just as he is about to squeeze the trigger, Simon tells him: "I know you are a man of honor." The man pauses and asks Bianca to translate for him. *"Isse a ritto cà sìn'omm d'onore."*

No, there will be no miracle. But, novel or not, it will not be said that he just let it happen. Simon does not believe in salvation, he does not believe that he has a mission on earth, but he does believe that the future is unwritten and that, even if he is in the hands of a sadistic, capricious novelist, his destiny is not yet settled.

Not yet.

He must deal with this hypothetical novelist the way he deals with God: always act as if God did not exist because if God does exist, he is at best a bad novelist who merits neither respect nor obedience. It is never too late to try to change the course of the story. And it may well be that the imaginary novelist has not yet made his decision. It may well be that the ending of the story is in the hands of his character, and that that character is me.

I am Simon Herzog. I am the hero of my own story.

The Camorra henchman turns back to Simon, who tells him: "Your father fought the fascists. He was a partisan. He risked his life for justice and freedom." The two men turn to Bianca, who translates into Neapolitan: *"Pateto eta nu partiggiano cà a fatt'a Guerra 'a Mussolini e Hitler. A commattuto p' 'a giustizia e 'a libbertà."*

The politician becomes impatient, but the assassin signals him to shut up. The politician orders the second henchman to execute Simon, but the one with the rifle says calmly: *"Aspett'."* And apparently the one with the rifle is the boss. He wants to know how Simon knows his father.

As it happens, this was just an inspired guess: Simon recognized the model of rifle, a Mauser, the weapon used by elite German marksmen. (Simon has always been partial to Second World War stories.) He deduced from this that the young man had inherited it from his father and this offered two possible hypotheses: either his father had come into possession of the rifle by fighting for the Italian army alongside the Wehrmacht, or quite the opposite: he had fought against them as a partisan and taken the gun from the corpse of a German soldier. As the first hypothesis offered him no hope of being saved, he gambled on the second. But he is careful not to reveal his reasoning and, turning to Bianca, he says: "I also know you lost family members during the earthquake." Bianca translates: *"Isse sape ca è perzo à coccheruno int'o terremoto . . ."*

The politician shouts: *"Basta! Spara mò!"*

But the Camorra member, *o zi*—"the uncle," as the "system" calls the young men it gets to do its dirty work—listens attentively as Simon explains the role played by the man he has been ordered to protect in the tragedy of the *terremoto* that struck his family.

The politician protests: *"Nun è over'!"*

But the young "uncle" knows it is true.

Simon asks innocently: "This man killed members of your family. Does vengeance mean anything to you?"

Bianca: *"Chisto a acciso e parienti tuoje. Nun te miette scuorno e ll'aiuta?"*

How did Simon guess that the young "uncle" had lost his family in the *terremoto*? And how did he know that, one way or another, without having any proof to hand, the "uncle" would consider it plausible that the politician could be held responsible? In his critical paranoia, Simon does not want to reveal this. He does not want the novelist, if there really is a novelist, to understand how he did it. Let it not be said of him that anyone can read him like a book.

In any case, he is too busy taking care of his peroration: "People you loved were buried alive."

Bianca no longer needs to translate. Simon no longer needs to speak.

The young man with the rifle turns to the politician, who is pale as the volcano's clay.

He hits him in the face with the butt of his rifle and pushes him backward.

The corrupt politician, so paunchy and cultivated, overbalances and falls into the boiling mud pit. *"La fangaia,"* whispers Bianca, hypnotized.

While his body floats for a moment, emitting horrible noises, the politician is able, just before being swallowed by the volcano, to recognize Simon's voice, as toneless as death, telling him: "See? It's my tongue you should have cut off."

And the geysers of sulfur continue to burst from the bowels of the earth, billowing toward the sky and poisoning the atmosphere.